HARCOURT HORIZONS

About My World

TEACHER'S EDITION

VOLUME 1

**Harcourt**

SCHOOL PUBLISHERS

Orlando   Austin   New York   San Diego

Visit *The Learning Site*
www.harcourtschool.co

D1402867

HARCOURT HORIZONS

Video segments are provided by **Reading Rainbow**.
For a catalog of all **Reading Rainbow**
videos, CD-ROMs, and DVDs, contact:

Reading Rainbow
C/O GPN/University of Nebraska
P.O. Box 80669
Lincoln, NE 68501-0669
Call: 1-800-228-4630
E-mail: gpn@unl.edu
Internet: gpn.unl.edu

For permission to reprint copyrighted material, grateful acknowledgment is made to the following sources:

Dutton Children's Books, an imprint of Penguin Putnam Books for Young Readers, a division of Penguin Putnam Inc.: "Whew!" and "Recess Rules" from *Lunch Money and Other Poems About School* by Carol Diggory Shields. Text copyright © 1995 by Carol Diggory Shields.

Free Spirit Publishing Inc., Minneapolis, MN, 1-800-735-7323, www.freespirit.com: "I Can't Move It" from *I Like Being Me: Poems for Children About Feeling Special, Appreciating Others, and Getting Along* by Judy Lalli, M. S. Text © 1997 by Judy Lalli.

Harcourt, Inc.: "Meg's Egg" from *The Llama Who Had No Pajama: 100 Favorite Poems* by Mary Ann Hoberman. Text copyright © 1981 by Mary Ann Hoberman.

Elizabeth M. Hauser: "Spring Rain" from *Around and About* by Marchette Chute. Text copyright 1957 by E. P. Dutton & Co.; text copyright renewed 1985 by Marchette Chute.

McFarland & Company, Inc., Box 611, Jefferson, NC 28640, www.mcfarlandpub.com: From "Johnny's Hammers" in *Children's Counting-Out Rhymes, Fingerplays, Jump-Rope and Bounce-Ball Chants and Other Rhythms,* compiled by Gloria T. Delamar. Text © 1983 by Gloria T. Delamar.

The McGraw-Hill Companies: "Come, Let's Celebrate" by Jean Warren from *1001 Rhymes & Fingerplays For Working With Young Children.* Text © 1994 by Totline® Publications.

Scholastic Inc.: "Making Maps" by Elaine V. Emans and "Friends Around the World" by Blanche Jennings Thompson from *Poetry Place Anthology.* Text copyright © 1983 by Edgell Communications, Inc.

The Society of Authors as the Literary Representative of the Estate of Alfred Noyes: "Daddy Fell Into the Pond" by Alfred Noyes.

University of Missouri-Kansas City Libraries: "Our House" by Dorothy Brown Thompson.

Printed in the United States of America.

ISBN 0-15-339624-5

4 5 6 7 8 9 10 073 11 10 09 08 07 06 05

Contents

Harcourt Horizons
Components

For content updates and additional information for teaching Harcourt Horizons, see The Learning Site: Social Studies Center at www.harcourtschool.com.

STUDENT SUPPORT MATERIALS	K	1	2	3	4	5	6
Pupil Editions*		●	●	●	●	●	●
Big Book*	●						
Unit Big Books*		●	●				
Activity Books*	●	●	●	●	●	●	●
Time for Kids Readers*	●	●	●	●	●	●	●

TEACHER SUPPORT MATERIALS	K	1	2	3	4	5	6
Teacher's Editions*	●	●	●	●	●	●	●
Activity Books, Teacher's Editions*				●	●	●	●
Assessment Programs*		●	●	●	●	●	●
Skills Transparencies*		●	●	●	●	●	●
Reading and Vocabulary Transparencies*		●	●	●	●	●	●
Audiotext Collections*	●	●	●	●	●	●	●

TECHNOLOGY	K	1	2	3	4	5	6
The Learning Site: Social Studies Center	●	●	●	●	●	●	●
GeoSkills CD-ROM*		●	●	●	●	●	●
Field Trip Videos*		●	●	●	●	●	●

* Available in Spanish

HARCOURT HORIZONS

About My World

Harcourt
SCHOOL PUBLISHERS

Orlando   Austin   New York   San Diego   Toronto   London

Visit *The Learning Site!*
www.harcourtschool.com

HARCOURT HORIZONS

ABOUT MY WORLD

General Editor

Dr. Michael J. Berson
Associate Professor
Social Science Education
University of South Florida
Tampa, Florida

Contributing Authors

Dr. Sherry Field
Associate Professor
The University of Texas at Austin
Austin, Texas

Dr. Tyrone Howard
Assistant Professor
UCLA Graduate School of
    Education & Information Studies
University of California at Los
    Angeles
Los Angeles, California

Dr. Bruce E. Larson
Associate Professor of Teacher
    Education and Social Studies
Western Washington University
Bellingham, Washington

Series Consultants

Dr. Robert Bednarz
Professor
Department of Geography
Texas A&M University
College Station, Texas

Dr. Robert P. Green, Jr.
Professor
School of Education
Clemson University
Clemson, South Carolina

Dr. Asa Grant Hilliard III
Fuller E. Callaway Professor
    of Urban Education
Georgia State University
Atlanta, Georgia

Dr. Thomas M. McGowan
Chairperson and Professor
Center for Curriculum and
    Instruction
University of Nebraska
Lincoln, Nebraska

Dr. John J. Patrick
Professor of Education
Indiana University
Bloomington, Indiana

Dr. Cinthia Salinas
Assistant Professor
Department of Curriculum and
    Instruction
University of Texas at Austin
Austin, Texas

Dr. Philip VanFossen
Associate Professor,
    Social Studies
    Education, and
    Associate Director,
    Purdue Center for Economic
    Education
Purdue University
West Lafayette, Indiana

Dr. Hallie Kay Yopp
Professor
Department of
    Elementary, Bilingual,
    and Reading Education
California State
    University, Fullerton
Fullerton, California

Maps
researched and prepared by

Readers
written and designed by

Take a Field Trip
video tour segments provided by

ISBN 0-15-339615-6

1 2 3 4 5 6 7 8 9 10 032 13 12 11 10 09 08 07 06 05 04

Contents

A1 **Atlas**

iv

· UNIT ·

2

Good Citizens

 Prior Knowledge

· UNIT · 3

The Land Around Us

Focus Skill Categorize

· UNIT ·

4

All About People

Generalize

ix

Features You Can Use

Geography

Heritage

Science and Technology

Charts, Graphs, and Diagrams

Maps

Atlas

 ## World

United States

Geography Terms

A1

Atlas

Set the Purpose

Main Idea A map can be used to show where land and water exist around the world.

Why It Matters Ask a volunteer to read the title of the map. Encourage children to tell what they think they are going to learn by looking at this map. (where land and water can be found on Earth)

Q Why might a person need to know where land and water can be found on Earth?

A Children might say so that the person will know what kind of transportation is needed to get from one place to another.

Map Study

Geography Explain that the map shows what the world looks like. Ask children if they think the world is round or flat. (round) Then ask children how they think this map can show the world, since it is not round like a globe. Point out that a world map shows what a globe would look like if it were rolled out and laid flat on a sheet of paper.

Visual Learning

Map Invite children to name different types of land (hills, mountains, deserts) and then different types of water (rivers, lakes, seas, oceans).

Q How can you show these things on a map?

A Draw pictures of them; use different colors.

Q How can you tell which places are land and which are water on the map in your book?

A Water is shaded blue; land is green or brown.

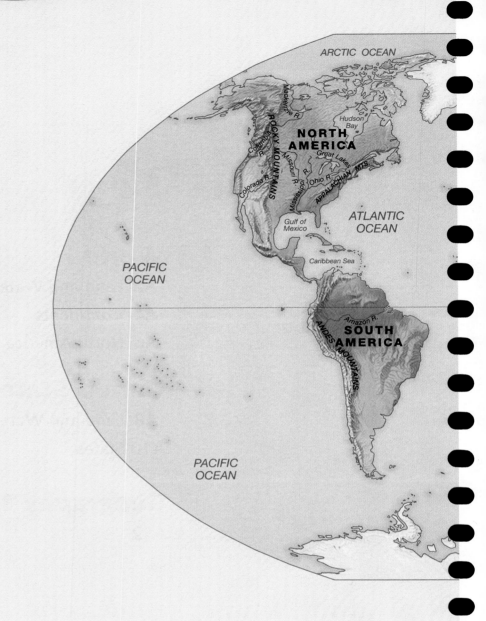

A2

INTEGRATE LANGUAGE ARTS

Descriptive Writing
Have children pick out a place on the map and then write a short paragraph to tell about the land and water features of the place. For example, "I am in western South America. I am at the top of a tall mountain. I can see the ocean on one side of the mountain and land on the other side."

REACH ALL LEARNERS

Tactile Learners Invite children to look through magazines to find and cut out pictures of different types of land and water. Have children take turns displaying and telling about one of their pictures. Then help children relate their pictures to places on the map so they will realize what the places on the map might actually look like.

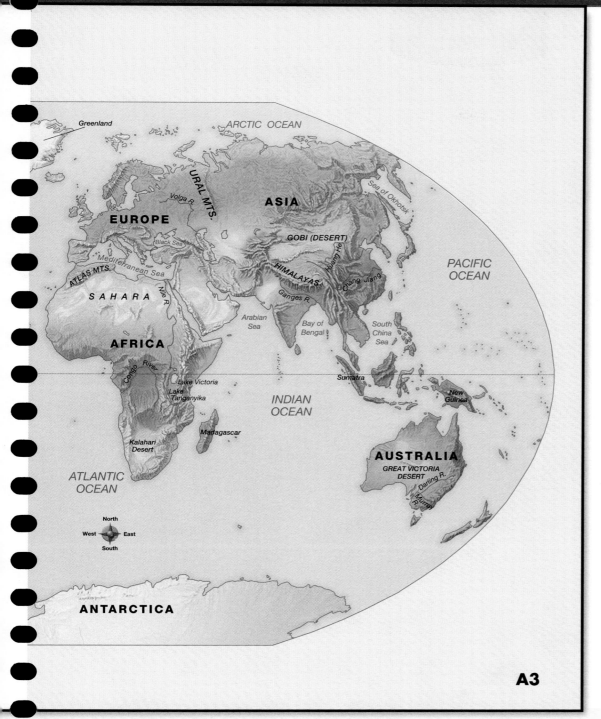

Greenland

ARCTIC OCEAN

URAL MTS.

Volga R.

EUROPE

ASIA

Black Sea

Sea of Okhotsk

Mediterranean Sea

GOBI (DESERT)

ATLAS MTS.

HIMALAYAS

Hwang He

PACIFIC
OCEAN

SAHARA

Nile R.

Ganges R.

Chang Jiang

AFRICA

Arabian
Sea

Bay of
Bengal

South
China
Sea

Congo River

Sumatra

Lake Victoria

Lake
Tanganyika

INDIAN
OCEAN

New
Guinea

Madagascar

Kalahari
Desert

AUSTRALIA

GREAT VICTORIA
DESERT

ATLANTIC
OCEAN

Darling R.

Murray R.

North

West   East

South

ANTARCTICA

A3

Visual Learning

Map Explain that the map shows
many different kinds of land and
water. Have children point to and
name the different rivers they see on
the map. Repeat with mountains,
deserts, seas, and other types of land
and water.

**Q How did the mapmakers make the
mountainous areas look different
from other areas?**

A The mountainous areas are bumpy
and uneven.

Map Study

Geography Point out the compass
rose on the map. Explain that a compass rose shows where things are on
a map based on the directions north,
south, east, and west. As you call out
each direction, have children point to
that general area on the map. Then ask
questions to help children continue to
identify north, south, east, and west.

**Q What is the name of the ocean that
is east of North America?**

A the Atlantic Ocean

CD-ROM

Explore GEOSKILLS CD-ROM to
learn more about map and
globe skills.

EXTEND AND ENRICH

Create a Land and Water Map
Have children create their own
world land and water maps. Provide
children with copies of the world
map on page T23, found in the
tabbed section Thinking Organizers
in this Teacher's Guide. Suggest
that children use different colors to
show areas of land and water.

GO ONLINE · INTERNET RESOURCES

THE LEARNING SITE

Go to
www.harcourtschool.com
for more information about
land and water maps.

Atlas

Set the Purpose

Main Idea A map can be used to show where continents are located on earth.

Why It Matters Ask a volunteer to read the title of the map. Explain that knowing how to find continents on a map helps you know where you are and where other places are in the world.

Visual Learning

Map Create a two-column chart on the board to help children identify the names of the large areas of land and water on Earth. Ask children to examine the map and name all the places shown in big type on the world map. As children name each place, encourage them to tell whether the feature is land or water. List the feature names in the appropriate column on the chart.

Land	Water
North America	Pacific Ocean
South America	Atlantic Ocean
Antarctica	Indian Ocean
Africa	Arctic Ocean
Europe	
Asia	
Australia	

Map Study

Geography Explain that the large areas of land on a world map are called continents.

Q How many continents are there on Earth?

A There are seven continents.

Q What are the names of the continents?

A North America, South America, Antarctica, Africa, Europe, Asia, Australia

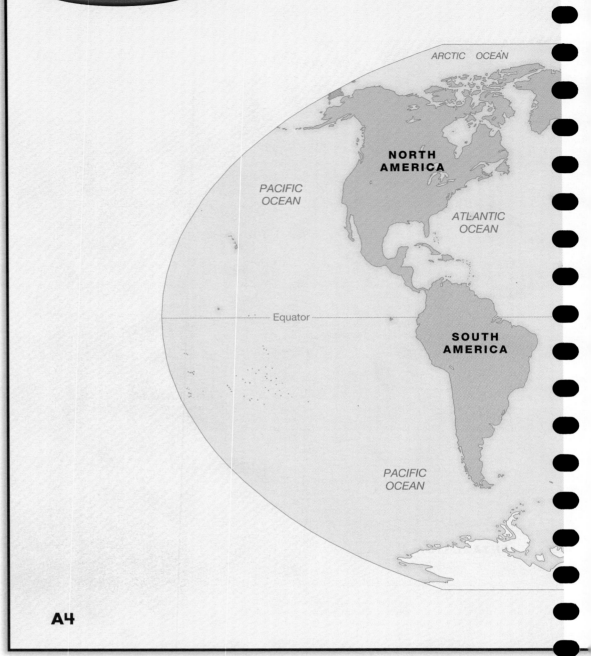

World
Continents

ARCTIC OCEAN

NORTH AMERICA

PACIFIC OCEAN

ATLANTIC OCEAN

Equator

SOUTH AMERICA

PACIFIC OCEAN

A4

BACKGROUND

Continents and Oceans Earth is divided into seven continents and three oceans. The seven continents vary greatly in size. Asia, the largest continent, is five times bigger than Australia. In order by size, the seven continents are Asia, Africa, North America, South America, Antarctica, Europe, and Australia. The three oceans are the Pacific, Atlantic, and Indian Oceans. The Arctic Ocean is actually part of the Atlantic Ocean.

REACH ALL LEARNERS

English as a Second Language Display a large world map on the wall, and cover the names of the continents. Provide each child with a label listing one of the continents. Then have children take turns reading their label and attaching it to the appropriate continent.

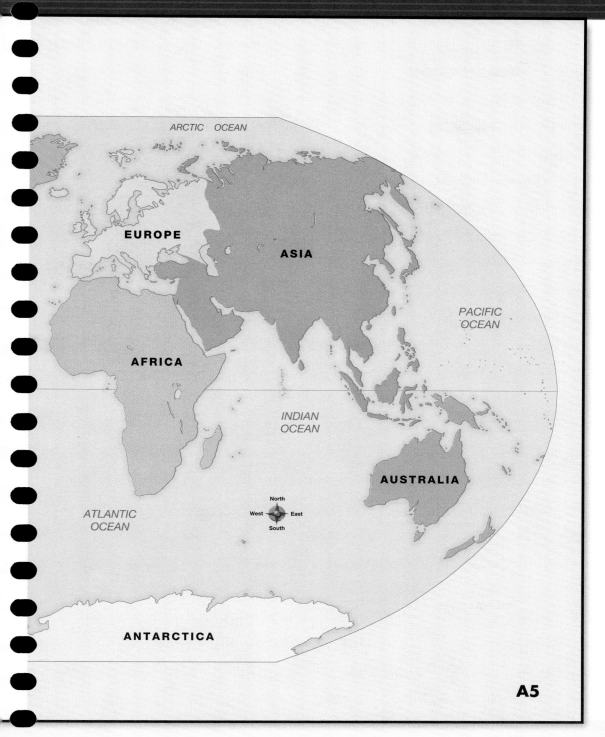

ARCTIC OCEAN

EUROPE

ASIA

AFRICA

PACIFIC OCEAN

INDIAN OCEAN

AUSTRALIA

North
West   East
South

ATLANTIC OCEAN

ANTARCTICA

A5

Map Study

Geography Ask volunteers to take turns tracing each continent and saying its name.

Q **How do you know where one continent ends and another begins?**

A The continents are shown in different colors.

Visual Learning

Map Direct attention to the continent of North America and have children name the oceans that surround it. Repeat this activity with the other continents.

Q **What continent is south of South America?**

A Antarctica

Q **What are the three continents that border each other?**

A Europe, Asia, and Africa

Q **On what continent is the United States?**

A North America

CD-ROM

Explore GEOSKILLS CD-ROM to learn more about map and globe skills.

REACH ALL LEARNERS

Tactile Learners Organize children into groups. Have each group trace the continents on paper and cut them out. Then tell children to shuffle the continent shapes. After the shapes have been mixed up, have children take turns holding up a shape and naming the continent. Then have the child find the continent on a wall map.

EXTEND AND ENRICH

Research and Report Have children work in groups to research one of the seven continents. Encourage them to record seven facts. Suggest children include the names of the countries that are part of their continent as one of the facts. Have children draw an outline of their continent on posterboard and then write on the outline the facts they discover. Display the continent posters around the room.

INTERNET RESOURCES

THE LEARNING SITE Go to **www.harcourtschool.com** to learn more about the continents.

Atlas

Set the Purpose

Main Idea A map can be used as a general view of a certain area of the world.

Why It Matters Have a child read aloud the title of the map. Then ask children why they might want to know more about North America than about the other continents. (because the United States is a part of North America)

Map Study

Geography Have children turn back to the world map on pages A4–A5 and find the continent of North America.

Q **How are the two maps alike? How are they different?**

A They both show places in the world. The map of North America shows only one continent.

Visual Learning

Map Tell children that North America is the third largest continent. Explain that most of the continents are divided into smaller parts. Point out to children that all parts of the United States are shown in pink. Then draw children's attention to the different bodies of water.

Q **What bodies of water that are part of and surround the North American continent are shown on the map?**

A Pacific Ocean, Atlantic Ocean, Gulf of California, Gulf of Mexico, Great Salt Lake, Hudson Bay, Lake Superior, Lake Michigan, Lake Huron, Lake Erie, and Lake Ontario

Geography Sometimes the southern portions of the Pacific, Atlantic, and Indian Oceans are referred to as the world's fifth ocean, or the Southern Ocean. However, this term is not universally used, and many major cartographers do not recognize it.

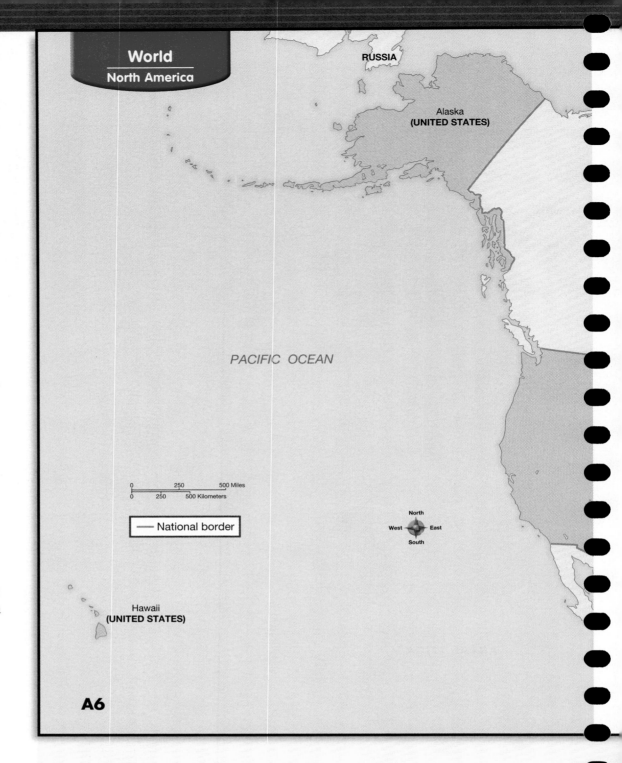

World
North America

RUSSIA

Alaska
(UNITED STATES)

PACIFIC OCEAN

| 0 | 250 | 500 Miles |
| 0 | 250 | 500 Kilometers |

— National border

North
West — East
South

Hawaii
(UNITED STATES)

A6

REACH ALL LEARNERS

Advanced Learners
Remind children that they live in the United States. Provide children with page T22 from the tabbed section Thinking Organizers in this Teacher's Guide. First, have children identify which part of the map is the United States by tracing its borders with a crayon. Next, challenge children to find approximately where their state is located within the United States, and have them write the name of the state in that general area.

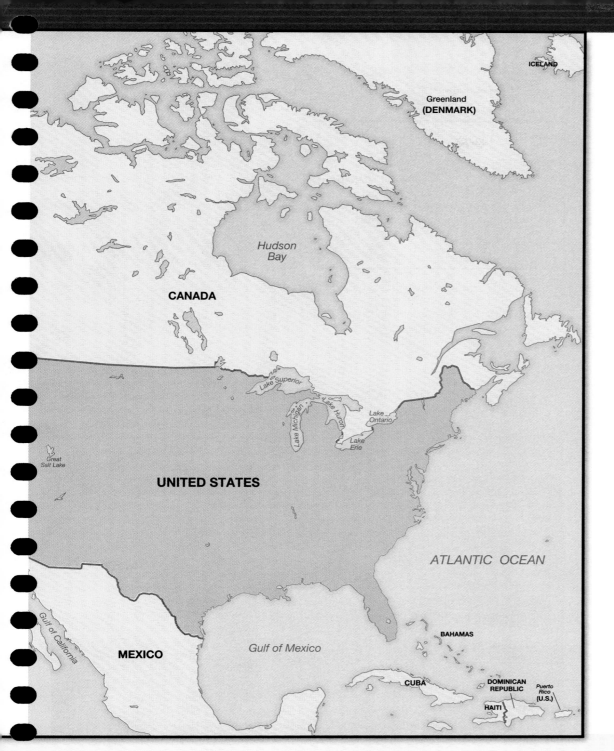

Map Study

Geography Ask volunteers to take turns tracing each country and saying its name.

Q How do you know where one country ends and another begins?

A The countries are separated by a dark line called a boundary line. Also, the United States is shown in a different color.

Visual Learning

Map Remind children that a compass rose shows where things are on a map, based on the directions north, south, east, and west. Explain that they should use the compass rose to help them identify where places are located on a map.

Q What country shares a border with Mexico on Mexico's north?

A the United States

Q What country shares a border with Canada on Canada's south?

A the United States

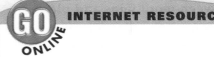

CD-ROM

Explore GEOSKILLS CD-ROM to learn more about map and globe skills.

BACKGROUND

North America One of the continents named for the Italian explorer Amerigo Vespucci, North America lies between the Arctic Circle and the equator. North America includes Mexico, the United States, Canada, Greenland, the Arctic Archipelago, the Bahamas, the Greater and Lesser Antilles, the Queen Charlotte Islands, the Aleutian Islands, and the countries of Central America. There are people from many cultures living in North America. The land is rich with natural resources.

EXTEND AND ENRICH

Riddle Game Organize children in pairs. Suggest that each pair make a riddle about one of the places on the map of North America for another pair to solve. For example, *Canada surrounds me. I am a body of water. I am south and west of Greenland. What am I? (Hudson Bay)* Have pairs take turns solving each other's riddles.

GO ONLINE   INTERNET RESOURCES

THE LEARNING SITE

Go to **www.harcourtschool.com** to learn more about North America.

Atlas

Set the Purpose

Main Idea A map can be used to show where land and water exist in the United States.

Why It Matters Ask a volunteer to read the title of the map. Encourage children to tell what they think they are going to learn by looking at this map. (about the kinds of land and water that can be found in the United States)

Map Study

Geography Point out that this map focuses on a part of North America called the United States. It also shows some of the other parts of North America that surround the United States. Smaller maps show the parts of the United States that are not connected to the other states.

Q What are the names of the states that are part of the United States but are not connected to them?

A Alaska and Hawaii

Visual Learning

Map Explain that this map shows the different kinds of land and water found in the United States. Have children point to and name the different rivers that they see on the map. Repeat with mountains, deserts, plains, lakes, and rivers.

Q If no words were on the map, how would you know the difference between mountains and plains?

A the mountain areas are bumpy and uneven and the plains are smooth and even; also, they are shown in different colors

Q What three large bodies of water surround the United States?

A the Pacific Ocean, the Atlantic Ocean, and the Gulf of Mexico

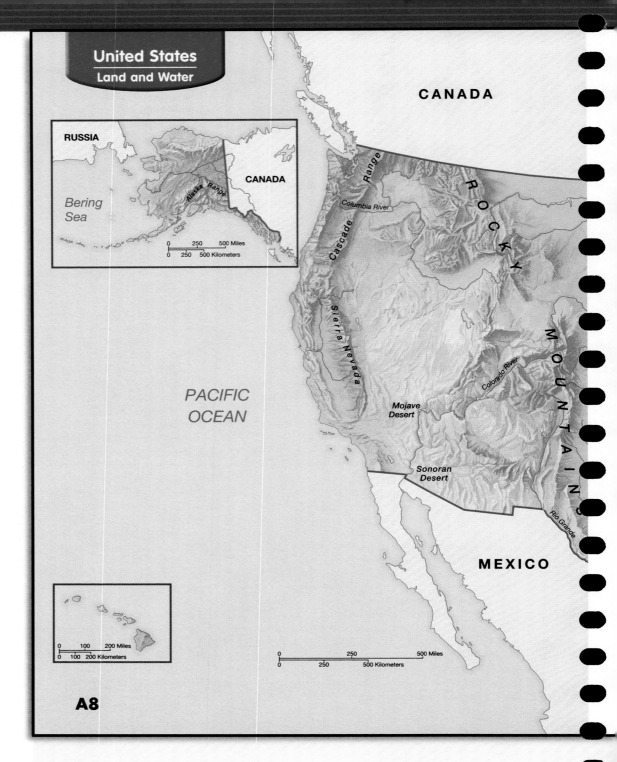

A8

INTEGRATE ART

Illustration Have children choose an area on the map and then draw a picture to show what they might see if they went to that spot. Invite volunteers to take turns displaying their pictures while class members guess which area the child has illustrated. Suggest that, before naming the area they drew, children provide clues to help the class guess.

REACH ALL LEARNERS

Tactile Learners Provide children with modeling clay. Have children form the clay to resemble the map of the contiguous United States. Then have them use plastic knives to form mountains, rivers, and other land and water forms to make a model of the United States.

A8 ■ ATLAS

CANADA

Lake Superior

Lake Michigan

Lake Huron

Lake Ontario

Lake Erie

GREAT PLAINS

Missouri River

Mississippi River

INTERIOR PLAINS

Missouri River

Ohio River

Mississippi River

APPALACHIAN MOUNTAINS

ATLANTIC OCEAN

COASTAL PLAIN

Rio Grande

North
West   East
South

Gulf of Mexico

BAHAMAS

Straits of Florida

CUBA

A9

Map Study

Geography Have a volunteer point out the compass rose on the map. Remind children that a compass rose shows where things are located on a map based on the directions north, south, east, and west. Explain that children can use directions and names of places on a map to help them find a location.

Q **What is the name of the desert that is south and east of the Mojave Desert?**

A the Sonoran Desert

Q **What is the name of the plains area that is north of the Gulf of Mexico?**

A the Coastal Plain

CD-ROM

Explore GEOSKILLS CD-ROM to learn more about map and globe skills.

INTEGRATE LANGUAGE ARTS

Descriptive Writing
Have children study the map of the United States. Then invite them to write a paragraph describing what the United States looks like, based on the information in the map.

EXTEND AND ENRICH

Land and Water in Your State
Provide reference resources and encourage children to find out about the kinds of land and water in their state. Then invite children to draw a map to show the types of land and water found in the state and approximately where they are located.

GO ONLINE INTERNET RESOURCES

THE LEARNING SITE

Go to **www.harcourtschool.com** for more information about land and water maps.

Atlas

Set the Purpose

Main Idea A map can be used to show where the different states are located in the United States.

Why It Matters Explain that a map can also be used to show where places are within a country. Have a child read aloud the title of the map. Then ask children what this map will show them. (the name and location of all the states in the United States)

Q **Why might we need to have different states in our country?**

A because it is a big place and having states makes it easier to tell someone else where you live within your country

Map Study

Geography Have children locate on the map and trace with their finger the state in which they live. Ask children how they know which state is theirs. (they could find the name of their state to identify it or they might know the shape of the state)

Q **How many states are part of the United States?**

A There are 50 states.

Q **What are the two states that are not attached to the other 48 states?**

A Alaska and Hawaii

Visual Learning

Map Draw attention to the letters listed in parentheses after each state name. Ask children what they think these letters mean. If children do not know, tell them that these letters are abbreviations for the states. Explain that abbreviations are usually used in a person's address. Invite children to practice writing their address on a sheet of paper using the correct abbreviation for their state.

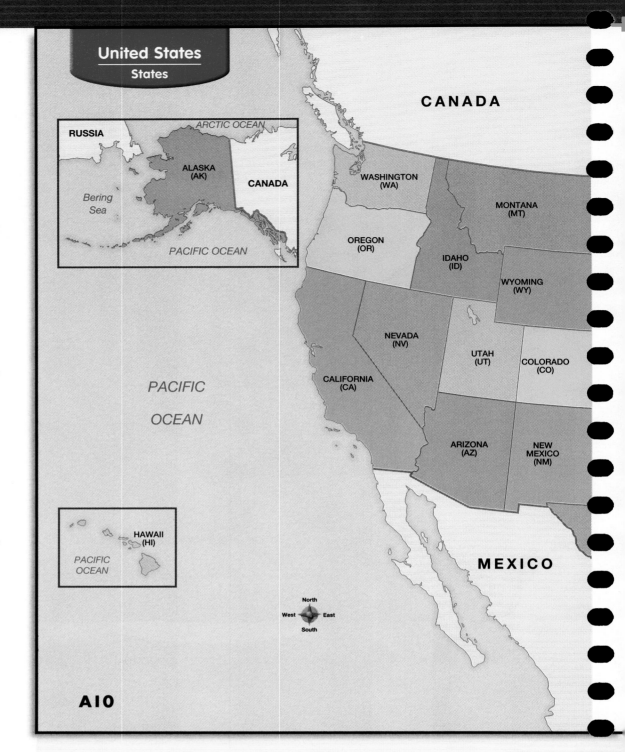

United States
States

A10

REACH ALL LEARNERS

English as a Second Language Have children make a set of flash cards for the 50 states. On one side of each card, tell them to write the name of a state. On the other side, have them draw an outline of the state. Suggest children take turns naming a state while a partner selects the card for that state.

REACH ALL LEARNERS

Tactile Learners Provide a puzzle map of the United States for children to put together. If a manufactured puzzle is not available, make one. Use a copy of page T21 from the tabbed section Thinking Organizers in this Teacher's Edition. Enlarge the map, write the names of the states in the appropriate places, and glue it on posterboard. Cut out each state and place the pieces in a plastic container. Allow children to work alone or with a partner to put the pieces together.

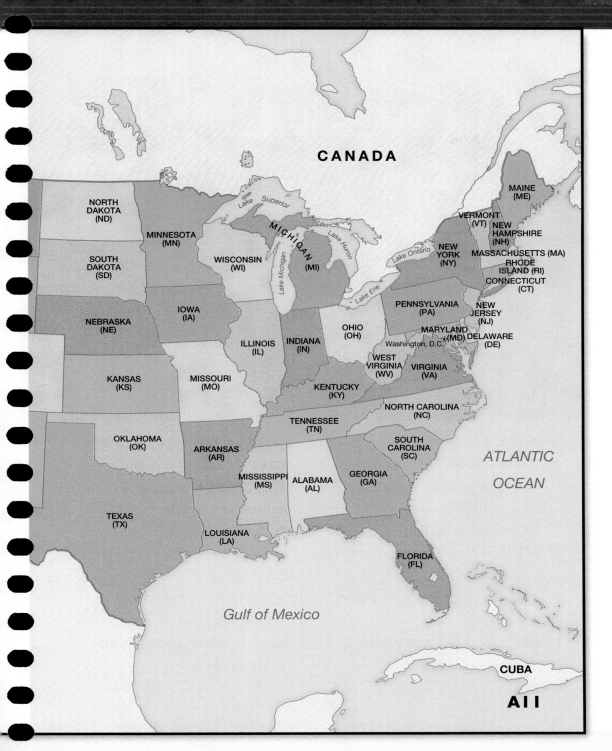

CANADA

NORTH DAKOTA (ND)

MINNESOTA (MN)

SOUTH DAKOTA (SD)

WISCONSIN (WI)

MICHIGAN (MI)

Lake Superior

Lake Huron

Lake Michigan

Lake Ontario

Lake Erie

MAINE (ME)

VERMONT (VT)

NEW HAMPSHIRE (NH)

NEW YORK (NY)

MASSACHUSETTS (MA)

RHODE ISLAND (RI)

CONNECTICUT (CT)

NEBRASKA (NE)

IOWA (IA)

OHIO (OH)

PENNSYLVANIA (PA)

NEW JERSEY (NJ)

MARYLAND (MD)

DELAWARE (DE)

ILLINOIS (IL)

INDIANA (IN)

Washington, D.C.

WEST VIRGINIA (WV)

VIRGINIA (VA)

KANSAS (KS)

MISSOURI (MO)

KENTUCKY (KY)

NORTH CAROLINA (NC)

TENNESSEE (TN)

OKLAHOMA (OK)

ARKANSAS (AR)

SOUTH CAROLINA (SC)

MISSISSIPPI (MS)

ALABAMA (AL)

GEORGIA (GA)

ATLANTIC OCEAN

TEXAS (TX)

LOUISIANA (LA)

FLORIDA (FL)

Gulf of Mexico

CUBA

A11

Map Study

Geography Encourage children to locate the compass rose on the map. Ask a volunteer to tell how they can use the compass rose. (It can help them locate places using the directions north, south, east, and west.)

Q Which state is south of Georgia?

A Florida

Q Which state has Tennessee on its west side and the Atlantic Ocean on its east?

A North Carolina

Visual Learning

Map Point out that all the states have different shapes and that this can help them find and identify their own state as well as others.

Q What might happen if all the states were the same shape and size?

A It might be harder to find each state, especially if the names were not on the map.

CD-ROM

Explore GEOSKILLS CD-ROM to learn more about map and globe skills.

Atlas

Set the Purpose

Main Idea A geographical diagram and dictionary can be used to illustrate and define terms for a variety of landforms and bodies of water.

Why It Matters Tell children that this dictionary and diagram can be used to help them learn to identify and remember different landforms and bodies of water.

Visual Learning

Diagram Point out that a dictionary provides a term or word and then tells what the word means. Read aloud the word *desert* and then the definition. Ask children which picture in the diagram shows what a desert looks like. Repeat this process with the other words until each word, definition, and picture has been matched.

Map Study

Geography Suggest that children compare the diagram and definitions on this page with the maps on pages A2–A3 and A8–A9. Help children relate the landforms and bodies of water in the dictionary and on the diagram to the areas shown on the maps.

Q **How might the diagram and the dictionary help you imagine what the land and water look like on the maps?**

A Seeing a picture of what each feature looks like can help me understand how the places on the map might look if I could be in those places. The definitions can also help me imagine each place.

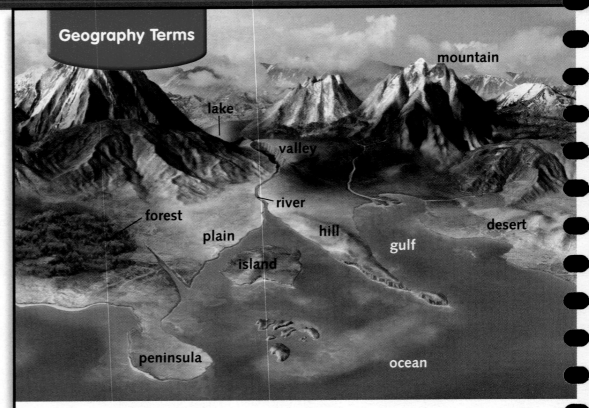

Geography Terms

mountain

lake

valley

river

forest

desert

plain

hill

gulf

island

peninsula

ocean

desert a large, dry area of land

forest a large area of trees

gulf a large body of ocean water that is partly surrounded by land

hill land that rises above the land around it

island a landform with water all around it

lake a body of water with land on all sides

mountain highest kind of land

ocean a body of salt water that covers a large area

peninsula a landform that is surrounded on only three sides by water

plain flat land

river a large stream of water that flows across the land

valley low land between hills or mountains

A12

Going to School

Eagle on Uncle Sam's Hat
Tradesign, 1870

Unit 1 Planning Chart Going to School

Unit 1 helps introduce children to the school environment. Children will explore school rules and why they are important, school workers and what they do, and schools around the world. In addition, children will discover what schools were like long ago and how they compare with schools today.

LESSON	PACING	OBJECTIVES	VOCABULARY
Introduce the Unit pp. 1R–1 **Preview the Vocabulary** pp. 2–3A **Start with a Poem** pp. 4A–5A	3 Days	■ Use a visual to predict content. ■ Interpret a quotation. ■ Use a table to prepare for the unit. ■ Use visuals to determine word meanings. ■ Use words and visuals to predict the content of the unit. ■ Obtain information about a topic using a variety of visual sources such as pictures and literature. ■ Explain why schools are important.	school **Word Work,** p. 3A
Going to School pp. 6A–7A	1 Day	■ Identify main ideas from visual sources. ■ Describe the role of self as a member of the class. ■ Express ideas orally based on knowledge and experiences.	learn share
READING SKILLS **Find the Main Idea** pp. 8A–9A	1 Day	■ Identify main ideas from oral and print sources. ■ Recognize details that support the main idea.	main idea detail
2 Rules at School pp. 10A–11A	1 Day	■ Explain the need for rules in the home, school, and community. ■ Give examples of rules that establish order, provide security, and manage conflict. ■ Explore appropriate behavior at school. ■ Compare rules made for different groups and situations.	rule fair
CITIZENSHIP SKILLS **Working Together** pp. 12A–13A	1 Day	■ Follow steps for working together in a group. ■ Use a decision-making process to identify a situation that requires a decision, gather information, identify options, predict consequences, and take action to implement a decision.	group

Time Management

READING	INTEGRATE LEARNING	REACH ALL LEARNERS	RESOURCES
Focus Skill Compare and Contrast, p. 1 **Reading Social Studies: Preview the Unit,** p. 2 **Make a Prediction,** pp. 4A, 5	**Theme Time,** p. 1I Art **Draw a School Mascot,** p. 1R Language Arts **Write Letters,** p. 1 Technology **Keyboard,** p. 3	**English as a Second Language,** pp. 1N, 2 **Advanced Learners,** p. 1N **Below-Level Learners,** p. 1N **Extension Activities For Home and School,** p. 5A	**Pupil Book/Unit Big Book,** pp. 1–5 **Audiotext** **Word Cards V1–V2** **Reading and Vocabulary Transparency 1–1** Internet Resources
Reading Social Studies: T-Chart, pp. 6A, 7	Mathematics **Add and Subtract,** p. 6	**Extend and Enrich,** p. 6 **Reteach the Lesson,** p. 7 **Extension Activities For Home and School,** p. 7A	**Pupil Book/Unit Big Book,** pp. 6–7 **Word Cards V1–V2** **Reading and Vocabulary Transparency 1–2** **Activity Book,** p. 1 Internet Resources
		Advanced Learners, p. 8 **Extend and Enrich,** p. 9 **Reteach the Skill,** p. 9 **Extension Activities For Home and School,** p. 9A	**Pupil Book/Unit Big Book,** pp. 8–9 **Word Cards V1–V4** **Skill Transparency 1–1** **Activity Book,** p. 2 Internet Resources
Reading Social Studies: Study Questions, pp. 10A, 11		**Extend and Enrich,** p. 10 **Reteach the Lesson,** p. 11 **Extension Activities For Home and School,** p. 11A	**Pupil Book/Unit Big Book,** pp. 10–11 **Word Cards V3–V4** **Reading and Vocabulary Transparency 1–3** **Activity Book,** p. 3 Internet Resources
	Reading **Literature,** p. 12A	**Advanced Learners,** p. 12 **Extend and Enrich,** p. 13 **Reteach the Skill,** p. 13 **Extension Activities For Home and School,** p. 13A	**Pupil Book/Unit Big Book,** pp. 12–13 **Word Cards V3–V4** **Skill Transparency 1–2** **Activity Book,** p. 4 Internet Resources

Unit 1 Planning Guide

LESSON	PACING	OBJECTIVES	VOCABULARY
3 School Workers pp. 14A–17A	2 Days	■ Identify school workers. ■ Identify the responsibilities of authority figures in the home and school. ■ Recognize that children depend on school workers. ■ Describe the work role of children in school and at home.	**teacher** **principal**
4 Where Are You? pp. 18A–19A	1 Day	■ Describe location of self and objects relative to other locations in the classroom and school. ■ Use relative location words to describe where things are.	**location** **Word Work,** p. 18
MAP AND GLOBE SKILLS **Looking at Maps** pp. 20A–21A	1 Day	■ Create and use simple maps to identify the location of places in the classroom and school. ■ Recognize the use of symbols on maps to represent real things. ■ Create visual and written material including pictures and maps.	**map** **symbol**
5 Schools Long Ago and Today pp. 22A–27A	3 Days	■ Compare and contrast schools of long ago with schools of today. ■ Recognize tools for learning in the classroom.	**tool** **Word Work,** p. 22

READING	INTEGRATE LEARNING	REACH ALL LEARNERS	RESOURCES
Reading Social Studies: **K-W-L Chart,** pp. 14A, 17	Language Arts **Expressive Writing,** p. 15	**Below-Level Learners,** p. 14 **English as a Second Language,** p. 15 **Advanced Learners,** p. 16 **Extend and Enrich,** p. 16 **Reteach the Lesson,** p. 17 **Extension Activities For Home and School,** p. 17A	**Pupil Book/Unit Big Book,** pp. 14–17 **Word Cards V5–V6** ⊘**Reading and Vocabulary Transparency 1–4** **Activity Book,** p. 5 **Activity Pattern P1** ⊜Internet Resources
Reading Social Studies: **Word Web,** pp. 18A, 19	Art **Draw a Picture,** p. 18	**Extend and Enrich,** p. 18 **Reteach the Lesson,** p. 19 **Extension Activities For Home and School,** p. 19A	**Pupil Book/Unit Big Book,** pp. 18–19 **Word Cards V5–V6** ⊘**Reading and Vocabulary Transparency 1–5** **Activity Book,** p. 6 ⊜Internet Resources
	Language Arts **Narrative Writing,** p. 20	**Below-Level Learners,** p. 20 **Extend and Enrich,** p. 21 **Reteach the Skill,** p. 21 **Extension Activities For Home and School,** p. 21A	**Pupil Book/Unit Big Book,** pp. 20–21 **Word Cards V5–V8** ⊘**Skill Transparency 1–3** **Activity Book,** p. 7 ⊘**GeoSkills CD-ROM** ⊜Internet Resources
Reading Social Studies: **Venn Diagram,** pp. 22A, 27 (Focus Skill) **Compare and Contrast,** p. 24	Language Arts **Informative Writing,** p. 24 Physical Education **Play Historic Games,** p. 25 Mathematics **Word Problems,** p. 26	**Advanced Learners,** p. 23 **English as a Second Language,** p. 26 **Extend and Enrich,** p. 26 **Reteach the Lesson,** p. 27 **Extension Activities For Home and School,** p. 27A	**Pupil Book/Unit Big Book,** pp. 22–27 **Word Cards V7–V8** ⊘**Reading and Vocabulary Transparency 1–6** **Activity Book,** p. 8 **Activity Pattern P2** ⊜Internet Resources

Unit I Planning Guide

LESSON	PACING	OBJECTIVES	VOCABULARY
CHART AND GRAPH SKILLS **Put Things into Groups** pp. 28A–29A	**1 Day**	■ Read and interpret a table. ■ Categorize information.	**table** **Word Work,** p. 28
6 Learning Around the World pp. 30A–33A	**2 Days**	■ Compare schools around the world. ■ Discover that people learn in places outside of school.	**world**
Visit A School for Firefighters pp. 34A–35	**1 Day**	■ Describe the requirements of jobs and the characteristics of a job well-performed. ■ Obtain information about a topic using a variety of visual sources, such as pictures, television, and computer images.	
Unit 1 Review and Test Preparation pp. 36–40	**3 Days**		

READING	INTEGRATE LEARNING	REACH ALL LEARNERS	RESOURCES
	Science **Living/Nonliving Table,** p. 28	**Advanced Learners,** p. 28 **Extend and Enrich,** p. 29 **Reteach the Skill,** p. 29 **Extension Activities For Home and School,** p. 29A	**Pupil Book/Unit Big Book,** pp. 28–29 **Word Cards V7–V8** 🌐 **Skill Transparency 1–4** **Activity Book,** p. 9 **Activity Pattern P1** 💻 Internet Resources
Reading Social Studies: **Anticipation Guide,** pp. 30A, 33 (Focus Skill) **Compare and Contrast,** p. 31	**Music** **Sing a Song,** p. 30 **Reading** **Getting to School,** p. 30 **Languages** **"Hello" Around the World,** p. 32	**Extend and Enrich,** p. 32 **Reteach the Lesson,** p. 33 **Extension Activities For Home and School,** p. 33A	**Pupil Book/Unit Big Book,** pp. 30–33 **Word Cards V7–V8** 🌐 **Reading and Vocabulary Transparency 1–7** **Activity Book,** p. 10 💻 Internet Resources
Reading Social Studies: **Make Predictions,** p. 34A		**English as a Second Language,** p. 34 **Extend and Enrich,** p. 35	**Pupil Book/Unit Big Book,** pp. 34–35 💻 Internet Resources **Take a Field Trip Video**
(Focus Skill) **Compare and Contrast,** p. 36			**Pupil Book/Unit Big Book,** pp. 36–40 **Activity Book,** pp. 11–12 🌐 **Reading and Vocabulary Transparency 1–8** ✔ **Assessment Program, Unit 1 Test,** pp. 1–4 💻 Internet Resources

Unit I Skills Path

Unit 1 features the reading skills of comparing and contrasting and finding the main idea. It also highlights the social studies skills of working together, looking at maps, and putting things into groups.

FOCUS SKILLS

UNIT 1 READING SKILL

 COMPARE AND CONTRAST

- INTRODUCE p. 1
- APPLY pp. 24, 31, 36

READING SOCIAL STUDIES

- Preview the Unit, p. 2
- Make a Prediction, pp. 4A, 5, 34A
- T-Chart, pp. 6A, 7
- Study Questions, pp. 10A, 11
- K-W-L Chart, pp. 14A, 17
- Word Web, pp. 18A, 19
- Venn Diagram, pp. 22A, 27
- Anticipation Guide, pp. 30A, 33

MAP AND GLOBE SKILLS

LOOKING AT MAPS

- INTRODUCE pp. 20A–21A
- APPLY p. 39

CITIZENSHIP SKILLS

WORKING TOGETHER

- INTRODUCE pp. 12A–13A

CHART AND GRAPH SKILLS

PUT THINGS INTO GROUPS

- INTRODUCE pp. 28A–29A
- APPLY p. 38

READING SKILLS

FIND THE MAIN IDEA

- INTRODUCE pp. 8–9

STUDY AND RESEARCH SKILLS

- Use Reference Sources, p. 1R
- Skimming and Scanning, p. 22
- Preview Pictures and Title, p. 28A

Theme Time: Classmates

MATH CENTER

Classmate Comparison

Provide interlocking cubes and either a mat or towel on which children can lie down. Have partners take turns using the cubes to measure and record the length of each other's feet, hands, arms, legs, and overall height. Tell partners to compare their measurements and decide in what ways they are similar and different. Ask children to think of a way to record their comparisons and display their results in the center.

SCIENCE CENTER

Puffing Power

Provide drinking straws and either paper or foam cups. Have children take turns laying the cup down and blowing through a straw into the open end of the cup. Then have two or three children use straws to blow into the cup at the same time. Ask children to compare the results of the two methods and to discuss reasons for the difference. Point out that when children work together, it can make their job easier.

READING/LANGUAGE ARTS CENTER

Advice for a Classmate

Place a recording of "Mary Had a Little Lamb" in the center. After children listen to the poem, ask them to discuss with a partner why bringing the lamb to school was not a good idea. Partners then brainstorm other things that are fine to have at home but that might cause problems if Mary brought them to school. Ask children to imagine they are talking to Mary as they make a recording giving advice about items that are fun and helpful to bring to school and others that should be left at home.

BULLETIN BOARD: COOPERATION

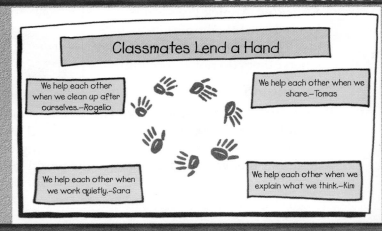

Have children help create a bulletin board, titled *Classmates Lend a Hand*, which tells ways classmates help each other learn and get things done. Invite each child to trace the outline of his or her hand onto a sheet of construction paper or colorful wrapping paper. Help children cut out their handprints. Then ask each to complete the sentence frame *We help each other when we _____.* Create a wreath by arranging the handprints in a circle, and surround the wreath with children's sentence frames.

Multimedia Resources

The Multimedia Resources can be used in a variety of ways. They can supplement core instruction in the classroom or extend and enrich children's learning at home.

Independent Reading

Easy

Bauld, Jane Scoggins. **We Need Principals.** Pebble Books, 2000. Full-color photos and simple, repetitive text help beginning readers learn about a principal's job.

Bloom, Suzanne. **The Bus for Us.** Boyds Mills Press, 2001. An older sibling makes sure that his younger sister gets on the right vehicle to go to school.

Floyd, Lucy. **Rabbit and Turtle Go to School.** Harcourt, 2000. In this humorous innovation on Aesop's fable, Rabbit races to school while Turtle relaxes on the school bus.

Murphy, Stuart J. **Get Up and Go!** HarperCollins, 1996. Sammie the dog creates time lines to help his friend and owner get ready for school. He doesn't rest for a minute until her school bus has disappeared.

Simmons, Jane. **Ebb and Flo and the New Friend.** McElderry Books, 1999. A little dog resents sharing with Bird but finds she misses Bird when she flies away.

Winters, Kay. **Did You See What I Saw?** Penguin Putnam, 2001. This entertaining collection includes twenty-four poems about the fun and difficulties of school life.

Average

Brown, Laurene. **Rex and Lilly Schooltime.** Little, Brown, 2001. Three short episodes present humorous school experiences at lunch, show-and-tell, and reading time.

Couric, Katie. **The Brand New Kid.** Doubleday, 2000. Two girls show caring and compassion for Lazlo S. Gazky, a new kid in school and a recent immigrant from Hungary. Carrie and Ellie teach their classmates that Lazlo is the same as them.

Feldman, Heather. **My School Bus: A Book About School Bus Safety.** Rosen Publishing Group, 1998. A young girl shows the safe way to wait for, ride, and get off the bus.

Havill, Juanita. **Jamaica and the Substitute Teacher.** Houghton Mifflin, 1999. A substitute teacher helps Jamaica learn that she does not need to have a perfect spelling paper to be special.

Henkes, Kevin. **Wemberly Worried.** Greenwillow Books, 2000. Wemberly's concerns about starting school disappear when she makes a friend.

Howe, James. **The Day the Teacher Went Bananas.** Puffin, 1992. The new teacher who is full of fun activities turns out to be a gorilla.

Lionni, Leo. **Swimmy.** Knopf, 1991. A school of small fish join together to protect themselves from a larger fish.

Maccarone, Grace. **Sharing Time Troubles.** Scholastic, 1997. Sam solves the problem of finding something special for show-and-tell by sharing his little brother.

Oppenheim, Joanne. **The Show-and-Tell Frog.** Gareth Stevens, 1998. As Allie searches for her lost frog, readers enjoy finding its hiding places in the illustrations.

Poydar, Nancy. **First Day, Hooray!** Holiday House, 1999. Workers and students are busy preparing for the first day of school.

Scieszka, Jon. **Baloney.** Viking, 2001. When a teacher asks an outer-space alien boy to explain why he is late, he spins a wild yarn. Children will enjoy using context and the decoder at the back of the book to decipher the alien vocabulary words.

Snihura, Ulana. **I Miss Franklin P. Shuckles.** Annick Press, 1998. Molly learns the importance of loyalty to her friend Franklin even when others do not accept him.

Challenging

Baer, Edith. **This Is the Way We Go to School: A Book About Children Around the World.** Econo-Clad Books, 1999. This rhyming text describes the way children all over the world get to school.

Cuyler, Margery. ***100th Day Worries.*** Simon & Schuster, 2000. Jessica's family comes to the rescue when she has trouble finding 100 items for her school assignment.

Peck, Jan. ***The Giant Carrot.*** Dial Books, 1998. In this adaptation of a Russian folktale, Isabelle sings and dances to help her family grow an enormous carrot.

Roop, Peter and Connie. ***A School Album.*** Heinemann Library, 1998. Pairs of photographs help children compare modern schools to those of long ago.

Wells, Rosemary. ***Timothy Goes to School.*** Puffin, 2000. During his first week of school, Timothy finds out how good it feels to be accepted.

Audiocassettes

1, 2, 3 Four-Ever Friends. North Side Music. Colleen and Uncle Squatty sing songs about making and keeping friends.

Huggabug Club Friends Forever. Audrey Landers sings songs about sharing, getting along, expressing feelings, and about family and friends.

I'm a Can Do Kid. John Archambault and David Plumer share songs and activities that build self-esteem, respect, and an appreciation of diversity.

School Days Songs. The Cedarmont Kids sing traditional school favorites.

Computer Software

Arthur's Teacher Trouble. Broderbund, 1992. Mac/Windows. This living book about Arthur's school experiences provides stories with clickable hotspots.

Choices, Choices: On the Playground. Tom Snyder Productions. Mac/Windows. This program helps children use problem-solving and goal-setting skills in playground situations.

Kelly Bear Teaches About Feelings. The Bureau for At-Risk Youth. Mac/Windows. This program includes video clips of children talking about their feelings and then offers users opportunities to relate the stories to their own feelings and to seek solutions.

Videos and DVDs

Cooperation.
BFA. Three children show how cooperation helps them have fun and get lots done at work, play, and school.

I Had It First! Learning to Share. Library Video, 1997. This video uses humor to show the importance of sharing.

Minding Your Manners at School. United Learning, 1996. Children learn important dos and don'ts in school situations through animated scenarios and the comments of young moderators.

Today Was a Terrible Day. Library Video, 1988. Ronald Morgan's school day is a disaster as he has one bad experience after another until something positive changes the ways he feels.

Additional books are recommended at point of use throughout the unit.

Note that information, while correct at time of publication, is subject to change.

ISBNs and other publisher information can be found at **www.harcourtschool.com**

The Learning Site: Social Studies Center

The Learning Site at www.harcourtschool.com offers a special Social Studies Center. The center provides a wide variety of activities, Internet links, and online references.

Here are just some of the HARCOURT Internet resources you'll find!

Multimedia Biographies
www.harcourtschool.com

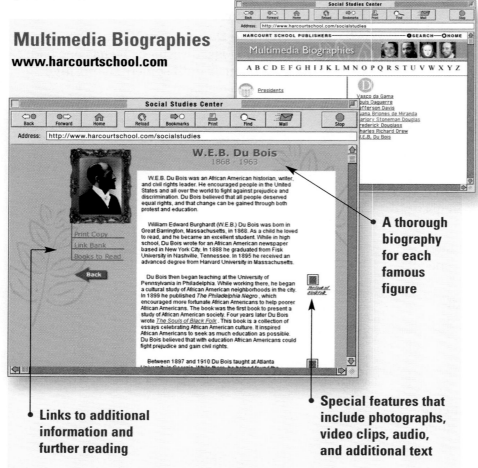

A thorough biography for each famous figure

Links to additional information and further reading

Special features that include photographs, video clips, audio, and additional text

INTERNET RESOURCES

Find all this at
The Learning Site at
www.harcourtschool.com
- Activities and Games
- Content Updates
- Current Events
- Free and Inexpensive Materials
- Multimedia Biographies
- Online Atlas
- Primary Sources
- Video Updates
- Virtual Tours
- Your State

and more!

Free and Inexpensive Materials
- Addresses to write for free and inexpensive products
- Links to unit-related materials
- Internet maps
- Internet references

www.harcourtschool.com

Primary Sources
- Artwork
- Clothing
- Diaries
- Government Documents
- Historical Documents
- Maps
- Tools

and more!

www.harcourtschool.com

Houston, TX Map

Virtual Tours
- Capitols and Government Buildings
- Cities
- Countries
- Historical Sites
- Museums
- Parks and Scenic Areas

and more!

www.harcourtschool.com

A School in Thailand

Integrate Learning Across the Curriculum

Use these topics to help you integrate social studies into your daily planning. See the page numbers indicated for more information about each topic.

Art

Draw a School Mascot, p. 1R
Draw a Picture, p. 18

Science

Puffing Power, p. 1I
Living/Nonliving Table, p. 28

Languages

"Hello" Around the World, p. 32

Language Arts

Advice for a Classmate, p. 1I
Write Letters, p. 1
Expressive Writing, p. 15
Narrative Writing, p. 20
Informative Writing, p. 24

Reading/Literature

"School Bus," p. 4
All Kinds of Schools, p. 5
Where Paper Comes From, p. 5
Garett Morgan, p. 5
Swimmy, p. 12A
This Is the Way We Go to School, p. 30
Get Up and Go!, p. 40
First Day, Hooray!, p. 40
A School Album, p. 40

Social Studies

Computer/Technology

Keyboard, p. 3
Go Online, pp. 5, 20, 31, 35
GeoSkills CD-ROM, p. 21
Take a Field Trip Video, p. 35

Music

"It's a Small World," p. 30

Physical Education

Play Historic Games, p. 25

Mathematics

Classmate Comparison, p. 1I
Add and Subtract, p. 6
Word Problems, p. 26

Reach All Learners

Use these activities to help individualize your instruction. Each activity has been developed to address a different level or type of learner.

English as a Second Language

20 minutes

Materials
■ picture cards showing classroom items

PRACTICE PRONUNCIATION Use the pictures as flash cards to model the names of classroom items and to have children practice pronunciation.

- Display a card and give clues or riddles about the pictures on it with words, with gestures, or by pantomiming. Give as many clues as children need to guess the item.
- Repeat for the other pictures on the cards.
- Have pairs make up their own clues or riddles about a few of the items.
- Invite children to take turns telling their clues or riddles for the group to guess.

Advanced Learners

30 minutes

Materials
■ paper
■ art materials

MAKE A CLASS "FIX-IT" BOOK Have children work together to make a book showing problems that arise in a classroom and how the class rules help "fix" the problems.

- Have partners draw pairs of pictures—one showing a problem situation and one showing a happy solution.
- Ask partners to organize the pictures in book form so that paired pictures are on facing pages.
- Have children bind the ordered pictures into a book.
- Ask children to choose a title and design a cover that reflects the contents of the book.

Fix-It Book for Ms. Johnson's Room

It's too noisy. Ms. Johnson can't hear what anyone is saying.

We can be heard if we follow the rule.

Below-Level Learners

30 minutes

Materials
■ film and camera
■ recorded messages from school helpers

PLAY "WHAT'S MY JOB?" Have children match photographs of school helpers with tape-recorded clues to their identity.

- Take children on a tour of the school to introduce them to people who do jobs around the school.
- Help children take photographs of each school helper.
- Display the photographs in the classroom, and play prerecorded messages in which the school helpers give clues about the job they do.
- Ask children to match each voice and set of clues with the correct photograph.
- Help children label each photograph with the school helper's name and job.

Mr. Herrera
Librarian

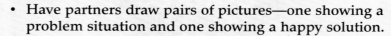

Assessment Options

The assessment program gives all learners many opportunities to show what they know and can do. It also provides ongoing information about each child's understanding of social studies.

Formal Assessment

- **LESSON REVIEWS:** pp. 7, 11, 17, 19, 27, 33
- **UNIT REVIEWS AND TEST PREPARATION,** pp. 36–39
- **UNIT ASSESSMENT**
  Standard Test,
  Assessment Program, pp. 1–3
  Individual Performance Task,
  Assessment Program, p. 4

Student Self-Evaluation

- **GEOGRAPHY THEME QUESTIONS**
  within lessons of Pupil Book
- **INDIVIDUAL END-OF-PROJECT CHECKLIST**
  Assessment Program, p. viii
- **GROUP END-OF-PROJECT CHECKLIST**
  Assessment Program, p. ix
- **INDIVIDUAL END-OF-UNIT CHECKLIST**
  Assessment Program, p. x

Informal Assessment

- **THINK ABOUT IT,** p. 5
- **SOCIAL STUDIES SKILLS CHECKLIST**
  Assessment Program, p. vi–vii

- **SKILLS**
  Practice the Skill, pp. 8, 13, 21, 28
  Apply What You Learned, pp. 9, 13, 21, 29

Performance Assessment

- **PERFORMANCE ACTIVITY IN LESSON REVIEWS**
- **UNIT ACTIVITIES,** p. 40
- **COMPLETE THE UNIT PROJECT,** p. 40
- **INDIVIDUAL PERFORMANCE TASK ASSESSMENT PROGRAM,** p. 4

Portfolio Assessment

STUDENT SELECTED ITEMS MAY INCLUDE:
- **THINK AND WRITE,** p. 36
- **UNIT ACTIVITIES,** p. 40
- **COMPLETE THE UNIT PROJECT,** p. 40

TEACHER SELECTED ITEMS MAY INCLUDE:
- **UNIT ASSESSMENT**
  Assessment Program, pp. 1–4
- **PORTFOLIO SUMMARY**
  Assessment Program, p. xv
- **GROUP END-OF-PROJECT CHECKLIST**
  Assessment Program, p. ix
- **INDIVIDUAL END-OF-UNIT CHECKLIST**
  Assessment Program, p. x

Unit 1 Test

STANDARD TEST

· Unit ·

Name _____ Date _____

1 Test

Vocabulary (4 points each)

Circle the picture that belongs with each sentence.

1. Someone who helps people learn is a _____.

2. Things that we must or must not do are _____.

   Class Schedule
   Tardy bell - 8:30
   Announcement - 8:35
   Pledge of Allegiance - 8:45

   Class Rules
   Raise hand
   Respect others
   Keep classroom clean

3. Our _____ is the leader of our school.

   PRINCIPAL

   NOTES

4. A _____ is a number of people working together.

5. We _____ when we find out something new.

Unit 1 Test

Assessment Program ▪ 1

STANDARD TEST

Name _____ Date _____

Main Ideas (10 points each)

6. Which tool helps you learn?
   - ● A map
   - ○ B box
   - ○ C fork
   - ○ D hammer

7. Which was used in schools long ago?
   - ○ F calculator
   - ○ G CD player
   - ● H book
   - ○ J computer

Draw a line from each school worker to something he or she might say.

8. "I serve your lunch."

9. LIBRARIAN "I work to keep our school looking its best."

10. "I help you find books."

11. "I take care of children who are sick or hurt."

(continued)

2 ▪ Assessment Program

Unit 1 Test

NOTES

_____
_____
_____
_____
_____
_____
_____
_____

Name _____ Date _____

Skills (5 points each)

Use the map to answer the questions.
Children should color the sink blue and draw a book or bookshelves on the map.

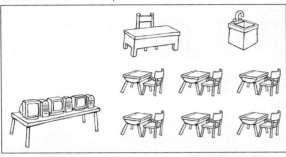

Teacher's desk   Child's desk   Sink   Computer center

12 How many computers are shown? _____ three

13 How many children's desks are there? _____ six

14 Think of a symbol for a reading area. Draw it on the map.

15 Find the sink in the classroom. Color it blue.

(continued)

Unit 1 Test   **Assessment Program ▪ 3**

Name _____ Date _____

Performance Task

There are different rules for different places at your school. Look at the pictures below. Think of a rule for each one and write it on the line below.

 Clean up after yourself. Use dining room manners.
_____
_____

 Wait your turn to play. Don't walk in front of swings.
_____
_____

 Be quiet at railroad crossings. Stay seated while the bus is moving.
_____
_____

(continued)

4 ▪ Assessment Program   Unit 1 Test

RUBRICS FOR SCORING

SCORING RUBRIC The rubric below lists the criteria for evaluating the tasks above. It also describes different levels of success in meeting those criteria.

INDIVIDUAL PERFORMANCE TASK

Score **4**	Score **3**	Score **2**	Score **1**
• Rules reflect strong understanding of possible problems and consequences. • Details provide strong examples of reasons for having rules. • Sentences are well developed.	• Rules reflect understanding of possible problems and consequences. • Details provide examples of reasons for having rules. • Sentences are fairly well developed.	• Rules reflect some understanding of possible problems and consequences. • Details provide some examples of reasons for having rules. • Sentences are minimally developed.	• Rules reflect no understanding of possible problems and consequences. • Details provide no examples of reasons for having rules. • Sentences are not developed.

Introduce the Unit

Access Prior Knowledge

Invite children to tell one fact about your school they would tell a newcomer to the school. Record responses on a list titled "All About Our School." Children can use the list as they make comparisons for their table.

All About Our School
Principal—Mrs. Green
Grades 1-5
Named after Dr. Martin Luther King, Jr.

Visual Learning

Call attention to the picture of the school on pages 1R and 1.

Q Who are the people in the picture?

A They are probably children who go to the school and their teachers or principal.

Q Why do you think the sign says "Home of the Eagles"?

A The eagle is the school mascot or symbol. The athletic teams are probably called the Eagles.

Q Does your school have a symbol or mascot? What is it?

A Children should be able to name the school mascot.

INTEGRATE ART

Draw a School Mascot
Discuss why the eagle makes a good mascot. Then tell children to choose and draw an animal mascot for your class. Have children begin by thinking about characteristics your class would like to be known for. Then have them choose an animal that represents one of those important traits.

STUDY/RESEARCH SKILLS

Using Reference Sources Have small groups research information about your school's history. Suggest that children include the date when the school was built and interesting stories about the building and its people. Have children write and illustrate the facts they find and bind the pages together to make a school history book.

Unit 1

Going to School

❝Enter to Learn Depart to Serve❞

—signs entering and leaving Mary McLeod Bethune's school in Daytona Beach, Florida, 1914

(Focus Skill) Compare and Contrast

As you read this unit, do the following.

- List what you learn about school.
- Use the list to show how schools are alike and different.

Schools
Alike	Different

1

INTEGRATE LANGUAGE ARTS

Write Letters Help children correspond with students in other schools to find out how schools are alike and different. Children may write to people they know who go to other schools. You may also wish to help children write class letters or use the Internet to correspond with classes in different places across the country and the world.

AUDIOTEXT

Use the Unit 1 AUDIOTEXT for a reading of the Unit narrative.

Analyze Primary Sources

Wooden Eagle Tradesign Help children identify the artifact at the beginning of the unit as a tradesign. Tell children that the bald eagle was adopted as our national symbol in 1782. Explain that the eagle is standing on an old-fashioned hat called a stovepipe hat.

Quotation Read aloud the quotation. Explain that the signs are posted at a college in Daytona Beach, Florida, a historically black college that was founded in 1904 by Mary McLeod Bethune.

Explain that *enter* means "to go in" and *depart* means "to leave." Point out that the words apply to students of any age.

Q **What does the first sign say is the reason students go to school?**

A When students enter school, their job is to learn.

Q **What does the second sign say students should do when they leave school?**

A When students finish school, they should use what they learned to help others.

(Focus Skill) Compare and Contrast

Tell children that in this unit they will be reading about schools in different times and places. As they read, children can think about the ways that schools are alike and different. Explain that a table is a chart children can use to compare these similarities and differences. Then, together with children, fill in the chart.

- A blank graphic organizer appears on page 11 of the Activity Book.
- A complete graphic organizer can be found on page 36 of this Teacher's Edition.

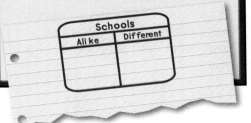

Schools
Alike	Different

Preview the Vocabulary

PAGES 2–3

Preview the Vocabulary

learn To find out something new. (page 6)

rule An instruction telling what must or must not be done. (page 10)

group A number of people working together. (page 12)

2

OBJECTIVES

- Use visuals to determine word meanings.
- Use words and visuals to predict the content of the unit.

Access Prior Knowledge

Have children examine the pictures on pages 2 and 3. Ask children to tell where they think the people in the pictures are. (school) Then encourage children to tell how they think the school in the pictures is like their school and how it is different.

Make Connections

Link Pictures and Words Display the word cards for *learn, rule, group, teacher,* and *principal.* Read each word aloud. Then have children match each word with the correct word and picture on pages 2 and 3. Have children describe each picture and share what it tells them about the word that matches it. Point out that pictures can help children figure out what words mean.

Visual Learning

Picture Focus children's attention on the picture of a child next to the word *learn.* Read aloud the definition, and ask what this picture shows. (a child learning) Have children compare the activity in this picture with a similar activity in their classroom.

Point out the picture of the group working together, and read aloud the definition of *group.*

Q How is working in a group different from working on your own?

A When you work in a group, you share ideas and jobs. When you work on your own, you use your own ideas and do everything yourself.

READING SOCIAL STUDIES

Preview the Unit Write the word *school* on the board, and read it aloud. Then ask children to name words that go with the word *school* to create a word web. Reread the words aloud, and have volunteers share what they think about when they hear each word.

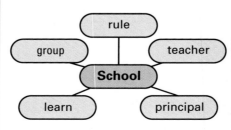

REACH ALL LEARNERS

English as a Second Language Suggest that children whose first language is not English begin a vocabulary word card file using index cards. Have children draw and label a picture for each vocabulary word. Invite them to write the word in their first language if they know it or to have a family member record it for them. Encourage children to add other words to their vocabulary files as they work through the unit.

---

2 ■ **Unit 1**

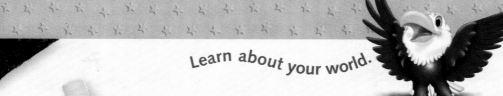

Learn about your world.

teacher A person who helps others learn. (page 14)

principal The leader of a school. (page 14)

3

Visual Learning

Pictures Ask children to look at the picture of the children raising their hands next to the term *rule*.

Q Why is it important to have rules in a school?

A Rules help keep everyone at a school in order so the children can learn. Rules also help keep people safe.

Ask children to tell what they see in the last two pictures on page 3. (a person in a classroom and a person in a school office) Then read aloud the words *teacher* and *principal* and their definitions. Have children identify teachers they have this year, such as art teachers, music teachers, and physical education teachers, as well as teachers they had in kindergarten. Then ask children to name the principal at your school.

CITIZENSHIP

DEMOCRATIC VALUES
Common Good

Point out the mascot, Earnest Eagle, on page 3. Tell children that they will see Earnest throughout the book and that each time it appears, the mascot will offer a message for children to think about. Read aloud what Earnest says. Then invite children to comment on how they can learn about their world and then use their new knowledge to help others learn.

INTEGRATE TECHNOLOGY

Keyboard Suggest that children use a word processing program to type the vocabulary words. If available, have children use a draw-and-paint program or clip art to illustrate their words. Alternatively, have them print their word list and illustrate each word to indicate the word's meaning.

SCHOOL TO HOME

Use the Unit 1 SCHOOL TO HOME NEWSLETTER on pages S1–S2 to introduce the unit to family members and suggest activities they can do at home.

Word Work

The following activities may be used to preteach vocabulary. You may also wish to duplicate and distribute the word cards found in the back of this book on pages V1–V8. Children can use them as flash cards to practice saying and defining each word. Remind children to use the glossary at the back of their book to help them define these words.

SCHOOL'S IN! BOARD GAME

Draw a simple path on a file folder to create a board game. On some spaces, write directions that include the vocabulary words, such as *You **share** with your friends. Move ahead two spaces.* Or *You forgot your **location**. Move back two spaces.* Also, make a set of word cards for the vocabulary words. Include the number "1," "2," or "3" on each card. To begin, players place markers, such as coins or buttons, on the board. Then children take turns drawing a word card. They read the word, use the word in a sentence, and move the number of spaces indicated on the card.

TABLE TALK

Guide children in using a table to compare their school with another school. Draw a table such as the one shown. Include items or people in the first column that are at your school as well as items or people that are not at your school. Have children place check marks to show where they might find each item or person. Then ask children to tell what the main idea of the table is and the details that tell them what it is about.

Person/Thing		Our School	Another School
tools		✓	✓
Principal Felkins		✓	
map		✓	✓
Mrs. Ezell, our teacher		✓	

MAP IT!

Read aloud the following poem. Then ask children to tell what they know about maps, the symbols on maps, and how we use maps.

Making Maps

I love to make maps!
I think it's great fun—
Making the boundaries,
And then, one by one,
Putting in railroads,
And each river bend,
And the tiny towns
Where little roads end.
I draw in the mountains,
And often a lake,
And I've even had
Long bridges to make!
I like to do highways,
And when they are drawn
I dream that they take me
Where I've never gone.
by Elaine V. Emans

SCHOOLHOUSE VOICES

JOURNAL Ask children to record the following words in their vocabulary journals. Then have children work with a partner or a small group. Invite children to take turns pointing to each word and using it in a sentence that shows the word's meaning.

 learn
 rule
 group
 teacher
 principal

School Bus

OBJECTIVES

- Obtain information about a topic using a variety of visual sources such as pictures and literature.
- Explain why schools are important.

RESOURCES

Pupil Book/Unit Big Book, pp. 4–5

Word Cards V1–V2

🖱 **Reading and Vocabulary Transparency 1–1**

💻 **Internet Resources**

Audiotext, Unit 1

Vocabulary

school p. 4

Summary

This poem is about going to school on a bus for the first day of the school year. The poet focuses on numbers of boys, girls, sleepy eyes, and school supplies.

1 Motivate

Set the Purpose

Read aloud the title of the poem and the poet's name. Explain to children that they can decide before they read what they want to learn from the reading. Point out that most poems are read for enjoyment. To help children set a purpose for reading, model the process:

> **I can tell from the title that the poem is about a school bus. I want to read to find out who is on the bus and where they are going.**

Access Prior Knowledge

Lead children in singing a variation of "The Wheels on the Bus" that focuses on a school bus. Invite children to share what they know about school buses.

READING SOCIAL STUDIES

Graphic Organizer Begin a chart about predictions about the poem. Complete the chart during Close.

Our Prediction	What the Poem Says
The poem is about kids on a bus going on a field trip or to school.	

🔴 **USE READING AND VOCABULARY TRANSPARENCY 1–1**

1–1
TRANSPARENCY

2 Teach

Read and Respond

Understand the Poem Ask children to think about how they got ready on the first day of school. Invite volunteers to share their preparations.

Culture and Society Point out that many different people are involved in preparing for the first day of school. Children and their family members buy school supplies and new clothes. Teachers organize their materials and fix up their rooms while other school workers ready other parts of the school.

Q What are two ways the poem mentions of getting ready for the start of a new school year?

A Someone painted the school bus. The children have many school supplies.

Q Why are schools important?

A They teach children about things they need to know, such as how to read and write and how to do math.

Ask children to jot down phrases that tell how they got ready for the new school year. Then help small groups of children compile their phrases to create a non-rhyming poem. Invite groups to share their work.

Visual Learning

Illustration Direct children's attention to the school bus scene.

Q What do you notice first in the picture? second?

A The children; they are on a bus.

Q Why did the artist show children on a school bus?

A The picture needed to match the words.

START with a POEM

School Bus

by Lee Bennett Hopkins
illustrated by Lori Lohstoeter

This wide-awake
freshly-painted-yellow
school bus

readied for Fall

carries us all—

    Sixteen boys—
    Fourteen girls—

    Thirty pairs of sleepy eyes

and

hundreds
upon
hundreds
of
school supplies.

4

BACKGROUND

About the Poet Lee Bennett Hopkins is an author, anthologist, and poet. He is especially known for his anthologies of poems for children. Hopkins has said, "Good poetry is by a master craftsman who knows the rules of his craft. He/She gets the maximum impact from a minimum number of words." Along with compiling collections of poems, Hopkins has written books for educators, fiction for young adults, and nonfiction for adults.

Yellow School Buses Frank W. Cyr is considered to be "the Father of the Yellow School Bus." In 1939 Cyr organized a conference at which national school bus standards, including the color yellow, were established. Until that time children rode to school in a variety of trucks and buses of all colors. The color yellow was chosen because black lettering on that color stands out in semidark conditions of early morning and late afternoon, when children typically ride school buses.

Think About It

1. What does the poem tell you about these children?

2. How do you get ready for school?

Read a Book

Start the Unit Project

A Classroom Scrapbook Your class will start a scrapbook. As you read this unit, draw and write about the new things you learn.

Use Technology

 Visit The Learning Site at **www.harcourtschool.com** for additional activities, primary sources, and other resources to use in this unit.

5

Think About It

Answers

1. Children's responses should include that they are going to school in a bus, there are 16 boys and 14 girls, they are sleepy, and they have many school supplies.

2. Children's responses may include that they eat breakfast, get dressed, and gather their school supplies.

 INTERNET RESOURCES

THE LEARNING SITE
Visit The Learning Site at **www.harcourtschool.com** to view Internet resources for this unit.

TIME FOR KIDS
Go to **www.harcourtschool.com** for the latest news in a student-friendly format.

---

3 Close

Summarize the Reading

- Some children ride a school bus to school.
- Workers and children get ready for a new school year.

READING SOCIAL STUDIES

Graphic Organizer Revisit the chart begun in Motivate. Invite children to share what they learned. Add these ideas to the chart.

Our Prediction	What the Poem Says
The poem is about kids on a bus going on a field trip or to school.	Children are riding in a school bus. They are sleepy because it is the first day of school. They have many school supplies.

● USE READING AND VOCABULARY TRANSPARENCY 1–1

 1–1 TRANSPARENCY

Read a Book

Children may enjoy reading these leveled independent Readers. Additional books are listed on pages 1J–1K of this Teacher's Edition.

Easy *All Kinds of Schools* by Susan Ring. This book explores unusual and highly specialized schools.

Average *Where Paper Comes From* by Susan Ring. The history of the paper-making process is introduced.

Challenging *Garrett Morgan* by Susan Ring. This biography tells about the African American inventor of the traffic light.

Start the Unit Project

Hint Before children begin their unit project, suggest that they look over page 1. As they read each lesson, help children make a list of the new words and concepts they are learning.

Extension Activities For Home and School

School Bus

Materials: construction paper, magazines, small box or milk carton, scissors, crayons or markers

Ask children to make a picture or model at home of a school bus. For example, they might draw and cut out a school bus, paste a magazine picture of a school bus on construction paper, or make a simple school bus model from a small box or clean milk carton. Have children discuss with family members why schools are important. Invite children to bring their school bus creations to school. As they share, encourage children to tell why they think schools are important. **(TACTILE/VISUAL)**

School Bus Safety Song

Materials: student handbook for your school

Display pages 4–5, and point out that the children are riding safely on the bus. Ask what the children are doing to be safe as they ride the bus. List ideas on the board. Then read aloud the rules for school bus safety in your school's student handbook. Invite children to add other ideas about how to stay safe as they ride a school bus. Organize children into small groups, and have each group make up a song about ways to stay safe on the bus. Suggest they use a familiar tune, such as "The Wheels on the Bus," "The Bear Went over the Mountain," or "She'll Be Coming Around the Mountain." Invite each group to share their song with the class. **(VISUAL/AUDITORY)**

School Bus Safety
1. Always walk to or from the bus.
2. Wait for the driver's signal to cross.
3. Cross at least 10 feet in front of the bus.
4. Always stay seated when the bus is moving.

Pencil Holders

Materials: instructional poster, cardboard, index card, scissors, crayons or markers, tape

Display an instructional poster, such as the one shown. Have children follow the directions on the poster to make a pencil holder. **(TACTILE/VISUAL)**

1. Cut a sheet of cardboard in half.
2. Fold the paper into three parts.
3. Fold up the paper a little at the bottom. Make small cuts at each section.
4. On each part of the paper, draw a picture about school and write why school is important.
5. Fold the paper into a triangle and tape it together. Then tape the flaps to an index card.
6. Store school supplies in your pencil holder.

Going to School

OBJECTIVES

- Identify main ideas from visual sources.
- Describe the role of self as a member of the class.
- Express ideas orally based on knowledge and experiences.

 Focus Skill **Compare and Contrast**
pp. 1, 36

RESOURCES

Pupil Book/Unit Big Book, pp. 6–7

Word Cards V1–V2

Activity Book, p. 1

📀**Reading and Vocabulary Transparency 1–2**

💻**Internet Resources**

READING SOCIAL STUDIES

Graphic Organizer Begin a T-chart about what people do at school. Complete the chart during Close.

Learn	Share

●USE READING AND VOCABULARY
TRANSPARENCY 1–2   **1–2**
TRANSPARENCY

Vocabulary

learn p. 6

share p. 7

 When Minutes Count

Have children examine the pictures on pages 6 and 7. Use the pictures to discuss the Big Idea of the lesson.

Quick Summary

The lesson focuses on school. It describes what children learn in school and what they share.

1 Motivate

Set the Purpose

Big Idea Before starting the lesson, read the Big Idea statement aloud. As you read and discuss the lesson, help children identify ways they learn and share at school.

Access Prior Knowledge

Before reading the lesson, invite children to think about the things they do at school every day. Ask children to choose one of the things and to draw a picture of that event. After children finish their drawing, invite them to share their work and to express orally what they are doing in the picture.

Read and Respond

Culture and Society After reading pages 6 and 7, ask children to tell what the word *learn* means. Repeat with the word *share*.

Q What are some ways that we learn new things?

A by reading, writing, drawing, using math materials, sharing

Q What kinds of things do children share at school?

A stories, school supplies, ideas

Point out the children on page 7 who are working with the math materials. Explain that those children are using class supplies.

Q What class supplies do we use?

A books, crayons, math materials

Visual Learning

Pictures Focus attention on the pictures on pages 6 and 7. Ask children to identify which children in the pictures are learning and which ones are sharing. Remind children about the main idea for this lesson. Invite children to identify where they see the main idea supported in the pictures.

Invite children to take turns pretending to tell someone who has never been to their school what it is like to be part of their class and what they do at school.

NOTE: Some children may not feel comfortable sharing personal or family experiences. Classroom instruction should respect all rights of privacy.

Diagram Invite children to point to the labels *lesson number, title, new word, picture,* and *question.* Explain that each lesson will be organized in the same way. Point out that knowing what these words mean and how to recognize and use them will help children become better readers in social studies.

Lesson 1

Going to School

1. lesson number

2. title

Big Idea
School is a place to learn and share.

Vocabulary
learn
share

3. new word

Our school is where we learn. When we **learn**, we find out something new. We read at school to learn. We write, draw, and tell stories, too.

6

INTEGRATE MATHEMATICS

Add and Subtract Have children use math problems to compare and contrast the children in the pictures. First, have children count the number of children doing each activity. Next, have them figure out how many more children are working with math materials than are writing a thank-you note. Then ask them to determine whether there are fewer children reading a book or playing show-and-tell.

EXTEND AND ENRICH

Write Goals Lead children in discussing things they would like to learn this year at school and some things they might like to share with classmates or family members. Record their responses on the board. Then encourage children to write in their journals the goals they like best. Children can refer to them throughout the year to track their progress or add new goals.

Our school is where we share. We **share** what we know and who we are.

4. picture

5. question

LESSON 1 Review

① **Vocabulary** What do you want to **learn** in school?

② What do the pictures tell you about how children in this classroom learn?

③ Draw a picture of something you did today in school.

7

ACTIVITY BOOK

Name _____ Date _____
School Pictures
Write a caption to tell something about each school picture.

We learn new things.

We help each other read.

We paint pictures.

Use with Unit 1, Lesson 1.   Activity Book • 1

PAGE 1

3 Close

Summarize Key Content

• We learn by reading, writing, drawing, and doing many things.

• We share what we know and who we are with others.

• School is a place to learn and share.

READING SOCIAL STUDIES

Graphic Organizer Revisit the T-chart begun in Motivate. Invite children to share new ideas they learned. Add these ideas to the chart.

Learn	Share
by reading	with classmates
by writing	what we know
by drawing	who we are

● USE READING AND VOCABULARY TRANSPARENCY 1–2

1–2 TRANSPARENCY

Assess

Lesson 1 Review—Answers

① Responses may include skills that children want to learn, such as being a better reader or writer, or may be about a specific topic.

② Responses may include that the children write, use math manipulatives, read, and share things they like to do.

③ **Performance Assessment Guidelines** Children's drawings should show an activity in which they learned something or shared something during the day.

Extension Activities For Home and School

Super Student T-Shirts

Materials: construction paper, scissors, crayons or markers

Have each child cut a T-shirt shape from construction paper. Then have children design shirts that use words and pictures to show that they are super students in the class. Suggest children and family members work together to brainstorm ideas for the shirt design. Have children use markers to create their shirt designs.
(TACTILE/VISUAL)

I am a good speller.

I show others how to use the computer.

File Folder Books

Materials: file folders, magazines, scissors, glue, crayons or markers

Organize children into small groups. Assign children roles to make a four-page file folder book. Have children choose a theme for their book, such as *What We Learn in Music* or *Things to Do on the Playground*. Two children should draw or cut and paste pictures on the pages. Another child can give each page a heading. A fourth child can dictate or write a sentence that tells what the main idea of the picture is.
(TACTILE/VISUAL)

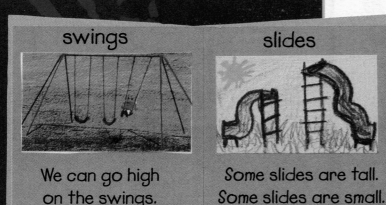

swings

slides

We can go high on the swings.

Some slides are tall. Some slides are small.

Student Starters

Materials: index cards

Invite children to give speeches about their school experiences. On index cards, write sentence starters to serve as speech starters for children. Have each child choose a card, and help him or her read it. Allow children a few minutes to think about what they would like to say. Then invite children to make their speeches. Encourage them to express their own ideas to complete each sentence starter.
(AUDITORY)

The best thing about being in this class is _____.

It is important to be a good student because _____.

When something you are learning is hard, you should _____.

A good book can help you _____.

When you are working in a group, you should _____.

Find the Main Idea

OBJECTIVES

- Identify main ideas from oral and print sources.
- Recognize details that support the main idea.

RESOURCES

Pupil Book/Unit Big Book, pp. 8–9

Word Cards V1–V4

Activity Book, p. 2

⊙ **Skill Transparency 1–1**

Vocabulary

main idea p. 8

detail p. 8

1 Motivate

Encourage children to help you prepare for a whole-class activity, such as math time. Assign tasks to children, such as distributing math manipulatives, paper, and pencils. As each child does the assigned task, ask the others to tell what the child is doing. Repeat as each task is done, and finally ask children what the group of children is doing together.

Why It Matters

Explain to children that thinking about the main idea helps readers make sense of what they are reading. It helps keep the reader focused. Then point out that a reader should look for details that explain what the main idea is about. Ask children to think back to the activity in Motivate. Was it easier to guess what the group was doing by first understanding what each child was doing?

MAKE IT RELEVANT

At Home Invite children to choose a favorite book to read to family members. Encourage them to talk to family members about what the book was mostly about. Suggest that they point out the details that helped them know the main idea.

2 Teach

What You Need to Know

Remind children that a paragraph is a group of sentences about a particular subject. Explain that the details help build up the main idea of the paragraph. Draw a pyramid graphic such as the one below and show children how the details support the main idea.

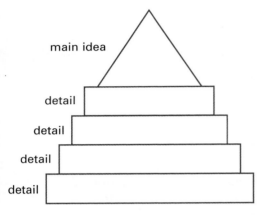

main idea

detail

detail

detail

detail

On the board or an overhead transparency, write a brief paragraph about your school. Include at least three detail sentences. Read the paragraph aloud with children. Help them identify the main idea, and write it in the graphic organizer. Then help them identify the detail sentences, and chart them as well. Remind children that the main idea is what the paragraph or other text is mostly about, and that details give more information to help explain the main idea.

Skills **READING**

Find the Main Idea

Vocabulary

main idea

detail

▶ Why It Matters

The **main idea** tells you what you are reading about.

▶ What You Need to Know

A paragraph has a main idea. Paragraphs also have detail sentences. A **detail** gives more information. Details help explain the main idea.

▶ Practice the Skill

1. Read the paragraph on page 9. What is the main idea?

2. What is one detail in the paragraph?

Braille watch

8

BACKGROUND

Louis Braille Louis Braille was born in 1809 near Paris, France. When he was 3 years old, he was blinded while playing with tools in his father's harness shop. He attended the National Institute for Blind Children in Paris and later taught there. At the age of 15, Braille adapted a writing system of raised coded dots. This new system was named for him and is still used today. An accomplished organist and cellist, Braille also adapted his system for use with musical notation.

REACH ALL LEARNERS

Advanced Learners Write the paragraph from page 9 on chart paper. Cut it apart sentence by sentence. Help children read the paragraph on page 9. Then have them use the sentence strips to assemble a main idea web. Draw a web on the board with a center oval and four leader lines. Have children attach the sentences on the web to show the main idea and details.

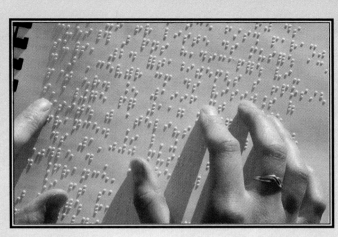

Braille

People who cannot see can use the Braille alphabet to read and write. Groups of small, raised dots stand for letters in the alphabet. The dot letters spell out words. People read Braille by running their fingers along the dots. ■

▶ **Apply What You Learned**

Read a children's magazine article. Look for main ideas and details.

9

Practice the Skill—Answers

❶ Braille is a way for people who cannot see to read and write.

❷ Children's responses should be one of the following: Groups of small, raised dots stand for letters in the alphabet. Braille is read by running fingers along the dots.

3 Close

Apply What You Learned

Children should be able to correctly identify the main idea and several details of a short magazine article.

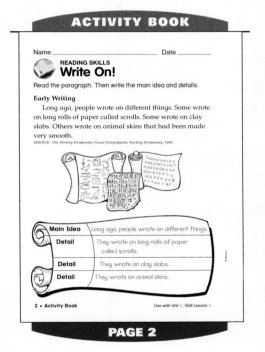

TRANSPARENCY

Use SKILL TRANSPARENCY 1–1.

EXTEND AND ENRICH

Write a Teaser Invite small groups of children to read a child's encyclopedia article on a social studies topic. Tell them to write a "teaser" for the article as if it were a magazine article. Have children write a title for the article that tells the main idea. Then have them list three details that support the main idea. You may wish to have children add illustrations to their writing.

RETEACH THE SKILL

Main Idea and Detail Questions
Read aloud a paragraph from a children's magazine or children's encyclopedia. To focus on the main idea, ask children what the paragraph is mostly about. Then focus on details by asking them how they knew. Explain to children that when they are reading, they should ask themselves questions, such as

What seems to be the big idea?
What are all the sentences about?
What do all the details explain?

Extension Activities For Home and School

Picture It

Materials: reading material, paper, crayons or markers

Invite children to read a short story or newspaper article at home with family members and then to draw a picture representing the main idea of what they read. Ask them to write the title of the book or article on the page. Encourage children to bring their illustrations to school to share with classmates.
(TACTILE/VISUAL)

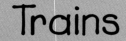

What's the Main Idea?

Materials: reading material

Organize children into small groups. Give each group a children's encyclopedia article to read and discuss. Have them identify the main idea and details that explain the main idea. Ask children to pretend that the content of their article has just been discovered and is making the news. Have children use the main idea and details to deliver a news report. Suggest that one group member state the main idea at the beginning of the report to introduce it, and that other group members share details that support the main idea. One group member could also pretend to interview another group member about the discovery.
(VISUAL/AUDITORY)

Main Idea Walk

Materials: chart paper, reading material, sentence strips, markers, masking tape

Copy a short paragraph from a children's magazine onto chart paper. Read the paragraph to children. Organize them into groups, and give each group a sentence strip. Encourage each group to write a different detail from the paragraph on the sentence strip. Then have them make a "walking paragraph" by taping the sentence strips to the floor. Invite groups to walk along the sentence strips, reading the sentence strips as they go. Then as a class, determine the main idea and add that to the walking paragraph.
(AUDITORY/KINESTHETIC)

Families enjoy spending time together.

Families play together.

Families work together.

Families cook and eat together.

2 Rules at School

OBJECTIVES

- Explain the need for rules in the home, school, and community.
- Give examples of rules that establish order, provide security, and manage conflict.
- Explore appropriate behavior at school.
- Compare rules made for different groups and situations.

 Compare and Contrast pp. 1, 36

RESOURCES

Pupil Book/Unit Big Book, pp. 10–11

Word Cards V3–V4

Activity Book, p. 3

● Reading and Vocabulary Transparency 1–3

▢ Internet Resources

READING SOCIAL STUDIES

Study Questions To help prepare children for the lesson, pose the following questions.

What are rules?	
What does it mean to be fair?	

Discuss the questions. Tell children to think about these questions as you read the lesson.

● USE READING AND VOCABULARY TRANSPARENCY 1–3

1–3 TRANSPARENCY

Vocabulary

rule p. 10

fair p. 11

 When Minutes Count

Have children skim the lesson to find the meanings of the lesson vocabulary words. Encourage children to tell how each word relates to the Big Idea of the lesson.

Quick Summary

The lesson focuses on what rules are and how they help everyone act in a fair way.

 1 Motivate

Set the Purpose

Big Idea Before starting the lesson, read the Big Idea statement aloud. As children read and discuss the lesson, have them think about what it means to be fair.

Access Prior Knowledge

Before reading the lesson, invite children to share some rules they follow at home, in school, or in the community.

Read and Respond

Civics and Government Remind children that there is usually someone in charge of helping and guiding a group of people. This person makes sure the group's rules are followed. Ask children to identify who does that in the classroom, at school, and at home.

Have children explain the need for rules at home and at school. Then lead a discussion on the differences between rules at home and rules at school.

Q What would happen if the school had no rules?

A It would probably be noisy. People would be doing all different things. It would be hard to learn. Someone could get hurt.

Q Which school rules might prevent problems from happening?

A Rules such as talking quietly, raising hands before speaking, walking in the hallways, taking turns, and following directions can help prevent problems.

CITIZENSHIP

DEMOCRATIC VALUES

Justice

Call attention to Earnest. Ask children to explain why they think Earnest says "Follow the rules." Point out that rules are important to follow at home, at school, or in the community. Invite children to explain the need for rules in the home, school, and community. Help children understand that following rules is a lifelong skill we must all learn.

Lesson

2 Rules at School

Big Idea
Good rules are fair and help people work together.

Vocabulary
rule
fair

We have rules in our classroom. A **rule** tells what you must do. Rules help us work and play safely.

Class Rules
Talk quietly.
Take turns.
Follow directions.
Be kind.

10

MAKE IT RELEVANT

At Home Have children discuss rules they have at home. List the following categories in a chart on the board to aid in the discussion: *Rules About Health, Rules About Safety, Rules About Bedtime, Rules About Property.* Record under the appropriate headings rules that children name. Point out that even though rules might vary from family to family, it is important to respect each other's rules, especially when children are visiting their friends. Have children explain the need for these rules at home.

EXTEND AND ENRICH

Create Rules Make a three-column chart with the headings *Keep Order, Provide Safety,* and *Get Along.* Discuss examples of classroom rules that belong in each category. Then have small groups of children write a rule for each category for a setting outside school, such as park rules, swimming pool rules, or public library rules.

Rules help us listen, share, and work together in a fair way. **Fair** means acting in a way that is right and honest.

Follow the rules.

LESSON 2 Review

1. **Vocabulary** How do **rules** help people be **fair**?

2. Explain why we need rules at school.

3. Choose a school rule. Draw a picture of children following that rule.

11

RETEACH THE LESSON

Write About Rules Share the Golden Rule with children: "Do unto others as you would have them do unto you." Discuss the meaning of the rule with children. Ask them to write about how they could apply this rule in classroom and home situations.

ACTIVITY BOOK

Name _____ Date _____

Following Rules

Read the paragraph, and then answer the questions.

Victor's class has rules for using the computer. One rule is to finish school work before using the computer. Victor did not follow this rule. The next day, he could not use the computer.

1. What rule did Victor break? — Finish your work before using the computer.

2. What happened because he broke the rule? — He could not use the computer the next day.

3. Why would it have been better for Victor to follow the rule? — He would not have missed any computer time.

Use with Unit 1, Lesson 2.   Activity Book • 3

PAGE 3

---

3 Close

Summarize Key Content

- A rule tells what must be done.
- Rules help us work and play in safe and fair ways.
- To be fair is to act in a way that is right and honest.

READING SOCIAL STUDIES

Study Questions Revisit the questions posed in Motivate. Invite children to share answers to the questions. Add these answers to the chart.

What are rules?	Rules tell us what we must do.
What does it mean to be fair?	Fair is giving everyone the same chance.

● USE READING AND VOCABULARY TRANSPARENCY 1–3

Assess

Lesson 2 Review—Answers

1. Rules help people be fair by telling what everyone must do.

2. Responses should include the fact that rules are needed because they help us work and play safely.

3. **Performance Assessment Guidelines** Children's drawings should show someone following a school rule.

Extension Activities For Home and School

Recess Rules Poem

Read the following poem aloud to children.

Recess Rules

No sliding down the handrails.
  No climbing up the slide.
No bouncing on the seesaw.
  No throwing sand outside.
No twisting on the swings.
  No climbing up the trees.
No jumping from the fences.
  No hanging by your knees.

Max slides down the handrails.
  He climbs right up the slide.
Max bounces on the seesaw.
  He throws sand outside.
Max twirls the swings up double.
  He calls me from a tree.
I climb up. Who gets in trouble?
  Max sure doesn't.
Only me.

by Carol Diggory Shields

Lead children in a discussion about the rules in the poem. Have them tell why these are important playground rules. Then invite children to make a list of playground rules without using the word "no."
(TACTILE/VISUAL)

Personal Report Card

Materials: construction paper, markers

Suggest that children work with a family member to create a report card for themselves at home that evaluates their behavior for the day. Direct them to focus on two or three rules. For each rule, have children give themselves a rating and write comments about their behavior.
(TACTILE/VISUAL)

Ratings

1 = Excellent
2 = Good
3 = Needs to improve

Rules Report for Sarah

Rule	Rating	Comments
Listen and follow directions.	2	I need to keep my eyes on the speaker more.
Respect others.	1	I think about treating others as I would like to be treated.
Be kind.	3	Today I said I didn't want to play with one of my friends and it hurt her feelings. I will not say that again.

Puppets Tell the Rules

Materials: paper bags or paper plates, crayons or markers

Organize children into small groups. Have each group create a puppet show that explains the need for a particular school or class rule. Have children make paper bag puppets and practice their puppet show before performing it for a classroom audience.
(AUDITORY/VISUAL/KINESTHETIC)

SKILLS

Working Together

Vocabulary

group p. 12

1 Motivate

Read aloud the following poem.

I Can't Move It

I can't move it,
You can't move it,
It won't move an inch.
But if we work together,
Moving it's a cinch.

by Judy Lalli

Reread the poem aloud, and invite small groups of children to act it out. Encourage them to tell what object they are trying to move. Then have children tell about times when they did a job that was easier because someone helped them do it.

Why It Matters

Explain that it is important to learn to work well with other people. Point out that this is not only important at school, but also outside of school. Help children identify some situations in which people might need to work together, such as Scout troops, clubs, sports, work, and home.

INTEGRATE READING

Literature Read aloud *Swimmy* by Leo Lionni (Knopf, 1991), and discuss how the fish in the story cooperated to survive. Give children red fish cutouts. Ask each child to write on a cutout how he or she works well with others. Model for children by writing on a black fish cutout how you work well with others. Then assemble the cutouts on a bulletin board in the shape of a fish with the black one for the eye, as in *Swimmy*.

2 Teach

What You Need to Know

Read aloud the steps for working in a group and discuss what they mean. Select several volunteers to help you demonstrate the process. First, present a task or problem, such as the classroom needs a new bulletin board. Next, lead the group in brainstorming several ideas for the board. Encourage children to respect each other's ideas. After several ideas are presented, invite children to raise a hand to show which idea they like best. Explain that although all the ideas are good ones, a decision must be made so the group can complete the task. Next, point out that the group needs to decide what each person should do to perform the task. Then, have children pantomime their roles. Finally, discuss how well everyone worked together.

Q Why is it important to think about how well your group worked together?

A It will help you the next time you work in a group.

Invite new volunteers to participate in another role-play. Have this group pretend they want to make a book about their class. Point out that the group will need someone to lead the group and assign roles. Remind children to demonstrate each step of the process. Repeat with other similar tasks until each child has a chance to participate as a follower and a leader.

Q Why is it important for each person to take a part in the group?

A It makes it easier to get the job done.

Q Would you rather work alone or in a group? Why?

A Responses might include that some jobs are best for one person and others need several people.

Skills
CITIZENSHIP

Working Together

Vocabulary

group

▶ Why It Matters

In school, children may work alone or with others in a **group**. People in a group need to know how to work together.

▶ What You Need to Know

These steps help group members work together.

Step 1 Plan together.

Step 2 Act together.

Step 3 Think about how well your group worked together.

12

▶ Practice the Skill

❶ Study the picture.

❷ Work in a group to write rules the children in this playground can use.

▶ Apply What You Learned

Work with family members to plan an activity. Use the steps you learned.

13

Practice the Skill—Answers

❷ Children's rules should reflect ways to make the playground a better place for children to play. They should focus on fairness and safety. Some suggestions: Take turns (holding the rope and jumping, using the ball); move away from the bottom of the slide so another child can safely slide down.

3 Close

Apply What You Learned

Children should work with family members to plan an activity.

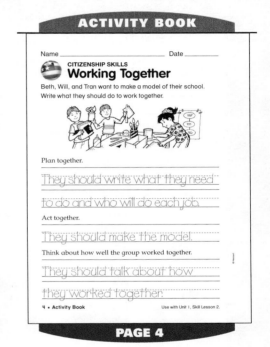

ACTIVITY BOOK

Name _____ Date _____

CITIZENSHIP SKILLS
Working Together
Beth, Will, and Tran want to make a model of their school.
Write what they should do to work together.

Plan together.

They should write what they need

to do and who will do each job.

Act together.

They should make the model.

Think about how well the group worked together.

They should talk about how

they worked together.

4 • Activity Book   Use with Unit 1, Skill Lesson 2.

PAGE 4

TRANSPARENCY

Use SKILL TRANSPARENCY 1–2.

EXTEND AND ENRICH

Make a List Have children make a list of rules they might use while working in a group. Encourage them to think of rules that are fair and will encourage their classmates to be respectful of each other and their ideas. For example, everyone must help complete the task or problem, the group will use the idea that most of the group likes best, and so on. Invite children to help choose the best rules, and then post them for future use.

RETEACH THE SKILL

Make a Circle Chart Give each child a paper plate. Show children how to divide it into three sections. Have them write one of the steps for working in a group in each section of the circle chart, beginning at the top right and going clockwise. Help children attach a paper clip to a brad in the middle of the circle to serve as a pointer. Discuss what should happen at each step, in order, as children move the pointer around the circle chart.

Extension Activities For Home and School

Mural, Mural, on the Wall

Materials: butcher paper, crayons or markers, paint and paintbrushes

Organize children into small groups. Tell them that the group is responsible for designing and creating a hallway mural about working together. Remind groups to follow the steps for working together in a group to create the mural. From time to time, ask for reports from the group, such as how they decided what to include in their mural, how they decided which jobs group members would do, and what might happen if everyone in the group did not perform his or her job. After children share their completed murals, have them share with classmates how their group worked well together.
(AUDITORY/TACTILE)

Earth Keepers Club

To be a member, you must be willing to help take care of Earth. Sign up here.

_____

_____

_____

_____

Here's what club members will do.

- Pick up litter on the playground once a week after school.
- Make posters to tell others how they can take care of Earth.
- Have a community project once a month.

A New Group

Materials: posterboard, crayons or markers

Organize children into small groups. Have children imagine that they are beginning a new club, team, or group for the school. You may wish to offer choices, such as a book club, a nature club, a music club, or an art club. Suggest that children work together to make decisions about the club, such as the name, how children can become members, and what the club will do. Then have children create posters to tell about their club.
(AUDITORY/TACTILE/VISUAL)

Work at Home Experience

Materials: will vary

Suggest that children work with family members on a family project, such as cleaning a closet, building a bird feeder, or having a family game night. Provide a copy of the steps for working together in a group for each child to take home. Have children draw pictures to show what they did at home.
(VISUAL/KINESTHETIC)

School Workers

OBJECTIVES

- Identify school workers.
- Identify the responsibilities of authority figures in the home and school.
- Recognize that children depend on school workers.
- Describe the work role of children in school and at home.

 Compare and Contrast pp. 1, 17, 36

RESOURCES

Pupil Book/Unit Big Book, pp. 14–17

Word Cards V5–V6

Activity Book, p. 5

Activity Pattern P1

⊕ **Reading and Vocabulary Transparency 1–4**

💻 **Internet Resources**

READING SOCIAL STUDIES

Graphic Organizer Begin a K-W-L chart about school workers. Complete the chart during Close.

What We Know	What We Want to Know	What We Learned
Teachers teach children. The principal makes sure the children follow the rules.	Who are some other school workers? Does every school have the same workers?	

⏺ **USE READING AND VOCABULARY TRANSPARENCY 1–4**

 1–4 TRANSPARENCY

Vocabulary

teacher p. 14

principal p. 14

 When Minutes Count

Direct children to examine the pictures in the lesson. Have them predict what they think the Big Idea of the lesson is. Encourage them to read the lesson to find out if they were correct.

Quick Summary

The lesson shares how many school workers, including teachers and principals, help children learn and make school a safe place. Children will learn that students are also school workers.

 # 1 Motivate

Set the Purpose

Big Idea Before starting the lesson, read the Big Idea statement aloud. As children read and discuss the lesson, encourage them to connect school workers discussed in the text with school workers they know.

Access Prior Knowledge

Invite children to think about the adults they see at school every day and to suggest what they think their jobs might be. Also ask children to name some qualities a person who enjoys working in a school might possess.

2 Teach

Read and Respond

Culture and Society Point out that all schools need many workers, and that each school worker does a special job that helps make school a place where children are safe and can learn. Name several different jobs that need to be done around the school such as driving the buses, cleaning the bathroom, teaching music or art, cooking the food, and others, and ask children to tell who does those jobs.

Q **What might happen if school workers did not do their jobs?**

A Children would not learn. The school might not be a nice place or a safe place.

Q **Could only one person or a few people do all the jobs in a school? Why or why not?**

A No, because there is too much to do. Also, many of the jobs require special training.

Visual Learning

Pictures Ask children to examine the pictures on pages 14 and 15 and to discuss what they see. Have children identify which one shows a principal and which one shows a teacher. Then ask children to tell what they know about each job. Point out that in addition to keeping schools safe, principals manage the business of the school. They hire teachers and other workers and spend money to keep the school in operation.

Next, ask children to tell who else they see in each picture. Lead children to conclude that there are children in each picture as well.

Q **What jobs are the children doing?**

A Their main jobs are to learn and to behave well. They might also have jobs in the classroom, such as line leader or supply helper.

Point out that since children have jobs at school, they are school workers, too. Invite children to compare jobs they do at school with jobs they do at home.

School Workers

Big Idea
There are many workers at a school.

Vocabulary
teacher
principal

Our school has many workers. Our **teacher** helps us learn. Our **principal** helps make our school a safe place.

teacher

14

REACH ALL LEARNERS

Below-Level Learners
Take children on a brief walk around the school. Encourage them to notice people who are working. Once you return to the classroom, have children recall the workers they saw and what they were doing. Make a list of children's responses.

MAKE IT RELEVANT

At Home Encourage children to discuss with family members how family members can help with their learning. Point out that family members sometimes help with homework, attend performances and other school functions, or volunteer at school. Ask children how they think these activities might help each student be a better school worker.

principal

• BIOGRAPHY •

Mary McLeod Bethune
1875–1955
Character Trait: Perseverance

When Mary McLeod Bethune was young, there were few schools for African American children. When she found one, she worked hard and became a teacher. She later opened a school and then a college where African Americans could go to learn.

GO ONLINE

MULTIMEDIA BIOGRAPHIES
Visit The Learning Site at
www.harcourtschool.com to
learn about other famous people.

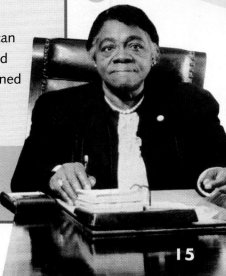

15

• BIOGRAPHY •

Mary McLeod Bethune

Perseverance Explain to children that the people who get the most things done in life are people who have *perseverance*. In other words, they are people who are determined to get something done and they do not give up even when times are difficult. After reading about Mary McLeod Bethune on page 15, ask children whether they think she had perseverance. Children may point out that she would have had to have perseverance in order to go to school during a time when most African Americans did not and to found a school for African Americans.

Call attention to the numbers after Mary McLeod Bethune's name. Tell children that the numbers tell the years she lived. Share with children that when Bethune died, *Time* magazine printed that "nothing on earth could stop Mary Bethune."

REACH ALL LEARNERS

English as a Second Language Write captions for the pictures on pages 14 and 15. Read the captions aloud, and help children match the captions to the pictures. Then have small groups of children act out the scenes depicted in the pictures.

INTEGRATE LANGUAGE ARTS

Expressive Writing Invite children to write a poem about a school worker. Suggest that children follow a pattern for their poetry, such as listing four or five describing words and then naming the school worker on the last line. Point out that the poems do not have to rhyme. When children complete their poems, have each child make a copy of the poem and give it to the appropriate school worker.

Visual Learning

Pictures Ask children to examine the pictures on pages 16 and 17 and to discuss what they see. Have children link the school workers in the pictures to school workers in their school. Ask children who in your school does each job.

Read and Respond

Culture and Society Help children identify authority figures at school, such as *nurse, custodian, teacher aide, librarian,* and *food server.* Have children identify how they depend on each worker.

Q What might happen if there were no custodian?

A Broken equipment would not be fixed, so no one could use it; the school would be dirty.

Repeat the question for each worker. Encourage children to answer the question at the top of the page about how each worker is helping the children.

Q Is there one school worker who has the most important job? Why do you think the way that you do?

A Every school worker has an important job. A school will not run well unless every worker does his or her job.

Lead children in a matching activity. Copy and distribute to small groups of children the pictures from Activity Pattern P1 in the tabbed section at the back of the book. Invite children to color and cut out the pictures. Have children paste the pictures in one column on a sheet of posterboard. Write locations in the school that correspond with the workers on the board, and have children copy those locations in a second column on the posterboard. Finally, have children draw lines to match each worker with the appropriate location.

Point out to children that there are also authority figures at home. Have children identify these authority figures and describe their responsibilities.

How are these school workers helping?

nurse

custodian

teacher aide

16

REACH ALL LEARNERS

Advanced Learners
Organize children into small groups. Assign each group a school worker to interview. Have children prepare several questions to ask the person. Arrange a time for the interview. Encourage children to take notes to record the person's answers to the questions. Then invite groups to share their interviews with classmates.

EXTEND AND ENRICH

Compile a School Directory Have children work in small groups to create a school directory. Encourage them to think of as many school workers as they can. Then suggest each child make a page for the directory. Have each child list three of the workers they named on their page and then include their own name. After each name, they should record the person's job title and a brief description of his or her job. Bind the completed directory pages together to make a book.

librarian

food server

① Compare and Contrast How are the jobs of a teacher and of a librarian alike? How are their jobs different?

② Vocabulary How does a **teacher** help children?

③ Make a list of people who help you at school. Write a thank-you card for a worker from your list.

17

RETEACH THE LESSON

Make a Chart Take photos of several school workers, and record them on audiotape making brief statements about their jobs, such as *I make sure the meals are ready on time. I am the cafeteria manager.* Tape the pictures in one column of a two-column chart. After listening to the audiotape, have children name each worker's job title. Write the title in the second column to complete the chart.

ACTIVITY BOOK

Name_____ Date_____

Who Am I?

Fill in the blank. Tell what job each person has.

I am a librarian   I am a teacher

I am a nurse   I am a student

Use with Unit 1, Lesson 3.   Activity Book • 5

PAGE 5

3 Close

Summarize Key Content

- A school has many workers.
- School workers have many responsibilities.
- All the workers must do their jobs in order to make school a safe place where children can learn.
- Children are also school workers.

READING SOCIAL STUDIES

Graphic Organizer Revisit the K-W-L chart children began in Motivate. Invite children to share new ideas they learned. Add these ideas to the chart.

What We Know	What We Want to Know	What We Learned
Teachers teach children. The principal makes sure the children follow the rules.	Who are some other school workers? Does every school have the same workers?	Other workers are librarians, nurses, cafeteria workers, and custodians. Schools have many of the same workers.

● USE READING AND VOCABULARY TRANSPARENCY 1–4

1–4 TRANSPARENCY

Assess

Lesson 3 Review—Answers

① **Compare and Contrast** Responses may include that teachers and librarians both help children. Teachers help children learn; librarians help children find books.

② A teacher helps children learn.

③

Performance Assessment Guidelines Children's lists should include a variety of school workers. Children's thank-you cards should reflect an understanding of the responsibilities of authority figures in the schools.

Extension Activities For Home and School

School Worker Appreciation

Materials: paper, markers, other art materials (optional)

Organize children into small groups. Have children in each group select a school worker to whom they would like to show their appreciation. Encourage children to explain why that worker is important to them. Then have children design a sign that can be posted in the school to honor the worker. Children can choose to draw a picture, write a poem, or write a thank-you message on the sign. Display the signs outside your classroom or in another prominent place in the school.
(TACTILE/KINESTHETIC)

We go to school and home safely each day, thanks to our bus driver, Ms. Kemp.

Now we can read. We can do math, too. All because of you! Mr. Nolan, our teacher!

Jobs at School and Home

Materials: paper, pencils

Invite children to work with family members to compare the work they do at home with the work they do at school. Help children draw and label Venn diagrams to compare the two. Encourage children to bring their completed diagrams to school to share with classmates.
(VISUAL/TACTILE)

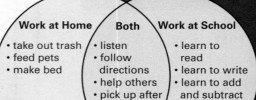

Work at Home
- take out trash
- feed pets
- make bed

Both
- listen
- follow directions
- help others
- pick up after self

Work at School
- learn to read
- learn to write
- learn to add and subtract
- work in groups

School Worker Card Game

Materials: Activity Pattern P1 (school workers), scissors

Organize children into pairs or small groups. Copy Activity Pattern P1 (school workers), and distribute two copies to each group. Direct children to cut out both sets of cards. Then have them mix up the cards and turn them facedown. Invite children to play a game in which they take turns turning over two cards. If children turn over a like pair, they can take the cards away from the pile. If the cards are unlike, children turn them back over. Play continues until all pairs are matched.
(TACTILE/VISUAL)

Where Are You?

OBJECTIVES

- Describe location of self and objects relative to other locations in the classroom and school.
- Use relative location words to describe where things are.

 Compare and Contrast pp. 1, 36

RESOURCES

Pupil Book/Unit Big Book, pp. 18–19

Word Cards V5–V6

Activity Book, p. 6

⊕ Reading and Vocabulary Transparency 1–5

⊟ Internet Resources

READING SOCIAL STUDIES

Graphic Organizer Begin a web about location words. Complete the web during Close.

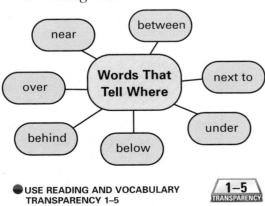

● USE READING AND VOCABULARY TRANSPARENCY 1–5

1–5 TRANSPARENCY

Vocabulary

location p. 18

 When Minutes Count

Have pairs of children work together to find the answers to the review questions.

Quick Summary

The lesson focuses on how to give directions to a certain place. It defines the word *location*.

1 Motivate

Set the Purpose

Big Idea Before starting the lesson, read the Big Idea statement aloud. As children read and discuss the lesson, help them note words that help to describe the relative location of a place.

Access Prior Knowledge

Invite children to look around the classroom and describe where objects and other children are located. Point out that the words they use, such as *near, between, over,* and *under,* are words that tell *location.*

Read and Respond

Geography Ask children to notice where you are standing in the room. Then use some of the location words children mentioned in Motivate to describe where you are standing. Tell children they can also use these words to give people directions to places. Read the text on page 18. Then say the name of one of the rooms in the drawing on pages 18–19, and have children point to it. Use direction words to have children point out other rooms in relation to that room, such as *the room across the hall* or *the room next to it on the right.*

Visual Learning

Diagram As children examine the drawing on pages 18–19, ask them how this school is like their school. Have them name all the rooms in the school in the picture that are also at their school. Then name a room, such as the cafeteria, and have children tell what rooms are next to and across from it at their school. Suggest children close their eyes and imagine the area. Have children make a sketch to show the cafeteria and the rooms next to it. Have children repeat the activity with other locations at their school.

CAPTION ANSWER: The cafeteria

Lesson

4

Where Are You?

Big Idea
You can describe a location.

Vocabulary

location

The **location** of a place is where the place is. The drawing shows where the rooms are in this school. Describe the location of each room. Use words such as <u>next to</u>, <u>beside</u>, and <u>across from</u>.

18

Draw a Picture Invite children to choose an object in the school, such as the water fountain. Have children draw a picture of the item. Then invite volunteers to use location words they have learned to describe the location of the object in their picture relative to the locations of other objects in the school.

Glossary Explain that the glossary is located in the back of the book and contains a definition for each vocabulary word. Model using the glossary for children by looking up the word *location.* Guide children in comparing their glossary to a dictionary.

Respond to Directions Organize children in pairs. Give each partner a picture of the same scene, such as a classroom. Have each partner add an object, such as a pencil, to the picture by drawing it. Direct children to draw without letting their partner see their work. Then have partners take turns describing their object's location. The other child should select the location and draw the object in the picture based on their partner's description. Then have partners compare their pictures.

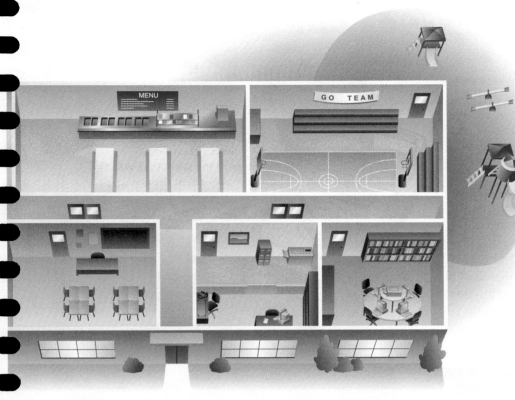

 Which room is between the music room and the gym?

LESSON 4 Review

1. **Vocabulary** Describe the **location** of the music room.

2. How is this school like your school?

3. Imagine you are helping a child who is new to your school. Describe the location of rooms he or she might need to find.

19

RETEACH THE LESSON

Demonstrate Location Words
Give each child a slip of paper on which a location is described, such as *in back of the teacher's desk,* or *to the right of the closet.* Have children take turns standing in the location and describing their location relative to other locations in the classroom. Then have children describe the location of objects relative to other locations in the classroom.

ACTIVITY BOOK

Name _____ Date _____
Where Is It?
Color to show location.

1 Color blue the object between the two closets.
2 Color green the sign over the science table.
3 Color red the object under the pencil sharpener.
4 Name something in your classroom. Write a location word for it. *Item and location words will vary.*

6 • Activity Book   Use with Unit 1, Lesson 4.

---

3 Close

Summarize Key Content
- Location is where a place is.
- Special words are used to describe a location.

READING SOCIAL STUDIES

Graphic Organizer Revisit the web begun in Motivate. Invite children to share new ideas they learned. Add these ideas to the web.

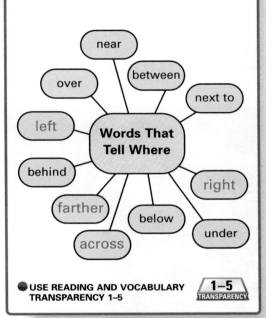

near
between
over
next to
left
Words That Tell Where
behind
right
farther
below
under
across

● USE READING AND VOCABULARY TRANSPARENCY 1–5   **1–5** TRANSPARENCY

Assess

Lesson 4 Review—Answers

1. Responses should include relative location words that accurately describe the music room's location, such as *The music room is across from a classroom and next to the cafeteria.*

2. Responses should note similarities between the two schools, such as the presence of various classrooms and other areas.

3. 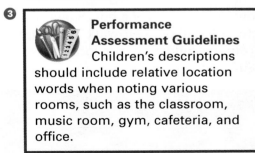 **Performance Assessment Guidelines** Children's descriptions should include relative location words when noting various rooms, such as the classroom, music room, gym, cafeteria, and office.

LESSON 4 ▪ 19

Extension Activities For Home and School

Where Are We?

Materials: audiocassette player, audiocassette tape

Organize children into small groups, and assign each group an area of the school, such as the playground, the cafeteria, the gymnasium, or the music room.

Encourage groups to keep their location a secret. Take children on a tour of the school. Tell children to look at their location in relation to other areas of the school. Back in the classroom, have groups write a set of at least three clues in riddle form using location words to describe their area. Ask groups to record their clues on an audiocassette tape. After recording their clues, have children state the location. Invite classmates to listen to each group's clues. Turn off the tape before each answer is revealed. After children share their answers, listen to the answer on the tape.
(AUDITORY/KINESTHETIC)

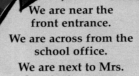

We are near the front entrance.
We are across from the school office.
We are next to Mrs. Scott's classroom.
Where in the school are we?
We are in the computer lab!

Location Labels

Materials: index cards, markers, tape

Choose a part of the classroom, such as a door, a window, or the teacher's desk. Have children write location words or phrases on index cards. Using tape, have the children attach each card to an item, in that area, whose position matches that location word.
(VISUAL/TACTILE)

Neighborhood Walk

Materials: drawing paper, crayons

Suggest that children take a neighborhood walk with a family member. Encourage children to use location words to describe what they see, for example: a tow truck *in front of* a bus. Suggest that when they return home, children draw pictures based on their walk. Have them bring the pictures to school to share. Encourage children to use location words to tell about their pictures.
(VISUAL/AUDITORY/KINESTHETIC)

Looking at Maps

OBJECTIVES

- Create and use simple maps to identify the location of places in the classroom and school.
- Recognize the use of symbols on maps to represent real things.
- Create visual and written material including pictures and maps.

RESOURCES

Pupil Book/Unit Big Book, pp. 20–21

Word Cards V5–V8

Activity Book, p. 7

⊙ **Skill Transparency 1–3**

GeoSkills CD-ROM

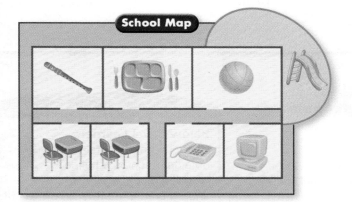

School Map

Vocabulary

map p. 20

symbol p. 20

1 Motivate

Tell children that they have been asked to draw a picture to show a place, but they are supposed to use only one object in the drawing. Invite children to do a quick sketch of one object to stand for a park. Point out that sometimes people use a picture of a single object to stand for a place.

Why It Matters

Explain to children that **maps** are small drawings of real places that people use to find where they need to go. Display a map of your town. Point out that if you were new in town, you would not know how to find places such as the police station or the school. Explain that a map can help you find a place that you have never been to.

MAKE IT RELEVANT

At Home Encourage children to notice maps outside of school, such as those at bus or train stations, shopping malls, amusement parks, or those used on television weather forecasts or in other news reports. Also, have children look at any maps they may have at home, such as a city map, road map, United States map, or world map. Suggest they ask a family member why they think maps are important.

2 Teach

What You Need to Know

Remind children of the picture they drew in Motivate to stand for a park. Explain that maps use pictures called **symbols** to stand for places, too. Point out that if a map did not use small symbols to stand for things, the map would be too big and would not be useful. Have children look at the map symbols on page 20 and tell what each symbol stands for.

Q **What are some other rooms that could be added to this school?**

A Possible answers might include an art room and bathrooms.

Explain that maps show how places look from above. Then invite children to examine the map on page 21 and compare it to the picture on pages 18 and 19. Help children recognize that the rooms and the symbols are in the same place in both the picture on pages 18 and 19 and the map on page 21.

Q **What is next to the library?**

A office

Q **What is across from the music room?**

A classroom

Skills MAP AND GLOBE

Looking at Maps

Vocabulary
map
symbol

▶ Why It Matters

A **map** is a drawing that shows where places are. Maps help you find places.

▶ What You Need to Know

Mapmakers use **symbols**, or pictures, to stand for real things.

playground

music room

cafeteria

gym

classroom

office

library

20

INTEGRATE LANGUAGE ARTS

Narrative Writing Invite children to write a class story in which a character goes from place to place looking for a lost pet or toy. After the story is complete, have pairs of children draw a map of the places and retrace the character's route on the map.

GO ONLINE INTERNET RESOURCES

THE LEARNING SITE

Go to **www.harcourtschool.com** to find links to sites where children can print maps of your town or other familiar places.

REACH ALL LEARNERS

Below-Level Learners Give children several small objects, such as a ball, a wooden block, a pencil, and an eraser. Instruct them to cut out paper shapes to serve as symbols for each object. Direct children to arrange the objects on a sheet of paper. Then have them replace each object with the cutout and glue the cutout to the paper to create a map of their objects.

▶ Practice the Skill

❶ Look at the map. Where is the playground? How do you know?

❷ What rooms are next to the cafeteria?

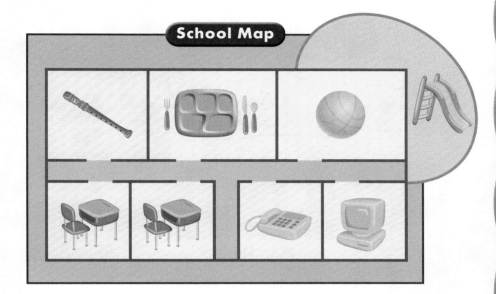

School Map

▶ Apply What You Learned

Make a map of your classroom. Use symbols to show where things are in the room.

 Practice your map and globe skills with the **GeoSkills CD-ROM**.

21

Practice the Skill—Answers

❶ The playground is next to the gymnasium. The symbol for the slide shows where it is.

❷ The music room and gymnasium are next to the cafeteria.

3 Close

Apply What You Learned

Children should select symbols that seem appropriate to each area of the classroom. The symbols should be placed in a fairly accurate representation of the classroom.

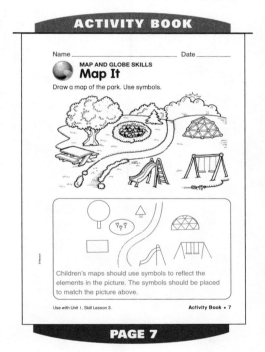

ACTIVITY BOOK

Name _____ Date _____

MAP AND GLOBE SKILLS
Map It

Draw a map of the park. Use symbols.

Children's maps should use symbols to reflect the elements in the picture. The symbols should be placed to match the picture above.

Use with Unit 1, Skill Lesson 3.   Activity Book • 7

PAGE 7

TRANSPARENCY

Use SKILL TRANSPARENCY 1–3.

CD-ROM

Explore GEOSKILLS CD-ROM to learn more about map and globe skills.

EXTEND AND ENRICH

Role-Play Mapmakers Have children imagine that three new rooms have been added to their school. Encourage them to pretend they are mapmakers who have been asked to make a map of the new rooms. Suggest they begin by listing the names of the rooms and deciding where the new rooms are located. Then they should create symbols for those rooms and finally draw a map using the symbols they created. Invite children to share their map with classmates.

RETEACH THE SKILL

Make a Map Have children make a map of their classroom. Remind them to include important areas of the classroom and to show each area with a symbol. Encourage children to use the map to identify the location of places in the classroom such as where he or she sits. Then have children make a map of the school. Finally, help children write a sentence identifying the location of the classroom in the school map they drew.

Extension Activities For Home and School

Map an Area

Materials: outline map of school, crayons or markers

Organize children in small groups and assign each a common area of the school, such as the cafeteria, the library, the computer lab, the music room, the gymnasium, and so on. Give each group a map of the school. Take a tour of the school, asking children to pay close attention to their assigned space. Back in the classroom, have children use symbols to make a map of their area.
(VISUAL/TACTILE)

ELM STREET SCHOOL

Map Hunt

Materials: maps brought from home

My living room

Invite children to have family members help them find maps at home to bring to school. Suggest that children look at newspapers, magazines, direct mail pieces, and invitations, or that they print out maps from the Internet. Alternatively, children and family members could draw a map of their street, their home, or a room in their home. Invite children to bring in the maps and share them with classmates. Discuss the symbols used on the maps.
(VISUAL/TACTILE)

Map Game

Materials: maps, index cards, crayons or markers, paper bags

Organize children into small groups and give each group a map, such as a map of the school, your community, or an attraction in your area. Discuss the map symbols with the group. Invite groups to draw each symbol from the map on an index card to create a map game. Have groups place their cards in a bag and switch maps and cards with another group. To play the map game, players take turns pulling a symbol from the bag, finding its match on the map, and discussing its meaning.
(VISUAL/TACTILE)

Schools Long Ago and Today

OBJECTIVES

- Compare and contrast schools of long ago with schools of today.
- Recognize tools for learning in the classroom.

 Compare and Contrast
pp. 1, 24, 27, 36
Focus Skill

RESOURCES

Pupil Book/Unit Big Book, pp. 22–27

Word Cards V7–V8

Activity Book, p. 8

Activity Pattern P2

⊕ **Reading and Vocabulary Transparency 1–6**

💻 **Internet Resources**

READING SOCIAL STUDIES

Graphic Organizer Begin a Venn diagram about schools long ago and today. Complete the diagram during Close.

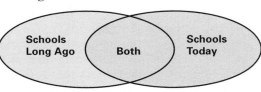

● USE READING AND VOCABULARY TRANSPARENCY 1–6

1–6 TRANSPARENCY

Vocabulary

tool p. 24

 When Minutes Count

Invite children to examine the pictures and captions in this lesson. Then have them tell which pictures belong in the following categories: *Then* and *Now.*

Quick Summary

Schools long ago were different from those today. Long ago, children often attended a one-room school and had few tools to use. Today, there are many kinds of schools. Children today use many tools to learn.

Motivate

Set the Purpose

Big Idea Before starting the lesson, read the Big Idea statement aloud. As children read and discuss the lesson, help them compare and contrast schools long ago with schools today.

Access Prior Knowledge

If you know it, teach children the song "School Days." Then invite them to tell what they know about schools long ago. Encourage children to speculate about how schools might have looked, what kind of work the children did, and what kinds of tools they used.

2 Teach

Visual Learning

Pictures Have children examine the pictures on pages 22 and 23. Ask them which pictures show schools from long ago and which show schools today. Guide them to compare the schools from long ago with schools today. Encourage them to tell how they are alike and how they are different.

Q How are the school and classroom on page 22 like our classroom?

A Both have desks, books, chalkboards.

Q How is the school different from our school?

A The school of long ago has only one room.

Read and Respond

Link Culture and Society with History After children have read pages 22 and 23, ask them why they think schools of long ago had only one room. Explain that most towns were small, so few school-age children lived in them. The people of the community often built the school themselves.

Q Why do you think some children learned at home?

A Some children probably lived too far away to go to school.

Big Idea
Schools long ago were like schools today in some ways. They were also different.

Vocabulary

tool

Schools Long Ago and Today

Then

Long ago, some children learned at home. Other children went to one-room schools. There, children of all ages learned together.

22

Skimming and Scanning Before children begin reading, suggest they glance over the first few pages, looking at important words, photos, and illustrations. Ask them to predict what they think the lesson might be about. Then have children read to find out if they were right.

Identify Important Words Ask children which words stand out on pages 22–23, leading them to focus on the headings *Then* and *Now*. Help children identify the meanings of the words to realize that *then* refers to something that happened long ago and *now* refers to something that is happening in the present. Point out that these words are opposite in meaning.

Q Why do most schools have vacation time in summer?

A Long ago, many families had farms. The school year was set up so that children were home to help with the harvesting and other farm work that took place in the summer. Today, many schools follow the tradition of ending the school year before summer.

Now

Some ways of learning are the same today as they were long ago. Some ways are different. Today there are many more kinds of schools.

Hebrew school

Special-needs school

Home school

Multiage class

23

Read and Respond

Link Culture and Society with History Help children realize that there are many different kinds of schools today. Ask them to name as many kinds as they can, such as public, private, high school, middle school, elementary school. Point out that some children still learn at home, too. Lead children in a discussion about why schools were important long ago and why they are still important today.

Q Why do you think there are more schools today than there were long ago?

A because there are a lot more children

Q How can you find out more about schools of long ago?

A from books, encyclopedias, Web sites, paintings, journals, or other writings by students of long ago

---

BACKGROUND

The Early Schoolhouse The one-room schoolhouse was a common fixture of the rural American landscape by the 1800s. Usually, the structure was wooden with a few windows, benches, and desks. Sometimes a wood stove was used to heat the room. Children up to eighth grade were often grouped together in one classroom with one teacher. A great deal of the class work was based on memorization, with children often being called on to recite what they had learned. Much focus was put on reading, writing, arithmetic, and penmanship. Besides teaching, the teacher was also responsible for keeping the building clean. The students were often asked to help the teacher with chores, such as cleaning the blackboards or bringing in wood.

REACH ALL LEARNERS

Advanced Learners Invite children to use what they have discovered about classrooms of long ago and from the pictures in the book to build a shoe-box diorama of a one-room school.

Read and Respond

History Read the text on page 24 aloud. Then ask children why the schools did not have many tools for the children to use. Help children realize that money was scarce and supplies were expensive. Explain that there were not many factories at that time, so producing paper and other school items would have been time-consuming and expensive. Books were not readily available either, so many children had to share a few books.

Q What do you think it would have been like to attend a school with so few tools?

A It probably would have been difficult to learn some things because there were so few tools to help you learn or to help you practice what you were learning.

Culture and Society Explain that discipline in schools long ago was strict. Learning was meant to be hard work and not much fun. Point out that most of the materials read aloud were often meant to teach lessons about how to behave.

Then

A **tool** is something people use. Some tools are used for learning. Long ago, children had few tools.

24

READING SKILL

Compare and Contrast As children read the lesson, they will have the opportunity to practice the skill of comparing and contrasting. Direct children to write one sentence comparing and contrasting *schools* of long ago and today and another sentence comparing and contrasting *school tools* of long ago and today.

INTEGRATE LANGUAGE ARTS

Informative Writing Give children a piece of black construction paper. Have them glue a frame of craft sticks around the edge of the paper to create the look of an old-fashioned slate. Tell children to use chalk to write some facts they learned about schools of long ago on their "slate."

MAKE IT RELEVANT

In Your School Share with children your school's history, including when the school was built and how many children attended at the time of the school's opening. Lead children in a discussion about how the school may have changed over time and how it may change in the future.

FAST FACT An abacus is a very old tool used for counting. Today most people use a calculator, but some people still use an abacus.

Artifacts Explain that people who study history, called *historians*, learn much about the past by examining artifacts such as those in the pictures on pages 24–25. Help children realize that when they study about things from the past, they are historians, too.

Lead children in a discussion about the school tools in the pictures. Encourage children to think about what it would have been like to use each tool.

Q Why do you think students used slates instead of paper?

A Paper was expensive and there was not much of it. A slate could be used over and over again.

Q What problems can you imagine having if you were trying to learn to write your letters and you had to use pen and ink?

A It would be difficult to write with a pen that you had to dip into ink, and it could be messy because the ink might drip or spill.

25

Play Historic Games Share some games children played in schools long ago, such as a marble game called "ringtaw." Take children outside and draw a large ring with a smaller ring inside. Use chalk on the sidewalk or a stick in dirt. Place several marbles in the small ring. Have players take turns crouching outside the large ring and flicking a large marble, called a shooter, into the small ring. Explain that the object of the game is to knock the other marbles out of the small ring. Players keep the marbles they knock out. The player with the most marbles at the end of the game wins. Encourage children to compare this game with games they play today.

School Books The Bible and other religious books were commonly used in early classrooms. In 1836 the first in a set of books was published that was designed to appeal to children while still teaching good values. This set of books was written by Dr. William H. McGuffey and became known as *McGuffey's Readers.*

Read and Respond

History Guide children to consider how school tools have changed over time. Have them review the school tools from long ago and compare them to the tools we use today.

Q What do you think caused the tools used in schools to change over time?

A Inventions, such as electricity, became commonplace; supplies, such as books and paper, became less expensive and more available; new books were written.

Visual Learning

Pictures Encourage children to compare the tools in the pictures to the actual tools they use in school.

Q What one tool at school would be the hardest for you to do without? Why?

A Responses should reflect children's understanding of the importance of the tool they select.

Now

Today children use many tools to learn.

26

Word Problems Model writing word problems about the class and classroom tools, such as *Three students worked in a group. Two more students joined them. How many students were there in all?* Organize children in pairs, and direct them to write several word problems. Have them switch problems with another pair and solve the problems.

English as a Second Language Place an assortment of school tools on a tray or work surface. Ask children questions about the objects, such as *Is this an eraser? Is this a pencil or a book? What is this?* Have children answer in complete sentences using the name of the object in the sentence. After identifying all the objects, have children study their arrangement. Then, while children close their eyes, remove one object. Ask children to tell which object is missing.

Write a Story Display photographs of schools from long ago (many can be found and printed from online sources) or fine art images, such as Winslow Homer's painting "New England Country School." Have children examine the images and imagine what it must have been like to live during that time period. Then invite children to write a short story using their ideas. Have children illustrate their stories and share them with the class.

LESSON 5 Review

Focus Skill

① **Compare and Contrast** How were schools different long ago?

② **Vocabulary** What **tools** do you use in school?

③ Write three sentences that describe your school.

27

RETEACH THE LESSON

Human Chart On index cards, write the names of school tools that were used long ago and those that are used today. Pass one card out to each child. Then make three signs: one that says *Then,* another that says *Both,* and a third that says *Now.* Space these signs out along one wall of the classroom and attach them. Have children read their cards and stand under the appropriate headings to make a human graph comparing schools long ago with schools of today.

ACTIVITY BOOK

Name _____ Date _____

Schools Then and Now

Write *then* or *now* to tell about each object.

now	accept either answer
then	then
then	now

8 • Activity Book   Use with Unit 1, Lesson 5.

PAGE 8

---

3 Close

Summarize Key Content

- Schools long ago were often just in one room with many grades learning together. Students had few tools.
- Schools today are larger and more varied. Students today have many tools.
- Schools long ago and today are the same in that children attend school to learn.

READING SOCIAL STUDIES

Graphic Organizer Revisit the Venn diagram begun in Motivate. Invite children to share new ideas they learned. Add these ideas to the diagram.

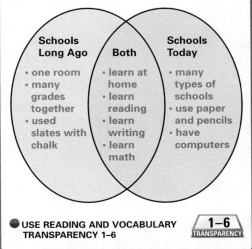

Schools Long Ago
- one room
- many grades together
- used slates with chalk

Both
- learn at home
- learn reading
- learn writing
- learn math

Schools Today
- many types of schools
- use paper and pencils
- have computers

● USE READING AND VOCABULARY TRANSPARENCY 1–6

1–6 TRANSPARENCY

Assess

Lesson 5 Review—Answers

① **Focus Skill** **Compare and Contrast** Schools long ago were often in one room. Schools long ago had fewer tools for students to use.

② Children should mention items like paper, pencils, textbooks, workbooks, calculators, computers, and art supplies.

③ **Performance Assessment Guidelines** Children's responses should accurately describe their school setting.

Extension Activities For Home and School

Time Travel Skit

Materials: classroom objects

Organize children into small groups. Direct them to put on a skit in which several children pretend to be first graders from long ago who have traveled through time to meet a group of first graders from today. Encourage children to think about what children from the past would say and would ask about a modern classroom. Give children time to organize and practice their skits before performing them for the class. Encourage groups to use classroom objects as props.
(KINESTHETIC/AUDITORY)

Write a Letter

Materials: stationery, envelopes, stamps

Suggest that children and family members write letters about their school experiences to an elderly family member. Suggest that children describe what they do at school, including what subjects they study and what tools they use. Encourage children to ask the family member questions about what first grade was like for him or her. Invite children to share replies they may receive with classmates.
(VISUAL/TACTILE)

September 8, 2005

Dear Grandma,

I love first grade. My favorite subjects are social studies and reading. We use journals, notebooks, and workbooks to do our work. We even have computers in our classroom! I like working on the computer. What was school like for you in first grade? Please write back and tell me all about it.

Love,

Mitchell

Schoolhouse Scenes

Materials: Activity Pattern P2 (schoolhouse), construction paper, scissors, glue, crayons or markers

Give each child two copies of Activity Pattern P2 (schoolhouse). Show children how to cut the slit and fold back the doors. Have children glue one precut pattern to each side of a piece of construction paper. Remind children not to glue down the doors. Direct children to fold back the doors and to draw a schoolhouse scene from long ago on one side of their paper, and a classroom scene from today on the other side. Invite children to share their work, comparing classrooms of long ago to classrooms of today.
(VISUAL/TACTILE/KINESTHETIC)

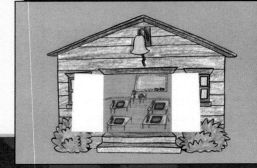

Put Things into Groups

OBJECTIVES

- Read and interpret a table.
- Categorize information.

RESOURCES

Pupil Book/Unit Big Book,
  pp. 28–29

Word Cards V7–V8

Activity Book, p. 9

Activity Pattern P1

Skill Transparency 1–4

Vocabulary

table p. 28

1 Motivate

Provide an index card for each child, and ask children to draw on the card a picture that shows how they get to school. Do they walk? ride the bus? ride in a car? ride a bike? Have children stand and hold up their card. Ask children to look around at the cards the other children are holding to see how each child gets to school. Then have children categorize the information by standing together in groups according to what is drawn on their cards. Direct children to look around again to see how each classmate gets to school. Ask children which way was easier to get the information: when children were standing by their seats or when they were standing in groups.

Why It Matters

Remind children that they have learned about one kind of group—a number of people working together. Tell them that a group can also be a number of things that are alike. Have children recall the grouping exercise they just did on ways they travel to school. Explain to children that information also can be arranged on paper in a way that makes it easier to understand.

STUDY/RESEARCH SKILLS

Preview Pictures and Title Ask children whether they have ever seen a movie preview. Encourage them to explain the purpose of a preview. Point out that children can also preview information they are about to read. Share the lesson title with children and have them examine the photos. Help children realize that previewing can help them understand what they are about to read.

2 Teach

What You Need to Know

Direct children to look at the table and read the titles along the top to find out what is being grouped in the chart. Help children understand that everything that is part of the group will appear under that group title. Then have children look at all the entries under the *Long Ago* title. Ask them what is the same about all the objects. Repeat for the *Today* column.

Q **If you had been in charge of making this table, what would you have to know about each tool to decide where it should be placed?**

A You must know whether the tool was used long ago or today.

Tell children to look at the table to find objects that children used for math long ago and objects they use for math today. Guide children in comparing the objects. Have children continue comparing school tools from long ago with those used for the same purpose today.

Q **Why might it be easier to compare these objects in a table than on separate pages?**

A Because it is easier to see how they are alike and different when they are side by side.

Skills **CHART AND GRAPH**

Put Things into Groups

Vocabulary

table

▶ Why It Matters

Putting things into groups helps you see how they are alike and different.

▶ What You Need to Know

A **table** is a chart that shows things in groups. Labels tell you what is in each group.

▶ Practice the Skill

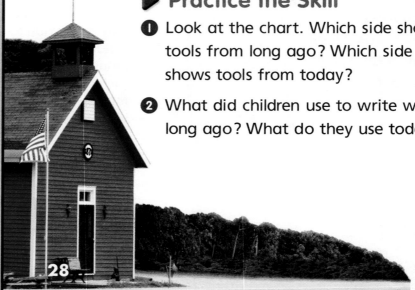

❶ Look at the chart. Which side shows tools from long ago? Which side shows tools from today?

❷ What did children use to write with long ago? What do they use today?

28

WORD WORK

Multiple Meanings Explain to children that the word *table* has more than one meaning. Point out that the meaning children are most familiar with (a piece of furniture) is only one meaning of the word. A table can also be a kind of graphic organizer that presents information in a way that makes it easy to understand.

INTEGRATE SCIENCE

Living/Nonliving Table On chart paper, draw a table with the column headings *Living Things* and *Nonliving Things*. Provide children with a variety of magazine pictures of both living and nonliving things, such as people, pets, plants, furniture, and tools. Invite children to attach their pictures in the appropriate column on the table and to explain why that is the correct spot for the picture.

REACH ALL LEARNERS

Advanced Learners Invite children to make a table to indicate their favorite subject area in school. On chart paper, draw a table with children's names in a column labeled *Student* and additional columns for subject areas such as *Math, Reading, Spelling, Science,* and *Social Studies.* Show children how to find their name in the table and look across the column to find their favorite subject. Have children place a checkmark to indicate their favorite subject.

28 ■ **UNIT 1**

School Tools

Long Ago	Today

▶ **Apply What You Learned**

Make a table that shows Reading Tools and Writing Tools. Use the tools on the Today side of the table on this page to make your new table.

29

Practice the Skill—Answers

❶ The left side shows tools from long ago. The right side shows tools used today.

❷ Long ago, children used a pen and inkwell and a slate board and chalk to write. Today, children use pencil and paper or a computer.

3 Close

Apply What You Learned

Children's tables should include tools from the *Today* group on page 29.

Reading Tools	Writing Tools

ACTIVITY BOOK

Name _____ Date _____

CHART AND GRAPH SKILLS
Which Room?

Mrs. Garza and Mr. Todd have new school supplies. Mrs. Garza teaches music. Mr. Todd teaches art.

Look at the picture. Which items go in each room? Draw pictures to complete the table.

New School Supplies	
Mrs. Garza's Room	**Mr. Todd's Room**

Use with Unit 1, Skill Lesson 4.   Activity Book • 9

PAGE 9

TRANSPARENCY

Use SKILL TRANSPARENCY 1–4.

EXTEND AND ENRICH

Conduct a Survey Have children brainstorm a list of favorite after-school activities, such as practicing sports, eating a snack, playing with friends, or watching TV. Direct children to ask one student from another first-grade classroom to identify his or her favorite activity. After the survey, guide children to tabulate the results and present them in a table titled *Favorite After-School Activities.* Display the table and help children compare results.

RETEACH THE SKILL

Build a Picture Table On chart paper, draw a table titled *School Workers* with the column heads *Classroom* and *Other Places.* Provide labeled pictures of school workers, such as *teacher, bus driver,* and *secretary.* You may want to use Activity Pattern P1. Have volunteers attach each picture in the appropriate place in the table. Encourage them to explain why each picture belongs in that part of the table.

Extension Activities For Home and School

School Supply Sort

Materials: assortment of school supplies, large sheets of paper

Organize children into small groups. Provide a variety of school supplies to represent various curriculum areas. For example, you might include counters, a calculator, and pattern blocks to represent mathematics and a hand lens and a medicine dropper to represent science. Give each group large sheets of paper with the title of a curriculum area, such as math, science, art, or social studies, on each one. Invite children to work together to sort items. Point out that some objects could possibly fit in more than one group. Encourage groups to discuss as they work why each item should be placed in a particular category.
(TACTILE/KINESTHETIC)

Personal Work Table

Materials: grids duplicated on paper, crayons or markers

Give each child a blank table grid to take home. Suggest children have a family member help them make a table to keep track of jobs they might do at home. Encourage them to brainstorm a list of tasks. Show children how to write the days of the week down the left column of the table and the jobs they plan to do across the top of the table. Encourage children to draw a happy face on the table each time they complete a job.
(VISUAL/TACTILE)

Day	Make bed	Take out trash	Do homework	Walk dog
Sunday	☺	☺	☺	☺
Monday	☺	☺		
Tuesday				
Wednesday				
Thursday				
Friday				
Saturday				

Pocket Chart Sort

Materials: pocket chart, sentence strips, marker, tape, small objects or pictures

Organize children into small groups. Provide groups with an assortment of small objects or pictures. Tell children to work together to sort the objects or pictures into two groups based on criteria they choose. Point out that there may be several ways to sort the objects. Have children use the sentence strips to make labels for their categories. Direct them to attach the labels to the pocket chart and to put the objects in the pocket chart to make a kind of table.
(TACTILE/KINESTHETIC)

Learning Around the World

OBJECTIVES

- Compare schools around the world.
- Discover that people learn in places outside of school.

Compare and Contrast
Focus Skill
pp. 1, 31, 36

RESOURCES

Pupil Book/Unit Big Book, pp. 30–33

Word Cards V7–V8

Activity Book, p. 10

📖 **Reading and Vocabulary Transparency 1–7**

💻 **Internet Resources**

READING SOCIAL STUDIES

Anticipation Guide Find out what children know by having them categorize the following statements as true or false.

—— The world is all the people and places on our planet.

—— Schools everywhere look the same.

—— All learning happens indoors.

—— Only children in the United States go on field trips.

 ● USE READING AND VOCABULARY TRANSPARENCY 1–7

1–7
TRANSPARENCY

Vocabulary

world p. 30

 When Minutes Count

Have pairs of children read the lesson together. Then ask them to write a summary sentence for the lesson.

Quick Summary

Schools all over the world can be quite different, but one thing is the same—school is a place where children learn.

 1 Motivate

Set the Purpose

Big Idea Before starting the lesson, read the Big Idea statement aloud. As children read and discuss the lesson, help them look for ways that each school is like theirs. Also help them understand that even though some schools are not like theirs, this does not mean the schools are better or worse; they are merely different.

Access Prior Knowledge

Pose a question for children to quickwrite about, such as *What do you think it would be like to go to school in Mexico?* or some other faraway place. Encourage each child to make a sketch and to write words, phrases, and captions to go with the sketch. Invite children to share their work.

2 Teach

Read and Respond

Geography Show children a globe and explain that it is a model of Earth. Point out the different bodies of land and water on the globe. Show children your approximate location on the globe. Then after reading the text on page 30, point out on the globe the places the children in the pictures are located. Lead children in a discussion about the different climates and land features around the world. For example, some places have mountains, others are surrounded by ocean or are on a coast, some are near rivers, and so on. Point out that some places are extremely hot, while others are very cold.

Culture and Society Explain to children that the beliefs and values of a group of people are often taught in schools. For example, most schools teach the history of the people or country where they are located as well as the traditional arts and crafts made by the people of their area.

Q How would a school's location in the world affect what children do at school?

A Possible responses: The weather can affect what children do. For example, in a very cold place, children probably would not play outdoors much. Also, they would wear clothing that is different from the clothing of children in a warm place. The arts and crafts of people in different places might be different because of the different materials people would have.

Lesson

6 Learning Around the World

Big Idea
Schools around the world are the same in many ways.

Vocabulary
world

The **world** is all the people and places on our planet. Around the world, children learn. Some schools may look like yours, and some may be very different.

Germany

Mexico

30

INTEGRATE MUSIC

Sing a Song Lead children in singing the song "It's a Small World." Then guide children in a discussion about the meaning of the expression "It's a small world." Encourage them to tell how this idea applies to schools around the world.

INTEGRATE READING

Getting to School Share with children *This Is the Way We Go to School: A Book About Children Around the World* by Edith Baer (Econo-Clad Books, 1999). Told in rhyme, the book explores different transportation methods to schools around the world. Some of the methods of transportation and places included are a ferryboat in New York City, a trolley in San Francisco, and a vaporetto in Italy.

·SCIENCE AND TECHNOLOGY·

The Internet

The Internet makes it easy for people to learn and share. With this tool, you can find information about many things. You can see art in a museum far away. You can even send messages around the world.

Togo

Brazil

31

Read and Respond

Culture and Society Ask children to think of themselves in one of the pictures on pages 30–33. Have them imagine they are attending school with these children. Encourage children to tell which picture they chose and to explain the reasons for their choice.

Q How would school in that place be different from school here?

A Responses will vary and should indicate children's understanding of similarities and differences in the learning environments.

Q What might be difficult if you had to attend school in another country next week?

A Possible responses: I might not understand the words used. The food might be different. It might be hard to make new friends.

Visual Learning

Pictures Focus children's attention on the pictures on pages 32 and 33. Point out that some of these children are on field trips. The group in Egypt is visiting the Kom Ombo Temple, and the group in Italy is visiting a castle. Help children realize that learning can take place in different settings and in different ways, but that the reason for learning is always the same—so children can find out about and understand their world.

Q Why is it important to learn about people in other places?

A It helps us understand that while people around the world are different in many ways, we are also alike in many ways. This can help us accept and be prepared to meet new people.

Some learning happens outside of the classroom. How are these children learning?

Venezuela

Japan

Egypt

32

INTEGRATE LANGUAGES

"Hello" Around the World
Tell children that it is helpful to know greetings in other languages. Use these pronunciations to share greetings in other languages.

Language	Greeting
Spanish	hola (OH•la)
French	bonjour (bohn•JOUR)
German	guten tag (GOO•ten TAHG)
Hebrew	shalom (sha •LOHM)

EXTEND AND ENRICH

Research and Report Have children choose one of the countries from this lesson and research to find out more about schools in that country. Then have children report to the class about their findings. Encourage children to tell about ways schools in that country are like and different from their school.

Italy

LESSON 6 Review

❶ **Vocabulary** What is the **world**?

❷ How are the ways these children learn the same as the ways you learn?

❸ Write a letter telling someone far away about your school.

33

RETEACH THE LESSON

Write Captions Invite children to write their own captions for the pictures on pages 30–33. Then have children share their captions with a partner and discuss the similarities and differences between the settings and activities in the pictures and those of their school.

ACTIVITY BOOK

Name _____ Date _____

Schools Near and Far

Look at the picture. How is this classroom the same as yours? How is it different? Write same or different to complete the chart.

different	same	accept either answer
different	same	accept either answer

10 • Activity Book — Use with Unit 1, Lesson 6.

3 Close

Summarize Key Content

- The world is all the people and places on our planet.
- All around the world, children learn.
- Schools can look the same or different, but everywhere school is a place to learn.

READING SOCIAL STUDIES

Anticipation Guide Revisit the anticipation guide begun in Motivate. Invite children to change any wrong answers.

true The world is all the people and places on our planet.

false Schools everywhere look the same.

false All learning happens indoors.

false Only children in the United States go on field trips.

● USE READING AND VOCABULARY TRANSPARENCY 1–7   **1–7 TRANSPARENCY**

Assess

Lesson 6 Review—Answers

❶ The world is all the people and places on our planet.

❷ Responses may include that children read, write, ask questions, study, and go on field trips.

❸ **Performance Assessment Guidelines** Children's letters should include details and descriptions about what it is like to attend their school.

Extension Activities For Home and School

Around the World

Materials: drawing paper, crayons or markers, computers

Read the following poem aloud to children.

Friends Around the World

If I should go to London
  I'd find a child like me;
He'd probably play cricket
  And have bread and jam for tea.

If I should go to Holland
  When winter's on the sea,
I'd find the children skating
  Upon the Zuyder Zee.

If I should go to China,
  Or down to Mexico
I'd find kites or balls or marbles
  Or something I would know.

It's curious to think of it—
  Wherever I might be,
In Spain or France or Russia,
  I'd find children just like me.

*by Blanche Jennings
Thompson*

Point out that the poem tells about things they would see in places around the world. Have children choose one of the places mentioned in the poem and then draw a picture to show what they think school might be like there. Have them compare their pictures to those in the lesson. Allow time for children to look up more information on the Internet if needed. You may also want to guide children in performing a choral reading of the poem.
(AUDITORY/VISUAL/TACTILE)

Guest Speaker

Materials: paper, marker, container

Invite children to brainstorm a list of questions they would like to ask someone who attended school in another country. Write the questions on slips of paper, and put them in a container. Invite a person (perhaps a family member of a student) to share their experiences and some items that they might have from their native country. Suggest that the visitor focus on how schools in this country and in the other country are alike and different. Invite volunteers to draw a question from the container and read it aloud to the speaker. After the visit, help children write thank-you notes that tell the speaker their favorite part of the presentation.
(AUDITORY/TACTILE)

September 30, 2005

Dear Mr. Rojas,

Thank you for telling us about going to school in Brazil. I liked the part when you told us about Carnival. School in Brazil sounds exciting.

    Your friend,
    Eli Wooden

Alphabet Posters

Materials: books, magazines, encyclopedias, posterboard, scissors, glue

Invite children to work with family members to collect print samples of different languages from around the world. Encourage children to compare the different alphabets. Suggest that families visit libraries to make copies of pages from books and magazines to show examples of the different characters. Suggest that children and family members at home glue the print samples to posterboard and label them. Encourage children to bring their completed posters to school for display.
(VISUAL/TACTILE)

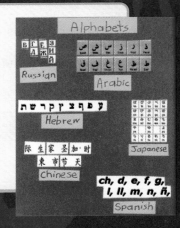

VISIT

A School for Firefighters

OBJECTIVE

■ Describe the requirements of various jobs and the characteristics of a job well-performed.

■ Obtain information about a topic using a variety of visual sources, such as pictures, television, and computer images.

RESOURCES

Pupil Book/Unit Big Book,
  pp. 34–35
Video
💻**Internet Resources**

Summary

In this lesson, children visit a school where men and women learn and train to become firefighters.

1 Motivate

Get Ready

Explain to children that they will be visiting a school for firefighters where students take special classes, study, and train to learn how to fight fires, how to keep people safe, and how to work as a team. Invite children to tell what they know about the jobs of firefighters. Record their responses in a web such as the one below.

fight fires

rescue people

check buildings

teach fire safety

READING SOCIAL STUDIES

Make Predictions Ask children to review the web they helped to create and then predict what they will learn about skills taught at a school for firefighters. Record their ideas and save. At the end of the lesson, have children review their list and make changes and additions.

What to See

Invite children to study the picture on page 34 and then follow along as you read aloud the caption.

Q Why do you think it is important for these student firefighters to work together as a team?

A The hose is thick and heavy and the water comes out so fast and hard that it takes more than one person to hold the hose steady and point it toward the fire.

Next, focus attention on the students using a ladder. Point out that the ladder with its built-in hose is attached to a turntable on the fire truck. It can be raised and lowered to reach different floors of a building. Ask what these firefighters would be wearing and carrying if they were fighting an actual fire. (helmets, boots, protective clothing, gloves, face masks, air tanks, and special tools)

Q Why do you think the students must practice?

A So they will know how to operate the ladder and how to climb it quickly and safely

Point out that a fire department may have several types of trucks including pumpers, ladder trucks, and rescue trucks. Explain that the pumper trucks have powerful pumps that take water from a fire hydrant (point out the hydrant in the next picture) and force it through the hoses under great pressure.

Q What do you think the students are learning about this fire truck?

A Children's responses may include how to operate the pump, what the dials mean, how to connect the hose to the pump.

As children study the last photograph, remind them that another important job of firefighters is to help prevent fires by making sure special fire safety codes are followed in buildings. They also teach people about fire safety. Ask children to state some of the fire safety rules they have learned.

VISIT
A School for Firefighters

Get Ready

There are many kinds of schools. At a school for firefighters, people learn how to fight fires and keep others safe. They also learn how to work together as a team.

What to See

Students help each other use a fire hose.

34

BACKGROUND

Early Fire Fighting in America
In 1648, Peter Stuyvesant, the governor of New Amsterdam, selected four men to serve as fire wardens. They had the authority to check homes and chimneys for fire hazards and to fine those who violated the rules. Later, in 1658, eight men were appointed to patrol and watch for fires at night. They were known as the "rattle watch" because they used wooden rattles to alert citizens when a fire was spotted. As citizens responded, the rattle watch would form a bucket brigade to fight the fire.

REACH ALL LEARNERS

English as a Second Language Have children make a set of cards for the terms *water hose, ladder, firefighter, fire truck,* and *fire hydrant.* Display pages 34 and 35. As you point to the ladder, for example, and say the word, have children repeat it and hold up the correct card. Later, have children randomly pick a card, read it, and then match it to the correct picture. You may want to have children draw a picture on the back of each card to help them recall what each term means.

Students practice using a ladder.

There is a lot to learn about the fire truck.

The water hose hooks up to the fire hydrant.

Students study fire safety rules.

Take a Field Trip

A VIRTUAL TOUR
Visit The Learning Site at **www.harcourtschool.com** to take virtual tours of other kinds of schools.

A VIDEO TOUR
Check your media center or classroom library for a video featuring a segment from Reading Rainbow.

35

3 Close

Invite children to role-play being instructors and student firefighters at a school for firefighters. As children pretend, encourage the instructors to discuss why it is important for the students to learn to work together as a team.

Take a Field Trip

A Virtual Tour Depending on the availability of computers, have children work individually, in pairs, or in small groups to view the virtual tour. Suggest they research how other kinds of schools and their school are alike and different.

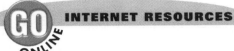

INTERNET RESOURCES

THE LEARNING SITE
Visit The Learning Site at **www.harcourtschool.com** to take virtual tours of other kinds of schools.

A Video Field Trip Tell children that after they watch the Reading Rainbow video on a school for firefighters in Dallas, Texas, they should jot down three or four questions about information covered in the video. Then invite children to exchange questions with a partner and answer their partner's questions. You may want to show the video a second time before children answer the questions.

VIDEO

Use the Reading Rainbow TAKE A FIELD TRIP videotape of a school for firefighters.

EXTEND AND ENRICH

Conduct an Interview Ask children to think about the kind of job or career they might like to have as an adult. Then encourage children to interview someone they know with that job or career. Help them come up with questions such as the following: *Did you go to a special school to become a _____? What kind? Where? What did you study? How long did it take?* After children conduct their interviews, invite them to share what they learned.

MAKE IT RELEVANT

At School Invite children to act as fire safety inspectors and to identify all the different things in and around the school that will help in case of a fire. Does the school have a sprinkler system? Where are the fire alarms located? Are the exits clearly marked? Are there fire extinguishers handy? Is there a fire hydrant near the school?

Unit I Review and Test Preparation

PAGES 36–40

 Compare and Contrast

Children's tables should include in each column several entries that reflect ideas from the text and from class discussions. Children should be able to use ideas from the table to compare and contrast schools around the world. In the Alike column, children may write a statement such as *Schools help children learn*. In the Different column, children may write a statement such as *Schools can look different*.

ACTIVITY BOOK

Name _____ Date _____
Going to School
Finish the table to show how schools are alike and different.

Schools	
Alike	**Different**
Schools have teachers.	Schools are different sizes.
Everyone uses tools to learn.	Some schools have computers.
Schools help children learn.	Schools can look different.
All schools have students.	Schools can teach children different things.

Use with Unit I.   Activity Book • 11

PAGE 11

Think & Write

Children should choose a tool that is available in your classroom. Their label should tell how the tool is used in their daily school activities.

TRANSPARENCY

This graphic organizer appears on READING AND VOCABULARY TRANSPARENCY 1–8.

Unit 1 Review and Test Preparation

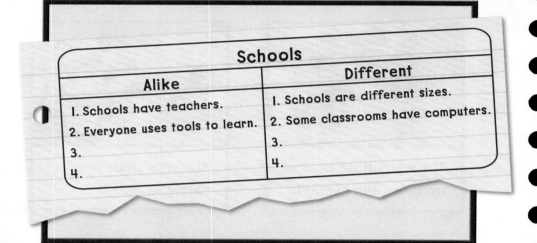

 Compare and Contrast

Fill in the chart about schools. List things that are alike and different such as ways you learn, school workers, and tools you use.

Schools	
Alike	**Different**
1. Schools have teachers.	1. Schools are different sizes.
2. Everyone uses tools to learn.	2. Some classrooms have computers.
3.	3.
4.	4.

 THINK & WRITE

Make a Choice Choose a tool you use every day in school.

Write a Label Write the name of the tool. Tell how it is used.

36

TEST PREPARATION

Review these tips with children.

- Read the directions before reading the questions.
- Read each question twice, focusing the second time on all the possible answers.
- Take the time to think about all the possible answers before deciding on an answer.
- Move past questions that are giving you trouble, and answer the ones you know. Then return to concentrate on the difficult items.

Use Vocabulary

Write the word that goes with each meaning.

❶ a number of people working together

❷ the leader of a school

❸ an instruction telling what must be done

❹ a person who helps others learn

❺ to find out something new

learn
(p. 6)
rule
(p. 10)
group
(p. 12)
teacher
(p. 14)
principal
(p. 14)

Recall Facts

❻ Name a school rule that helps children be fair.

❼ What tools help you learn?

❽ Tell two ways schools today are different from schools long ago.

❾ Which of these school workers helps you find a book?

  A nurse   **C** custodian

  B librarian   **D** food server

❿ Which of these is a good symbol for a cafeteria?

F   **H**

G   **J**

37

Use Vocabulary

❶ group

❷ principal

❸ rule

❹ teacher

❺ learn

Recall Facts

❻ Children may name a rule in their own school or a rule from the unit.

❼ Children should name at least two school tools that were discussed in this unit.

❽ Children should write two statements that contrast modern schools with long ago schools.

❾ B—librarian

❿ F—food tray

Think Critically

⓫ Children may say that people might be confused, might not be safe, and might not get much done.

⓬ Children may say that people who work alone make their own decisions but have no one to help them do the work. People who work in groups must agree on what to do and how to do it, but group members help each other do the work.

Apply Chart and Graph Skills

⓭ Rules

⓮ School—the left side; Home—the right side

⓯ a home rule

⓰ the left (School) side

⓫ What can happen when people do not follow rules?

⓬ How is working in a group different from working alone?

Apply Chart and Graph Skills

Rules	
School Rules	**Home Rules**
Raise hand	Make bed
Stand in line	Feed fish
Hang up backpack	Keep room clean

⓭ What is the title of this table?

⓮ Which side shows rules at school? Which side shows rules at home?

⓯ Is **Feed fish** a school or home rule?

⓰ On which side would the rule **Take turns** go?

38

Study these symbols.

| Art center | Child's desk | Lunch boxes | Reading corner | Teacher's desk |

Joe's Classroom

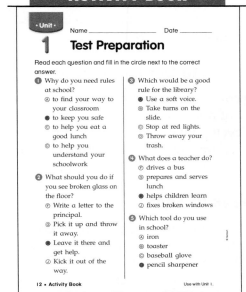

17 What does this map show?

18 What is the symbol for the reading corner?

19 What is the brush a symbol for?

20 What is between the art center and the reading corner?

39

Apply Map and Globe Skills

17 Joe's classroom

18 a book

19 the art center

20 the teacher's desk

ACTIVITY BOOK

· Unit · Name _____ Date _____

1 **Test Preparation**

Read each question and fill in the circle next to the correct answer.

1 Why do you need rules at school?
Ⓐ to find your way to your classroom
● to keep you safe
Ⓒ to help you eat a good lunch
Ⓓ to help you understand your schoolwork

2 What should you do if you see broken glass on the floor?
Ⓕ Write a letter to the principal.
Ⓖ Pick it up and throw it away.
● Leave it there and get help.
Ⓘ Kick it out of the way.

3 Which would be a good rule for the library?
● Use a soft voice.
Ⓑ Take turns on the slide.
Ⓒ Stop at red lights.
Ⓓ Throw away your trash.

4 What does a teacher do?
Ⓕ drives a bus
Ⓖ prepares and serves lunch
● helps children learn
Ⓘ fixes broken windows

5 Which tool do you use in school?
Ⓐ iron
Ⓑ toaster
Ⓒ baseball glove
● pencil sharpener

12 • Activity Book   Use with Unit 1.

PAGE 12

ASSESSMENT

Use the UNIT 1 TEST on pages 1–4 of the Assessment Program.

Unit Activities

Organize the class into three groups, according to whether they prefer to draw the classroom, the cafeteria, or the library. Have children close their eyes for a few minutes and visualize the place they will draw. Then allow time for children to discuss tools and workers they might include in their pictures.

Where to Get Information

Encourage children to use a wide variety of reference sources, including encyclopedias, library books, travel brochures, social studies books, picture atlases, magazines, and the Internet.

Ways to Share

Have group members design a cover for their scrapbook. Suggest that each child make a page for the book. Use yarn and a hole punch to help children bind their pages together. Call on volunteers from each group to describe their pictures as you read their scrapbook to the class. Have children name the school workers and tools in each picture.

 Performance Assessment Guidelines Observe to see that children have included school workers and school tools in their drawings and that they have chosen appropriate workers and tools for their setting.

Visit Your Library

Encourage independent reading with these books or others of your choice after children have completed their study of school. Additional resources are listed in the Multimedia Resources on pages 1J–1K of this Teacher's Edition.

Easy *Get Up and Go!* by Stuart J. Murphy. HarperCollins, 1996. With encouragement from her dog, the story character finds that time lines are a useful way to keep track of time while getting ready for school.

Average *First Day, Hooray!* by Nancy Poydar. Holiday House, 1999. Children are not the only ones who enjoy getting ready for the beginning of school. School workers look forward to the first day, too.

Challenging *A School Album* by Peter and Connie Roop. Heineman Library, 1998. School in the olden days was like modern school in some ways. In others it was very different.

Unit Activities

Complete the Unit Project Work with your group to finish the unit project. Decide what you want to show in your scrapbook. Make a cover.

 Visit The Learning Site at **www.harcourtschool.com** for additional activities.

Choose a Place

Choose one of these places in your school. Draw a picture of it.
- classroom
- cafeteria
- library

Match Workers and Tools

Draw pictures of school workers. Find or draw pictures of the tools they use at work. Match the workers to their tools.

Visit Your Library

 Get Up and Go! by Stuart J. Murphy. Follow a young girl as she gets ready for school on a busy morning.

First Day, Hooray! by Nancy Poydar. Workers and students are getting ready for the first day of school.

 A School Album by Peter and Connie Roop. See how schools long ago and today are alike and different.

40

Good Citizens

An airplane hood ornament
for car, 1915

Unit 2 Planning Chart Good Citizens

Unit 2 is the story of our country's government. Children will explore rules and laws, voting, our local, state and national leaders, and American symbols. In addition, children will discover that they have both rights and responsibilities as citizens and ways they can be good citizens.

LESSON	PACING	OBJECTIVES	VOCABULARY
Introduce the Unit pp. 41R–41 **Preview the Vocabulary** pp. 42–43A **Start with a Song** pp. 44A–45A	4 Days	■ Use a visual to predict content. ■ Interpret a quotation. ■ Use a K-W-L chart to prepare for the unit. ■ Use visuals to determine word meanings. ■ Use words and visuals to predict the content of the unit. ■ Obtain information about a topic using a variety of visual sources such as pictures and literature. ■ Communicate information through words and visuals. ■ Learn a patriotic song.	**Word Work,** pp. 42, 43A
Rules and Laws pp. 46A–47A	2 Days	■ Explain the need for rules and laws in the community. ■ Give examples of rules or laws that establish order, provide security, and manage conflict. ■ Recognize that breaking rules or laws has consequences.	**law** **community**
2 Who Are Our Leaders? pp. 48A–51A	3 Days	■ Identify leaders of different groups. ■ Identify the responsibilities of authority figures in the home, school, and community. ■ Identify leaders in the community and state. ■ Describe the roles of public officials, including mayor and governor.	**leader** **mayor** **city** **governor** **government** **Word Work,** p. 49
MAP AND GLOBE SKILLS **Find States on a Map** pp. 52A–53A	2 Days	■ Locate places of significance on maps. ■ Use simple maps to identify the location of places beyond the classroom, school, and community. ■ Recognize their state on a United States map.	**country** **state** **border**

Time Management

READING	INTEGRATE LEARNING	REACH ALL LEARNERS	RESOURCES
Prior Knowledge, p. 41 *(Focus Skill)* Reading Social Studies: **Make a Prediction**, p. 42 **Personal Response**, pp. 44A, 45	**Theme Time**, p. 41I Reading **Stars and Stripes**, p. 41R Art **Good Citizen Mural**, p. 41 Music **Recognize Music**, p. 43 **Patriotic Songs**, p. 44	**English as a Second Language**, p. 41N **Advanced Learners**, p. 41N **Below-Level Learners**, p. 41N **Extension Activities For Home and School**, p. 45A	**Pupil Book/Unit Big Book**, pp. 41–45 **Audiotext** ●**Reading and Vocabulary Transparency 2–1** **Activity Pattern P3** 💻 Internet Resources
Reading Social Studies: **Concept Web**, pp. 46A, 47		**Extend and Enrich**, p. 46 **Reteach the Lesson**, p. 47 **Extension Activities For Home and School**, p. 47A	**Pupil Book/Unit Big Book**, pp. 46–47 **Word Cards V9–V10** ●**Reading and Vocabulary Transparency 2–2** **Activity Book**, p. 13 💻 Internet Resources
Reading Social Studies: **K-W-L Chart**, pp. 48A, 51 **Prior Knowledge**, p. 48 *(Focus Skill)*	Language Arts **Descriptive Words**, p. 48 Music **Conductors**, p. 49	**English as a Second Language**, p. 48 **Advanced Learners**, p. 50 **Extend and Enrich**, p. 50 **Reteach the Lesson**, p. 51 **Extension Activities For Home and School**, p. 51A	**Pupil Book/Unit Big Book**, pp. 48–51 **Word Cards V9–V12** ●**Reading and Vocabulary Transparency 2–3** **Activity Book**, p. 14 💻 Internet Resources
		Advanced Learners, p. 52 **Extend and Enrich**, p. 52 **Reteach the Skill**, p. 53 **Extension Activities For Home and School**, p. 53A	**Pupil Book/Unit Big Book**, pp. 52–53 **Word Cards V11–V14** ●**Skill Transparency 2–1** **Activity Book**, p. 15 **GeoSkills CD-ROM** 💻 Internet Resources

Unit 2 Planning Guide

LESSON	PACING	OBJECTIVES	VOCABULARY
3 Our Country's Presidents pp. 54A–57A	3 Days	■ Identify leaders in the nation. ■ Describe the role of public officials, including the President. ■ Identify George Washington as the first President of our country. ■ Know past Presidents.	**President**
CITIZENSHIP SKILLS **Make a Choice by Voting** pp. 58A–59A	1 Day	■ Recognize the democratic process of voting. ■ Identify how people in the United States choose their leaders. ■ Use voting as a way of making choices and decisions.	**vote** **ballot**
4 America's Symbols pp. 60A–65A	4 Days	■ Explain selected national and state patriotic symbols. ■ Recite and explain the meaning of a pledge of allegiance and a flag. ■ Identify anthems and mottoes of countries and states. ■ Explain how symbols reflect an American love of individualism and freedom. ■ Identify ways in which Americans show respect for and honor their country.	**flag**
READING SKILLS **Fiction or Nonfiction** pp. 66A–67A	1 Day	■ Distinguish between fiction and nonfiction. ■ Recognize facts in nonfiction writing.	**fiction** **nonfiction** **fact** **Word Work,** p. 66A

READING	INTEGRATE LEARNING	REACH ALL LEARNERS	RESOURCES
Reading Social Studies: **Study Questions,** pp. 54A, 57 (Focus Skill) **Prior Knowledge,** p. 54		**Advanced Learners,** p. 55 **Below-Level Learners,** p. 55 **Extend and Enrich,** p. 56 **Reteach the Lesson,** p. 57 **Extension Activities For Home and School,** p. 57A	**Pupil Book/Unit Big Book,** pp. 54–57 **Word Cards V13–V14** **Reading and Vocabulary Transparency 2–4** **Activity Book,** p. 16 Internet Resources
Extend and Enrich, p. 59 **Reteach the Skill,** p. 59 **Extension Activities For Home and School,** p. 59A	**Mathematics** **Charts and Graphs,** p. 58		**Pupil Book/Unit Big Book,** pp. 58–59 **Word Cards V13–V16** **Skill Transparency 2–2** **Activity Book,** p. 17 Internet Resources
Reading Social Studies: **K-W-L Chart,** pp. 60A, 65 **Paraphrase,** p. 62	**Art** **Draw a Symbol,** p. 60 **Mathematics** **Measurement,** p. 61 **Music** **Sing the National Anthem,** p. 62 **Learn a Song,** p. 63	**Advanced Learners,** p. 61 **English as a Second Language,** p. 63 **Extend and Enrich,** p. 64 **Reteach the Lesson,** p. 65 **Extension Activities For Home and School,** p. 65A	**Pupil Book/Unit Big Book,** pp. 60–65 **Word Cards V15–V16** **Reading and Vocabulary Transparency 2–5** **Activity Book,** p. 18 Internet Resources
	Reading **Tall Tales,** p. 66	**Extend and Enrich,** p. 67 **Reteach the Skill,** p. 67 **Extension Activities For Home and School,** p. 67A	**Pupil Book/Unit Big Book,** pp. 66–67 **Word Cards V15–V18** **Skill Transparency 2–3** **Activity Book,** p. 19 Internet Resources

Unit 2 Planning Guide

LESSON	PACING	OBJECTIVES	VOCABULARY
5 Portraits of Good Citizens pp. 68A–71A	3 Days	■ Identify characteristics of good citizenship such as a belief in equality and responsibility for the common good. ■ Identify historic figures and ordinary people who have exemplified good citizenship. ■ Identify contributions of historical figures who have influenced the community, state, and nation. ■ Identify historic figures who have exhibited a love of individualism.	**citizen**
6 Rights and Responsibilities pp. 72A–73A	2 Days	■ Identify some of the rights people have. ■ Explore some of the responsibilities that accompany rights. ■ Predict what might happen if you did not act responsibly.	**right** **responsibility**
Visit How Communities Honor Their Citizens pp. 74A–75	1 Day	■ Identify and describe ways that communities honor people who have made a difference. ■ Identify historical figures who have influenced the community, state, and nation. ■ Explain how selected customs and symbols reflect an American love of individualism, inventiveness, and freedom. ■ Obtain information about a topic using a variety of visual sources, such as pictures, television, and computer images.	
Unit 2 Review and Test Preparation pp. 76–80	4 Days		

READING	INTEGRATE LEARNING	REACH ALL LEARNERS	RESOURCES
Reading Social Studies: **Graphic Organizer,** pp. 68A, 71 **Use Context Clues,** p. 68		**Extend and Enrich,** p. 70 **Reteach the Lesson,** p. 71 **Extension Activities For Home and School,** p. 71A	**Pupil Book/Unit Big Book,** pp. 68–71 **Word Cards V17–V18** **Reading and Vocabulary Transparency 2–6** **Activity Book,** p. 20 Internet Resources
Reading Social Studies: **Make a Prediction,** pp. 72A, 73		**Extend and Enrich,** p. 72 **Reteach the Lesson,** p. 73 **Extension Activities For Home and School,** p. 73A	**Pupil Book/Unit Big Book,** pp. 72–73 **Word Cards V17–V18** **Reading and Vocabulary Transparency 2–7** **Activity Book,** p. 21 **Activity Pattern P4** Internet Resources
	Language Arts **Write a Description,** p. 75	**Advanced Learners,** p. 74 **Extend and Enrich,** p. 75	**Pupil Book/Unit Big Book,** pp. 74–75 Internet Resources **Take a Field Trip Video**
Prior Knowledge, p. 76			**Pupil Book/Unit Big Book,** pp. 76–80 **Activity Book,** pp. 22–23 **Reading and Vocabulary Transparency 2–8** **Assessment Program, Unit 2 Test,** pp. 5–8 Internet Resources

Unit 2 Skills Path

Unit 2 features the reading skills of accessing prior knowledge and understanding the concepts of fiction or nonfiction. It also highlights the social studies skills of finding states on a map and making a choice by voting.

FOCUS SKILLS

UNIT 2 READING SKILL

 PRIOR KNOWLEDGE

- INTRODUCE p. 41
- APPLY pp. 48, 54, 76

READING SOCIAL STUDIES

- Synonyms, p. 41R
- Make a Prediction, pp. 42, 72A, 73
- Personal Response, pp. 44A, 45
- Concept Web, pp. 46A, 47
- K-W-L Chart, pp. 48A, 51, 60A, 65
- Study Questions, pp. 54A, 57
- Paraphrase, p. 62
- Graphic Organizer, pp. 68A, 71
- Use Context Clues, p. 68

MAP AND GLOBE SKILLS

FIND STATES ON A MAP

- INTRODUCE pp. 52A–53A
- APPLY p. 79

CITIZENSHIP SKILLS

MAKE A CHOICE BY VOTING

- INTRODUCE pp. 58A–59A

READING SKILLS

FICTION OR NONFICTION

- INTRODUCE pp. 66–67

STUDY AND RESEARCH SKILLS

- Using Reference Sources, pp. 52, 56
- Using the Internet, p. 63

Theme Time: Rights and Responsibilities

MATH CENTER

Class Vote

Each day have children vote to decide on how to handle various details of the classroom routine. For example, have children vote on which of two books they would like to hear at story time the next day or which of two snacks they would like at snack time. Post the two choices and label them *Choice A* and *Choice B*. Provide ballots with an *A* and a *B* printed on them and have children use a hole punch to put a hole next to the letter of their choice. At the end of the day, have one group of children count and tally the ballots and a second group do a recount to check the results.

SCIENCE CENTER

Neighborhood Nature Project

Provide small pots, soil, and a variety of seeds for plants that grow well in your area. Invite children to plant and tend the seeds so they can later use the plants to beautify the community. Have children place their seedlings in a sunny place and check them daily to make sure they do not dry out. When seedlings are mature, either have children take them home to plant or get permission to allow children to plant them somewhere in the community.

READING/LANGUAGE ARTS CENTER

Good Neighbor Puppet Show

Ask children to imagine that a new family has moved in on their street. Have them think about things the family would need to know, such as where to buy things, where to find community helpers, when the mail comes, and when to put out the trash. Point out that they could also explain to the family what people do to make the community a nice place to live and have fun. Have children use their ideas to plan and present a puppet show about a good neighbor who helps a new family.

BULLETIN BOARD: RESPONSIBILITY

I Do My Part

I sweep.
DeShaun
Lori
Mia
Andy
Tanya

I make my bed.
Tien
Miguel
Mia
Sandra
Will

I set the table.
Tanya
Alexis
Jesse

Ask children to help you create an "I Do My Part" bulletin board showing responsibilities they have at home and at school. As children name ways they help, list the chores on a chart. Ask volunteers to illustrate each chore. Then have children post their name under each job they do.

Multimedia Resources

The Multimedia Resources can be used in a variety of ways. They can supplement core instruction in the classroom or extend and enrich children's learning at home.

Independent Reading

Easy

Hoban, Tana. *I Read Symbols.* William Morrow and Company, 1999. Photographs show important symbols that help people communicate and follow rules without words.

Munro, Roxie. *The Inside-Outside Book of Texas.* SeaStar Books, 2001. Interesting pictures with short captions show the attractions of the state.

Munro, Roxie. *The Inside-Outside Book of Washington, D.C.* SeaStar Books, 2001. Interesting pictures with short captions give a visual tour of the nation's capital.

Saunders-Smith, Gail. *Communities.* Pebble Books, 1998. This nonfiction book describes workers in the community and the services they provide.

Average

Brown, Marc. *Arthur Meets the President.* Little, Brown, 1992. Arthur is a proud American when he wins an essay contest and is rewarded by reading it to the President in Washington, D.C.

Farmer, Patti. *To Tell the Truth.* General Distribution, 1997. Benjamin learns an important lesson about how and when to tell the truth.

Gibbons, Gail. *Soaring with the Wind: The Bald Eagle.* William Morrow, 1998. The author presents a fact-filled introduction to the magnificent bald eagle, the official symbol of the United States. She provides interesting facts and statistics about the bald eagle and tells of efforts to save it from extinction.

Hassett, Ann. *Cat Up a Tree.* Houghton Mifflin, 1998. As one cat after another gets stuck in Nana's tree, she asks community helpers and townspeople for help. Children will see why it is important for real community helpers to cooperate and help.

Lewison, Wendy Cheyette. *A Trip to the Firehouse.* Grosset & Dunlap, 1998. Colorful photos and simple descriptions show a class visit to a local firehouse. The book contains action photos, which capture the daily lives of the firefighters.

Penner, Lucille Recht. *The Statue of Liberty.* Random House, 1995. The construction and symbolism of the skyscraper-sized Statue of Liberty are explored with simple text and illustrations.

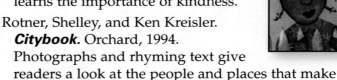

Stier, Catherine. *If I Were President.* Albert Whitman, 1999. This book tells what several children would do if they were the President of the United States.

Treays, Rebecca. *My Street.* EDCP, 1999. This book presents bright illustrations showing a child's view of the workings and architecture of all kinds of streets.

Challenging

Kottke, Jan. *A Day with Police Officers.* Children's Press, 2000. This nonfiction book describes different kinds of jobs officers do.

McKissack, Patricia. *The Honest-to-Goodness Truth.* Atheneum Books, 2000. When Libby finds that telling the truth can go too far, she learns the importance of kindness.

Rotner, Shelley, and Ken Kreisler. *Citybook.* Orchard, 1994. Photographs and rhyming text give readers a look at the people and places that make up a city.

Santella, Andrew. *George Washington.* Compass Point, 2000. The author presents a brief biography of George Washington, a Virginia farm boy who grew up to be President.

Ward, Stasia. *I Live in a City.* PowerKids Press, 2000. An eight-year-old girl tells about her school, the city government, local sights, and neighborhood activities.

Audiocassettes

Building Character.
Twin Sisters Productions. The songs on this cassette teach positive values and making good choices.

Changing Channels. Rounder Records, 1998. Cathy Fink and Marcy Marxer combine positive messages about conflict resolution with lots of fun music.

I Pledge Allegiance. Live Oak Media. This cassette explains the history and meaning of the Pledge of Allegiance.

One Voice for Children. Educational Activities. This upbeat musical collection teaches respect, caring, and multicultural sensitivity.

Computer Software

Conflict Resolution:
Fun to Share. Boulden Publishing. Mac/Windows. Children explore positive ways to resolve conflict.

Kid Pix Activity Kit Volume 2. The Learning Company. Mac/Windows. In addition to the Kid Pix drawing tools and slide show, the module includes Community Workers and My Country activities.

Thinkin' Things: All Around FrippleTown. Edmark. Mac/Windows. Children use creative thinking skills as they design flags, go door-to-door, and solve problems around FrippleTown.

Videos and DVDs

Flag Day/
Citizenship Day. GPN Educational Media. After describing America's flag and the ways people feel about it, the video ends with a Flag Day parade and the National Anthem.

My America: A Pledge Is a Promise. Sunburst. Children in this video discuss pledges that are made by Scouts, doctors, brides and grooms, and presidents. Viewers learn how the Pledge of Allegiance was written.

My America: What Is a Flag? Sunburst, 2000. This video tells the story of the flag and explains the symbolism of the stars, stripes, and colors.

What's Respect? Sunburst. As viewers watch episodes of a young boy's experiences, he narrates and explains how each situation taught him what it means to respect others.

Why We Have Elections. Coronet. After the rule of an unjust king, the people of Snark decide the best way to choose a leader.

ISBNs and other publisher information can be found at
www.harcourtschool.com

The Learning Site: Social Studies Center

The Learning Site at www.harcourtschool.com offers a special Social Studies Center. The center provides a wide variety of activities, Internet links, and online references.

Here are just some of the HARCOURT Internet resources you'll find!

Multimedia Biographies
www.harcourtschool.com

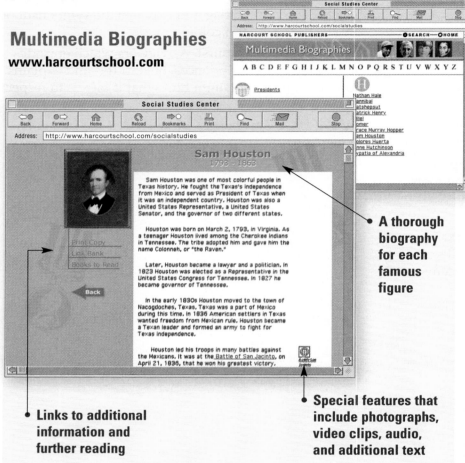

A thorough biography for each famous figure

Links to additional information and further reading

Special features that include photographs, video clips, audio, and additional text

INTERNET RESOURCES

Find all this at
The Learning Site at
www.harcourtschool.com

- Activities and Games
- Content Updates
- Current Events
- Free and Inexpensive Materials
- Multimedia Biographies
- Online Atlas
- Primary Sources
- Video Updates
- Virtual Tours
- Your State

and more!

Free and Inexpensive Materials
- Addresses to write for free and inexpensive products
- Links to unit-related materials
- Internet maps
- Internet references

www.harcourtschool.com

Primary Sources
- Artwork
- Clothing
- Diaries
- Government Documents
- Historical Documents
- Maps
- Tools

and more!

www.harcourtschool.com

Voting Machine

Virtual Tours
- Capitols and Government Buildings
- Cities
- Countries
- Historical Sites
- Museums
- Parks and Scenic Areas

and more!

www.harcourtschool.com

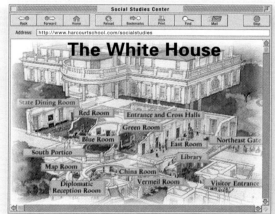

The White House

Integrate Learning Across the Curriculum

Use these topics to help you integrate social studies into your daily planning. See the page numbers indicated for more information about each topic.

Art

Good Citizen Mural, p. 41
Draw a Symbol, p. 60

Science

Neighborhood Nature Project,
p. 41I

Reading/Literature

***Stars and Stripes: The Story of
the American Flag,*** p. 41R
Philadelphia, Home of Liberty,
p. 45
Visit the Capitol, p. 45
At the Eiffel Tower, p. 45
Paul Bunyan, p. 66
***The Inside-Outside Book of
Washington, D.C.,*** p. 80
If I Were President, p. 80
The Flag We Love, p. 80

Language Arts

Good Neighbor Puppet Show,
p. 41I
Descriptive Words, p. 48
Write a Description, p. 75

Social Studies

Music

"Hail to the Chief," p. 43
"You're a Grand Old Flag,"
p. 44
"Yankee Doodle," p. 44
"This Land Is Your Land," p. 44
Sousa marches, p. 44
Conductors, p. 49
"The Star-Spangled Banner,"
p. 62
Learn a Song, p. 63

Computer/Technology

Go Online, pp. 45, 50, 55,
61, 75
GeoSkills CD-ROM, p. 53
Take a Field Trip Video, p. 75

Mathematics

Class Vote, p. 41I
Charts and Graphs, p. 58
Measurement, p. 61

Reach All Learners

Use these activities to help individualize your instruction. Each activity has been developed to address a different level or type of learner.

English as a Second Language

Materials
- drawing paper
- crayons or markers

LEARN A CHEER Have children learn a cheer about things good citizens do.

- Explain the meaning of each of the following: *vote, obey the law, be fair.*
- Have children draw pictures to illustrate each phrase.
- When children are familiar with the phrases, have them make up gestures to go with the cheer.
- Have small groups perform verses of the cheer, taking turns, using the gestures and holding up the pictures at the appropriate times.

Good Citizens' Cheer

Red, white, and blue!
What do citizens do?
Good citizens vote,
And obey the law.
Red, white, and blue!

Red, white, and blue!
What do citizens do?
They're fair to others,
And do their part.
Red, white, and blue!

Red, white, and blue!
We're good citizens, too.
We follow the rules
And do what's fair.
Red, white, and blue!

Advanced Learners

Materials
- note cards
- markers
- art materials

TEACH A CLASS Have children present a lesson to tell other children about leaders and government in the United States.

- Have children find out the names of their mayor, governor, and President, and where these leaders work.
- Have children make flash cards and visuals of the information they find that they will use in explaining their lesson.
- Invite children from another classroom to listen to the presentation.

Below-Level Learners

Materials
- pictures of U.S. symbols
- clay and other art materials

CREATE A PATRIOTIC MUSEUM Use clay and other art materials to re-create U.S. symbols for a class patriotic museum.

- Display pictures of U.S. symbols and discuss the shape of each.
- Have children choose one symbol to create from clay or other art materials.
- Display the finished symbols in a center designated as a class museum.
- Have children explain to those who visit the museum how they made their creation and why it is important to the United States.

Assessment Options

The assessment program gives all learners many opportunities to show what they know and can do. It also provides ongoing information about each child's understanding of social studies.

Formal Assessment

- **LESSON REVIEWS:** pp. 47, 51, 57, 65, 71, 73
- **UNIT REVIEWS AND TEST PREPARATION,** pp. 76–79
- **UNIT ASSESSMENT**
  Standard Test,
    Assessment Program, pp. 5–7
  Individual Performance Task,
    Assessment Program, p. 8

Student Self-Evaluation

- **GEOGRAPHY THEME QUESTIONS**
  within lessons of Pupil Book
- **INDIVIDUAL END-OF-PROJECT CHECKLIST**
  Assessment Program, p. viii
- **GROUP END-OF-PROJECT CHECKLIST**
  Assessment Program, p. ix
- **INDIVIDUAL END-OF-UNIT CHECKLIST**
  Assessment Program, p. x

Informal Assessment

- **THINK ABOUT IT,** p. 45
- **SOCIAL STUDIES SKILLS CHECKLIST**
  Assessment Program, p. vi–vii

- **SKILLS**
  Practice the Skill, pp. 53, 59, 67
  Apply What You Learned, pp. 53, 59, 67

Performance Assessment

- **PERFORMANCE ACTIVITY IN LESSON REVIEWS**
- **UNIT ACTIVITIES,** p. 80
- **COMPLETE THE UNIT PROJECT,** p. 80
- **INDIVIDUAL PERFORMANCE TASK ASSESSMENT PROGRAM,** p. 8

Portfolio Assessment

<u>STUDENT SELECTED ITEMS MAY INCLUDE:</u>
- **THINK AND WRITE,** p. 76
- **UNIT ACTIVITIES,** p. 80
- **COMPLETE THE UNIT PROJECT,** p. 80

<u>TEACHER SELECTED ITEMS MAY INCLUDE:</u>
- **UNIT ASSESSMENT**
  Assessment Program, pp. 5–8
- **PORTFOLIO SUMMARY**
  Assessment Program, p. xv
- **GROUP END-OF-PROJECT CHECKLIST**
  Assessment Program, p. ix
- **INDIVIDUAL END-OF-UNIT CHECKLIST**
  Assessment Program, p. x

Unit 2 Test

STANDARD TEST

· Unit ·

Name _____ Date _____

2 Test

Vocabulary (5 points each)

Circle the picture that goes with each word.

1 state

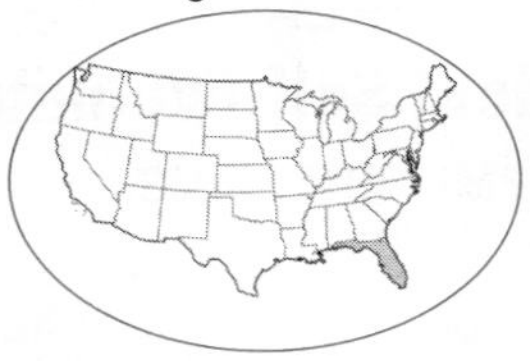

2 law

Puppies for Sale

SPEED LIMIT 50

3 citizen

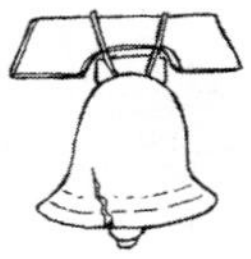

4 country

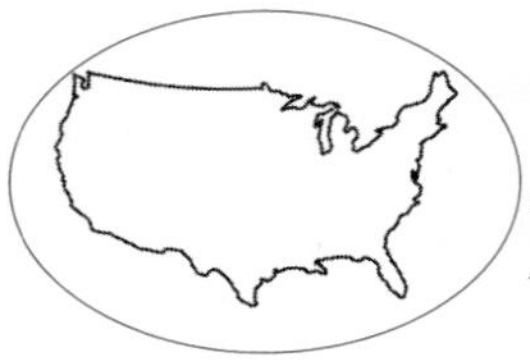

Unit 2 Test

Assessment Program ■ 5

(continued)

STANDARD TEST

Name _____ Date _____

Main Ideas (5 points each)

5 We have laws to—
○ A help us find things. ○ C help children read.
● B keep people safe.   ○ D make us healthy.

6 "The Star-Spangled Banner" is—
○ F a motto.   ○ H a nickname.
● G a national anthem. ○ J a pledge.

7 Draw a line under two pictures that show good citizens.

Draw a line to the word that ends each sentence.

8 A governor is the leader of a—   country.

9 The President is the leader of the—   state.

10 A mayor is the leader of a—   city.

11 Circle two pictures that are symbols for our country.

12 Circle the sentence that is true.

A state is part of a neighborhood.

A state is part of a country.

6 ■ Assessment Program

Unit 2 Test

(continued)

NOTES

Name _____ Date _____

Skills (10 points each)

Using the map, follow the directions below.

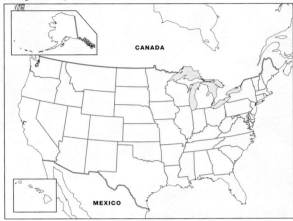

⓭ Color your state green. Students should color their state green.

⓮ Trace the border between the United States and Canada in brown. Students should trace the United States/Canada border in brown.

⓯ Trace the border between the United States and Mexico in red. Students should trace the United States/Mexico border in red.

(continued)

Unit 2 Test   Assessment Program ▪ 7

Name _____ Date _____

Performance Task

George Washington

Thomas Jefferson

Betsy Ross

Harriet Tubman

Think about these famous Americans. Write a sentence that tells how people can be good citizens.

Answers will vary but should involve
patriotism, responsibility, kindness, or fairness.

_____

_____

_____

8 ▪ Assessment Program   Unit 2 Test

RUBRICS FOR SCORING

SCORING RUBRIC The rubric below lists the criteria for evaluating the tasks above. It also describes different levels of success in meeting those criteria.

INDIVIDUAL PERFORMANCE TASK

Score **4**	Score **3**	Score **2**	Score **1**
• Rich description is provided. • Sentences reflect strong understanding of characteristics of good citizens. • Historical figures are strongly linked to characteristics of good citizens. • Sentences are well developed.	• Some description is provided. • Sentences reflect an understanding of characteristics of good citizens. • Historical figures are linked to characteristics of good citizens. • Sentences are fairly well developed.	• Little description is provided. • Sentences reflect little understanding of characteristics of good citizens. • Historical figures are somewhat linked to characteristics of good citizens. • Sentences are minimally developed.	• No description is provided. • Sentences reflect no understanding of characteristics of good citizens. • Historical figures are not linked to characteristics of good citizens. • Sentences are not developed.

Introduce the Unit

- Use a visual to predict content.
- Interpret a quotation.
- Use a K-W-L chart to prepare for the unit.

Access Prior Knowledge

Write U.S.A. on the board and circle it. Elicit from children that U.S.A. stands for United States of America, the name of our country. Ask children to name words that make them think of our country. In smaller circles around the center circle, write the words children say, and connect the smaller circles to the center circle to make a word web.

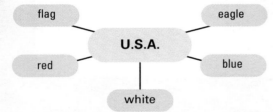

```
  flag              eagle
        U.S.A.
  red               blue

         white
```

Visual Learning

Have children look at the picture on pages 41R and 41.

Q What do you notice about the decorations on the houses?

A The houses are decorated with American flags.

Q Where do you often see American flags?

A Children may say that they have seen flags on houses in their own neighborhood, in front of the school, and in front of other public buildings.

Q Why do you think people fly American flags?

A Children may say that Americans fly flags to celebrate special holidays such as Independence Day, to show that they are proud to be Americans, or to show that they support our government.

BACKGROUND

Writing the Pledge Francis Bellamy was the circulation manager of a children's magazine called *The Youth's Companion.* In 1892, the magazine published the Pledge of Allegiance so children could recite it in school to celebrate Columbus Day. The Pledge, with a few small changes, was recited over the years, but it was not officially recognized until Congress adopted it in 1942.

INTEGRATE READING

Stars and Stripes Read aloud to the class *Stars and Stripes: The Story of the American Flag* by Sarah L. Thomson, a book that traces the history of the American flag. Point out that our flag has not always looked as it does today, but it has always stood for loyalty and pride for the United States. Then invite children to contribute to a class story that tells about the American flag.

Good Citizens

Unit 2

> **"I pledge allegiance to my flag."**
>
> —Francis Bellamy, in the magazine *Youth's Companion*, September 8, 1892

(Focus Skill) Prior Knowledge

Before you read this unit, do the following.

- List what you already know about how to be a good citizen.
- List what you want to know about how to be a good citizen.

As you read this unit, do the following.

- List what you learned about how to be a good citizen.

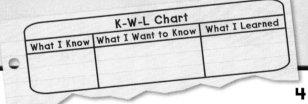

41

INTEGRATE ART

Good Citizen Mural
Mount a large sheet of paper on the wall and invite children to make a good citizen mural. Have children draw pictures of people being good citizens or of American symbols. When the mural is complete, call on volunteers to tell about their drawings. Encourage children to add to the mural as they learn new ways to be good citizens.

AUDIOTEXT

Use the Unit 2 AUDIOTEXT for a reading of the Unit narrative.

Analyze Primary Sources

Flag Hood Ornament Explain to children that the artifact is called a hood ornament. Long ago, most cars had some kind of decoration at the end of their hood and some cars still do today.

Quotation Read aloud the quotation. Then invite children to say it with you. Explain that the words are the first part of the Pledge of Allegiance as it was originally written. Today we say the Pledge a little differently. The words *my flag* have been replaced with *the flag of the United States of America*.

Q What does the quotation mean?

A "I promise to be loyal to the flag, which stands for my country."

Q When do Americans say the Pledge?

A at the beginning of the school day or special ceremonies

(Focus Skill) Prior Knowledge

Explain to children that in this unit they will be reading about what it means to be a good citizen. Ask children to think about what they already know about citizenship. Explain that a K-W-L chart can help readers organize their thoughts. The letter *K* stands for (what you already) *Know*, the letter *W* stands for (what you) *Want to Know*, and the *L* stands for (what you) *Learned*. Together with children, fill in the chart.

- A blank graphic organizer appears on page 22 of the Activity Book
- A complete graphic organizer can be found on page 76 of this Teacher's Edition.

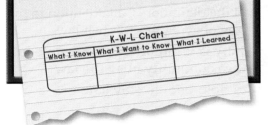

Preview the Vocabulary

PAGES 42–43

Access Prior Knowledge

Have children tell the names of their community, state, and country. Tell children that they are citizens. Explain that most citizens take pride in the place where they live. They show their pride in words and actions. Discuss ways that good citizens can show their pride in their home, such as by celebrating holidays like Independence Day, saluting the flag, saying the Pledge of Allegiance, voting, and following laws and rules that help the members of the community live together safely and happily. Invite children to tell things they like about their community, state, and country.

Make Connections

Link Pictures and Words Point to *citizen*, read the word aloud, and have children repeat it. Explain that *citizens* are people who live in and belong in a certain place. Ask what the citizens in the picture are doing together. Tell children that all the other words name things that are important to citizens.

Visual Learning

Picture Point to *law* and read the word aloud. After children repeat the word, read the definition. Call attention to the citizen obeying the seat belt law.

Q Why is it important that people in the community obey the law?

A to help people stay safe

Preview the Vocabulary

law A rule that people in a community must follow. (page 46)

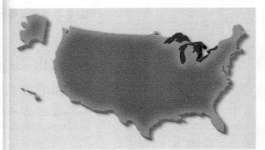

country An area of land with its own people and laws. (page 52)

state A part of a country. (page 52)

42

READING SOCIAL STUDIES

Make a Prediction Encourage children to look again at the words and the pictures on pages 42–43. Then ask children to predict what they will learn about in the unit. Record their ideas on chart paper and save their work so children can check later to see if they were right.

WORD WORK

Preview Vocabulary Write each of the vocabulary words on a separate index card. Flash the cards, and have children read the words. Call on volunteers to define the terms in their own words. Have other children use the vocabulary words in sentences. Then write on the board the categories *People, Places,* and *Things*. Have children place each card below the correct heading to sort the words.

Be proud of your country!

President The leader of the United States government. (page 54)

flag A piece of cloth with a special design that stands for a country or group. (page 62)

citizen A person who lives in and belongs to a community. (page 68)

43

Visual Learning

Map Tell children that they are not only citizens of their community, they are also citizens of their state and country. Ask what country the map shows. (the United States) Point to Georgia and explain that a state is a smaller part of a country. Ask what country Georgia is part of. (the United States) Then help children locate their own home state on a map.

INTEGRATE MUSIC

Recognize Music Tell children that special music is played when the President of the United States appears at an official function. Write *"Hail to the Chief"* on the board. Underline *Chief* and compare a chief, or boss, to a President. Hum the first few lines of "Hail to the Chief." Write the vocabulary words on the board. Point to each word. Tell children to hum "Hail to the Chief" when you point to *President*.

BACKGROUND

Our Flag Display an American flag. Help children count the stars. Explain that the U.S. flag has 50 stars because the country has 50 states. Have children look at a map to see all the states. Then have children count the stripes. Explain that the United States began with 13 colonies. Tell children that the number of stripes is 13 to remind us of the first 13 colonies that became states.

SCHOOL TO HOME

Use the Unit 2 SCHOOL TO HOME NEWSLETTER on pages S3–S4 to introduce the unit to family members and suggest activities they can do at home.

Word Work

The following activities may be used to preteach vocabulary. You may also wish to duplicate and distribute the word cards found in the back of this book on pages V9–V18. Children can use them as flash cards to practice saying and defining each word. Remind children to use the glossary at the back of their books to help them define these words.

WORD RIDDLES

Display the vocabulary words on a chart or bulletin board. Model clues such as *This word names something you must or must not do.* Do not enter *and* no littering *are examples of this word.* Have children guess the word. (law) Then invite volunteers to give clues to describe other words for the class to guess.

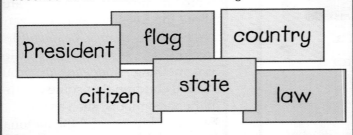

VOTING DAY ROLE-PLAY

Assign children the parts of citizens and candidates for President. Begin the role-play by having children act out as you narrate the action on Election Day. Describe how the citizens line up and cast their ballots one by one. Demonstrate how the votes are counted and the new President is announced. Then invite volunteers to help narrate Election Day role-plays for electing the governor.

PICK-A-WORD RELAY

Have two relay teams at a time line up to play while the rest of the class watches. In front of each team, display the same four vocabulary word cards on the chalk rail. Give a cloze sentence as a clue for one of the words, and have the first member of each team go to the chalk rail and pick the correct word. Replace those two cards with new ones and repeat until all the team members have had a turn. The team with the most correct choices wins.

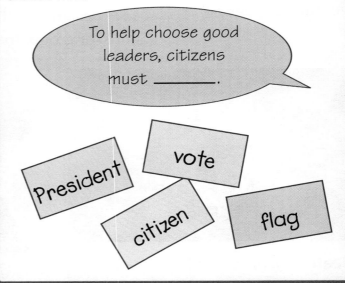

PATRIOTIC PARADE

JOURNAL Ask children to imagine and draw a patriotic parade and celebration in their community. Then ask them to write a description of the celebration. Display the vocabulary words and challenge children to use as many of them as they can in describing the people, sights, and events of the special day.

America

OBJECTIVES

- Obtain information about a topic using a variety of visual sources such as pictures and literature.
- Communicate information through words and visuals.
- Learn a patriotic song.

RESOURCES

Pupil Book/Unit Big Book, pp. 44–45

Activity Pattern P3

⊙ **Reading and Vocabulary Transparency 2–1**

▢ **Internet Resources**

Audiotext, Unit 2

Summary

The traditional song "America" has been sung since 1832 by citizens who want to express their appreciation of the United States.

1 Motivate

Set the Purpose

Read aloud the title of the song, and invite children to look at the illustration. Remind children that illustrations often give clues to what something is about. Encourage children to think about the song's title and to look at the illustration. Remind children that setting a purpose before they read can help them focus on what they want to learn from the song. To help children set a purpose for reading, model the process:

> **I can tell from the title that this song is about the United States. I want to read to find out what the songwriter has to say about our country.**

Access Prior Knowledge

READING SOCIAL STUDIES

Graphic Organizer Begin a Personal Response chart about the song "America." Complete the chart during Close.

Things the Songwriter Loves About America	Things Students Love About America
Its name	
Its woods and hills	

● USE READING AND VOCABULARY TRANSPARENCY 2–1

2–1 TRANSPARENCY

2 Teach

Read and Respond

Understand the Song Read the song aloud and then invite children to sing it with you. Ask children to paraphrase the author's message.

Visual Learning

Illustration Have children look at the illustration on pages 44 and 45. If children recognize the Statue of Liberty, ask them to tell what they know about it. Add background as necessary (see page 60 of this Teacher's Edition) by explaining that the statue is a symbol of liberty, or freedom. Americans are proud that the citizens of their country are free.

Read and Respond

Culture and Society Point out the United States on a world map. Have children note the large size of the country compared to smaller countries in Europe. Ask children to read the title of the song and then share things they know about America, such as places they have visited, history, or things they like about their country.

Tell children that even though the United States is large and diverse, its people share many traditions. One tradition that children can share with Americans from different parts of the country and even from past generations is singing patriotic songs like "America."

Q Why do people enjoy writing and singing songs about their country?

A Writing and singing songs about America is one way Americans show their love for their country, pass on their country's history, tell why they love their country, and join in on a cultural tradition.

START with a SONG

America

by Samuel F. Smith
illustrated by Erika LeBarre

My country, 'tis of thee,
Sweet land of liberty,
Of thee I sing.
Land where my fathers died,
Land of the Pilgrims' pride,
From every mountainside
Let freedom ring!

My native country, thee,
Land of the noble free,
Thy name I love.
I love thy rocks and rills,
Thy woods and templed hills;
My heart with rapture thrills
Like that above.

44

INTEGRATE MUSIC

Patriotic Songs Introduce other patriotic songs, such as "You're a Grand Old Flag," "Yankee Doodle," "This Land Is Your Land," and the marches of John Philip Sousa. Ask children to name holidays when they might celebrate our country by singing or listening to these types of songs. Then invite children to line up and march around the room as they sing one of these songs.

BACKGROUND

About "America" The music for the song "America" is really the tune of the British anthem, "God Save the Queen." It was probably composed in the late 1500s. The melody became so popular in Europe that many different lyrics were written for it. Around 1832, Samuel F. Smith, a U.S. citizen, wrote the words of "America" to be sung to the British tune.

Think About It

1 What does the author tell us about America?

2 How does the song make you feel?

Read a Book

Start the Unit Project

Proud Citizens Mobile Your class will make a mobile that shows people being proud citizens. As you read this unit, think about how we show pride in our community, state, and country.

Use Technology

Visit The Learning Site at **www.harcourtschool.com** for additional activities, primary sources, and other resources to use in this unit.

45

Think About It

Answers

1 The author loves that America is a place for freedom and loves the landscape of America.

2 Children may say that the song reminds them of things they love about America or that it gives them a feeling of pride in our country.

GO ONLINE **INTERNET RESOURCES**

THE LEARNING SITE Go to **www.harcourtschool.com** to view Internet resources for this unit.

TIME FOR KIDS Go to **www.harcourtschool.com** for the latest news in a student-friendly format.

3 Close

Summarize the Reading

- Writing and singing patriotic songs is one way for citizens to show that they love their country.

- Some reasons to love America include liberty and freedom and the country's natural beauty.

READING SOCIAL STUDIES

Graphic Organizer Revisit the Personal Response chart begun in Motivate. Invite children to share new ideas they learned. Add these ideas to the chart.

Things the Songwriter Loves About America	Things Students Love About America
Its name	The mountains and lakes
Its woods and hills	The colors of the flag

● USE READING AND VOCABULARY TRANSPARENCY 2–1 **2–1** TRANSPARENCY

Read a Book Children may enjoy reading these leveled independent Readers. Additional books are listed on pages 41J–41K of this *Teacher's Edition.*

Easy *Philadelphia, Home of Liberty* by Lisa Trumbauer. History comes alive in historic Philadelphia.

Average *Visit the Capitol* by Lisa Trumbauer. Tour the United States Capitol and learn what happens there.

Challenging *At the Eiffel Tower* by Lisa Trumbauer. Learn about the structure of the Eiffel Tower and why it was built.

Start the Unit Project

Hint Before children begin their Unit Project, remind them that they will be making a mobile to show people being good citizens. Have them begin a file of ideas and pictures they can use in their mobiles.

Extension Activities For Home and School

In Love with America

Materials: Activity Pattern P3 (U.S. map), drawing paper, glue, markers or crayons

Provide children with copies of the outline map that is on Activity Pattern P3. Have them glue the map in the center of a sheet of drawing paper and write the title *I Love America* at the top of the paper. Tell children to decorate the border around the outline map with drawings and words that show things they love about America.
(VISUAL/TACTILE)

See the U.S.A.

Materials: U.S. map, self-sticking stars or tacks

Have children interview family members about places in the United States that they particularly enjoy. The places may be close to home, or they may be places that family members have visited on a vacation or have lived in at an earlier time. If possible, have family members send in photographs or souvenirs of the places they describe. Call on volunteers to tell the class what they learned from the interview, find the place on the map, and show the photograph or souvenir.
(AUDITORY/VISUAL)

Class Songbook

Materials: paper, pencils, audiocassette recorder, blank audiocassette tape, hole punch, yarn

Suggest that children perform "America" for family members, then ask family members to teach them a patriotic song they learned as a child. Explain that the songs can be about a community, state, or any country. Have children ask their family members to write down the words so children can bring them to class. Call on volunteers to teach the songs they learned. Group together children who learned the same song, and make an audio recording of children performing the songs. For each song, have children work together to copy the words onto lined paper and to illustrate the song. Bind children's pages together in the order the songs appear on the audiocassette. Title the class book *Our Class Book of Songs Citizens Sing*. Place the audiocassette and songbook in a listening center. Suggest that children listen and follow along with the words in the songbook in their free time.
(AUDITORY/VISUAL)

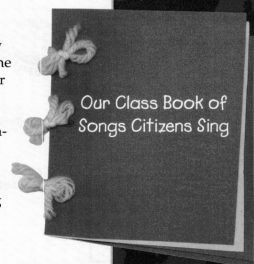

Rules and Laws

OBJECTIVES

- Explain the need for rules and laws in the community.
- Give examples of rules or laws that establish order, provide security, and manage conflict.
- Recognize that breaking rules or laws has consequences.

 Prior Knowledge pp. 41, 76

RESOURCES

Pupil Book/Unit Big Book, pp. 46–47

Word Cards V9–V10

Activity Book, p. 13

⊘**Reading and Vocabulary Transparency 2–2**

⊟**Internet Resources**

READING SOCIAL STUDIES

Graphic Organizer Begin a concept web about the consequences of not following laws. Complete the web during Close.

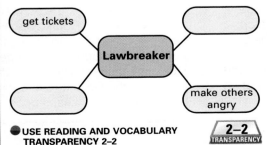

●**USE READING AND VOCABULARY TRANSPARENCY 2–2**

2–2 TRANSPARENCY

Vocabulary

law p. 46

community p. 46

 When Minutes Count

Have pairs of children quiz each other on the meanings of the signs on page 46. Use the signs and the photo on page 47 to discuss the Big Idea in the lesson.

Quick Summary

In this lesson, children learn about rules, laws, and the reasons citizens need laws. They discuss how laws are enforced and the consequences for breaking laws.

1 Motivate

Set the Purpose

Big Idea Before starting the lesson, read the Big Idea statement aloud. As children read, have them look for rules and laws in the text that are the same as rules and laws in their community.

Access Prior Knowledge

Remind children of some of the rules they have at home, in the classroom, and in the community. Ask them to name some consequences of breaking classroom rules. Encourage children to name any community laws they know.

2 Teach

Read and Respond

Civics and Government Explain to children that laws and rules are alike because they both tell things that people should do, but they are also different. Remind children that any group of people, such as a school, a club, or even a group of children playing a game together, can make rules. However, explain that laws are made by people in our government, such as the city council or Congress. Point out that laws are always written down and can be enforced by a police officer. Both laws and rules help people in a community get along with each other and stay safe.

Q **What are some examples of rules you obey in school that establish order, provide security, manage conflict, or show respect toward others?**

A Some examples of school rules are that children must stay in their seats, walk quietly in the halls, raise their hand to talk, play fairly, and come in from recess when the bell rings.

Q **What are some examples of laws a police officer might enforce that establish order, provide security, or manage conflict?**

A Examples of laws include obeying speed limits, wearing a seat belt when riding in a car, crossing streets at the proper place and time, and not littering.

Visual Learning

Artifacts Explain that some signs help us understand and remember to follow laws. To make sure that everyone can understand the laws, some signs are written in symbols instead of words. Call on volunteers to tell what each sign means and where they would see the sign.

Lesson

1

Rules and Laws

Big Idea
Communities have rules called laws.

Vocabulary
law
community

A community has rules called laws. A **law** is a rule that people in a community must follow. A **community** is a group of people who live or work together. It is also the place where those people live.

46

MENTAL MAPPING

Ask children to visualize an intersection they pass regularly and name things they see that tell about laws. Have children draw a map of the intersection. Tell them to include signs and symbols, such as stop signs and traffic lights, that help people remember and obey laws. Have children share their maps and tell why we should obey laws at an intersection.

EXTEND AND ENRICH

Role-Play Have partners work together to name a law and think about the reason for it. Suggest they predict what will happen if the law is broken. Tell the partners to prepare Do and Don't skits. Have them present the Don't skit first to show what happens when people disobey the law. Then have them present the Do skit to show how obeying the law keeps people safe.

Police officers work to keep people safe. They make sure that people obey the laws.

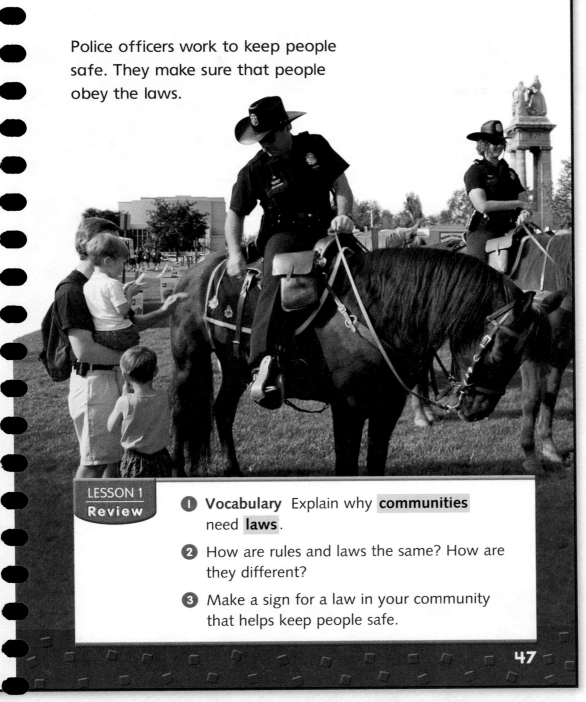

LESSON 1 Review

❶ **Vocabulary** Explain why **communities** need **laws**.

❷ How are rules and laws the same? How are they different?

❸ Make a sign for a law in your community that helps keep people safe.

47

3 Close

Summarize Key Content

- Laws are rules for people in a community to live by.
- Police officers help their community by making sure people obey laws.
- Signs remind people of the laws.

READING SOCIAL STUDIES

Graphic Organizer Revisit the web begun in Motivate. Invite children to share new ideas they learned. Add these ideas to the web.

● USE READING AND VOCABULARY TRANSPARENCY 2–2

2–2 TRANSPARENCY

Assess

Lesson 1 Review—Answers

❶ Communities have laws to help people live together.

❷ Both rules and laws help people live together peacefully and stay safe. Laws are made by the government and enforced by the police. Anyone can make rules.

❸ 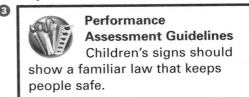 **Performance Assessment Guidelines** Children's signs should show a familiar law that keeps people safe.

ACTIVITY BOOK

Name _____ Date _____

Who Is Obeying the Law?

Color each person who is obeying the law. Draw an X on each person who is not.

Use with Unit 2, Lesson 1.

Activity Book • 13

PAGE 13

Extension Activities For Home and School

Meet a Police Officer

Materials: reference books, index cards, pencils

Many community police forces provide speakers for organizations and schools. If possible, invite a police officer to speak to the children about laws in their community and how the laws make the community a good place to live. Have children prepare for the visit by reading books about police officers at work. You may also wish to guide children in preparing a list of interview questions to ask the speaker. Have each child select a question, and help him or her write it on an index card to better remember it. After the speaker's visit, help children summarize what they learned. Then follow up by having children dictate a class thank-you letter. Encourage them to mention what they learned about why we need laws.
(AUDITORY/VISUAL/TACTILE)

Rules and Laws Charades

Materials: paper strips, pencils, bowl

Have each child write a rule or a law on a strip of paper and fold it in half. Place all the strips in a bowl. Invite children to take turns selecting a strip and then acting out that rule or law, while the others guess what it is. Suggest that children also play this game at home with family members.
(AUDITORY/KINESTHETIC)

Law Hunt

Materials: notebooks, pencils

Suggest that children tell their families what they have learned about rules and laws. Then encourage children to go for a walk or a drive around their neighborhood or town with a family member. Tell children to have their family member help them look for signs that tell about rules and laws. Have children draw pictures to show the signs they saw. Ask children to notice whether they observed any citizens obeying rules and laws or breaking them. Encourage them to discuss what might happen to the people who break the rules or laws.
(VISUAL/TACTILE/KINESTHETIC)

Who Are Our Leaders?

OBJECTIVES

- Identify leaders of different groups.
- Identify the responsibilities of authority figures in the home, school, and community.
- Identify leaders in the community and state.
- Describe the roles of public officials, including the mayor and governor.

 Prior Knowledge pp. 41, 48, 51, 76

RESOURCES

Pupil Book/Unit Big Book, pp. 48–51

Word Cards V9–V12

Activity Book, p. 14

● **Reading and Vocabulary Transparency 2–3**

▭ **Internet Resources**

READING SOCIAL STUDIES

Graphic Organizer Begin a K-W-L chart about leaders. Complete the chart during Close.

What We Know	What We Want to Know	What We Learned
Leaders tell us what to do. Leaders make rules. Leaders answer our questions.	Who are our community leaders? What are their jobs?	

● USE READING AND VOCABULARY TRANSPARENCY 2–3

2–3 TRANSPARENCY

Vocabulary

leader p. 48   **mayor** p. 50   **city** p. 50

governor p. 51   **government** p. 51

 When Minutes Count

Invite pairs of children to examine the pictures in the lesson. Then have them come up with one question they think will be answered by reading the lesson. Encourage children to read the lesson to find the answer to their question.

Quick Summary

All groups have leaders whose job is to be in charge of the group. Government leaders work with other community leaders to help the citizens of that community.

 1 Motivate

Set the Purpose

Big Idea Before starting the lesson, read the Big Idea statement aloud. Remind children that community rules and laws make a community run smoothly. Explain that communities need to have leaders who make the laws and who make sure the laws are followed. Tell children to read to find out who the leaders are in a community and why having good leaders is important.

Access Prior Knowledge

Ask children to name the leaders of their school (principal), classroom (teacher), and home (parent or guardian). Encourage children to discuss what things would be like if these leaders were not there. Ask children why it is important that these leaders enforce the rules.

2 Teach

Visual Learning

Pictures Have children look at the pictures on pages 48–49 and describe the group in each scene. Lead children to identify the service club, sports team, and church group.

Read and Respond

Link Culture and Society with Civics and Government Read aloud the text with children. Point out the definition of the word *leader*. Ask children who are the leaders in their lives. (parents, grandparents, teachers, coaches, religious leaders) Point out to children that leaders in community groups are often chosen by members of the group they will lead. Have children identify leaders in their community.

Q Who are some leaders of clubs and organizations?

A Children should mention club officers.

Q Who are the leaders of sports groups?

A Children should include coaches and team captains.

Q Who are some leaders in religious organizations?

A Children may mention pastors, rabbis, priests, nuns, choir directors, or youth group leaders.

Who Are Our Leaders?

Big Idea
Leaders help people follow rules and laws.

Vocabulary
leader
mayor
city
governor
government

You belong to many groups. You are a member of a family, a class, and a school. Most groups have leaders. A **leader** is in charge of helping a group of people follow rules.

48

★ Focus Skill — READING SKILL

Prior Knowledge Ask children to recall great leaders they have heard about. If your classroom has pictures of famous historical figures, such as George Washington, Abraham Lincoln, Rosa Parks, or Benjamin Franklin, use the pictures as a starting point. Ask children to tell why they think great leaders are remembered.

REACH ALL LEARNERS

English as a Second Language Write *Follow the Leader* on the board. Point to *Leader* and have each child read the word. Remind children that a leader shows group members what to do. Write *Leader* on an index card, and tape the card onto your shirt. Show how to play *Follow the Leader* as you lead the class around the room. Have children take turns wearing the *Leader* card and leading the game.

INTEGRATE LANGUAGE ARTS

Descriptive Words Draw an outline of a person's head on chart paper. Above the outline write the title *A Good Leader Is. . . .* Have children suggest descriptive words that tell about a good leader, such as *smart, helpful,* and *fair.* Inside the outline, write the words that children dictate. Reread the words and discuss why each characteristic is important.

Read and Respond

Link Culture and Society with Civics and Government Have children identify the responsibilities of various authority figures in the community.

Q **What are some of the responsibilities of leaders of clubs and organizations?**

A Possible responses: They have meetings to talk about how to get things done.

Q **What are some of the responsibilities of leaders of sports groups?**

A Possible responses: They help players get along and play fairly.

Q **What are some of the responsibilities of leaders in religious organizations?**

A Possible responses: They organize people to work with and help others.

49

WORD WORK

Suffix Write *leader* on the board and circle the suffix. Tell children that the suffix means "someone who does something." Tell students that a *leader* is "someone who leads." List other words, such as *player, teacher,* and *speaker.* Call on volunteers to circle the suffixes and define the words.

INTEGRATE MUSIC

Conductors Choose a song children know well. Tell children to sing the song, but do not start the song for them. If children had difficulty singing without a leader, discuss why a musical group needs a leader. If children solved the problem on their own by following the lead of a strong singer, discuss what happened. Then take the role of conductor and have the group sing the song again.

MAKE IT RELEVANT

In Your Community Help children list groups they belong to, including family, class, school, clubs, sports teams, city, state, and the United States. Have children copy the list and write the title and name of the leader for each group. Help children as necessary with names and spellings.

Read and Respond

Civics and Government Ask children if they know what a mayor or a governor is. (the mayor is the leader of a city or town; the governor is the leader of a state) Ask children if they can identify who their mayor or governor is.

 Children can research their state-elected officials. Have them visit The Learning Site at **www.harcourtschool.com**

Discuss ways the local government works for its citizens. Explain that besides making sure people obey laws, the government also takes care of the town by keeping streets and parks clean, building roads, picking up trash, warning people about dangerous weather situations, planning where things should go in a town, and running clinics, schools, and libraries. Explain that the government pays for some of these services through taxation and some by charging user fees.

Q How would you describe the roles of public officials, including the mayor and governor?

A They are in charge of leading the community and making certain that there are workers to keep the community clean, safe, and educated.

Write *government workers* on the board at the center of a word web. Lead children in brainstorming about government workers, and tell what each worker does to help the community.

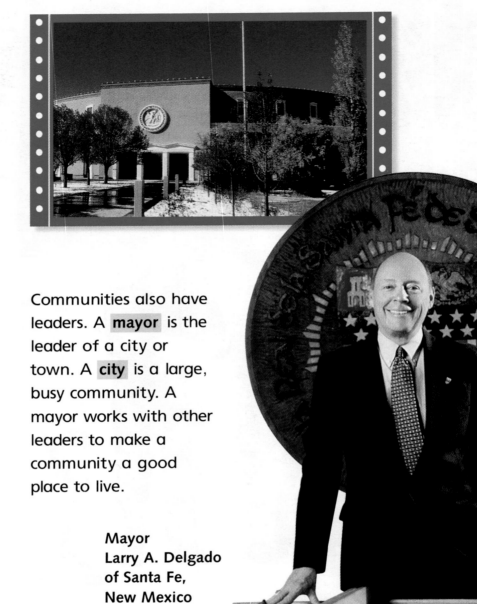

Communities also have leaders. A **mayor** is the leader of a city or town. A **city** is a large, busy community. A mayor works with other leaders to make a community a good place to live.

**Mayor
Larry A. Delgado
of Santa Fe,
New Mexico**

50

DEMOCRATIC VALUES
Popular Sovereignty

Call on a volunteer to read Earnest Eagle's words. Remind children that the leader of a group is often chosen by group members. Point out that many state and national leaders are chosen by members of the community, too. Leaders, such as mayors and governors, are chosen to represent the interests of the community members who chose them. Working with our leaders lets them know what is important to us.

REACH ALL LEARNERS

Advanced Learners Give a group of children a local phone book and point out the government pages. Explain that children are not expected to read and understand all the listings, but they should be able to find some familiar words. Have children list some services they find, such as animal control and the fire department. Discuss ways citizens might use the phone to get help from the government.

EXTEND AND ENRICH

Research and Report Explain to children that a mayor is the leader in local government, a governor is the leader in state government, and the President presides over the federal government. Explain that these three governments must work together for all citizens. Divide the class in thirds and have each research one of these three governments. Each group should prepare an outline showing its government's organization, responsibilities, and functions.

A **governor** is also a leader. The governor works for many communities.

Mayors and governors are part of the government. The **government** is a group of people who make laws. Government workers also do other jobs in a community, such as repairing roads, keeping parks in good condition, and helping when there is a fire.

Work with your leaders.

LESSON 2 Review

Focus Skill ❶ **Prior Knowledge** How have you helped leaders at school and in the community?

❷ **Vocabulary** What does a **mayor** do?

❸ Pretend you are the leader of a group. Tell how you would help the group members.

51

RETEACH THE LESSON

Revisit the Pictures Have children take another close look at the pictures on pages 48–51. Call on volunteers to point out the leaders and describe what the leaders are doing. Have them find a picture that shows any leader and a picture that shows something that is happening in a city.

ACTIVITY BOOK

Name _____ Date _____

Who Is the Leader?

Draw a line to match each clue with a leader. Then write the name of the leader on the line.

I tell a team how to play.

I am a coach

teacher

I make sure swimmers follow rules at the pool.

I am a lifeguard

coach

I am in charge of a city.

I am a mayor

lifeguard

I teach a class.

I am a teacher

mayor

14 • Activity Book   Use with Unit 2, Lesson 2.

PAGE 14

---

3 Close

Summarize Key Content

• Groups have leaders who help people follow the group's rules or laws.

• Mayors and governors are government leaders.

• Government leaders are in charge of all the people who provide services for the community.

READING SOCIAL STUDIES

Graphic Organizer Revisit the K-W-L chart begun in Motivate. Invite children to share new ideas they learned. Add these ideas to the chart.

What We Know	What We Want to Know	What We Learned
Leaders tell us what to do. Leaders make rules. Leaders answer our questions.	Who are our community leaders? What are their jobs?	The mayor leads our city. The mayor is in charge of the community.

● USE READING AND VOCABULARY TRANSPARENCY 2–3

2–3 TRANSPARENCY

Assess

Lesson 2 Review—Answers

❶ **Focus Skill** **Prior Knowledge** I have shown respect for my leaders, listened to them, and followed rules or laws.

❷ A mayor leads a city or town.

❸ **Performance Assessment Guidelines** Children may say they would make sure group members follow the rules and help them do their jobs.

Extension Activities For Home and School

Our Teacher

Ms. Harper makes the rules.

Ms. Harper teaches us new things.

Ms. Harper shows us how to get along.

Leader Posters

Materials: pictures of various leaders, posterboard, drawing paper, glue, scissors, crayons or markers

Organize children into groups. Assign each group one of the following locations: home, school, or community. Ask children to select one or two leaders from the assigned location to profile on a poster. Suggest they cut and paste or draw a picture of the person or persons on a sheet of posterboard. Have them add pictures and words to tell about the leader or leaders, the important job they do, and the people they lead. Designate a wall as the Leader Hall of Fame and have children display their posters.
(VISUAL/TACTILE)

Now Hiring!

Materials: chart paper, paper, pencils

Have children talk about the roles of mayor and governor. Help children recognize the ways the two positions are alike and different. Remind children that the mayor works in the city or town and the governor works in the state capital. Then organize the class into small groups to create want ads to find a person who would make a good mayor or governor. On chart paper write a want ad frame similar to the one shown. Have children copy the frame and work together to decide what to write in it.
(AUDITORY/VISUAL/TACTILE)

Help Wanted
Job Title:
Location:
Duties:
SKills Needed:

Leadership Bulletin Board

Materials: newspapers, magazines, scissors

Encourage children to look through newspapers and magazines with a family member at home. Suggest that they find and cut out pictures and articles about different kinds of leaders in action. Have children bring their clippings to school and display them on a bulletin board. Encourage children to continue to search for related news items at home as they complete Unit 2 and to add updated news items to the bulletin board when they find them. Periodically review aloud the contents of the bulletin board. Specifically, point out the various duties mentioned that the leaders perform.
(VISUAL/TACTILE)

SKILLS

Find States on a Map

OBJECTIVES

- Locate places of significance on maps.
- Use simple maps to identify the location of places beyond the classroom, school, and community.
- Recognize their state on a U.S. map.

RESOURCES

Pupil Book/Unit Big Book, pp. 52–53

Word Cards V11–V14

Activity Book, p. 15

⊕**Skill Transparency 2–1**

GeoSkills CD-ROM

Vocabulary

country p. 52   **state** p. 52

border p. 52

1 Motivate

Have children pretend they need to tell a new student how to get from the school's front door to a particular location in your school, such as the office, the lunchroom, or the classroom. Choose a location that requires children to follow several steps. Then draw a simple map on the board that shows the same information. Help children conclude that maps are useful because they show clearly how to get from one place to another.

Q Why might a map be better than spoken directions if the student got lost along the way?

A With a map, the student could see where she or he is and go on from there.

Why It Matters

Tell children that knowing the country, state, and community where they live is important. Children can use maps to see exactly where they live in relation to other people and places. They find out how to visit a friend or relative, discover how to get to a favorite vacation spot, or even find important places in their own town or city.

MAKE IT RELEVANT

In Your State Display a map of your state. Point out your community on the map. Find the borders of your county and point these out to the children. Invite children to locate familiar places within the borders of your community.

Welcome to
FL RIDA
THE SUNSHINE STATE

2 Teach

What You Need to Know

Have children look at the map. Invite them to trace some of the lines on the map with their finger. Explain that the lines show where one state (or country) ends. Remind children that the lines appear only on maps. If children went to a state border, they would not see a line to step over. But if they were driving on a highway, they might see a sign that shows where the border is.

Point to Alaska and Hawaii on the map. Explain that even though Alaska and Hawaii are part of the United States, they are not part of the continental United States, or the states that touch each other. Trace the states that are part of the continental United States to show what you mean. Then use a globe to show the actual positions of Alaska and Hawaii in relation to the continental United States. Explain that Alaska is bordered by water and by Canada and that Hawaii is surrounded by water.

Skills

MAP AND GLOBE

Find States on a Map

Vocabulary

country

state

border

▶ Why It Matters

A **country** is an area of land with its own people and laws. Our country is the United States of America. The United States is made up of 50 states. A **state** is one part of our country.

▶ What You Need to Know

On a map, lines called borders separate states and countries. A **border** shows where a state or country ends. The countries of Canada and Mexico have borders that touch the United States.

Welcome to **FLORIDA**

THE SUNSHINE STATE

52

STUDY/RESEARCH SKILLS

Using Reference Sources Point out that two other countries border the United States. Help children locate Canada on the northern border and Mexico in the south. Have them use children's encyclopedias and easy reading books to find facts about Canada and Mexico. Allow time for children to report their findings to the class.

REACH ALL LEARNERS

Advanced Learners
Provide children with a political map of the United States that shows cities. Point out the symbol, often a star, that indicates that a city is a state capital. Discuss the idea that the capital is where the state's government is located. Have children locate their state capital. Next, have children locate Washington, D.C. Point out that it is shown as a star within a circle. Explain that this means it is the nation's capital, or where the federal government is located.

EXTEND AND ENRICH

Identify and Label States Teach children the postal abbreviations for your state and for the surrounding states. Have children write the abbreviations on small sticky notes. Point to a state on a large map and have children show the appropriate sticky note. Call on a volunteer to place a sticky note with the appropriate abbreviation on the state you pointed to.

United States

Map labels: CANADA, WASHINGTON, OREGON, NEVADA, CALIFORNIA, IDAHO, MONTANA, WYOMING, UTAH, ARIZONA, NEW MEXICO, COLORADO, NORTH DAKOTA, SOUTH DAKOTA, NEBRASKA, KANSAS, OKLAHOMA, TEXAS, MINNESOTA, IOWA, MISSOURI, ARKANSAS, LOUISIANA, WISCONSIN, ILLINOIS, MICHIGAN, INDIANA, OHIO, KENTUCKY, TENNESSEE, MISSISSIPPI, ALABAMA, GEORGIA, FLORIDA, NEW HAMPSHIRE, VERMONT, MAINE, NEW YORK, MASSACHUSETTS, RHODE ISLAND, CONNECTICUT, PENNSYLVANIA, NEW JERSEY, DELAWARE, MARYLAND, WEST VIRGINIA, VIRGINIA, NORTH CAROLINA, SOUTH CAROLINA, Washington, D.C., Lake Superior, Lake Michigan, Lake Huron, Lake Ontario, Lake Erie, ATLANTIC OCEAN, Gulf of Mexico, PACIFIC OCEAN, MEXICO

▶ **Practice the Skill**

❶ Which state shares a border with Maine?

❷ Locate your state. Name a state that is near yours.

❸ How many states share Florida's border?

▶ **Apply What You Learned**

List the states with borders that touch Canada or Mexico.

Practice your map and globe skills with the **GeoSkills CD-ROM.**

53

MAP AND GLOBE SKILLS

Practice the Skill—Answers

❶ New Hampshire

❷ Children should be able to point to their state and name states that touch it.

❸ Two

3 Close

Apply What You Learned

Have children trace their finger along the northern border of the continental United States. Tell children that areas below the line are part of the United States and areas above the line are part of Canada. Begin at the east coast of the United States and point to each border state. Have children name the states as you point to them. Next, have children trace the southern border. Point out that the areas above the line are part of the United States and the areas below the line are part of Mexico. Then have children point to and name the states that border Mexico. Ask children to compare the length of the borders and the number of states along each one.

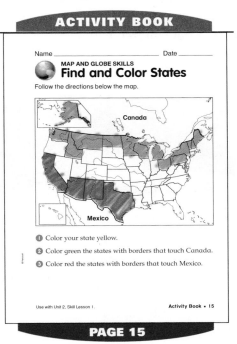

ACTIVITY BOOK

Name _____ Date _____

MAP AND GLOBE SKILLS
Find and Color States

Follow the directions below the map.

Canada

Mexico

❶ Color your state yellow.
❷ Color green the states with borders that touch Canada.
❸ Color red the states with borders that touch Mexico.

Use with Unit 2, Skill Lesson 1.   Activity Book • 15

PAGE 15

Extension Activities For Home and School

Your State

Materials: map of your state, modeling clay, star and circle stickers

Display a map of your state. Trace the border around your state with your finger, and invite students to do the same on their map on Pupil Edition pages 52 and 53. Have children work in pairs to create a clay model of their state. Encourage children to find the name and location of their state capital. Then have them gently press a star sticker into the clay model to mark the location of the capital. Suggest that children mark their community's location with a circle sticker.
(TACTILE/VISUAL)

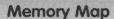

Memory Map

Materials: several U.S. maps, drawing paper, pencils and crayons

Give groups of children a U.S. map. Have them look at the map and find a state they have never visited. Tell children they will draw from memory the outline of the state they chose. First, encourage children to trace the border of their chosen state with a finger. After children have had some time to trace the state's outline, have them put the maps away. Then ask children to draw the state from memory. After children have completed their maps, allow them to compare their drawings to the map.
(VISUAL/TACTILE/KINESTHETIC)

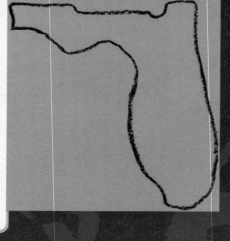

A New Country

Materials: drawing paper, crayons or markers

Tell children to work with a family member to design a make-believe country. Have them include at least seven states. Encourage children to name their new country and states. Remind them to draw borders between the states. Invite volunteers to share the drawings of their new country with the class.
(TACTILE)

LESSON 3

Our Country's Presidents

OBJECTIVES

- Identify leaders in the nation.
- Describe the roles of public officials, including the President.
- Identify George Washington as the first President of our country.
- Know past Presidents.

 Prior Knowledge pp. 41, 54, 76

RESOURCES

Pupil Book/Unit Big Book, pp. 54–57

Word Cards V13–V14

Activity Book, p. 16

Reading and Vocabulary Transparency 2–4

Internet Resources

READING SOCIAL STUDIES

Study Questions To help prepare children for the lesson, pose the following questions:

What does the President of the United States do?	
Can you name some past Presidents?	

Discuss the questions. Tell children to think about these questions as you read the lesson.

● USE READING AND VOCABULARY TRANSPARENCY 2–4

Vocabulary

President p. 54

 When Minutes Count

Have children read pages 56–57. Then invite them to tell in their own words what they just read.

Quick Summary

The leader of the United States is called the President. George Washington was our first President. Since Washington, there have been many other Presidents. Another famous President was Thomas Jefferson.

Motivate

Set the Purpose

Big Idea Before starting the lesson, read the Big Idea statement aloud. Remind children that leaders are people who are in charge of groups, and groups of all sizes have leaders. In our country, the President is the leader of the United States. The President is in charge of the country and all its citizens.

Access Prior Knowledge

Review what children learned about leaders.

Q What have you learned that government leaders do?

A They help citizens plan what to do and follow the laws. They make sure that the government provides services to the citizens.

2 Teach

Read and Respond

Geography Show children a map of the United States. Point out Washington, D.C., on the map. Ask children between which two states is Washington, D.C. (Maryland and Virginia) Explain that Washington, D.C., is the only American city or town that is not part of a state.

Visual Learning

Pictures Point to the pictures that show the White House. Explain that the White House is both the President's office and the home of the President's family. Tell children that even though the President uses the White House while in office, the White House really belongs to the people of the United States.

Explain that the President spends much time working in the Oval Office. Then point out that the President also has a special airplane called *Air Force 1* and a special helicopter called *Marine 1*. Explain that the President always travels in special vehicles.

Q Why do you think the President has so many special things?

A The special things help the President save time, and they also help keep the President safe.

Lesson

3

Our Country's Presidents

Big Idea
The President is the leader of our country.

Vocabulary

President

The **President** is the leader of our country. The President and other government leaders work together to decide on laws.

Much of the President's work is done at the White House. The White House is also the home of the President.

54

QUESTIONS KIDS ASK

Q Why does the President need a special house?

A The President needs to live right beside the office because a President must always be ready to go to work. Whenever a problem happens in the United States or in another country, the President hears about it right away. The President must be able to get to work very quickly.

BACKGROUND

The White House The White House has been the official home of the President of the United States since 1800. The first President to live in the White House was John Adams. Although George Washington managed the building of the White House, he was out of office by the time it was completed.

READING SKILL

Prior Knowledge Ask children to think of people, places, or things they already know that are associated with the Presidency. Create a class list. (Responses will vary but may include the following: *The First Lady*—the President's wife; *Air Force One*—the President's plane; *1600 Pennsylvania Avenue*—address of the White House)

The President meets with people and leaders from around our country. The President visits leaders in other countries, too.

The White House

55

Read and Respond

Civics and Government Ask children to name the current President and recall things they have seen or heard about the President on TV or in magazines and newspapers.

Q How would you describe the President's role?

A The President is the leader of the people of the United States of America.

Explain to children that the President sometimes has special dinners and parties at the White House with leaders of other countries.

Q What do you think the President talks about in meetings with other leaders?

A He might talk about how to solve problems in our country and in other countries. He might talk about ways to help people in all parts of the world and how to keep peace in the world.

Discuss the kind of work the President does. Create a word web and help children brainstorm characteristics of a good President.

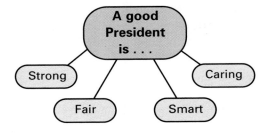

A good President is . . .

Strong

Caring

Fair

Smart

Read and Respond

History Explain that George Washington is often called the Father of Our Country. Besides being the first President and the first person to sign the Constitution, Washington was also a great and famous general who led the colonial troops in a war that created the United States. He served as President from 1789 to 1797. After two terms, Washington could have been reelected, but he chose to retire.

Q Where have you seen pictures of George Washington?

A on money, in books

· BIOGRAPHY ·

Thomas Jefferson

Responsibility Introduce and develop the concept of responsibility. Help children see that people who are responsible look for things that need to be done and then they try to make sure those things get done. They take on hard jobs and see them through to the end. Have children identify the contributions of Thomas Jefferson to our nation. (He wrote the Declaration of Independence and was President.)

George Washington was the first President of the United States of America. He did not live in the White House, but he helped decide where to build it.

George Washington was the first person to sign the Constitution of the United States. The Constitution is the plan for our country's government. Our country still follows this plan today.

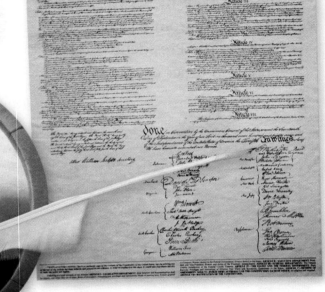

The Constitution of the United States of America

56

BACKGROUND

The Constitution The Constitution is the foundation of law and government in the United States. It describes how the American government is to be run. It gives the American people a set of laws to live by and protects certain rights and freedoms. Each state also has its own constitution, which describes how the state government is to be run. Use the Internet to find your state's constitution. Read and review it as a class.

STUDY/RESEARCH SKILLS

Using Reference Sources Provide a list of U.S. Presidents and have children choose a President to research. Have them use children's encyclopedias or books and the Internet to find at least two facts about the President that they chose. Have children report their information to the class.

EXTEND AND ENRICH

Discuss Governments Explain to children that an *unlimited* government, also known as a totalitarian government, has no way to restrain the powers of its rulers. These non-constitutional governments regulate every part of the lives of individuals. The United States government is a *limited*, or constitutional, government, which protects the rights of individuals and has effective controls over the power of people in authority. One example of these controls is the checks and balances system of the Executive, Judicial, and Legislative branches.

· BIOGRAPHY ·

Thomas Jefferson
1743–1826
Character Trait: Responsibility

Thomas Jefferson was the third President of our country. In 1776 he helped write the Declaration of Independence, which started the United States.

GO ONLINE

MULTIMEDIA BIOGRAPHIES
Visit The Learning Site at
www.harcourtschool.com
to learn about other famous people.

The Constitution says that Americans can choose who will be President. Every four years Americans choose the next President.

LESSON 3 Review

❶ **Vocabulary** Who is our country's **President** now?

❷ What makes a good President?

❸ Draw and write to show something you know about our President.

57

ACTIVITY BOOK

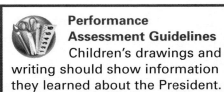

Name _____ Date _____
Know Your Presidents

Paste a picture of our President in the third box. Then write a fact about each President.

George Washington — He was our first President.

Thomas Jefferson — He wrote the Declaration of Independence.

Name of current President; one fact about the current President.

16 • Activity Book   Use with Unit 2, Lesson 3.

PAGE 16

---

3 Close

Summarize Key Content

- The President of the United States is the leader of our country.
- The United States has had many Presidents.
- George Washington and Thomas Jefferson were famous Presidents.

READING SOCIAL STUDIES

Study Questions Revisit the questions posed in Motivate. Invite children to share answers to the questions. Add these answers to the chart.

What does the President of the United States do?	The President is the leader of our country.
Can you name some past Presidents?	George Washington, Thomas Jefferson

● USE READING AND VOCABULARY TRANSPARENCY 2–4

2–4 TRANSPARENCY

Assess

Lesson 3 Review—Answers

❶ Children should be able to name the current President.

❷ Children's answers should include *responsibility*. Other characteristics they might name are intelligence, fairness, and honesty.

❸ **Performance Assessment Guidelines** Children's drawings and writing should show information they learned about the President.

Extension Activities For Home and School

Oral History

Materials: writing paper, pencil

Tell children to interview older adult family members about a President they remember. Help children prepare for the interview by writing a list of questions like the ones at right to use in their interview. When children bring their information back to the classroom, group them according to the President their interviewee recalled. Have children who learned about the same President share and compare their information.
(AUDITORY/TACTILE)

What President do you remember?

What do you think was the most important thing the President did?

What did you like best about the President?

Presidential Bulletin Board

Materials: reference books, Internet, drawing paper, crayons or markers

Invite children to make a bulletin board about the role of President. Encourage them to include great Presidents of the past, a picture of the White House, and duties that the President performs. You may want to help children find and print out pictures from the Internet or copy pictures out of reference books. You might also have children draw some pictures. As children make their bulletin board, encourage them to discuss why the United States needs a President.
(VISUAL/TACTILE)

The Office of the President

The President travels many places in an airplane.

The President lives and works in the White House.

If I Were President

Materials: paper, pencils

Ask children to pretend that they have grown up to be President. Suggest that they write three important things they would do. Then have children give a speech that begins, "If I were President, I would…"
(AUDITORY)

Make a Choice by Voting

Vocabulary

vote p. 58

ballot p. 58

1 Motivate

Invite children to suggest games the class might play at recess, such as softball or tag. Write their suggestions on the board. Then tell children the class can play only one game today, and ask them how to choose which game to play. Elicit the idea that each child will indicate his or her choice and the class will play the game that is chosen by the most children. Then take an informal vote as a way of making choices and talk about the results.

Why It Matters

Tell children that all citizens of the United States have a chance to choose, or elect, their leaders, including the President. Explain that by voting, the people help decide how their community, state, and country will be run. Each citizen has only one vote and each vote is secret. Point out that even though voters do not always get the results they hope for, it is important to vote. Voting is a fair way to choose leaders because the winner is the person most people want.

MAKE IT RELEVANT

At Home Ask children to think about a time when their family or a group of friends had to make a choice about something, such as what movie to see or what game to play. Encourage children to tell what choice had to be made, how the group made the choice, and how they felt about the choice. Discuss how they might use voting when making decisions at home or with friends.

2 Teach

What You Need to Know

Tell children that using a ballot is not the only way to vote. Some people vote using a special voting machine. Sometimes people vote by raising their hands or by a voice vote. To vote yes, they say "Aye." To vote no they say "Nay." The side that is louder wins. Explain that in large public elections, ballots or voting machines are almost always used. Point out that these methods are used in a way that allows Americans to vote in secret for the person they choose.

Q Before voting, what do you think people should do?

A Learn about each person on the ballot to decide who is best for the job.

Q Why do you think ballots are kept secret?

A So people can vote the way they want to vote and not the way someone else would like them to vote.

Tell children that before 1920, women did not have the right to vote in the United States. Also explain that there was a time when Native Americans and African Americans were not permitted to vote. Laws were finally passed to be fair to all citizens.

Q What would you think if all the girls in the class could vote, but the boys could not?

A That it would not be fair.

Skills CITIZENSHIP

Make a Choice by Voting

Vocabulary

Vocabulary

vote

ballot

▶ Why It Matters

Americans vote for many government leaders. When you **vote**, you make a choice. Americans also vote to make choices about laws.

▶ What You Need to Know

Americans use a **ballot** to vote. A ballot is a paper that shows all of the choices. You mark on it what your choice is. When voting time is over, the votes for each choice are counted. The choice with the most votes wins.

58

> ★ Ballot
> **Mr. Garcia's Class** ★
>
> To vote, fill in the arrow to your choice, like this: ◀━━ ◀━ ▸ pointing
>
> Para votar, complete la flecha ◀━ a la selección de la siguiente manera: ◀━ ▸ que apunta
>
> **Class Leader**
> **Líder de la clase**
> (Vote for One)   (Vote por uno)
>
> **Samuel** ◀━━ ◀━ ▸
> **Teresa** ◀━ ◀━ ▸
> **Olivia** ◀━ ◀━ ▸

BACKGROUND

Democracies Help children understand the difference between a direct democracy and a representative democracy. Explain that everyone votes on the rules in a direct democracy and that an elected group makes the rules in a representative democracy. Help children think of examples of both systems in their classroom, school, and community.

INTEGRATE MATHEMATICS

Charts and Graphs Hold a class vote on any issue, such as favorite sport, favorite color, favorite TV show, with three or four choices. Have children vote with a show of hands, and tally the votes. Next, help children graph the results. Ask questions such as the following to help children interpret the graph: *Which sport is the favorite in our class? Do more (or fewer) children like soccer or baseball? How do you know?*

▶ Practice the Skill

① Mr. Garcia's class used ballots to vote for a class leader. The choices were Samuel, Teresa, and Olivia. The votes were counted. Look at the chart to see who got the most votes.

② Who will be the class leader?

▶ Apply What You Learned

Have a class vote. Make a list of books your class would like to read. Make a ballot showing all of the choices. Count the votes each book gets. Show the counts on a chart. Which book does your class most want to read?

CITIZENSHIP SKILLS

Practice the Skill—Answers
② Olivia had the most votes, so she will be the class leader.

3 Close

Apply What You Learned

Have children name books they enjoy. Write three of the titles on the board, and tell children that they will vote for a class favorite. Children should create their own ballots, using the ballot on page 58 as a model. Show children how to fill in their ballots. Have them place the ballots in a ballot box. Then open the box and have a volunteer read the votes as another child makes a tally mark for each vote beside the title on the board. After all the votes have been counted, children should be able to name the winner of the vote and explain that the winner is the book with the most tally marks, or votes.

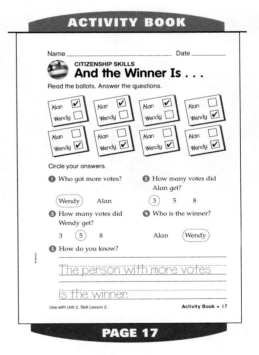

PAGE 17

TRANSPARENCY

Use SKILL TRANSPARENCY 2–2.

Extension Activities For Home and School

Try Out a Voting Booth

Call your local board of elections and arrange for children to go on a field trip to examine a voting machine and learn how it works. Or ask for a speaker to visit the class to demonstrate the process available to voters in your community. Ask the speaker to explain how ballots are kept secret. You might also ask the speaker to tell the class how and when people in your community can register to vote and how registering insures that no one can vote illegally.
(AUDITORY/KINESTHETIC)

Good Presidents

Materials: writing paper, pencils

With children, brainstorm personal characteristics that make a good President. Make sure the list includes a wide variety of choices, including things such as honesty, intelligence, being a good speaker, fairness, and having a sense of humor. Write the traits in a column on a chart. Have children copy the list and ask family members to vote for the characteristic they think is most important in a President. When children bring back their results, count the votes to see which characteristic seems most important to the voters in your community.
(VISUAL/TACTILE)

Class Favorites Book

Materials: notebook, pencil, drawing paper, crayons

Help children brainstorm topics for a class book titled *Our Favorite Things*. Topics might include favorite color, favorite snack food, favorite healthful food, favorite animal, and favorite sport. Organize the class into groups and assign each group a topic. Have the group make a ballot, poll their classmates, and tally the results. Have children report the results by drawing a page for the class book. Have them title the page *Our Favorite (insert name of topic)*. Make copies of the pages and help children bind the pages together to make their own copy of the class book. Encourage children to take the book home and explain to family members how the results were obtained.
(VISUAL/TACTILE)

America's Symbols

OBJECTIVES

- Explain selected national and state patriotic symbols.
- Recite and explain the meaning of a pledge of allegiance and a flag.
- Identify anthems and mottoes of countries and states.
- Identify ways in which Americans show respect for and honor their country.

 Prior Knowledge pp. 41, 76

RESOURCES

Pupil Book/Unit Big Book, pp. 60–65

Word Cards V15–V16

Activity Book, p. 18

🌐 **Reading and Vocabulary Transparency 2–5**

💻 **Internet Resources**

READING SOCIAL STUDIES

Graphic Organizer Begin a K-W-L chart about school workers. Complete the chart during Close.

What We Know	What We Want to Know	What We Learned
the U.S. flag the school mascot the eagle	What are some other U.S. symbols? Does our state have symbols?	

● **USE READING AND VOCABULARY TRANSPARENCY 2–5**

 2–5 TRANSPARENCY

Vocabulary

flag p. 62

 When Minutes Count

Have children read the Big Idea of the lesson. Then have them read the lesson and find at least one sentence that supports the Big Idea.

Quick Summary

Symbols are objects that remind us of, or stand for, other things or ideas. The United States has many symbols. Citizens respect these symbols because they represent our country.

 1 Motivate

Set the Purpose

Big Idea Before starting the lesson, read the Big Idea statement aloud. Explain that some symbols are meant to remind us of the importance of our country. People show respect for these symbols because they stand for the United States. As children read the lesson, encourage them to find out what some of these symbols are and why they are important to Americans.

Access Prior Knowledge

Ask children to brainstorm symbols with which they are familiar. These can be United States symbols or symbols affiliated with school or other areas. As symbols are mentioned, ask children to explain what they stand for.

2 | Teach

Visual Learning

Pictures Invite children to scan the pictures and name any that they recognize.

Q Have you ever seen any of these national symbols in person? Which one(s)?

A Children should relate their personal experiences.

Read and Respond

History After children share what they know about the symbols pictured, read aloud the text on the page and help children locate and name all the symbols. You may wish to share the additional information provided here.

The **Statue of Liberty** stands in New York Harbor on Liberty Island. The statue was a gift from the people of France and is a symbol of freedom. Many people came from faraway countries seeking freedom in the United States. For many who came by boat, the Statue of Liberty was the first thing they saw.

The **Liberty Bell** is also a symbol of freedom. In fact, the following motto is inscribed on it: *Proclaim liberty throughout all the land unto all the inhabitants thereof.* Explain that our forefathers believed they were not treated fairly by the King of England so they went against his rule. This love of individualism led to our country's formation. Tell children that the colonists in Philadelphia rang the bell when they read the Declaration of Independence for the first time. The bell is cracked and no longer rings. Many visit Philadelphia every year to see it.

The **bald eagle** became our national bird in 1782. This majestic-looking animal is native to North America.

America's Symbols

Big Idea
Symbols remind us to show respect for our country.

Vocabulary
flag

The United States of America has symbols that remind us of important people and events. Some of these symbols are places we can visit.

Bald eagle

Capitol building

FAST FACT A leader named Benjamin Franklin wanted the turkey to be a symbol of the United States. The bald eagle was chosen instead.

60

INTEGRATE ART

Draw a Symbol Point out that the symbols used in each state are different because the people and the places are different. Invite children to think of something that they admire. Have children draw a picture of the object to create their own symbol.

MAKE IT RELEVANT

Locate Symbols Display a U.S. map on a bulletin board. Write the name of each symbol except the eagle and Uncle Sam on an index card. Use tacks and yarn to connect the cards to the locations of the monuments named. (Statue of Liberty—New York City; Liberty Bell—Philadelphia; Washington Monument and the Capitol—Washington, D.C.; Mount Rushmore—Black Hills, South Dakota)

Mount Rushmore

Liberty Bell

Washington Monument

Uncle Sam

I WANT YOU

for the U.S. ARMY
ENLIST NOW

Statue of Liberty

61

The **Washington Monument** was built in Washington, D.C., between 1848 and 1884. It serves as a memorial to our first President, George Washington. Until the Eiffel Tower was completed in France in 1889, it was the tallest human-made structure in the world.

The **Capitol Building** is where one branch of our government, Congress, meets to make laws for the country. The Capitol Building is located on Capitol Hill in Washington, D.C. Congress began meeting there in 1800, when the north wing of the building was completed.

Uncle Sam is a national symbol who stands for the United States. The most well-known image of Uncle Sam is shown in this poster drawn by James Montgomery Flagg in 1916–1917.

Mount Rushmore is a huge sculpture on a cliff near Rapid City, South Dakota, in an area known as the Black Hills. Gutzon Borglum designed this spectacular sculpture to show his love for his country. Workers used dynamite and then drills to complete the sculpture. The faces of Presidents George Washington, Thomas Jefferson, Theodore Roosevelt, and Abraham Lincoln are depicted in the sculpture.

Encourage children to explain how these symbols reflect an American love of individualism and freedom.

Visual Learning

Pictures Explain to children that the United States has many other symbols. Point out that each state has its own symbols, too.

Children might enjoy researching other country and state symbols. Have them visit The Learning Site at **www.harcourtschool.com**

INTEGRATE MATHEMATICS

Measurement Tell children that the Statue of Liberty is just over 151 feet (46 m) tall, from the tip of her toes to the top of her torch. The base the statue stands on makes her even taller. Take children to a hallway or a large open space on the playground and work together to measure a distance of 151 feet (46 m). Have groups of children stand at each end of this distance to help them visualize the size of the statue.

REACH ALL LEARNERS

Advanced Learners
Remind children that Benjamin Franklin thought our national bird should be the turkey. Organize children into two groups. Have one group research turkeys, and the other, eagles. Tell children to organize their information about each bird into two categories: Why the Bird Should be a National Symbol and Why It Should Not. Then invite children to debate which bird makes a better national symbol.

Visual Learning

Picture Have children look at the picture of the U.S. flag or the actual flag, if you have one in your classroom.

Q **Where have you seen the flag displayed?**

A Children's answers may include the school, library, post office, government buildings, restaurants, stores, people's houses, sporting events.

Q **How many stars and stripes does the American flag have? Why?**

A The American flag has 50 stars. They stand for the 50 states. There are 13 stripes on the American flag. They remind us of the first 13 states.

Read and Respond

Culture and Society Have children read the Pledge of Allegiance aloud. Explain that in 1942 the Pledge of Allegiance became the official pledge to the flag of the United States. When saying the pledge, an individual is supposed to stand with his or her right hand over the heart. Invite children to stand and say the pledge together.

NOTE: You may have children who, because of religious or other beliefs, choose not to participate in certain celebrations or in pledging allegiance to the flag. This behavior should not be judged as a lack of good citizenship.

Our **flag** is a symbol of our country. It is red, white, and blue. Each star stands for one of the states in our country. The stripes stand for the first 13 states in the United States. When we say the Pledge of Allegiance, we show that our country is important to us.

The Pledge of Allegiance

I pledge allegiance to the Flag
of the United States of America,
and to the Republic
for which it stands,
one Nation under God, indivisible,
with liberty and justice for all.

62

READING SOCIAL STUDIES

Paraphrase To help children explain the meaning of the Pledge of Allegiance, guide them in paraphrasing it. For example: *I promise to be loyal to the flag and to the country the flag stands for. It is a country that cannot be divided. It is a country that God watches over. It is a country that gives its citizens freedom and treats them fairly.*

INTEGRATE MUSIC

Sing the National Anthem Play "The Star-Spangled Banner" for children and invite them to sing along. Explain that it is our national anthem, a song that stands for our country. Help children realize that, like the Pledge of Allegiance, the national anthem is a symbol of our country. When people stand to sing "The Star-Spangled Banner," they are standing to honor the United States of America.

Each state has its own flag.

· BIOGRAPHY ·

Betsy Ross
1752–1836
Character Trait: Patriotism

In 1776 the United States was a
new country and needed a flag.
George Washington knew the
right person for the job. Betsy Ross
did sewing work in Philadelphia,
Pennsylvania. Some people think
she sewed the first American flag.
Betsy Ross is a patriotic symbol for
our country.

MULTIMEDIA BIOGRAPHIES
Visit The Learning Site at
www.harcourtschool.com
to learn about other famous people.

GO
ONLINE

63

Visual Learning

Pictures Point to the picture that
shows all the state flags, and tell
children that although citizens in all
states honor the U.S. flag, they honor
their own state flag, too. If your school
displays your state flag, take children
on a walk to see it.

**Q Why do you think all the state
flags are so different?**

A Children may realize that
different things are important
to the people of different states.

Help children locate the picture of
their state flag. Then help them do
research to explain the symbols chosen
for the flag.

· BIOGRAPHY ·

Betsy Ross

Patriotism According to legend,
Betsy Ross made the first American
flag. Although it is possible that
she made the flag, there is no real
evidence to support this story.
Whoever made it, the flag was
called the Stars and Stripes and had
13 stars and 13 stripes. There was
no official arrangement for the
stars, so several different designs
were used. The Stars and Stripes
was adopted as the flag of the
United States by the Continental
Congress on June 14, 1777.

Read and Respond

Culture and Society Tell children that many countries, states, communities, and other groups have mottoes. Ask children where they may have seen the motto *In God We Trust*. You might pass around a quarter and a magnifying glass and let children read the motto.

Call on children to identify and read aloud the state mottoes on page 64. Note that South Carolina has two mottoes.

· HERITAGE ·

Florida's Day

Point out the state of Florida on a U.S. map. Florida became the twenty-seventh state in the United States on March 3, 1845. The state seal is in the center of the state flag. The seal was revised in 1985 and depicts a Seminole Indian woman, a steamboat, and a sabal palm.

Read and Respond

History Have children identify the anthem of the United States. ("The Star-Spangled Banner") Help children recall other songs they know that tell about America, such as "America," the song they sang at the beginning of the unit. Then explain that each state has its own song. Teach children your state song.

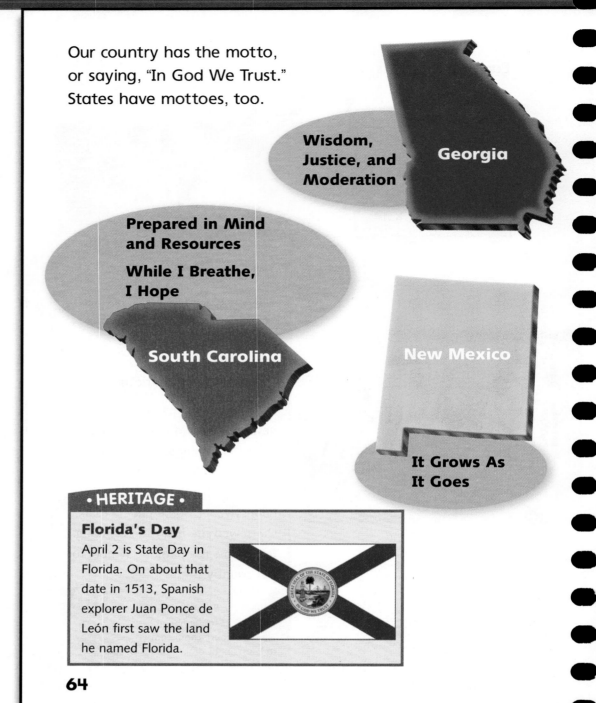

Our country has the motto, or saying, "In God We Trust." States have mottoes, too.

Wisdom, Justice, and Moderation — Georgia

Prepared in Mind and Resources

While I Breathe, I Hope

South Carolina

New Mexico

It Grows As It Goes

· HERITAGE ·

Florida's Day

April 2 is State Day in Florida. On about that date in 1513, Spanish explorer Juan Ponce de León first saw the land he named Florida.

64

BACKGROUND

The National Anthem "The Star-Spangled Banner" is the official patriotic song of the United States. The words for the anthem are from a poem written by Francis Scott Key in 1814.

"The Star-Spangled Banner"

Oh, say, can you see,
by the dawn's early light,
What so proudly we hailed
at the twilight's last gleaming,
Whose broad stripes and bright stars, through the perilous fight,
O'er the ramparts we watched
were so gallantly streaming?
And the rockets' red glare,
the bombs bursting in air,
Gave proof through the night
that our flag was still there.
Oh, say, does that star-spangled banner yet wave,
O'er the land of the free
and the home of the brave?

EXTEND AND ENRICH

Make a Bulletin Board Prepare a bulletin board titled "Symbols of the United States." Include the headings: *Objects, Places, People, Songs, Mottoes.* Ask children to write statements that tell about things that symbolize the United States. Have children illustrate their statements and display them in the appropriate column on the bulletin board.

We can sing songs that show how proud
we are of our country and our state.

1 **Vocabulary** Explain how the **flag** is a symbol for our country.

2 Do you think symbols are important? Why?

3 Make a poster to show symbols of your state.

65

Write a Postcard Have children write a postcard they might send if they visited one of the national monuments mentioned in the lesson. Suggest that children describe the monument, explain why it is an important symbol of our country, and tell how visiting the monument might make them feel.

Name _____ Date _____

National Symbols

Liberty Bell   Washington   Statue of   American
                Monument   Liberty   flag

Write the name of a symbol to complete each sentence.

1 The *Statue of Liberty* holds a torch.

2 The *Washington Monument* helps us remember our first President.

3 Each star stands for a state on the
American flag

4 The *Liberty Bell* stands for liberty and freedom.

18 • Activity Book   Use with Unit 2, Lesson 4.

3 Close

Summarize Key Content

- Symbols help us remember and show respect for our country.
- Citizens also show respect for their country and state by singing special songs.

READING SOCIAL STUDIES

Graphic Organizer Revisit the K-W-L chart begun in Motivate. Invite children to share new ideas they learned. Add these ideas to the chart.

What We Know	What We Want to Know	What We Learned
the U.S. flag the school mascot the eagle	What are some other U.S. symbols? Does our state have symbols?	Other symbols include songs, mottoes, and places.

● USE READING AND VOCABULARY TRANSPARENCY 2–5

2–5
TRANSPARENCY

Assess

Lesson 4 Review—Answers

1 When we see the flag, we think of the 50 states.

2 Children may say that symbols are important because they help us remember what our country stands for.

3 **Performance Assessment Guidelines** Children's posters should include their state flag, bird, and flower.

Extension Activities For Home and School

Citizenship Game Show

Materials: index cards, pencils

Divide the class into several large groups. Challenge the children in each group to brainstorm questions and answers that relate to patriotic symbols and ways Americans honor their country. Have children write each question on one side of an index card and the answer on the other side. Then have each group create a game-show format in which to incorporate their questions. Pair the groups. Have the children in one group take turns being contestants in the other group's game show.
(AUDITORY/KINESTHETIC)

> Q What are the colors of the American flag?
>
> Q How many stars are on the flag?
>
> Q What American symbol can be found in Philadelphia?
>
> A "America" is a song Americans sing to honor their country.
>
> A The Statue of Liberty is a symbol of freedom.

Symbol T-Shirts

Materials: paper, crayons, white T-shirts, fabric markers, pictures of various symbols

Have children design a symbol T-shirt. Suggest that they choose either a state or a national symbol to create their shirt. You may want to provide pictures to help children make their drawing. You may wish to have children practice drawing their symbol on a sheet of paper before drawing directly on the shirt. After children make their shirts, hold a symbol celebration day. Children should wear their shirt and be able to tell about the symbol and what it honors. Ask children to tell why they think all the symbols for states are so different. Then invite children to sing a few patriotic songs.
(VISUAL/TACTILE)

Come Visit Our State

Materials: paper, pencils, reference material about your state

Group children and tell them that their job is to convince people from other states to visit your state by writing a commercial or advertisement for the state. Tell children to begin by listing the best things about their state. Then tell children to find ways to make sure people in other states know about some of the good things your state has. Tell children to make use of state songs and symbols. Have children present their projects as if they were speaking to someone planning to visit their state.
(AUDITORY/KINESTHETIC)

Tourist Office

Fiction or Nonfiction

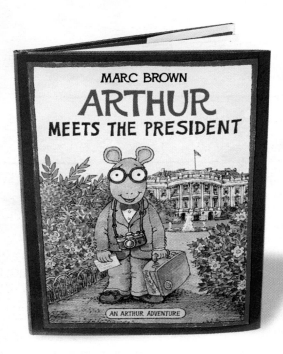

Vocabulary

fiction p. 66   **nonfiction** p. 66

fact p. 66

1 Motivate

Call on volunteers to name a favorite book and tell what the book is about. After each summary, ask the speaker whether they think the book tells about things that really happened or if the things are made up and did not happen.

Why It Matters

Explain that some stories in books are real and some are made-up. Both kinds of stories can be interesting and fun to read. It is important that readers are able to tell the difference between the two kinds of stories so they know whether they are learning facts they might want to remember or are reading just to have fun.

WORD WORK

Prefixes Write *fiction* and *nonfiction* on the board. Tell children that *fiction* is the name for made-up stories. Name some stories children have read in class that are fiction. Circle the prefix *non-* and explain that *non-* means "not" or "the opposite of." *Nonfiction* is the opposite of *fiction*. Since fiction is made up, nonfiction is the opposite of a made-up story. Nonfiction is a true story about something that really happened. Name some stories children have read in class that are non-fiction. Encourage children to name and define other words that include the prefix *non-*, such as *nonbreakable, nonliving, nonsmoking.*

What You Need to Know

Explain that if even one sentence in a book is not true or is about something that is not real, the book is considered fiction.

Q **What words in a title might let you know that a story is fiction?**

A Fiction titles may have words about things that cannot be real, such as *magic, elf,* or *dragon*.

Q **What kinds of pictures might be clues that a book is nonfiction?**

A The pictures may be photographs or drawings with many realistic details.

Show a selection of fiction and non-fiction books. Read the title of each book and page through the book to let children see the illustrations. Have them tell whether they think each book is fiction or nonfiction. Then have children tell what clues helped them make that choice.

Skills

READING

Fiction or Nonfiction

Vocabulary

fiction

nonfiction

fact

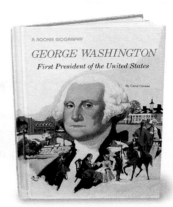

A ROOKIE BIOGRAPHY
GEORGE WASHINGTON
First President of the United States
By Carol Greene

▶ **Why It Matters**

Stories can be made up or real. Made-up stories are **fiction**. Books of real information are **nonfiction**. Nonfiction books tell only facts. A **fact** is something that is true.

▶ **What You Need to Know**

The title, pictures, and words of a book let you know if it's fiction or nonfiction.

Then, in 1789, George was elected the first president of the United States.

He didn't think he was good enough to be president. But he took the job.

66

INTEGRATE READING

Tall Tales Explain that a tall tale is an exaggeration. For example, instead of being "very tall," a character is "taller than a three-story building." Read a tall tale that is based on and includes some facts. A Paul Bunyan story, for instance, has Paul accidentally digging the Mississippi River because he was so tired he dragged his huge ax along the ground. Have children tell what parts of the story are based on fact (the Mississippi River is a real river) and what parts are fiction (Paul Bunyan was so big he could carry an ax as wide as a river). Remind children that if part of a story is fiction, the whole story is fiction, so tall tales are always fiction.

▶ Practice the Skill

1. Look at the two books.

2. Which book do you think is fiction? What makes you think so?

3. Which book do you think tells more facts? What makes you think so?

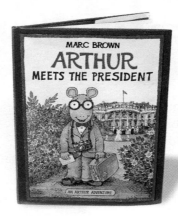

▶ Apply What You Learned

Choose a book, and look at the cover and the pictures. Do you think the book is fiction or nonfiction? How can you tell?

67

Practice the Skill—Answers

2. Children should mention the title, pictures, and words in the text as they explain why they think the book *Arthur Meets the President* is fiction.

3. Children should say that the nonfiction book, *George Washington, First President of the United States*, is most likely to have more facts.

3 Close

Apply What You Learned

Supply children with a selection of easy picture books that have obvious clues to their genre. Tell children to write a prediction about whether each book will be fiction or nonfiction. Children should be able to tell how looking through the books helped them confirm or disprove their predictions.

PAGE 19

TRANSPARENCY

Use SKILL TRANSPARENCY 2–3.

EXTEND AND ENRICH

Guess Nonfiction or Fiction Pair children and tell each partner to tell a story to the other partner. Have children tell about either a real event or a completely unreal event. Have the listener tell whether they think the story is fiction or nonfiction and why. Then have the storyteller tell whether or not the listener is correct.

RETEACH THE SKILL

Make a Chart Brainstorm genres with which children are familiar, such as plays, fables, poems, riddles, biographies, encyclopedia articles, and magazine articles. Make available samples to illustrate each one or have children visit the library to obtain samples. Allow time for children to explore the samples. Then draw a two-column chart and label the columns *Fiction* and *Nonfiction*. Help children list the samples in the appropriate column.

Extension Activities For Home and School

Tour a Library

Ask the school librarian or library aide to give children a tour of the library and explain how the books are arranged. Ask the librarian to show how fiction and nonfiction books are separated and to briefly explain how nonfiction books are grouped by category. After the tour, have children use what they learned about predicting whether a book is fiction or nonfiction to group the books in the classroom in an arrangement similar to the school library's.
(AUDITORY/VISUAL/KINESTHETIC)

Finding Facts

Explain that all the sentences in a nonfiction book are true, but not all sentences are facts. A fact often includes a number, a date, or the name of a place. A fact has specific information. Facts are ideas children might take notes on if they were writing a report. Some statements in nonfiction writing are opinions. They are not false statements, because they tell what the writer really believes. But they are not the same as facts. Write these sentences on the board:

This is a beautiful tree.
This tree has white flowers in the springtime.
This tree grows to be about 20 feet tall.

Read the sentences with children. Then explain that two sentences tell facts and one gives an opinion. After children identify the two sentences that are facts, have them circle the word in the opinion sentence that makes it an opinion.
(VISUAL)

Read to a Family Member

Materials: nonfiction books, index cards or paper, pencils

Take children to the library and have them choose a nonfiction book on a subject they think will be interesting to a family member. Tell children to take the book home and read it with the family member. Suggest that they tell the family member how they knew the book was a nonfiction book. Have children choose a fact in the book that they and their family member found interesting, write it on an index card or paper, and bring it back to school. Have children show the book they read and share the interesting fact.
(VISUAL)

Pandas are not really bears.

Portraits of Good Citizens

OBJECTIVES

- Identify characteristics of good citizenship, such as a belief in equality and responsibility for the common good.
- Identify historic figures and ordinary people who have exemplified good citizenship.
- Identify contributions of historical figures who have influenced the community, state, and nation.
- Identify historic figures who have exhibited a love of individualism.

 Prior Knowledge pp. 41, 76

RESOURCES

Pupil Book/Unit Big Book, pp. 68–71

Word Cards V17–V18

Activity Book, p. 20

🌐 **Reading and Vocabulary Transparency 2–6**

💻 **Internet Resources**

READING SOCIAL STUDIES

Graphic Organizer Begin a chart about Good Citizens. Complete the chart during Close.

Good Citizens	
Characteristics	**People**
responsibility	Thomas Jefferson

🔴 **USE READING AND VOCABULARY TRANSPARENCY 2–6**   **2–6 TRANSPARENCY**

Vocabulary

citizen p. 68

 ### When Minutes Count

Ask children to skim the lesson to find out traits of good citizens.

Quick Summary

We are all citizens. Some people are especially good citizens. Some good citizens become famous. But people do not need to be famous to be good citizens. Many ordinary people practice good citizenship every day.

 # 1 Motivate

Set the Purpose

Big Idea Before starting the lesson, read the Big Idea statement aloud. Remind children that they have already read about one responsible citizen, Thomas Jefferson, who took the responsibility of writing the Declaration of Independence and also took on the difficult job of being President. Tell children to read to find out about other responsible citizens and to think of ways to be good citizens themselves.

Access Prior Knowledge

Ask children to think of qualities a good citizen possesses. Begin a list and have children name people they know or have heard of who have these citizenship qualities.

Read and Respond

Civics and Government Read the text on page 68 and then ask children to name some citizens in your community. Help children realize that they are all citizens of their community.

Q What are some things good citizens do in your community?

A Children may say good citizens follow the laws to help keep the people in the community safe, they help other people, they raise money for good causes, and they help keep the community clean.

History Explain that a character trait is a quality a person has or the way a person acts. One character trait that Bernardo de Gálvez had that makes a good citizen was patriotism.

Q How was Bernardo de Gálvez a good citizen?

A He helped Americans fight to be free from England.

Q How can you show patriotism?

A Children may say by singing the national anthem or saying the Pledge of Allegiance.

Civics and Government Remind children that everyone can practice good citizenship by following rules and laws, being fair and honest, being a good sport, and treating others the way he or she wants to be treated. Invite children to role-play ways they can practice these good citizenship skills.

Help children identify local, state, and national leaders. Have children describe how these leaders serve as good examples for the communities they serve.

Lesson 5

Portraits of Good Citizens

Big Idea
Good citizens help others.

Vocabulary
citizen

A **citizen** is a person who lives in and belongs to a community. Good citizens do things to help people. Read about the ways these good citizens helped others.

Patriotism

Bernardo de Gálvez
1746–1786
Character Trait: Patriotism

Bernardo de Gálvez showed great patriotism, or love for his country. He was a Spanish leader in Louisiana who helped Americans fight to be free from the country of England.

68

READING SOCIAL STUDIES

Use Context Clues Have children put their finger on the word *Patriotism* beside the *Character Trait* label. Ask children to find the same word in the text. Explain that writers sometimes give readers clues about a word's meaning right in the same sentence. Reread the first sentence as children listen for the meaning of the word *patriotism*.

BACKGROUND

Bernardo de Gálvez Bernardo de Gálvez was the Spanish governor of the Louisiana territory that encompassed 13 of our present states. Before Spain entered the American Revolutionary War, Gálvez did much to aid the American patriots. Once Spain was in the war, Gálvez defeated the British in Alabama and Florida and secured the south. He has been honored with statues, and even a city was named for him — Galveston, Texas.

Kindness

Harriet Tubman
1820?–1913
Character Trait: Kindness

Harriet Tubman lived at a time when many African Americans were slaves. A slave is someone who is forced to work for another person without pay. She helped many slaves escape to freedom.

Responsibility

Henry Flagler
1830–1913
Character Trait: Responsibility

Henry Flagler built grand hotels in Florida. Some who visited decided to move to Florida. Henry Flagler made Florida's railroads better, too. He also gave money to build schools and hospitals.

69

BACKGROUND

Harriet Tubman At the age of 30, Harriet Tubman escaped slavery. She vowed to help others. Tubman led hundreds to freedom via the Underground Railroad, which aided slaves fleeing to free states or to Canada. She was never caught, and she never lost a slave.

Henry Flagler Henry Flagler recognized Florida's promise. He boosted the flagging railroad system and built palatial hotels to lure visitors to the Sunshine State. Thanks to Flagler, the tourism and agricultural industries flourished there.

INTEGRATE READING

Character Traits Remind children of the meaning of *perseverance* (determination to get something done, even when it is difficult). Ask children which citizens from this lesson showed perseverance. Then read aloud *Amazing Grace* by Mary Hoffman. Ask children to describe how Grace showed perseverance. Have children discuss any other character traits they feel she showed.

Read and Respond

History Read aloud the text about Harriet Tubman. Explain that showing kindness means doing something to help others.

Q How do you think Harriet Tubman showed kindness?

A She helped others become free.

Help children understand that there are many other ways to be good citizens. Give examples such as Rosa Parks, who helped spark the Civil Rights movement, and Barbara Jordan, a political leader. Explain that both of these African American women overcame obstacles because they persevered and because of the earlier work of people like Harriet Tubman, who risked her life so that others could experience freedom. Ask children to share with the class some good citizens they know.

After children read about Henry Flagler on page 69, help them locate St. Augustine, Florida, on a map. Explain that this is where Flagler built a grand hotel. Eventually, the Hotel Ponce de Leon closed. The former hotel is now a college named in his honor.

Q What contributions did Henry Flagler make to Florida?

A Children may say that he improved railroads in Florida and helped bring people to the state.

Explain to children that Bernardo de Gálvez, Harriet Tubman, and Henry Flagler also showed a love of *individualism*, being willing to take risks for something in which they believed. Encourage children to state, in their own words, how these people showed a love of individualism.

Read and Respond

History Read aloud the section on John Gonzales. Tell children that he pursued his artistic talent of pottery making later in life so that he could work side by side with his father and take care of his ailing mother.

Q In what ways does John Gonzales show respect?

A He is very loyal to the people he serves and had dedicated his career to the memory of his parents.

Q How is John Gonzales a great citizen?

A He is committed to serving his people and preserving their way of life.

Civics and Government As children read about Stephanie Kwolek, help them find the word *invent* in *inventiveness* and discuss its meaning.

Q Why is *inventiveness* an important trait for a citizen?

A Americans are always facing new problems. Inventive people help find ways to solve problems for everyone.

Q How does protecting police officers help protect all citizens?

A Police protect everyone. When the police are protected, they are able to protect us better.

Visual Learning

Picture Invite children to examine the picture on page 71 and discuss how the work firefighters do helps everyone. Explain that *citizenship* means doing things for the good of others in a community. Remind children of the definition of *individualism*. Point out that ordinary citizens often also risk their lives to do their civic duty. Have children identify ordinary people who exemplify good citizenship and exhibit a love of individualism.

Respect

John Gonzales
born in 1955
Character Trait: Respect

John Gonzales is a Native American leader in New Mexico. He is the governor of his village, San Ildefonso Pueblo. He believes that everyone should be treated fairly and with respect.

Inventiveness

Stephanie Kwolek
born in 1923
Character Trait: Inventiveness

Stephanie Kwolek made an important new fabric. This material is light but stronger than steel. It is used in the special vests police officers wear. Her discovery has helped save many lives.

70

Citizenship

Firefighters
Character Trait: Citizenship

Some citizens have dangerous jobs. When firefighters are called to work, they do all they can to help people. They will even give up their own safety.

Many firefighters lost their lives when buildings in New York City were attacked on September 11, 2001.

LESSON 5
Review

❶ **Vocabulary** What are some ways people can be good **citizens**?

❷ What are some character traits of good citizens?

❸ Think about a good citizen you know. Tell the class about him or her.

71

Perform a Skit Organize children into small groups and assign each group a characteristic of a good citizen from the lesson: patriotism, responsibility, compassion, fairness, or inventiveness. Have children read about the person with that characteristic in the lesson. Then help children think of a story that would demonstrate the characteristic. Allow time for children to develop and perform a skit of their story.

ACTIVITY BOOK

Name _____ Date _____

Good Citizens in Action

Look at the pictures. Write a word from the box below the picture that shows its meaning.

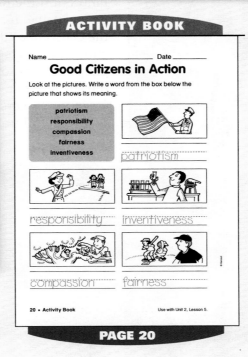

patriotism
responsibility
compassion
fairness
inventiveness

patriotism

responsibility   inventiveness

compassion   fairness

20 • Activity Book   Use with Unit 2, Lesson 5.

PAGE 20

---

3 Close

Summarize Key Content
- Good citizens help the whole community.
- Character traits that good citizens have include patriotism, responsibility, compassion, fairness, and inventiveness.
- Most people who are good citizens are not famous.

READING SOCIAL STUDIES

Graphic Organizer Revisit the chart begun in Motivate. Invite children to share new ideas they learned. Add these ideas to the chart.

Good Citizens	
Characteristics	**People**
responsibility	Thomas Jefferson and Sam Houston
fairness	Eleanor Roosevelt
inventiveness	Stephanie Kwolek
patriotism	Nathan Hale
compassion	Clara Barton

● **USE READING AND VOCABULARY TRANSPARENCY 2–6**   **2–6** TRANSPARENCY

Assess

Lesson 5 Review—Answers

❶ They can show their love for their country, take responsibility, be fair, and help people.

❷ Children should name some of the character traits from this lesson.

❸ **Performance Assessment Guidelines** Children should be able to explain why that person is a good citizen.

Extension Activities For Home and School

Family Citizen Search

Tell children to talk to family members about current or past relatives who show or have shown good citizenship. Make sure children understand that the relative does not need to be famous or heroic. Family good citizens can be immigrants who are studying to become citizens, soldiers, volunteer workers, or anyone else who shows love of country or helps the community in any way. Have children find out all they can about the relative. Then tell children to use the information to make a speech about being a good citizen, taking the role of the relative they studied. Tell children they may bring in pictures, use props, or wear costumes if they wish.
(AUDITORY/VISUAL/KINESTHETIC)

Learn About the Red Cross

Find out if the Red Cross in your area has speakers available. If so, invite a volunteer to speak to the class about the founding of the Red Cross and about ways the Red Cross continues to help people in this country and around the world. Ask the speaker to tell what characteristics they look for in volunteers and whether there are opportunities for children to help the Red Cross.
(AUDITORY)

Rights and Responsibilities

OBJECTIVES

- Identify some of the rights people have.
- Explore some of the responsibilities that accompany rights.
- Predict what might happen if you did not act responsibly.

 Prior Knowledge pp. 41, 73, 76

RESOURCES

Pupil Book/Unit Big Book, pp. 72–73

Word Cards V17–V18

Activity Book, p. 21

Activity Pattern P4

⊛**Reading and Vocabulary Transparency 2–7**

⌧**Internet Resources**

READING SOCIAL STUDIES

Make a Prediction Read aloud the lesson title. Then have children look at the pictures and read the review questions. Ask children to predict what they think they will learn in the lesson. Write their predictions and save them for use during Close.

Our Prediction	What the Lesson Says
People have responsibilities, such as walking their dogs.	

●USE READING AND VOCABULARY TRANSPARENCY 2–7

2–7
TRANSPARENCY

Vocabulary

right p. 72   **responsibility** p. 73

 ### When Minutes Count

Have children skim the lesson to find the meanings of the lesson vocabulary words.

Quick Summary

In this lesson, children learn that citizens of the United States have rights, things they have the freedom to do. They also learn that by having rights citizens also have responsibilities, things they should do.

1 Motivate

Set the Purpose

Big Idea Before starting the lesson, read the Big Idea statement aloud. Tell children to think about the things they like to do and the responsibilities that go with these activities as they read and discuss the lesson.

Access Prior Knowledge

Help children think of things we are free to do in this country such as tell people what we think and go to religious services. Explain that these things are also called our rights.

2 Teach

Visual Learning

Pictures Ask children to tell what is taking place in the picture on page 72. The picture shows the right of free speech. Tell children that many people who moved to this country in the early days came so they could enjoy freedoms that they did not have in their own countries. People still move to the United States for these reasons. Discuss some other rights citizens have in the United States, such as the right to privacy, the right to vote, and the right to a fair trial.

Q What are some ways you use your rights?

A Children may say they go to church, they keep private some personal belongings, they buy what they want, or they read what they want.

Q What rights are most important to you? Why?

A Children should give reasons for their choices.

Read and Respond

Culture and Society Discuss with children that citizens may enjoy their rights and they should not violate the rights of others, such as the right to privacy. Point out the importance of respecting other people and their rights.

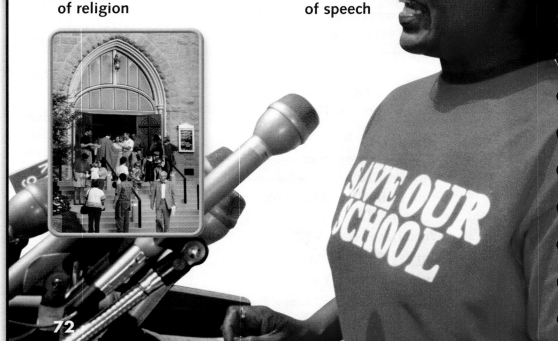

Lesson 6

Rights and Responsibilities

Big Idea
Citizens have rights and responsibilities.

Vocabulary
right
responsibility

Citizens of our country have special rights. A **right** is something people are free to do. They can choose their leaders. They can belong to groups. They can live where they want to live.

Freedom of religion

Freedom of speech

SAVE OUR SCHOOL

72

BACKGROUND

The Bill of Rights The first ten amendments of the U.S. Constitution are known as the Bill of Rights. They were added to the Constitution in 1791. The Bill of Rights protects our freedoms. Among the freedoms protected by the Bill of Rights are the freedoms of religion, speech, and the press, the right to assemble and to petition, and the right to a fair trial.

Personal Rights The right to privacy is a personal right guaranteed by the United States Constitution. This right is explained in the fourth Amendment. The right to privacy can be expected in our homes. Only under certain exceptions can a law officer search a person's home and property without a search warrant issued by a judge. There must be a valid reason for the search, and the warrant must describe the place to be searched.

EXTEND AND ENRICH

Role-Play Help children think of problems in which one person's rights might conflict with another's. For example: You have the right to play music in your apartment, and your neighbor has a right to a quiet place to sleep without being disturbed. Organize the class into small groups. Have each group choose a problem and act out a solution that respects both people's rights.

When people have rights, they also have responsibilities. A **responsibility** is something you should take care of or do. One responsibility is to obey laws. This keeps the community safe.

LESSON 6 Review

Focus Skill

1 Prior Knowledge What responsibilities do you have at school?

2 Vocabulary What is one **right** that Americans have?

3 Draw a picture that shows a responsibility you have at home.

73

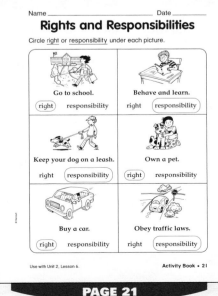

ACTIVITY BOOK

Name _____ Date _____

Rights and Responsibilities

Circle right or responsibility under each picture.

Go to school.
(right)   responsibility

Behave and learn.
right   (responsibility)

Keep your dog on a leash.
right   (responsibility)

Own a pet.
(right)   responsibility

Buy a car.
(right)   responsibility

Obey traffic laws.
right   (responsibility)

Use with Unit 2, Lesson 6.

Activity Book • 21

PAGE 21

Visual Learning

Pictures Have children describe the activities in the pictures on page 73. Explain that the bottom picture shows a responsibility that comes from a right. People have the right to keep pets, but they have the responsibility to clean up after them.

3 Close

Summarize Key Content

• United States citizens have rights.
• United States citizens have responsibilities.

READING SOCIAL STUDIES

Make a Prediction Reread the predictions children made in Motivate. Ask children to summarize the lesson and to tell whether their predictions were correct.

Our Prediction	What the Lesson Says
People have responsibilities, such as walking their dogs.	Citizens have rights, or things they are free to do. Citizens have responsibilities, or things they should do.

● USE READING AND VOCABULARY TRANSPARENCY 2–7

2–7 TRANSPARENCY

Assess

Lesson 6 Review—Answers

1 Prior Knowledge
Focus Skill Children may mention responsibilities such as following class rules.

2 Children may mention the right to religious freedom or the right to say what they like.

3 **Performance Assessment Guidelines** Children's pictures should show them engaged in a task for which they are responsible at home.

Extension Activities For Home and School

Let Freedom Ring

Materials: Activity Pattern P4 (bell template), construction paper, scissors

Remind children of the line *Let freedom ring* in the song "America" on pages 44–45. Tell children that the songwriter is comparing our enjoyment of our rights to the sound of ringing bells. Suggest that children ask family members at home what freedoms they enjoy most and take notes about their answers. When children bring back their notes, have them trace and cut out bells and write the favorite freedoms of their family members on the bells. Have children read aloud the rights they wrote about, before attaching their bells to a bulletin board with the title *Let Freedom Ring*. **(AUDITORY/TACTILE)**

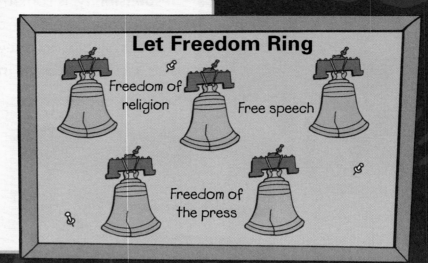

What a Country!

Materials: drawing paper, pencils

Review the responsibilities that citizens have and how responsible citizens help their community and country. List on the board the responsibilities children name. Then ask children to imagine what would happen if citizens did not act responsibly. Give the example that if all citizens tossed their trash onto the street, soon the whole country would be covered with litter. Have children choose a responsibility and draw a picture that shows the consequences that would happen if citizens did not take on the responsibility. Encourage them to write captions for their drawings, and display them in the classroom or the hallway. **(TACTILE)**

Be a responsible citizen!
Don't Litter

Do You Have the Right?

Remind children that even though they have many rights, they must use those rights responsibly so they do not violate the rights of others. Organize the class into groups of three. Have each group think of a situation in which one citizen does not use their rights responsibly. Give this example.

The kids on Elm Street like to play baseball. They play in Julio's backyard. But Mrs. Jackson's kitchen window looks out on Julio's yard. Her window has been broken three times by the baseball players. Once her cat was almost hit by a ball.

Have the group choose two group members to play the roles of the citizens involved and one child to take the role of a judge. Have them practice a skit in which both citizens tell their side of the story and the judge helps them come up with a solution. Have children perform their skits for the class. **(KINESTHETIC)**

How Communities Honor Their Citizens

OBJECTIVES

- Identify and describe ways that communities honor people who have made a difference.
- Identify historical figures who have influenced the community, state, and nation.
- Explain how selected customs and symbols reflect an American love of individualism, inventiveness, and freedom.
- Obtain information about a topic using a variety of visual sources, such as pictures, television, and computer images.

RESOURCES

Pupil Book/Unit Big Book,
pp. 74–75

Video

📖 **Internet Resources**

Summary

In this lesson, children see how a community honors people who have made a difference.

1 Motivate

Get Ready

Explain to children that they will visit a school, a park, and a mural to discover how a community—the city of Chicago—honors three people who each did something special during their lives. Ask children to think about streets, buildings, and other places in their community. Have any of them been named for people? Who? What? Why? Record their responses on a chart such as the following:

Celebrating People in Our Community

Who?	What?	Why?
George Washington	Washington Avenue	first U.S. President

Encourage children to explain how the custom of naming a school or a park after someone reflects an American love of individualism, inventiveness, and freedom.

MAKE IT RELEVANT

In Your Community Display a map of the community. As children name streets, buildings, parks, monuments, and statues that celebrate people who have done something special, mark them on the map. Then use the map to help plan a route that the class can take to tour some of the different places they identified.

2 Teach

What to See

Invite children to look at the picture and tell where the children are going. Point out that they are going to school. Then read aloud the text as children look at the picture of Gwendolyn Brooks. Explain that by the time she was 13 years old, Brooks had published one of her poems in a well-known children's magazine. Emphasize that Gwendolyn Brooks went on to win the Pulitzer Prize for poetry and that her many works celebrate black culture. Tell children that she lived in Chicago her entire life, from 1917 to 2000.

Display a map of the United States, and help children locate Chicago, Illinois. Then have children read about Daniel Burnham, another Chicago resident, and look at a mural panel that honors his work. Explain that Daniel Burnham developed a plan for Chicago during the early 1900s. He wanted to protect the waterfront from industrial development and keep it for public use, create more parks and playgrounds, and build museums and monuments along the lakeshore.

Show milk, juice, or other food containers that indicate that the contents have been pasteurized. Then have children read about French scientist Louis Pasteur and the Chicago park that was named for him. Tell them that Pasteur proved that germs cause diseases. Explain that a pasteurized food is one that has been heated to the right temperature for the right amount of time to kill germs that cause it to spoil and cause disease in people.

Have children summarize the contributions made to the community, state, and nation by Gwendolyn Brooks, Daniel Burnham, and Louis Pasteur. Then have children identify how these people exhibited a love of individualism, inventiveness, or freedom, and how the school, mural, and park named for them can be symbols for the same.

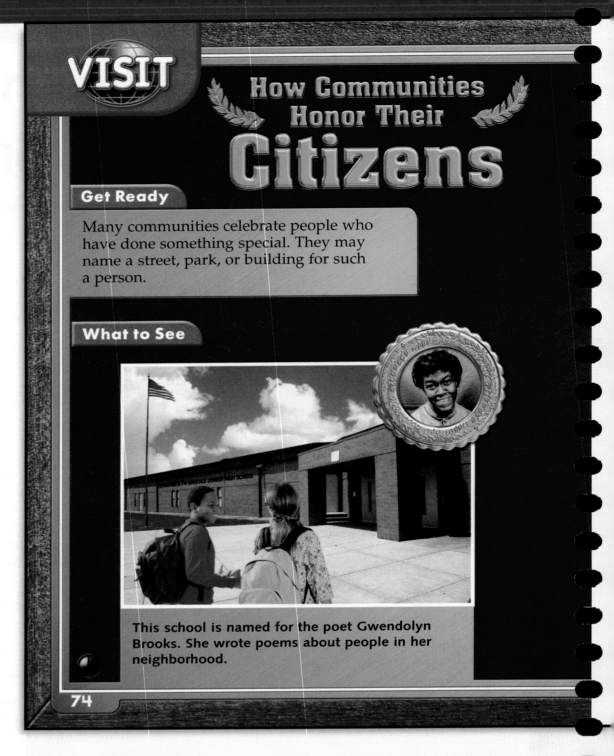

VISIT

How Communities Honor Their Citizens

Get Ready

Many communities celebrate people who have done something special. They may name a street, park, or building for such a person.

What to See

This school is named for the poet Gwendolyn Brooks. She wrote poems about people in her neighborhood.

74

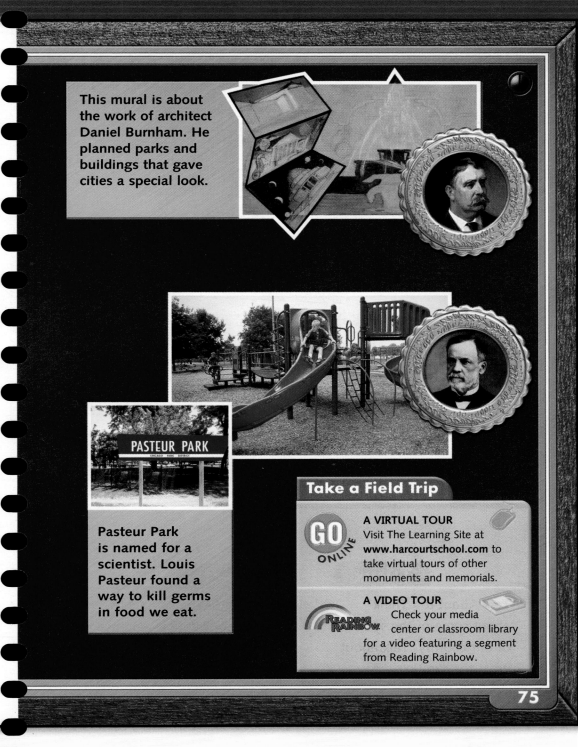

This mural is about the work of architect Daniel Burnham. He planned parks and buildings that gave cities a special look.

Pasteur Park is named for a scientist. Louis Pasteur found a way to kill germs in food we eat.

Take a Field Trip

GO ONLINE **A VIRTUAL TOUR** Visit The Learning Site at **www.harcourtschool.com** to take virtual tours of other monuments and memorials.

READING RAINBOW **A VIDEO TOUR** Check your media center or classroom library for a video featuring a segment from Reading Rainbow.

75

Invite children to write several sentences that tell about the three people in this lesson and how Chicago celebrates or honors them. Next, have children rewrite each sentence, omitting an important word or name. Then have children exchange sentences with a partner, read each other's work, and fill in the missing word or name.

Take a Field Trip

A Virtual Tour Depending on the availability of computers, have children work individually, in pairs, or in small groups to view the virtual tour. Suggest they research other monuments and memorials. Children should use what they learn on their virtual tours as background information for the unit project.

GO ONLINE **INTERNET RESOURCES**

THE LEARNING SITE Visit The Learning Site at **www.harcourtschool.com** to take virtual tours of other monuments and memorials.

A Video Field Trip Explain to children that as they watch the Reading Rainbow video, they should note three or four facts they learned about Louis Armstrong and about making a mural. After children watch the video, tell them to write questions about what they learned, exchange questions with a partner, and then answer each other's questions. You may want to show the video a second time before you have children answer the questions.

VIDEO

Use the Reading Rainbow TAKE A FIELD TRIP videotape about the construction of a mural that celebrates Louis Armstrong.

EXTEND AND ENRICH

Create a Mural Invite children to create a mural about a person they admire. Have children brainstorm a list of people they might like to include. Then have children form small groups. Each group should choose a different person and plan and create a panel for the mural. Provide each group with a large sheet of paper and art materials to create a panel. Then arrange the completed panels on a classroom wall. Ask each group to tell the name of the person they chose and why they admire that person.

INTEGRATE LANGUAGE ARTS

Write a Description Ask children to think about the people they listed on their chart at the beginning of the lesson and the three people they read about in this lesson. What qualities do children think these people share? Why do children think that communities should honor these people? Have children write a general description of the kind of person they would want their community to celebrate.

Unit 2 Review and Test Preparation

PAGES 76–80

 Prior Knowledge

Children's charts should have entries in all three columns. Entries in the last column should include ideas from the reading and from class discussions and activities, such as *Everyone in a community must follow laws.* Children should be able to tell which questions from the second column were answered as they completed the unit.

ACTIVITY BOOK

Name _____ Date _____

Good Citizens

Finish the chart to show what you have learned about being a good citizen.

K-W-L Chart		
What I Know	**What I Want to Know**	**What I Learned**
We have laws.	Does everyone have to follow laws?	Everyone in a community must follow laws.
We have a President.	Who is our President?	Children should write the name of the current President.
The Liberty Bell is an American symbol.	Why is the Liberty Bell an important symbol?	The Liberty Bell is a symbol of America's freedom.

22 • Activity Book   Use with Unit 2.

PAGE 22

Think & Write

Children should discuss at least three United States symbols that were mentioned in the unit, such as the flag, an eagle, and the White House. They should write a complete sentence that tells why the symbol was chosen and what it represents.

TRANSPARENCY

This graphic organizer appears on READING AND VOCABULARY TRANSPARENCY 2–8.

Unit

2 Review and Test Preparation

 Prior Knowledge

Finish the chart. Show what you learned about being a good citizen.

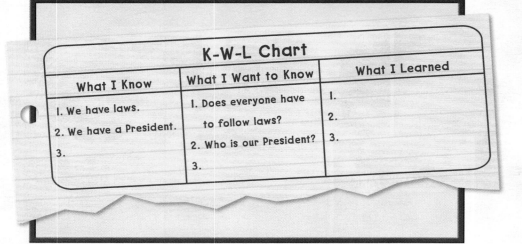

K-W-L Chart		
What I Know	**What I Want to Know**	**What I Learned**
1. We have laws.	1. Does everyone have to follow laws?	1.
2. We have a President.	2. Who is our President?	2.
3.	3.	3.

THINK & WRITE

Talk About It   Think about some of the symbols of our country. Talk about what the symbols mean.

Write a Sentence   Choose a symbol. Write a sentence telling why it is a good symbol for our country.

76

TEST PREPARATION

Review these tips with children.

■ Read the directions before reading the questions.

■ Read each question twice, focusing the second time on all the possible answers.

■ Take the time to think about all the possible answers before deciding on an answer.

■ Move past questions that are giving you trouble, and answer the ones you know. Then return to concentrate on the difficult items.

Use Vocabulary

Write the word that goes with each picture.

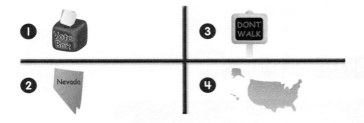

law
(p. 46)
country
(p. 52)
state
(p. 52)
citizen
(p. 68)

Recall Facts

5 What is a law?

6 Name leaders in your community and state.

7 How are a country and a state different?

8 Who was the first President of the United States?

9 Which of these is the home of the President of the United States?
- **A** Capitol building
- **B** Washington Monument
- **C** Alamo
- **D** White House

10 Which of these tells about nonfiction books?
- **F** tell no facts
- **G** have no pictures
- **H** have real information
- **J** have made-up stories

77

Use Vocabulary

1 citizen

2 state

3 law

4 country

Recall Facts

5 A law is a rule that people in a community must follow.

6 Children may name a local government official or another leader, such as their principal or coach.

7 A country is an area of land with its own people and laws. A state is a part of a country.

8 George Washington

9 D—White House

10 H—have real information

Think Critically

11 Children may say that leaders help citizens solve problems, run city services, and see that laws are obeyed.

12 Children may say that good citizens vote, obey laws and follow rules, get along together, and work together to make the community better.

Apply Chart and Graph Skills

13 They are voting to decide where to go on a class field trip.

14 The choices are the museum, the zoo, and the park.

15 The museum has four votes.

16 The zoo has the most votes.

Think Critically

11 How do leaders help citizens?

12 What are some things that good citizens do?

Apply Chart and Graph Skills

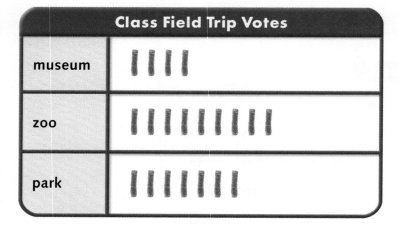

13 What are the children in Mrs. Johnson's class voting about?

14 What are the choices?

15 How many votes does the museum have?

16 Which choice has the most votes?

78

United States

17 Find New Mexico. Name the states that share borders with New Mexico.

18 What countries share borders with the United States?

19 Which state is closer to Canada, Oregon or Mississippi?

20 Which state shares a border with Nebraska, Iowa or Louisiana?

79

Apply Map and Globe Skills

17 Arizona, Colorado, Oklahoma, Texas

18 Canada, Mexico

19 Oregon

20 Iowa

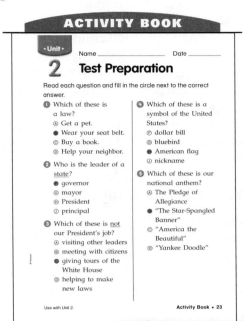

ACTIVITY BOOK

• Unit •

Name _____ Date _____

2 Test Preparation

Read each question and fill in the circle next to the correct answer.

1 Which of these is a law?
ⓐ Get a pet.
● Wear your seat belt.
ⓒ Buy a book.
ⓓ Help your neighbor.

2 Who is the leader of a state?
● governor
ⓖ mayor
ⓗ President
ⓘ principal

3 Which of these is not our President's job?
ⓐ visiting other leaders
ⓑ meeting with citizens
● giving tours of the White House
ⓓ helping to make new laws

4 Which of these is a symbol of the United States?
ⓕ dollar bill
ⓖ bluebird
● American flag
ⓘ nickname

5 Which of these is our national anthem?
ⓐ The Pledge of Allegiance
● "The Star-Spangled Banner"
ⓒ "America the Beautiful"
ⓓ "Yankee Doodle"

Use with Unit 2.   Activity Book • 23

PAGE 23

ASSESSMENT

Use the UNIT 2 TEST on pages 5–8 of the Assessment Program.

Unit Activities

Organize the class into small groups. Suggest that each group appoint one child to act as recorder. Have the other group members begin by looking through the unit to find ideas for symbols of good citizenship and of the United States. Tell children to work together to make a list of symbols to use on their mobiles. Then have the group assign several symbols for each group member to draw or cut out and paste on cards. Remind groups to also assign one member to make a title card for their mobile.

Where to Get Information

Encourage children to use a wide variety of reference sources, including encyclopedias, library books, travel brochures, social studies books, picture atlases, magazines, and the Internet.

Ways to Share

Distribute hangers and yarn. Have children cut the yarn into different lengths. Help group members punch holes in the cards, tie one end of a length of yarn to each card, and tie the other end on the hanger to assemble their mobiles. Have children tape or tie the title card on the top of the mobile. Before hanging the mobiles, invite a volunteer from each group to explain the symbols the group chose. Hang the mobiles at a level that allows children to examine them during their free time.

 Performance Assessment Guidelines Ask children to explain their reasons for choosing each symbol. Listen to find out whether their answers demonstrate an understanding of what it means to be a good citizen.

Visit Your Library

Encourage independent reading with these books or others of your choice after children have completed their study of good citizenship. Additional resources are listed in the Multimedia Resources on pages 41J–41K of this Teacher's Edition.

Unit Activities

Complete the Unit Project Work with your group to finish the unit project. Decide how you will show what good citizens do and what is special about our country.

 Visit The Learning Site at **www.harcourtschool.com** for additional activities.

Choose a Leader

Draw one of these leaders. Write a sentence telling why he or she is a good leader. Add your leader to the mobile.
- teacher
- principal
- coach

American Symbols

Draw or find pictures of American symbols. You can also use your state's symbols. Add the symbols to the mobile.

Visit Your Library

 The Inside-Outside Book of Washington, D.C. by Roxie Munro. Take a look at some of the important buildings in Washington, D.C.

 If I Were President by Catherine Stier. Read about what some children would do if they were President of the United States.

 The Flag We Love by Pam Muñoz Ryan. Find out facts about the flag of the United States.

80

Easy *The Inside-Outside Book of Washington, D.C.* by Roxie Munro. SeaStar Books, 2001. This book illustrates some of the historical and cultural attractions that visitors to Washington, D.C., would see.

Average *If I Were President* by Catherine Stier. Albert Whitman & Co., 1999. Reading about what children would do if they were President may inspire Presidential dreams in your own students.

Challenging *The Flag We Love* by Pam Muñoz Ryan. Charlesbridge, 2000. In this celebration of the American flag, each spread has beautiful illustrations and several facts about the flag and how it is used.

The Land Around Us

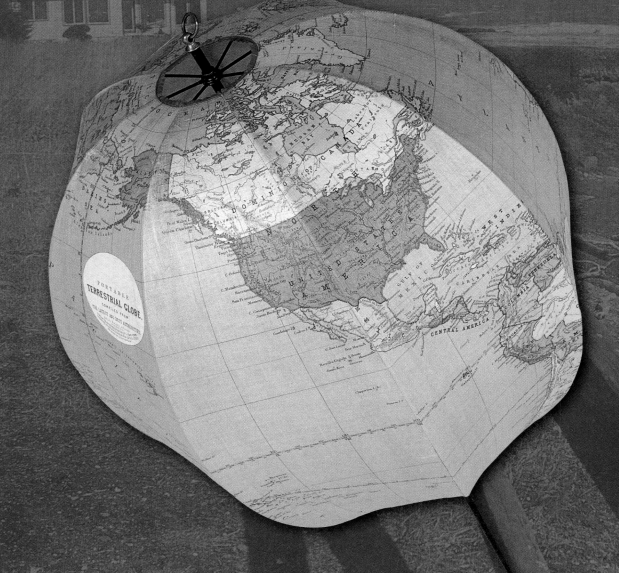

A folding
pop-up globe

Unit 3 Planning Chart The Land Around Us

Unit 3 focuses on the Earth. Children will explore the concept of neighborhood and the people who live in a community, as well as physical characteristics of Earth, such as landforms and bodies of water. They will explore how to use maps and globes to find places on Earth. In addition, children will explore some of Earth's resources, how people depend on them, and how we can help save them.

LESSON	PACING	OBJECTIVES	VOCABULARY
Introduce the Unit pp. 81R–81 **Preview the Vocabulary** pp. 82–83A **Start with a Story** pp. 84A–93A	4 Days	■ Use a visual to predict content. ■ Interpret a quotation. ■ Use a graphic organizer to prepare for the unit. ■ Use visuals to determine word meanings. ■ Use words and visuals to predict the content of the unit. ■ Obtain information about a topic using a variety of visual sources such as pictures and literature. ■ Locate places of significance on maps such as your local community, your state, and the United States. ■ Know own address and the areas it designates.	**address** **Word Work,** pp. 83A, 84, 88
A Neighborhood pp. 94A–95A	2 Days	■ Define a neighborhood as a place where people interact as they live, work, and play. ■ Compare a map to an aerial view.	**neighborhood**
MAP AND GLOBE SKILLS **Use a Map Key** pp. 96A–97A	1 Day	■ Create and use simple maps to identify the location of places in the community and beyond. ■ Use a map key to identify places on a map. ■ Access information from a map using colors and symbols in a map key.	**map key**
2 Land and Water pp. 98A–101A	3 Days	■ Identify and describe the physical characteristics of places such as landforms. ■ Identify and describe the physical characteristics of places such as bodies of water.	**valley** **mountain** **lake** **hill** **plain** **island** **river** **Word Work,** p. 98

Time Management

READING	INTEGRATE LEARNING	REACH ALL LEARNERS	RESOURCES
Categorize, p. 81 **Reading Social Studies:** **Make a Prediction,** pp. 82, 84A, 89, 93	**Theme Time,** p. 81I Music **Sing About Our Land,** p. 81R Language Arts **Write Riddles,** p. 83 **Speaking and Listening,** p. 84 **Informative Writing,** p. 86 **Journal Entry,** p. 91 Health **Nutrition,** p. 85 Mathematics **Number Order,** p. 86 **Counting,** p. 89 **Solids,** p. 91 World Languages **Spanish,** p. 88	**English as a Second Language,** pp. 81N, 81, 82, 85, 90 **Advanced Learners,** pp. 81N, 90 **Below-Level Learners,** p. 81N **Tactile Learners,** p. 89 **Extension Activities For Home and School,** p. 93A	**Pupil Book/Unit Big Book,** pp. 81–93 **Audiotext** **Word Cards V19–V20** **Reading and Vocabulary Transparency 3–1** Internet Resources
Reading Social Studies: **Personal Response,** pp. 94A, 95		**Kinesthetic Learners,** p. 94 **Extend and Enrich,** p. 94 **Reteach the Lesson,** p. 95 **Extension Activities For Home and School,** p. 95A	**Pupil Book/Unit Big Book,** pp. 94–95 **Word Cards V19–V20** **Reading and Vocabulary Transparency 3–2** **Activity Book,** p. 24 Internet Resources
		Below-Level Learners, p. 96A **Extend and Enrich,** p. 96 **Reteach the Skill,** p. 97 **Extension Activities For Home and School,** p. 97A	**Pupil Book/Unit Big Book,** pp. 96–97 **Word Cards V19–V20** **Skill Transparency 3–1** **Activity Book,** p. 25 **GeoSkills CD-ROM** Internet Resources
Reading Social Studies: **Graphic Organizer,** pp. 98A, 101 **Categorize,** p. 99		**Tactile Learners,** p. 98 **English as a Second Language,** p. 100 **Extend and Enrich,** p. 100 **Reteach the Lesson,** p. 101 **Extension Activities For Home and School,** p. 101A	**Pupil Book/Unit Big Book,** pp. 98–101 **Word Cards V19–V24** **Reading and Vocabulary Transparency 3–3** **Activity Book,** p. 26 **Activity Pattern P5** Internet Resources

Unit 3 Planning Guide

LESSON	PACING	OBJECTIVES	VOCABULARY
MAP AND GLOBE SKILLS **Find Land and Water on a Map** pp. 102A–103A	1 Day	■ Access information from a map using colors and symbols in a map key. ■ Create visual and written material including maps.	
3 Globes and Maps pp. 104A–105A	2 Days	■ Recognize the globe as a model of Earth. ■ Identify the continents and oceans of the world. ■ Locate places of significance on maps and globes.	**Earth** **globe** **continent** **ocean**
MAP AND GLOBE SKILLS **Find Directions on a Globe** pp. 106A–107A	1 Day	■ Locate places using the four cardinal directions. ■ Obtain information about a topic using a variety of visual sources such as maps. ■ Locate the North Pole and the South Pole.	**directions**
4 People and Resources pp. 108A–111A	3 Days	■ Identify examples of and uses for natural resources in the community, state, and nation. ■ Recognize how people depend on land and water. ■ Understand the importance of natural resources.	**resource** **farm** **forest**
READING SKILLS **Predict What Will Happen** pp. 112A–113A	1 Day	■ Use a decision-making process to identify a situation that requires a decision, gather information, and predict consequences. ■ Demonstrate the concept of scarcity.	**predict** **weather**

READING	INTEGRATE LEARNING	REACH ALL LEARNERS	RESOURCES
Reading Social Studies: **K-W-L Chart,** p. 102A	Reading **Solve Puzzles,** p. 102	**Extend and Enrich,** p. 102 **Reteach the Skill,** p. 103 **Extension Activities For Home and School,** p. 103A	**Pupil Book/Unit Big Book,** pp. 102–103 ⬤ **Skill Transparency 3–2** **Activity Book,** p. 27 ◉ **GeoSkills CD-ROM** ▣ Internet Resources
Reading Social Studies: **Study Questions,** pp. 104A, 105	Mathematics **Compare Sizes,** p. 104	**Extend and Enrich,** p. 104 **Reteach the Lesson,** p. 105 **Extension Activities For Home and School,** p. 105A	**Pupil Book/Unit Big Book,** pp. 104–105 **Word Cards V23–V26** ⬤ **Reading and Vocabulary Transparency 3–4** **Activity Book,** p. 28 ▣ Internet Resources
Reading Social Studies: **Make a List,** p. 106A	Physical Education **Simon Says,** p. 106	**Advanced Learners,** p. 106 **Extend and Enrich,** p. 107 **Reteach the Skill,** p. 107 **Extension Activities For Home and School,** p. 107A	**Pupil Book/Unit Big Book,** pp. 106–107 **Word Cards V25–V26** ⬤ **Skill Transparency 3–3** **Activity Book,** p. 29 ◉ **GeoSkills CD-ROM** ▣ Internet Resources
Reading Social Studies: **Graphic Organizer,** pp. 108A, 111	Science **What's in Soil?** p. 108 Art **Leaf and Bark Rubbings,** p. 109 Reading **Add to a Poem,** p. 109	**Tactile Learners,** p. 108 **Extend and Enrich,** p. 110 **Reteach the Lesson,** p. 111 **Extension Activities For Home and School,** p. 111A	**Pupil Book/Unit Big Book,** pp. 108–111 **Word Cards V25–V28** ⬤ **Reading and Vocabulary Transparency 3–5** **Activity Book,** p. 30 ▣ Internet Resources
		English as a Second Language, p. 112A **Below-Level Learners,** p. 112 **Extend and Enrich,** p. 113 **Reteach the Skill,** p. 113 **Extension Activities For Home and School,** p. 113A	**Pupil Book/Unit Big Book,** pp. 112–113 **Word Cards V27–V28** ⬤ **Skill Transparency 3–4** **Activity Book,** p. 31 ▣ Internet Resources

Unit 3 Planning Guide

LESSON	PACING	OBJECTIVES	VOCABULARY
5 Saving Our Resources pp. 114A–117A	3 Days	■ Recognize that we need to protect resources for the future. ■ Describe personal responsibility for protecting the environment.	**pollution** **litter** **recycle**
6 Houses and Homes pp. 118A–121A	3 Days	■ Identify and describe the physical characteristics of places such as landforms, bodies of water, natural resources, and weather. ■ Identify and describe the human characteristics of places such as types of houses. ■ Explain how the environment affects the types of homes people have.	**desert**
Visit A Butterfly Garden pp. 122A–123	1 Day	■ Recognize the importance of caring for our natural resources. ■ Sequence and categorize information. ■ Obtain information about a topic using a variety of visual sources, such as pictures, television, and computer images.	
Unit 3 Review and Test Preparation pp. 124–128	3 Days		

READING	INTEGRATE LEARNING	REACH ALL LEARNERS	RESOURCES
Reading Social Studies: **Study Questions,** pp. 114A, 117 (Focus Skill) **Categorize,** p. 116	Science **Acid Rain,** p. 114 Reading **Things To Do,** p. 114 Technology **Environmental Concerns,** p. 114	**Extend and Enrich,** p. 116 **Reteach the Lesson,** p. 117 **Extension Activities For Home and School,** p. 117A	**Pupil Book/Unit Big Book,** pp. 114–117 **Word Cards V29–V30** **Reading and Vocabulary Transparency 3–6** **Activity Book,** p. 32 **Activity Pattern P6** Internet Resources
Reading Social Studies: **Graphic Organizer,** pp. 118A, 121	Mathematics **Measurement,** p. 118 Reading **Making Comparisons,** p. 119	**Tactile Learners,** p. 119 **Extend and Enrich,** p. 120 **Reteach the Lesson,** p. 121 **Extension Activities For Home and School,** p. 121A	**Pupil Book/Unit Big Book,** pp. 118–121 **Word Cards V29–V30** **Reading and Vocabulary Transparency 3–7** **Activity Book,** p. 33 Internet Resources
		English as a Second Language, p. 122 **Advanced Learners,** p. 122 **Extend and Enrich,** p. 123	**Pupil Book/Unit Big Book,** pp. 122–123 **Take a Field Trip Video** Internet Resources
(Focus Skill) **Categorize,** p. 124			**Pupil Book/Unit Big Book,** pp. 124–128 **Activity Book,** pp. 34–35 **Reading and Vocabulary Transparency 3–8** **Assessment Program, Unit 3 Test,** pp. 9–12 Internet Resources

Unit 3 Skills Path

Unit 3 features the reading skills of categorizing and making predictions. It also highlights the social studies skills of using a map key, finding land and water on a map, and finding directions on a globe.

 FOCUS SKILLS

UNIT 3 READING SKILL

 CATEGORIZE

- INTRODUCE p. 81
- APPLY pp. 99, 116, 124

 READING SOCIAL STUDIES

- Make a Prediction, pp. 82, 84A, 89, 93
- Personal Response, pp. 94A, 95
- Graphic Organizer, pp. 98A, 101, 108A, 111, 118A, 121
- K-W-L Chart, p. 102A
- Study Questions, pp. 104A, 105, 114A, 117
- Make a List, p. 106A

 MAP AND GLOBE SKILLS

USE A MAP KEY

- INTRODUCE pp. 96A–97A
- APPLY p. 127

FIND LAND AND WATER ON A MAP

- INTRODUCE pp. 102A–103A
- APPLY pp. 126, 127

FIND DIRECTIONS ON A GLOBE

- INTRODUCE pp. 106A–107A
- APPLY p. 126

 READING SKILLS

PREDICT WHAT WILL HAPPEN

- INTRODUCE p. 112
- APPLY p. 113

Theme Time: Earth Talk

MATH CENTER

Save a Tree

Invite children to save a tree by recycling. Explain that a tree makes about one hundred pounds of paper. Each day, have children bring from home and gather from classrooms paper to be recycled. Have them bag the day's paper and weigh it on a bathroom scale. Have children use calculators to keep a running tally of the number of pounds brought in each day. When one hundred pounds have been collected, have a class celebration. Then challenge children to think of ways to reduce the amount of paper they use. List their suggestions on a class chart and display.

"Save Our Trees"

1. Use real plates instead of paper plates.
2. Recycle newspaper.
3. Use cloth napkins.
4. Save construction paper scraps for art projects.
5. Use cloth sacks to bag groceries.

SCIENCE CENTER

Water Filters

Provide clear plastic cups, colanders, coffee filters, wet sand, and clean gravel. Invite children to experiment with layering the materials in a colander to create a water filter. After they design a filter, have children "pollute" a cup of water by adding bits of trash and a few drops of vegetable oil. Have children draw a picture of their water before and after pouring it through their filter.

READING/LANGUAGE ARTS CENTER

Earth Verses

Post the poem below in the center. Have children think about the colors, plants, animals, and other things they like in nature. Have them work with a partner to replace the underlined words in the poem to make up their own verses about the Earth.

I'm Glad the Sky Is Painted Blue
I'm glad the <u>sky</u> is painted <u>blue</u>,
And the <u>earth</u> <u>is</u> painted green,
With such a lot of <u>nice fresh air</u>
All <u>sandwiched</u> in between.

Anonymous

I'm glad the moon is painted white,
And the trees are painted green,
With such a lot of puffy clouds
All floating in between.

BULLETIN BOARD: ECOLOGY

We Help the Earth

I help the Earth when I recycle paper.

I help the Earth when I don't waste water.

I help the Earth when I turn off lights.

I help the Earth when I pick up litter.

I help the Earth when I reuse things.

I help the Earth when I feed the birds.

I help the Earth when I plant trees.

Ask children to help you create a bulletin board telling how they take care of the air, water, plants, and other things Earth provides. Have each child draw a self-portrait of his or her face. If possible, provide mirrors for children to use. Then give each child a lined speech bubble and have them complete the following sentence frame: *I help the Earth when I _____.* Display the faces and speech bubbles on a bulletin board titled "We Help the Earth."

Multimedia Resources

The Multimedia Resources can be used in a variety of ways. They can supplement core instruction in the classroom or extend and enrich children's learning at home.

Independent Reading

Easy

Anholt, Laurence. **Summerhouse.** Dorling Kindersley, 1999. Ella's grandmother helps her get away from the winter snow and boredom by showing her how to escape to a tropical island paradise.

Benjamin, Cynthia. **Footprints in the Sand.** Scholastic, 1999. Pictures and easy-to-read text reveal the tracks of desert animals hurrying to their homes.

Costain, Meredith. **Clean Air.** Sundance, 2000. This non-fiction book gives a simple explanation of pollution and how to prevent it.

Glaser, Linda. **Compost! Growing Gardens from Your Garbage.** Millbrook, 1996. A little girl helps her family make a compost heap. Then she helps tend the pile until it is spring and time to spread the soil on the garden.

Ryan, Pam Muñoz. **Hello Ocean.** Talewinds, 2001. A young girl describes what she sees, hears, smells, and feels at the beach.

Average

Cuyler, Margery. **From Here to There.** Henry Holt, 1999. Maria describes where she lives in a special way—from her place in her house to her place in the universe.

Gibbons, Gail. **How a House Is Built.** Holiday House, 1996. Readers are introduced to the workers needed to build a house, from surveyor to plumber to electrician.

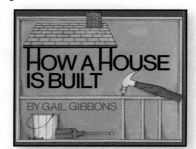

Maitland, Barbara. **Moo in the Morning.** Farrar, Straus & Giroux, 2000. A mother and her child take a trip to the country to escape the city noise. However, they discover that the country is full of different noises.

Marzollo, Jean. **I Am Water.** Scholastic, 1996. Bright cutout pictures and text describe the ways water is used.

Rockwell, Anne. **One Bean.** Walker, 1999. Readers discover what happens when a bean seed is soaked, planted, watered, and replanted.

Shulevitz, Uri. **Snow.** Farrar, Straus & Giroux, 1998. A boy and his dog wait and watch for snowfall. Beautiful illustrations show the transformation of a town as the snow gradually covers the landscape.

Spohn, Kate. **Turtle and Snake Go Camping.** Viking, 2000. Turtle and Snake pass one land feature after another until they reach their campsite but rush back through the same landscape when an owl's call frightens them.

Sweeney, Joan. **Me on the Map.** Dragonfly/Crown, 1998. A young girl explains maps beginning with her bedroom, then expands to her house, town, state, country, and finally the world.

Tews, Susan. **Lizard Sees the World.** Clarion, 1997. With the rhythm and sentiment of a traditional folk tale, this story tells about a lizard who goes off to see the world.

Venn, Cecilia. **On with the Show!** Millbrook Press, 1998. Four children try to plan a clean-up day for the park while they are baby-sitting a little sister.

Challenging

Atwell, Debby. **River.** Houghton Mifflin, 1999. After people pollute and destroy the life of a river habitat, they realize their mistake and clean up and reclaim the river.

Axelrod, Amy. **The News Hounds in the Great Balloon Race.** Simon & Schuster, 2000. Three "news dogs" cover a hot-air balloon race. The book includes maps and geography of Texas.

Geisert, Bonnie and Arthur. **Haystack.** Houghton Mifflin, 1995. The importance of the haystack to the people and animals that live on a farm is chronicled through the different seasons.

Hamilton, Kersten. **This Is the Ocean.** Caroline House/Boyds Mills Press, 2001. This rhyming text takes readers on a journey from the ocean to the clouds, mountains, streams, and rivers. After completing the cycle, the water returns to the ocean.

Miller, Debbie. **_River of Life._**
Clarion, 2000. This nonfiction book shows the importance of the river to the living things in and near it.

Van Allsburg, Chris. **_Just a Dream._** Houghton Mifflin, 1990. Walter starts to understand how important it is to care for the Earth after he has a dream about the future.

Audiocassettes

Earth Day.
Live Oak Media. This cassette explains why and how people began celebrating Earth Day.

Environmental Songs for Kids. Smithsonian Folkways. Coco Kallis sings songs to encourage children to think about and preserve the environment.

Hopping Around from Place to Place. Educational Activities. Ella Jenkins sings with the Chicago Children's Choir about states, countries, and cultures.

This Pretty Planet. Sony, 2000. Tom Chapin sings songs encouraging children to recycle and to take care of the planet.

Computer Software

Jack's Attic.
Grolier. Mac/Windows. Children enter Jack's attic to find it leads to the desert, the rain forest, and wild landscapes. Activities develop thinking skills in geography, science and math.

Kid Pix Activity Kit Volume 5. The Learning Company. Mac/Windows. In addition to the Kid Pix drawing tools and slide show, the module includes activities related to the environment.

Maps and Globes. Grolier. Children explore maps and how to use them. They also practice map skills using four interactive geography games.

Neighborhood Map Machine. Tom Snyder Productions. Mac/Windows. Children learn about direction, scale, and map symbols as they create maps of real or imaginary communities.

Videos and DVDs

Earth: A First Look.
Library Video, 2000. Children learn about Earth's landforms, air, water, and core.

Garbage Day! Library Video, 1994. Viewers take an outing to learn about landfills and recycling.

Maps and Landmarks. BFA. This video helps children learn how to use landmarks in finding their way or giving directions around the neighborhood. The film also shows how landmarks are shown on maps.

Additional books are recommended at point of use throughout the unit.
Note that information, while correct at time of publication, is subject to change.

ISBNs and other publisher information can be found at
www.harcourtschool.com

The Learning Site: Social Studies Center

The Learning Site at www.harcourtschool.com offers a special Social Studies Center. The center provides a wide variety of activities, Internet links, and online references.

Here are just some of the HARCOURT Internet resources you'll find!

Multimedia Biographies
www.harcourtschool.com

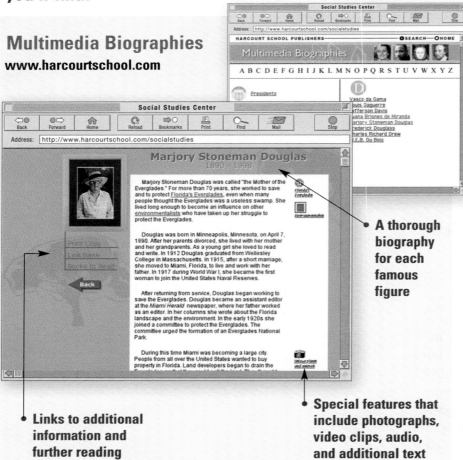

A thorough biography for each famous figure

• **Links to additional information and further reading**

Special features that include photographs, video clips, audio, and additional text

INTERNET RESOURCES

Find all this at
The Learning Site at
www.harcourtschool.com

- Activities and Games
- Content Updates
- Current Events
- Free and Inexpensive Materials
- Multimedia Biographies
- Online Atlas
- Primary Sources
- Video Updates
- Virtual Tours
- Your State

and more!

Free and Inexpensive Materials
- Addresses to write for free and inexpensive products
- Links to unit-related materials
- Internet maps
- Internet references

www.harcourtschool.com

Primary Sources
- Artwork
- Clothing
- Diaries
- Government Documents
- Historical Documents
- Maps
- Tools

and more!

www.harcourtschool.com

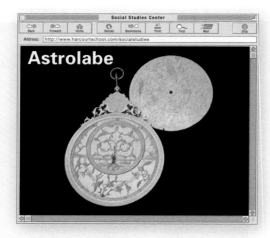

Virtual Tours
- Capitols and Government Buildings
- Cities
- Countries
- Historical Sites
- Museums
- Parks and Scenic Areas

and more!

www.harcourtschool.com

Integrate Learning Across the Curriculum

Use these topics to help you integrate social studies into your daily planning. See the page numbers indicated for more information about each topic.

Art

Leaf and Bark Rubbings, p. 109

Science

Water Filters, p. 81I
What's in Soil?, p. 108
Acid Rain, p. 114

Health

Nutrition, p. 85

Languages

Spanish, p. 88

Language Arts

Write Riddles, p. 83
Speaking and Listening, p. 84
Informative Writing, p. 86
Journal Entry, p. 91

Reading/Literature

"I'm Glad the Sky Is Painted Blue," p. 81I
From Here to There, p. 84
A Zoo Map, p. 93
National Parks, p. 93
The Sahara Desert, p. 93
The News Hounds in the Great Balloon Race: A Geography Adventure, p. 102
"What Do We Plant?" p. 109
Just a Dream, p. 114
Houses and Homes, p. 119
Compost! Growing Gardens from Your Garbage, p. 128
Me on the Map, p. 128
Haystack, p. 128

Social Studies

Computer/Technology

Go Online, pp. 93, 123
GeoSkills CD-ROM, pp. 97, 103, 107
Environmental Concerns, p. 114
Take a Field Trip Video, p. 123

Physical Education

Simon Says, p. 106

Mathematics

Save a Tree, p. 81I
Number Order, p. 86
Counting, p. 89
Solids, p. 91
Compare Sizes, p. 104
Measurement, p. 118

Music

"America the Beautiful," p. 81R

Reach All Learners

Use these activities to help individualize your instruction. Each activity has been developed to address a different level or type of learner.

English as a Second Language

Materials
- a U.S. map

TELL A TRAVEL STORY Use the map to tell a travel story.

- Introduce a story character, and create a story about a trip around the United States that the character takes.

- As you tell the story, point to the places that the character visits on the map.

- Have children complete story sentences. For example, use sentences such as *Sam started his trip in a state called* _____. *Next Sam crossed the* _____. *He spent the day on a small* _____.

Advanced Learners

Materials
- sample maps
- drawing paper
- crayons or markers

MAKE A TREASURE MAP Have children pretend they have buried treasure on an imaginary island.

- Ask children to make a map of the island, showing where the treasure is buried.

- Tell them to make up symbols and names for landforms and bodies of water on and around the island.

- Provide time for children to share and explain their maps.

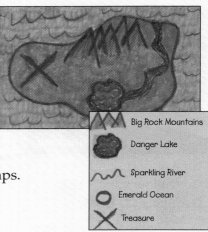

Below-Level Learners

Materials
- notecards
- crayons

PLAY A MATCHING GAME Have partners play a resource-to-product matching game.

- Have partners work together to make a pair of cards, one card showing a resource from their state and the other showing a product made from it.

- Put the group's cards in a hat and have each child reach in and take one.

- Ask children who take a product to find and stand by someone who has the matching resource.

- Have each pair explain why they belong together.

Assessment Options

The assessment program gives all learners many opportunities to show what they know and can do. It also provides ongoing information about each child's understanding of social studies.

Formal Assessment

- **LESSON REVIEWS:** pp. 95, 101, 105, 111, 117, 121
- **UNIT REVIEWS AND TEST PREPARATION,** pp. 124–127
- **UNIT ASSESSMENT**
  Standard Test,
      Assessment Program, pp. 9–11
  Individual Performance Task,
      Assessment Program, p. 12

Student Self-Evaluation

- **GEOGRAPHY THEME QUESTIONS**
  within lessons of Pupil Book
- **INDIVIDUAL END-OF-PROJECT CHECKLIST**
  Assessment Program, p. viii
- **GROUP END-OF-PROJECT CHECKLIST**
  Assessment Program, p. ix
- **INDIVIDUAL END-OF-UNIT CHECKLIST**
  Assessment Program, p. x

Informal Assessment

- **THINK ABOUT IT**, p. 93
- **SOCIAL STUDIES SKILLS CHECKLIST**
  Assessment Program, p. vi–vii

- **SKILLS**
  Practice the Skill, pp. 96, 102, 107, 113
  Apply What You Learned, pp. 97, 103, 107, 113

Performance Assessment

- **PERFORMANCE ACTIVITY IN LESSON REVIEWS**
- **UNIT ACTIVITIES,** p. 128
- **COMPLETE THE UNIT PROJECT,** p. 128
- **INDIVIDUAL PERFORMANCE TASK ASSESSMENT PROGRAM,** p. 12

Portfolio Assessment

STUDENT SELECTED ITEMS MAY INCLUDE:
- **THINK AND WRITE,** p. 124
- **UNIT ACTIVITIES,** p. 128
- **COMPLETE THE UNIT PROJECT,** p. 128

TEACHER SELECTED ITEMS MAY INCLUDE:
- **UNIT ASSESSMENT**
  Assessment Program, pp. 9–12
- **PORTFOLIO SUMMARY**
  Assessment Program, p. xv
- **GROUP END-OF-PROJECT CHECKLIST**
  Assessment Program, p. ix
- **INDIVIDUAL END-OF-UNIT CHECKLIST**
  Assessment Program, p. x

Unit 3 Test

· Unit ·

Name _____ Date _____

3 Test

Vocabulary (7 points each)

Circle the word that belongs on each line.

1. A _____ has houses and streets.
   (neighborhood)   farm

2. Fish and whales live in the _____.
   sky   (ocean)

3. The _____ is windy and rainy today.
   sun   (weather)

4. Gas is a natural _____.
   (resource)   tree

GAS

(continued)

Unit 3 Test   Assessment Program ▪ 9

Name _____ Date _____

Main Ideas (7 points each)

5. Which of these is a continent?
   ● A North America   ○ C North Carolina
   ○ B Washington, D.C.   ○ D United States

6. Which of these is not a natural resource?
   ○ F wood   ● H video
   ○ G soil   ○ J water

7. Tell how this child could use resources more wisely.
   _____
   - - - - - - - - - - Turn off water. - - - - - -

Draw a line from each sentence to the home it tells about.

8. Some families live close to the water.

9. There are many homes in this building.

10. People use wood to build their homes.

(continued)

10 ▪ Assessment Program   Unit 3 Test

NOTES

Name _____ Date _____

Skills (6 points each)

Use the map to answer the questions.

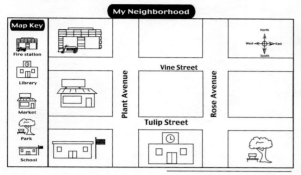

⑪ What is north of the market? _____ fire station

⑫ Which way is the park from the school? _____ east

⑬ Which building is closest to the park? _____ library

⑭ Draw a lake to the north of the park.
Students should draw a lake to the north of the park symbol on the map.

⑮ What is to the west of the library? _____ school

(continued)

Unit 3 Test   **Assessment Program ▪ 11**

Name _____ Date _____

Performance Task

Write the number of each place to show where it belongs on the map. Then color all land green and all water blue.

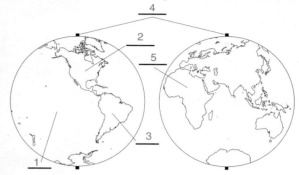

❶ Pacific Ocean
❷ North America
❸ South America
❹ North Pole
❺ Africa

Children should color all land areas green and all water areas blue.

12 ▪ **Assessment Program**   Unit 3 Test

RUBRICS FOR SCORING

SCORING RUBRIC The rubric below lists the criteria for evaluating the tasks above. It also describes different levels of success in meeting those criteria.

INDIVIDUAL PERFORMANCE TASK

Score **4**	Score **3**	Score **2**	Score **1**
• All places were correctly located and labeled. • All land and water areas were correctly identified and colored.	• Most places were correctly located and labeled. • Most land and water areas were correctly identified and colored.	• Some places were correctly located and labeled. • Some land and water areas were correctly identified and colored.	• No places were correctly located and labeled. • No land or water areas were correctly identified and colored.

Introduce the Unit

OBJECTIVES

- Use a visual to predict content.
- Interpret a quotation.
- Use a graphic organizer to prepare for the unit.

Access Prior Knowledge

Show children a world map. Explain that the blue areas show water and the other areas are land. The large blue areas are big bodies of water called oceans. The blue lines are rivers.

Q **What other kinds of water do you know about?**

A Children may mention lakes, ponds, streams, and creeks.

Explain that there are also different kinds of land.

Q **What kinds of land can you name?**

A Children may mention plains, mountains, deserts, and hills.

Then tell children that resources are things in nature, such as trees, that people use to make products.

Q **What are some other resources?**

A Children may mention oil, gas, water, soil, and coal.

Visual Learning

Have children look at the picture on pages 81R and 81. Tell them that the picture shows a house at Shelter Cove, California. Point out Shelter Cove on a map. Have children point to the land in the picture, and describe what the land is like there. Then ask a volunteer to point to the land around Shelter Cove on the map. Next have children point to the water in the picture and describe what the water looks like there. Then ask a volunteer to point to the same water on the map. Explain that the body of water is the Pacific Ocean.

INTEGRATE MUSIC

Sing About Our Land Write the words of "America the Beautiful" on chart paper and point to each word as you read it aloud. Have volunteers identify and underline words that name America's natural features. Call on volunteers to define each underlined word. Then sing the song with children.

O beautiful for spacious
  skies,
  For amber waves of
  grain,
For purple mountain majesties
  Above the fruited plain!

America, America!
  God shed His grace on thee;
And crown thy good with brother-
  hood
  From sea to shining sea.

Unit 3

The Land Around Us

"Enjoy the earth gently
Enjoy the earth gently
For if the earth is spoiled
It cannot be repaired
Enjoy the earth gently."

—Yoruba (African) song

⭐ Categorize

As you read this unit, do the following.

- Make a web to show what you learn about Earth.
- Group ideas under land, water, and natural resources.

Earth → Land, Water, Natural Resources

81

Analyze Primary Sources

Betts's Pop-up Globe Have children look at the artifact at the beginning of the unit. Explain that the globe is made of linen sewn over a frame that "pops" up, opening and closing the way an umbrella does. This allows the globe to be folded up when it is not in use. Tell children that the globe shows the same things other globes show, such as oceans, mountains, and rivers.

Quotation Read the quotation aloud. Tell children that the poem comes from the Yoruba people, who live in Nigeria and Benin in Africa. The Yoruba are agricultural people who care about the land. They are also known for producing great art.

Q What are some ways we can "use the earth gently"?

A Children may mention actions such as reusing and recycling, keeping water free from pollution, not littering, setting aside land for parks, and planting trees.

⭐ Categorize

Explain to children that in this unit they will be reading and learning about Earth and its resources. Tell children that using a graphic organizer such as a web can help them organize and remember what they read by putting information into categories. As you continue through the unit, complete the web together with children by adding types of land, water, and resources.

- A blank graphic organizer appears on page 34 of the Activity Book.
- A complete graphic organizer can be found on page 124 of this Teacher's Edition.

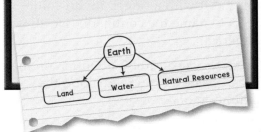

Earth → Land, Water, Natural Resources

Preview the Vocabulary

PAGES 82–83

Preview the Vocabulary

> **OBJECTIVES**
> - Use visuals to determine word meanings.
> - Use words and visuals to predict the content of the unit.

Access Prior Knowledge

Ask children to describe the area where they live and go to school. Then invite children to examine the pictures on pages 82–83 and tell how they think the pictures relate to "the land around us."

Make Connections

Link Pictures and Words Have children read with you the word *neighborhood* and its definition. As children study the picture, encourage them to share their observations.

Q How is this neighborhood like the one where you live? How is it different?

A Children should recognize that both neighborhoods are places where people live, work, and play, although the kinds of homes, buildings, and land, for example, may differ.

Tell children that all the words have to do with the world we share with others, both near and far away.

Visual Learning

Picture Ask children to describe the satellite photo. Explain that this photo was taken from space. Read aloud the definition of continent. Have children point to the land mass and trace around it with a finger. Invite volunteers to name the continent. (North America)

Next, focus children's attention on the ocean scene as you read aloud the definition of *ocean*.

neighborhood The part of a community in which a group of people lives. (page 94)

continent One of seven main land areas on Earth. (page 105)

82

READING SOCIAL STUDIES

Make a Prediction Invite children to use the words and pictures on these pages to predict what the main ideas of this unit will be. Record their ideas on a chart and save the chart. As children work through the lessons in this unit, encourage them to refer to the chart to assess and amend the main ideas they suggested.

REACH ALL LEARNERS

English as a Second Language Arrange Word Cards for *neighborhood, continent, ocean, resource,* and *weather* along the chalk ledge. Cover the words and definitions on pages 82–83. Hold up each Word Card and have children repeat the word after you. Then call on volunteers to match the Word Cards to pictures in their books and try to use each word in a sentence. Have children add these and other new words to a vocabulary notebook.

We share our world.

ocean A very large body of salty water. (page 105)

resource Anything people can use. (page 108)

weather What the air outside is like. (page 112)

83

INTEGRATE LANGUAGE ARTS

Write Riddles Invite children to create riddles for the vocabulary words. Encourage them to include clues that tell about meaning, the number of syllables or letters, and words within a word, for example. You may wish to use the following as a model:

I have two syllables. People often complain about me. What am I? (weather)

Invite children to read aloud their riddles for classmates to guess.

SCHOOL TO HOME

Use the Unit 3 SCHOOL TO HOME NEWSLETTER on pages S5–S6 to introduce the unit to family members and suggest activities they can do at home.

Visual Learning

Pictures Point out the picture of the truck carrying logs, and read aloud the definition of *resource*. Explain that the logs are from trees, a resource used to make things such as paper, furniture, and houses.

Q **For what do you think these logs will be used?**

A paper, furniture, houses

Focus attention on the picture for *weather*. Ask what the children are wearing and why they are dressed as they are. (raincoats and galoshes for a rainy day) Then read aloud the word *weather* and its definition.

Q **Why is it important to know about the weather?**

A Possible responses: so we know what to wear; so we can prepare for bad weather; so we can make plans

DEMOCRATIC VALUES

Common Good

Call attention to Earnest's words. Invite children to suggest some things we share. (land, water, air, neighborhoods, continents, oceans, resources) Emphasize that we also share the responsibility of taking care of our world now for those who come after us. Encourage children to tell what they do to show that they care about Earth. (recycle, reuse things, don't litter, use less)

Word Work

Use the following to preteach vocabulary. You may also wish to duplicate and distribute the word cards found in the back of this book on pages V19–V30. Children can use them as flash cards to practice saying and defining each word. Remind children to use the glossary at the back of their books to help them define these words.

SORT AND SHARE

Give a set of vocabulary Word Cards for the Unit to each small group of children. Have them find a way to sort the words into groups. Provide time for children to explain to the class how they sorted the words and how many categories they created. Then have them read the words in each of their categories.

BEAN BAG JOURNEYS

Provide a dry teabag or a spoonful of rice tied in a tissue as a small "beanbag." Lay a world map on the floor and have children take turns throwing the bag onto it. Players receive one point for landing in the ocean, two points for landing on a continent, and three points for landing on an island. When children know how to play, provide maps and beanbags for small groups and have them play until one player reaches fifteen points. After the game, have children describe the locations on which they landed.

WHERE'S MY TEACHER?

Have children imagine that you are traveling throughout the world. Explain that you will describe to them what you see and they will guess what kind of place you are visiting. For example, a clue for *island* might be *I see trees and shells and sand and there's ocean all around me. This piece of land is very small.* After you have given clues for several places, invite volunteers to give clues for others to guess.

PICTURE DICTIONARY

JOURNAL Have children choose ten of the vocabulary words and think of ways to illustrate them. Ask children to use a page of their journal to make a picture dictionary for their words. Then invite them to write rebus sentences using their dictionary pictures.

neighborhood

address

mountain

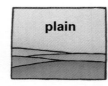
plain

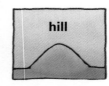
hill

Earth

From Here to There

OBJECTIVES

■ Obtain information about a topic using a variety of visual sources such as pictures and literature.

■ Locate places of significance on maps such as your local community, your state, and the United States.

■ Know your own address and the areas it designates.

RESOURCES

Pupil Book/Unit Big Book,
  pp. 84–93

Word Cards V19–V20

⊛**Reading and Vocabulary**
  Transparency 3–1

Thinking Organizers T21 and T22

▭**Internet Resources**

Audiotext, Unit 3

Vocabulary

address p. 84

Summary

Like most children, Maria Mendoza knows her street address, but Maria doesn't stop there. She includes her country, continent, hemisphere, and more to describe where she lives.

1 Motivate

Set the Purpose

Remind children that it helps to set a purpose for reading a story before they begin. Read aloud the book title and introduction on page 84. To help children set a purpose for reading, model the process.

> Now that I've read the title and introduction, I'm really curious about how Maria describes where she lives. I want to read *From Here to There* to find out more.

Access Prior Knowledge

READING SOCIAL STUDIES

Make a Prediction Read aloud the story title. Then have children look at the pictures. Ask children to predict what they think they will learn in this lesson. Write their predictions and save them for use during Close.

Our Prediction	What the Story Says
house number, street, town, state	

●USE READING AND VOCABULARY TRANSPARENCY 3–1

3–1
TRANSPARENCY

2 Teach

Visual Learning

Understand the Story Direct children's attention to the picture of the girl standing at the window. Tell children that she is Maria.

Q What is Maria doing?

A She is looking out the window.

Q What do you think Maria sees?

A Possible responses: her neighborhood, backyard, and front yard

Encourage children to suggest specific things Maria might see in her neighborhood as she looks out the window, such as other homes, a sidewalk, a street, cars, friends and neighbors, lawn, trees, a garden, and the sky.

Read and Respond

Geography Remind children that an address is a label that helps people find a house or building. Emphasize that every home and building has an address that is different from every other home and building.

Q Why is it important to know your address?

A to help someone find where you live; to get help if you are lost

Q Who might want to find you?

A a mail carrier, newspaper deliverer, firefighter, or new friend

---

START with a STORY

From Here to There

by Margery Cuyler
illustrated by Yu Cha Pak

People often use their **address** to tell where they live. In this book, Maria describes where she lives in a special way.

84

WORD WORK

Context Clues Read aloud the first sentence, noting that the word *address* is highlighted because it is an important word to know. Explain to children that if they come to an unfamiliar word when reading, they can often use the words and sentences around it to figure out what it means. Ask children to identify the words in the sentence that help them to know what *address* means.

BACKGROUND

About the Author Margery Cuyler was born in Princeton, New Jersey, and grew up in a large family—four brothers and sisters and four cousins who lived with them. This helped her learn how to fend for herself. Concerning her career, she says, "My passion has been editing children's books, but I also enjoy writing, since it exercises my imagination in a more personal and introspective fashion." Margery Cuyler edits under the pseudonym Daisy Wallace.

INTEGRATE LANGUAGES

Speaking and Listening Provide a toy telephone and invite partners to take turns pretending to make an emergency 911 call and giving their address. Have one partner act as the dispatcher, repeating the caller's address and asking the caller if the address is correct. Have the caller confirm the address or correct it as necessary.

My name is Maria Mendoza. I live with my father, my mother, my baby brother, Tony, and my older sister, Angelica,

85

Visual Learning

Understand the Story Read aloud the text as children follow along. Then direct attention to the illustration of the Mendoza family. Have children identify Maria, Angelica, Tony, and their parents and then tell what each family member is doing.

Q **What meal of the day do you think Maria's parents are preparing?**

A dinner or lunch

Q **How do you think your family is like the Mendoza family? How are they different?**

A the size of the families, ages and/or genders of the children, number of parents and/or grandparents living in the home

Emphasize that although families are different, they share some things in common—they care for one another and share their lives.

Read and Respond

Culture and Society Point out that one way family members show they care about one another is by sharing responsibilities and working together. Point out that Mr. and Mrs. Mendoza are working together to prepare a meal.

Invite children to tell about ways they cooperate and work together with family members at home.

MENTAL MAPPING

Draw a Neighborhood Point out that Maria is about to go outside. Invite children to close their eyes and imagine they are at the front door of their home or apartment building. Tell them to open the door, step outside, and walk down the street, noticing all the things in their neighborhood. Then have children open their eyes. Provide them with drawing paper and crayons to make maps of their neighborhood.

REACH ALL LEARNERS

English as a Second Language Help children identify the words for family members. Have them point to Maria's mother, for example, and say, "This is Maria's mother." List the words on the board. As you say each word, have children repeat it. Invite children to teach the class the words for *father, mother, brother, sister,* and other family members in their first language.

INTEGRATE HEALTH

Nutrition Draw attention to the different foods pictured. Ask children to identify any they know. Invite children to suggest what Mr. Mendoza might have made in the pot. Then discuss how important it is to eat the right foods to stay healthy. Display the U.S. government's food pyramid and talk about foods children can eat to create a balanced diet.

Read and Respond

Understand the Story Read aloud the text on pages 86–87 as children follow along. Tell children that there are various kinds of communities in which people live, such as cities, towns, and villages. Recall with children that the Mendoza family lives in a town. As children look at the pictures, help them to recognize that a town is usually smaller than a city. Discuss the ideas that people live and work there, the homes are closely grouped together, and the neighborhoods are quieter because there is less traffic than in a city. Invite children to compare their community to Splendora.

Visual Learning

Pictures Focus children's attention on the first picture and ask children to describe what Maria is doing. (putting a letter in the mailbox) Have children find the signal flag on the side of the mailbox. Explain that when the flag is up, it signals the mail carrier to stop and collect the mail. Then point out the number on the mailbox and help children recall that 43 is the number of the Mendoza family's house. Explain that no other house on Juniper Street has that number.

Q Why is it helpful for each street in a town to have a name and for each house or building on a street to have a different number?

A Street names and building numbers make it easier to find a house or building.

Mention to children that families who live in apartment buildings have another number or letter in their address that tells which apartment they live in.

at number 43 Juniper Street—

in the town of Splendora,

86

INTEGRATE LANGUAGES

Informative Writing Ask children to think about what they would write in a letter to Maria about their family and where they live. List their ideas on the board. Then have children write a letter to Maria. They may want to include drawings of themselves, their family, and their home. Invite children to share their letter and drawings with the class.

INTEGRATE MATHEMATICS

Number Order Write Maria's name and address on an envelope. Then address an envelope to each of six imaginary people who live at 39, 41, 45, 47, 49, and 51 Juniper Street, Splendora, Texas. Randomly display the envelopes along the chalk ledge. Then ask children to arrange the envelopes in order so the mail carrier can easily deliver them to the people on Maria's side of the street.

in the county of Montgomery,

in the state of Texas,

87

BACKGROUND

About Texas Texas is the second-largest state in the United States. Only Alaska is larger in area.

The **bluebonnet** is the state flower.

Austin is the state capital.

The Lyndon B. Johnson Space Center, at Houston, is the NASA headquarters for all manned space projects.

Many varieties of **cactus** grow in parts of Texas.

The Alamo is the site of the famous battle fought in 1836 during the Texas Revolution.

The **armadillo** is a small mammal with a shell of hard, bony plates. It is one of the wild animals that live in Texas.

The **longhorn** steer is a breed of cattle that was important to the American West until the 1900s.

Visual Learning

Understand the Story Recall with children that Maria and her family live at 43 Juniper Street in the town of Splendora. Then focus attention on the next picture as you point out that Splendora is in Montgomery County. Encourage children to describe the landscape and clusters of homes and buildings. Help them to recognize that Splendora is one of many communities in the county.

Read and Respond

Geography Focus children's attention on the top picture on page 87. Point out that some details in the picture are human-made and some are natural.

Q Which details show human-made features?

A water tower, roads, power lines, buildings, cars

Q Which details show natural features?

A hills, trees, grass, soil, river, lake

Have children identify which human-made and which natural features are found in their communities.

Display a map of Texas. Point out the border lines of the individual counties. Find Montgomery County, and then locate Splendora. Mention that most states in the United States are divided into counties. Ask children if they can name the county in which they live. Display a map of your state and help children locate their city or town.

Culture and Society Point out that although people living in your home state are very different from each other, they have many things in common as well. Lead children in a discussion about the attributes that people in your state have in common.

Visual Learning

Pictures Direct children's attention to the last picture. Point out that the picture shows special symbols, such as the state flower and the Alamo. Invite children to identify any state symbols they know.

Read and Respond

Understand the Story Read aloud the text as children study the map. Remind children that a country is a land and a state is one part of a country. Help children recognize that the green areas and the orange area represent the United States and that Texas is the state highlighted in orange. Children might compare the shape of Texas on this map with the shape of the state map pictured on the previous page.

Geography Have children name the state in which they live. Display an outline or map of your state and challenge children to locate it on the map in their book.

Have children point to the areas of blue on pages 88–89.

Q What do you think blue stands for on the map? Why do you think so?

A The blue stands for water or oceans; there are two ships in the picture and ships sail in water.

Q What are very large bodies of water called?

A oceans

Invite volunteers to name the two oceans in the picture. (Atlantic Ocean, Pacific Ocean)

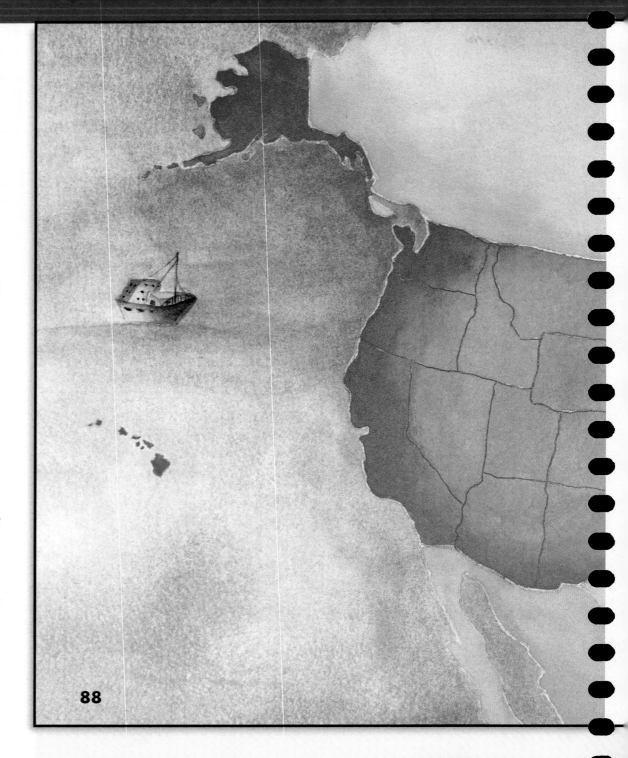

88

WORD WORK

Vocabulary Write the words *county* and *country* on the board. Underline the letter *r*. Then ask children to listen carefully as you say each word. Help them recognize that *ou* has more than one sound. Have children say each word and briefly review the meanings. Then ask children to complete these sentences:

Splendora is in Montgomery _____.
The United States is a _____.

INTEGRATE LANGUAGES

Spanish Explain to children that people in Mexico, Spain, and other countries where Spanish is spoken refer to the United States of America as "*los Estados Unidos de America.*" Invite children who speak other languages to teach the class how to say "United States of America" in those languages.

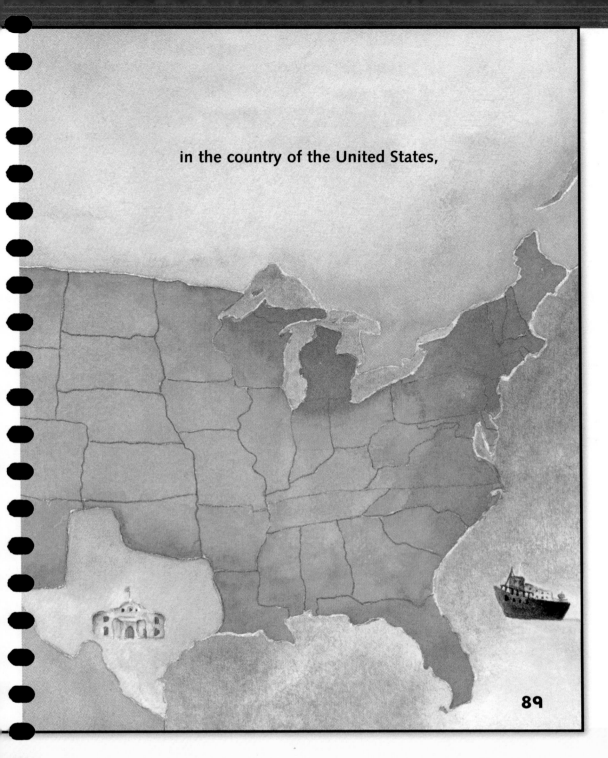

in the country of the United States,

89

Understand the Story Ask children to look again at the picture on pages 88–89 and tell what else they see. Have them point to the two red areas.

Q What do you think these two areas stand for?

A Possible responses: land or other countries

Verify that each area represents a different country and that both countries are considered to be our neighbors. As you point to each area, tell children that the country to the north of the United States is Canada and the country to the south is Mexico.

INTEGRATE MATHEMATICS

Counting Remind children that many states make up our country, the United States of America. Invite children to name as many states as they can. List them on the board in groups according to the letter they begin with. Start with the letter *A*. When children think they have named all 50 states, have them count to verify. You can have children circle groups of 2, 5, or 10 and then count.

REACH ALL LEARNERS

Tactile Learners Write each of the following on separate sentence strips and arrange the strips randomly along the chalk ledge:

I live at 43 Juniper Street,
in the town of Splendora,
in the county of Montgomery,
in the state of Texas.

Invite children to put them in order. As Maria tells more about where she lives, write each on a strip and have children add to the "address."

READING SOCIAL STUDIES

Make Predictions Discuss the special way Maria describes where she lives. Help children recognize that she starts out with her house and continues to move outward to include her street, town, county, state, and country. Ask children to predict what Maria might describe next. Then continue reading the story to find out. Follow a similar procedure as children complete each page of the story.

Read and Respond

Understand the Story Remind children that Maria is telling about where she lives in a special way.

Q What is so special about Maria's address?

A Maria starts with her house number, street, town, and state, like most people, but then she adds other things like the county, country, and now the continent where she lives.

Visual Learning

Pictures Focus children's attention on the picture of North America. Encourage children to describe in their own words what a continent is. Children may recall from Preview the Vocabulary that a continent is one of the seven main land areas on Earth.

Q What countries make up the continent of North America?

A the United States and the countries to the north and the south of the United States, including Mexico and Canada

Have children use their fingertip to trace North America. Then display a world map or globe and invite children to locate and identify North America and the United States.

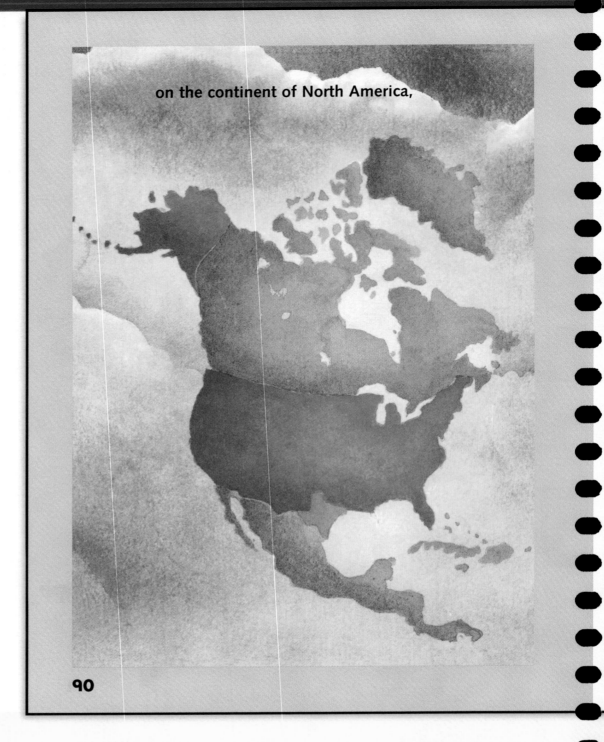

on the continent of North America,

90

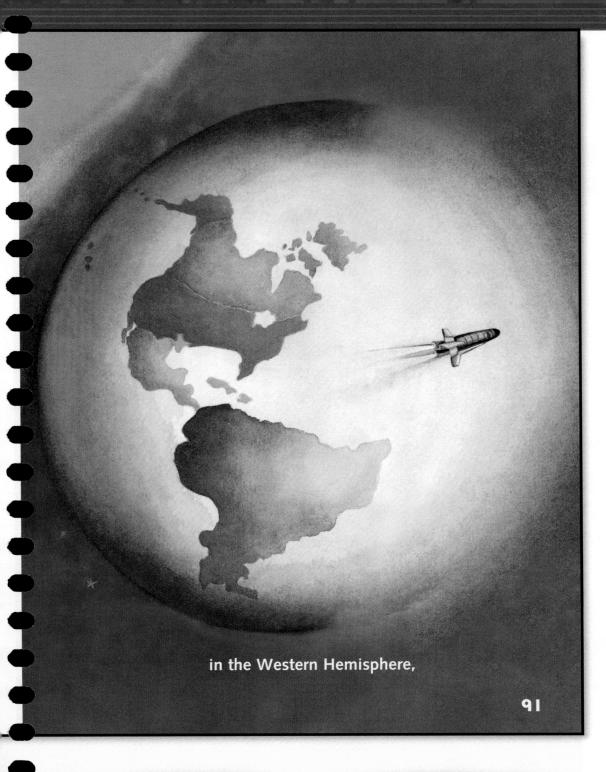

in the Western Hemisphere,

91

Read and Respond

Understand the Story Ask children to complete the following sentence to recall Maria's special way of describing where she lives: Maria lives at 43_____. (Juniper Street, in the town of Splendora, in the county of Montgomery, in the state of Texas, in the country of the United States, on the continent of North America) Then read aloud the text on page 91 to continue Maria's address.

Visual Learning

Pictures Ask children to point to Texas, the United States, and the countries to the north and to the south of the United States, noting that they make up the continent of North America. Then focus attention on the large land area to the south of North America, explaining that it is also a continent. Invite volunteers to name the continent. (South America) Point out that these two continents make up the Western Hemisphere.

Q **What makes up the Western Hemisphere?**

A the continents of North America and South America

Geography Explain to children that Earth is divided into halves called hemispheres.

- Using a globe, point out the equator, an imaginary horizontal line at the center of Earth.

- Explain that the equator divides Earth into the Northern and Southern Hemispheres. All countries north of the equator are in the Northern Hemisphere, while all countries south of the equator are in the Southern Hemisphere.

- Next, point out the vertical imaginary line at 0° longitude, called the Prime Meridian, and its twin line of longitude, which lies opposite the Prime Meridian at 180° longitude.

- Explain that these lines of longitude divide Earth into the Eastern and Western Hemispheres. Help children name some of the countries of the Eastern and Western Hemispheres.

INTEGRATE LANGUAGES

Journal Entry Invite children to imagine they are astronauts traveling far above Earth. Have them write a journal entry to describe what they see as they look toward Earth. Children can also include a drawing as part of their journal entry.

INTEGRATE MATHEMATICS

Solids Invite children to shape some clay into a ball. Write *hemisphere* on the board. Explain that *hemi-* means "half" and that a sphere is a round, solid object. Display the illustration of the Western Hemisphere. Then have children use a dull plastic knife to slice their clay balls in half. Explain that as they look at the picture of the Western Hemisphere, they are seeing only half of the world, similar to half of the clay ball.

Visual Learning

Understand the Story As you read the text on pages 92–93, focus children's attention on the illustration of Earth. Ask them to identify Texas, the United States, and North America.

Q What do you think the large brown areas are?

A land or other continents

Children may recall that there are seven continents. Explain that not all the continents can be seen in this illustration.

Q How would you describe the shape of planet Earth?

A round, like a ball

Read and Respond

Geography Point out that the solar system is the sun and the objects—planets, their moons, asteroids, comets, and meteoroids—that travel around it.

 Children might enjoy seeing pictures of the universe taken by the Hubble telescope. Have them visit The Learning Site at **www.harcourtschool.com**

on the planet Earth, in the solar system,

92

---

in the Milky Way galaxy,
in the universe
and beyond.

From here to there,
my name is
Maria Mendoza.

Think About It

1 How does Maria describe where she lives?

2 Write your address on an envelope.

Read a Book

Start the Unit Project

A Community Collage Your class will make a collage to show the kinds of land, water, and resources in and around your community. As you read this unit, remember how these things are important.

Use Technology

Visit The Learning Site at **www.harcourtschool.com** for additional activities, primary sources, and other resources to use in this unit.

93

3 Close

Summarize the Reading

• An address includes a house number, street, town or city, and state.

• You can describe where you live in a special way.

Read a Book

Children may enjoy reading these leveled independent Readers. Additional books are listed on pages 81J–81K of this Teacher's Edition.

Easy *A Zoo Map* by Lisa Trumbauer. Readers follow directions through a zoo and learn about the animals and their environments.

Average *National Parks* by Lisa Trumbauer. Learn about John Muir, a naturalist, and the national park system to which he contributed.

Challenging *The Sahara Desert* by Lisa Trumbauer. An introduction to the biggest desert in the world.

Start the Unit Project

Hint Before children begin their unit project, suggest that they look over page 81. As they read each lesson, help children look for, or make, pictures of the land, water, and resources they learn about.

Think About It

Answers

❶ Maria tells her street address, county, state, country, continent, hemisphere, planet, solar system, and galaxy.

❷ Children's addresses should include a name, house number and street, an apartment number if applicable, city or town, state, and Zip code.

INTERNET RESOURCES

THE LEARNING SITE Go to **www.harcourtschool.com** to view Internet resources for this unit.

TIME FOR KIDS® Go to **www.harcourtschool.com** for the latest news in a student-friendly format.

READING SOCIAL STUDIES

Make a Prediction Reread the predictions children made in Motivate. Ask children to summarize the story and tell whether their predictions were correct.

Our Prediction	What the Story Says
house number, street, town, state	house number, street, town, state, country, continent, planet, universe

● USE READING AND VOCABULARY TRANSPARENCY 3–1

3–1 TRANSPARENCY

Extension Activities For Home and School

Where I Live

Materials: large local street map, envelopes, crayons or markers, pushpins, yarn or ribbon

Display on the bulletin board a large street map of your community. Provide each child with an envelope on which to print his or her name and address and perhaps illustrate a postage stamp. As children take turns pinning their completed envelopes around the edge of the map to make a frame, have them read aloud their addresses. Then help each child locate his or her street on the map and connect the envelope and the street with a piece of yarn or ribbon.
(VISUAL/TACTILE)

Make a Book

Materials: drawing paper, construction paper, crayons or markers, Thinking Organizers T21 (United States) and T22 (North America), scissors, glue

Organize children into small groups. Have each group create its own version of *From Here to There* that describes the school address. Provide each group with five large sheets of drawing paper. At the bottom of each sheet, have children copy and complete one of the following statements:

We go to school at _____,   in the town [city, village] of _____,   in the state of _____, in the country of _____,   on the continent of _____.

Have children illustrate each page with a drawing or by coloring, cutting out, and gluing in place the maps of the United States and North America shown in the Thinking Organizers. Suggest they use one color for their state, another color for the rest of the states, and a third color for other countries. Children can then make a book cover with a title, their names, and any art they may want to include.
(TACTILE/VISUAL)

We go to school at
123 Pine Road.

Sentence Strip Fun

Materials: sentence strips, crayons or markers, large paper clips

Invite children to make one long sentence to describe where they live, in the same special way that Maria did in the story. You may wish to write a sentence across the board as a model for children to follow, beginning with *I live at 43 Juniper Street, in the town of Splendora* through *in the universe and beyond*. Provide each child with 11 sentence strips. Tell children to write each part of the sentence on a separate strip, making sure to replace Maria's house number and street, town, county, and state with their own. Provide children who live in an apartment with an additional strip to write their apartment number. Remind children to include commas, capital letters, and a period at the end of the sentence. When children have completed their strips, have them arrange them in order to make a sentence.
(TACTILE/VISUAL)

I live at number 704 East Street,	in the town of Roselle,	in the county of Union,	in the state of New Jersey,
in the country of the United States,	on the continent of North America,	in the Western Hemisphere,	on the planet Earth,
in the solar system,	in the Milky Way galaxy,	in the universe and beyond.	

A Neighborhood

OBJECTIVES

- Define a neighborhood as a place where people interact as they live, work, and play.

- Compare a map to an aerial view.

 Categorize pp. 81, 124

RESOURCES

Pupil Book/Unit Big Book, pp. 94–95

Word Cards V19–V20

Activity Book, p. 24

⊕**Reading and Vocabulary Transparency 3–2**

💻**Internet Resources**

READING SOCIAL STUDIES

Graphic Organizer Begin a personal response chart about what people in a neighborhood share. Complete the chart during Close.

Things People in a Neighborhood Share
streets
sidewalks
stores

●USE READING AND VOCABULARY TRANSPARENCY 3–2

3–2
TRANSPARENCY

Vocabulary

neighborhood p. 94

 When Minutes Count

Have children compare the map on page 95 with the aerial photo on page 94. Then ask children to think about what each main building might be (library, school, etc.) and label a copy of the map accordingly.

Quick Summary

In this lesson children explore what a neighborhood is and what the people in a neighborhood share. Children also observe an aerial photograph of a neighborhood in Houston, Texas, and compare it to a map of the neighborhood.

 Motivate

Set the Purpose

Big Idea Before starting the lesson, read the Big Idea statement aloud. As children read and discuss the lesson, encourage them to identify specific things people in a neighborhood share.

Access Prior Knowledge

Recall with children how Maria describes her address in the book *From Here to There*. Call on volunteers to say their addresses as Maria does. Then display page 86, noting that it shows the neighborhood where Maria and her family live in Splendora, Texas. Ask children how they would describe what a neighborhood is.

2 Teach

Read and Respond

Link Culture and Society with Geography Read aloud the paragraph at the top of page 94 and help children locate Splendora and Houston on a map of Texas. Note that both are communities—places where people live, work, and play. Some urban communities, like the city of Houston, are very big and have many neighborhoods. Others, like the rural town of Splendora, are smaller and have fewer neighborhoods. Display a map of the United States. Invite children to name their state and community, locate each on the map, and then describe their neighborhood and community.

Visual Learning

Pictures Focus attention on the aerial picture of the Houston neighborhood.

Q Where do you think this photo was taken from?

A from an airplane

As children study the picture, challenge them to identify some of the places in this Houston neighborhood that people share and to explain how they can tell. Children may recognize rooftops, streets, and treetops.

Q If you were to look at a picture of your neighborhood taken from the air, what do you think it would show?

A Possible responses may include houses, apartment buildings, streets, the school, the mall.

Invite children to look at the map on page 95 and compare it to the picture of Houston. Help them recognize that although both the picture and map show the same place from above, the map use shapes and colors to represent only some of the real objects, while the picture shows everything as it really looks. Show children a map of their community. Help children locate their homes and neighborhoods, school, and other important places.

Big Idea
People in a neighborhood share things.

Vocabulary
neighborhood

A Neighborhood

Not far from Splendora, where Maria lives, is the city of Houston. Houston is a large community with many neighborhoods. A **neighborhood** is a small part of a community in which people live. People in a neighborhood share schools, libraries, parks, and other places of the community.

Look at this picture of a Houston neighborhood taken from above.

94

REACH ALL LEARNERS

Kinesthetic Learners
Invite children to arrange several items on a tabletop, such as a toy car, a book, a jar of glue, and an action figure. Have children sit so they are looking at the items at eye level and then describe what they see. Next, arrange the same items similarly on the floor. This time ask children to stand, look at the items from above, and describe what they see. Tell children to imagine they are going to make a map. Ask which view they would use and why.

EXTEND AND ENRICH

Places on Maps Display maps of your community, state, the United States, North America, and the world. Challenge children to locate the street where they live on the community map, their community on the state map, their state on the map of the United States, their country on the map of North America, and their continent on the map of the world.

This is a map of the same neighborhood.

 How are places shown on this map?

LESSON 1
Review

❶ **Vocabulary** What is a **neighborhood**?

❷ How are a picture and a map the same? How are they different?

❸ List some places that people share in your neighborhood.

95

RETEACH THE LESSON

Make a Venn Diagram Draw a large Venn diagram on chart paper or on the board. Display an aerial photo and map of another community neighborhood, or use the photograph and map on pages 94 and 95. Invite children to use the diagram to record how the photo and map are alike and how they are different.

ACTIVITY BOOK

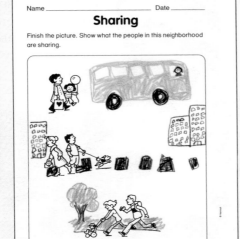

Name _____ Date _____

Sharing

Finish the picture. Show what the people in this neighborhood are sharing.

24 • Activity Book   Use with Unit 3, Lesson 1.

PAGE 24

---

3 **Close**

Summarize Key Content

• You can describe a neighborhood as a place in a community where people live, work, and play.

• You can tell how a map and an aerial view of the same place are alike and how they are different.

READING SOCIAL STUDIES

Graphic Organizer Revisit the personal response chart begun in Motivate. Invite children to share new ideas they learned. Add these ideas to the chart.

Things People in a Neighborhood Share	
streets	library
sidewalks	recreation
stores	center
playground	mall
school	church and
apartment	temple
buildings	park
office buildings	lake

● USE READING AND VOCABULARY TRANSPARENCY 3–2

3–2
TRANSPARENCY

Assess

Lesson 1 Review—Answers

❶ A neighborhood is a place in a community where people live, work, and play.

❷ A picture and a map show what a place looks like from above. A picture shows real things like trees, streets, and the roofs of buildings. A map uses shapes and colors to show some of the things and where they are in a place.

❸ **Performance Assessment Guidelines** Children's lists should include such things as streets, sidewalks, stores and other public buildings, parks and playgrounds, and schools.

Extension Activities For Home and School

Bird's-Eye View

Materials: boxes, wooden blocks, construction paper, crayons or markers, scissors, masking tape, toy vehicles, ladder, instant camera, mural paper

Invite children to work in groups to plan and create a tabletop neighborhood. Suggest that they first decide what kinds of buildings and features to include, such as homes, a playground, a school, stores, and trees. Encourage children to refer to the list they completed at the end of the lesson for ideas. Then have children construct the buildings and features with the provided materials. While some children build, others can prepare the tabletop by making streets out of black construction paper strips and then taping them in place to make a kind of grid. Once children finish construction, have them arrange the buildings in the areas outlined by the streets.

Use a ladder to take a series of "aerial" photographs of the tabletop neighborhood. Then invite children to use the photographs to create a simple map using shapes and colors to show the different buildings, streets, and features. Arrange the photographs around the completed map and encourage children to compare how they are alike and how they are different.
(TACTILE/VISUAL)

Our Neighborhood

Materials: bulletin board, street map of the community, pushpins, drawing paper, crayons or markers, photos (optional), yarn

Invite children to create a bulletin board display entitled "Welcome to the Neighborhood." Display a map of the community on a bulletin board and invite children to tell where they live. As they say their addresses, help them locate their homes, streets, or neighborhoods on the map and mark the location with a pushpin. Then ask children to draw pictures or bring in photos of something in their neighborhood. Discuss what the pictures show: people at home, at work, or at play; the things that the people share. Display the drawings and photos around the map to form a frame. Then attach a length of yarn from each child's home, street, or neighborhood on the map to his or her drawing or photo.
(VISUAL/TACTILE)

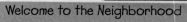
Welcome to the Neighborhood

Imagine That!

Materials: drawing paper, crayons or markers, map of the community

Encourage children to share with family members what they have learned about a neighborhood. Then ask children to invite everyone in the family to close their eyes and imagine they are floating high above the rooftops in their neighborhood, looking down. After a minute or two, they can open their eyes and work together to draw a picture that shows how they think their neighborhood looks from above. Ask children to bring their drawing to class to share. Then display a map of the community for children to compare with their drawings.
(VISUAL/TACTILE)

SKILLS

Use a Map Key

Map Key

Children's Museum

Community Center

Golf Course

Houston Museum of Natural Science

Japanese Garden

Rice University

Zoo

Street

Vocabulary

map key p. 96

1 Motivate

Have children turn to pages 94–95 in their books.

Review how the aerial view of the neighborhood in Houston, Texas, and the map of the neighborhood are alike and different. Help children recall that a map is a drawing that shows what a place looks like from above. As children look at the map on page 95, ask how they know what the pictures, shapes, and colors mean.

Why It Matters

Explain to children that knowing symbols and colors on a map helps us find places.

REACH ALL LEARNERS

Below-Level Learners Take children to a playground. Ask them to bring along a notebook and a pencil and to make a sketch that shows the positions of different items of play equipment. When they return to the classroom, help children make maps of the playground, drawing shapes to show the different features, such as the swing, slide, sandbox, and basketball hoop, as seen from above. Invite children to display their maps.

2 Teach

What You Need to Know

Ask children to look at the map and read aloud the title, *Hermann Park*. Explain that the map shows a real park in Houston, Texas. Read aloud the text and ask children to locate and point to the map key.

Q How many symbols are in this map key?

A eight

Call on volunteers to tell what each symbol stands for. Mention that some symbols may look like what they represent, or stand for, while others may not. Have children tell why they think the mapmaker chose each symbol.

Q How do you think you might use the map key?

A If I don't know what something means on the map, I can find out by looking at the map key.

As an example, ask children to find and point to the symbol for the Japanese Garden. Then have them find and point to that symbol on the map. Repeat with other symbols.

Skills MAP AND GLOBE

Use a Map Key

Vocabulary
map key

▶ Why It Matters

Symbols help you find places on a map.

▶ What You Need to Know

A **map key** lists the symbols used on a map. It shows you what they mean.

▶ Practice the Skill

❶ What is the symbol for the zoo?

❷ Find the Community Center. On what street is it located?

❸ What is near the lake?

96

Map Key

 Children's Museum

 Community Center

 Golf Course

 Houston Museum of Natural Science

 Japanese Garden

 Rice University

 Zoo

Street

Hermann Park

Caroline Street

Crawford Street

Main Street

Fannin Street

Binz Street

Hermann Drive

John P. McGovern Lake

Zoo Circle Drive

Golf Course Drive

Almeda Road

Carson Court

North Macgregor Drive

▶ **Apply What You Learned**

Make a map of your community.

Use symbols and a map key.

Practice your map and globe skills with the **GeoSkills CD-ROM**.

97

Practice the Skill—Answers

❶ The symbol is a tiger.

❷ The Community Center is at Almeda Road.

❸ The Japanese Garden is near the lake.

3 Close

Apply What You Learned

Children's maps should show a familiar area of the community and contain symbols—pictures and/or shapes as well as colors—to represent various features and landmarks.

ACTIVITY BOOK

Name _____ Date _____

MAP AND GLOBE SKILLS
A Neighborhood Map

Color the pictures in the map key and on the map. Then make a new symbol. Draw it in the map key and on the map.

Map Key

house   school   park   store   library

bank   street   stop sign   hospital

Use with Unit 3, Skill Lesson 1.

Activity Book • 25

PAGE 25

RETEACH THE SKILL

Find Places on the Map Invite children to work in pairs to find places on the map of Hermann Park. Have them use the map key and ask questions, such as *What is the symbol for the Houston Museum of Natural Science? How many museums are on this map? Which museum is near Caroline Street?*

TRANSPARENCY

Use SKILL TRANSPARENCY 3–1.

CD-ROM

Explore GEOSKILLS CD-ROM to learn more about maps and globe skills.

Extension Activities For Home and School

Make a Mural Map

Materials: mural paper, masking tape, crayons or markers, camera or camcorder (optional)

Take children on a walking tour of an area in the community, such as a business district, a park, or the school and the surrounding neighborhood. Encourage children to note street names and landmarks. You may want to use a camera or camcorder to record important landmarks. When children return to the classroom, invite them to make a large mural map to show the places they saw.

Tape mural paper to a section of wall that is easily accessible to children. After outlining the streets, ask children to name the places or landmarks they want to show on the map and decide what symbols and colors they want to use to represent each one. Call on volunteers to draw and label the symbols in the map key. Then help children identify where the symbols belong on the map before you call on volunteers to draw them in place. **(VISUAL/ TACTILE/ KINESTHETIC)**

Make a Map

Materials: Thinking Organizer T21 (map of the United States), crayons or markers

Challenge children to name some of the interesting places people enjoy visiting in the United States, such as the Grand Canyon, the Alamo, Colonial Williamsburg, the Statue of Liberty, Independence Hall, or the White House. Distribute maps of the United States to children and invite them to work with family members to create a map key with symbols that show some of the places in our country they have visited or would like to visit one day. To complete the map, suggest that children and family members draw in the appropriate state the symbol for each place listed in the map key. Ask children to bring their completed maps to school to share. **(VISUAL/ TACTILE)**

Where Is It?

Materials: large map of the community or state, index cards cut in half, crayons or markers

Invite children to play a game. To prepare, display a large map of your community or state on the bulletin board. Draw the symbols shown in the map key on individual cards and place them face down on a table. Then help children identify the symbols in the map key. Remind children that the map shows how their community or state looks from above and the symbols in the map key show what is on the ground in their community or state. Call on volunteers, in turn, to choose a symbol card, tell what it means, and then find that symbol on the map.

LESSON 2 Land and Water

OBJECTIVES

- Identify and describe the physical characteristics of places such as landforms.
- Identify and describe the physical characteristics of places such as bodies of water.

 Categorize pp. 81, 99, 101, 124

RESOURCES

Pupil Book/Unit Big Book,
pp. 98–101

Word Cards V19–V24

Activity Book, p. 26

⊕ **Reading and Vocabulary Transparency 3–3**

Activity Pattern P5

⊟ **Internet Resources**

READING SOCIAL STUDIES

Graphic Organizer Begin a chart about Earth's physical features. Complete the chart during Close.

Earth's Features	
Land	**Water**
mountains	ponds
hills	rivers

● USE READING AND VOCABULARY TRANSPARENCY 3–3

3–3
TRANSPARENCY

Vocabulary

valley p. 98   **mountain** p. 98   **lake** p. 99

hill p. 100   **plain** p. 100   **island** p. 101

river p. 101

 When Minutes Count

Direct children to examine the pictures in the lesson and to read the vocabulary words. Have pairs of children work together to match words to pictures.

Quick Summary

Earth has many different physical characteristics. This lesson focuses on some of its landforms and bodies of water.

1 Motivate

Set the Purpose

Big Idea Before starting the lesson, read the Big Idea statement aloud. As children read and discuss this lesson, encourage them to identify the different kinds of land and water in their community.

Access Prior Knowledge

Ask children to name any kind of land or water that they have seen or read about. Have them suggest activities that occur there. Invite children to share stories about activities they have tried.

2 Teach

Visual Learning

Pictures Focus attention on the photo of the mountain valley community and invite children to describe the scene. Encourage them to note the general characteristics of mountain regions—steep slopes, sharp or slightly rounded peaks, vegetation such as grass-covered slopes and trees, and snow.

Explain that a *region* is a land area with common characteristics that distinguish it from other regions. These characteristics could be geographic (mountains, deserts), political (counties, states, countries), or cultural (neighborhoods).

Read and Respond

Geography Display a map of the United States and help children locate Oregon. Then point to Mt. Hood on the map and mention that it is part of the Cascade Range.

Explain to children that mountains and other physical features on Earth's surface are the result of natural forces such as floods, earthquakes, volcanoes, and landslides. The scientific field of *geology* shows that the processes that shape the earth over time are still acting on it and that change is normal.

Help children list how mountains are important:

- Rain and melting snow flowing down steep mountain slopes bring water to many of our rivers and streams.
- Mountains are home to a wide variety of animals and plants, including trees found in mountain forests, which are a source of lumber and fuel.
- Mountains are a source of many important minerals, like gold.

Q Why else do you think mountains are important to people?

A Mountains are a good place for hiking, skiing, camping, climbing, and enjoying nature.

Lesson 2

Land and Water

Big Idea
There are many kinds of land and water.

Vocabulary
valley
mountain
lake
hill
plain
island
river

Communities can be in many places. This community is in a **valley** between mountains. A **mountain** is the highest kind of land.

Mount Hood

Dear Aunt Patty,
I'm having a great time in Hood River!
Love,
Tony

Visit
Hood River, Oregon

98

WORD WORK

Related Words Write the words *community* and *communities* on the board. Tell children that when they are reading and come to a word that ends in *-s* or *-es*, it often signals more than one of something—in this case, more than one *community*. Recall with children that a community is a place where people live, so *communities* means more than one place where people live. Point out how *y* changes to *i* before *-es*.

REACH ALL LEARNERS

Tactile Learners Have children work in pairs or small groups using clay or modeling dough to create models of mountains, hills, islands, plains, rivers, and lakes on sheets of heavy cardboard. When their clay or dough is dry, have children paint and label their model. Then invite children to display, discuss, and compare their models.

This community is near a lake. There is land all around the water of a lake. Lakes can be large or small, shallow or deep.

HOOD RIVER
Aug '04, 2005
Oregon, USA

Patty Hosley
1234 Sea Dr.
Orlando, FL 12345

Lake Maitland, Florida

99

Pictures Invite children to describe the neighborhood bordering the lake and to describe the physical characteristics of the lake. Point out the area of land near the water's edge. Explain that the area of land that borders a lake or other large body of water is called the shore. Encourage children to trace with a finger the shore of the lake in the photograph.

Q How is this lake like other lakes you have seen? How is it different?

A Children should recognize that all lakes are bodies of water with land around them but that they vary in size, shape, depth, type of plant and animal life, and the way people use them.

Read and Respond

Geography Locate Florida on a map of the United States. Have children point to various lakes in the state. Explain that central Florida has many lakes. Point out that Lake Maitland is located in the city of Maitland. At about 437 acres, it is the largest lake in the community.

Direct attention to the pictures on pages 98 and 99 that show both land and water.

Q Why do you think people choose to live in a community near a lake or a mountain?

A People might like the sports or other activities they can do there; they might want to work around the water or on a mountain.

Focus Skill

READING SKILL

Categorize After children have read the lesson, review with them the different kinds of land and water discussed in the lesson. Then have children work in pairs to create a chart. Have them put the lesson vocabulary words in the following two categories: *land* and *water*.

MAKE IT RELEVANT

In Your Community and State
Explain that lakes support a wide variety of water plants and animals—insects, snails, fish, frogs, snakes, crayfish, and waterfowl—and are a source of food and water for many land animals. Display pictures of typical lake wildlife. Then invite a local nature scientist to bring in photos or videotapes of wildlife found in your community or state.

Visual Learning

Pictures Have children examine the postcards on pages 100–101 and identify the different types of land and water. Guide them to compare the different types of land (valleys, mountains, hills, plains, and islands) and the different bodies of water (rivers and lakes) on pages 98–101. Emphasize that we often use words that tell about shape to describe the land.

Q **How are the land and water where we live like the land and water on the postcards in this lesson?**

A Accept all reasonable answers, such as the land where we live is rounded and hilly like the postcard picture with the hills or flat like the plains.

Read the captions on pages 100–101 with children and help them locate each place on a map.

Read and Respond

Geography Ask children to recall the different types of land they have learned about in this lesson. Explain that islands are found in rivers, lakes, and oceans; some are very small and others are very large. Using a map of the United States, help children locate the state of Hawaii and its many islands. Then point to the East Coast of the United States. Ask children if they can name the smallest state. (Rhode Island) Point out that it includes 36 islands.

There are other kinds of land. A **hill** is land that rises above the land around it. Hills are not as high as mountains.

The Hills of Georgia

A **plain** is land that is mostly flat. The land in most plains is good for growing food.

Main Street
Lawrence, Kansas

Across Kansas
Plains

100

An **island** is land that has water all around it.

DAUPHIN ISLAND, AL
PM
04 AUG

DAUPHIN ISLAND
Alabama, U.S.A.

Love,
Patty

575 Penn Lane
York, PA 17404

MISSISSIPPI RIVER

MISSISSIPPI, USA

A **river** is a long body of moving water that moves across the land. The water in some rivers flows very fast.

LESSON 2 Review

Focus Skill ❶ **Categorize** What kinds of land and water are near your community?

❷ **Vocabulary** What is the difference between a **mountain** and a **plain**?

❸ Choose a kind of land and a kind of water. Draw a picture of each.

101

RETEACH THE LESSON

Land and Water Picture Search
Provide small groups of children with a set of Word Cards for *valley, mountain, lake, hill, plain, island,* and *river*. Then invite children to find illustrations and photographs of each in magazines and books and mark them with the Word Cards. Ask children to describe the characteristics of each.

ACTIVITY BOOK

Name _____ Date _____

Finish the Picture

Is this town near mountains or hills? Is it on a plain? Is there a lake or a river nearby? Draw the land and water around the town.

26 • Activity Book   Use with Unit 3, Lesson 2.

PAGE 26

3 Close

Summarize Key Content

• You can describe land by its shape.

• Some types of land are plains, hills, mountains, and islands.

• You can identify and describe lakes and rivers.

READING SOCIAL STUDIES

Graphic Organizer Revisit the chart begun in Motivate. Invite children to share new ideas they learned. Add these ideas to the chart.

Earth's Features	
Land	**Water**
mountains	ponds
hills	rivers
plains	lakes
islands	oceans

● USE READING AND VOCABULARY TRANSPARENCY 3–3

 3–3 TRANSPARENCY

Assess

Lesson 2 Review—Answers

❶ *Focus Skill* **Categorize** Children should be able to distinguish mountains, hills, plains, islands, rivers, or lakes in their community.

❷ A mountain is the highest kind of land, and a plain is mostly flat.

❸ **Performance Assessment Guidelines** Children's drawings should depict the characteristics of the bodies of water and landforms they learned about in this lesson.

Extension Activities For Home and School

Puzzle Game

Materials: index cards, pencils, calendar photographs depicting landforms and bodies of water, posterboard, glue, scissors

Have small groups of children work together to generate a list of questions and answers about land and water. For example:

- What is the highest kind of land called?
- What is all around an island?
- What is high, but not as high as mountains?
- What word for a body of water can you make with the letters *KAEL*?

Have children write each question and answer on an index card. Then have each group glue a calendar photo of a scenic landscape to a sheet of posterboard and cut it into six puzzle pieces. Have children in two groups trade puzzle pieces, pool their questions, and pair up to play a game. Explain that to play the game, each player, in turn, must correctly answer a question in order to turn over a puzzle piece. When the puzzle is complete, players must identify the kind of land or water shown.
(VISUAL/TACTILE/AUDITORY)

> What kind of land is good for growing food?

> What has water all around it?

Bulletin Board

Materials: old postcards, greeting cards, magazines, and calendars

Ask children to look through postcards, greeting cards, magazines, and calendars with family members for pictures of different kinds of land and water. Encourage children to share what they know about land and water with their family members. Then have children bring a postcard, greeting card, magazine, or calendar picture to class for a bulletin board display entitled "Land and Water."
(VISUAL/TACTILE)

Land and Water

Make a Picture Dictionary

Materials: Activity Pattern P5 (picture dictionary), scissors, pencils, crayons or markers, construction paper cut in half

Invite children to make picture dictionaries for the words in this lesson as well as other words in Unit 3. Start by having children name the different kinds of land and water they discussed in this lesson. List the words on the board.

Then give each child two copies of Activity Pattern P5 (picture dictionary page) and have them cut along the dashed lines to make two dictionary pages from each pattern. Instruct children to write a word on the line, draw a picture in the box to illustrate the word, and then write a definition on the lines below the picture.
(VISUAL/ TACTILE)

The Land Around Us Picture Dictionary.

mountain
A mountain is the highest kind of land.

Find Land and Water on a Map

OBJECTIVES

■ Access information from a map using colors and symbols in a map key.

■ Create visual and written material including maps.

RESOURCES

Pupil Book/Unit Big Book,
pp. 102–103

Activity Book, p. 27

🌐 **Skill Transparency 3–2**

💿 **GeoSkills CD-ROM**

1 Motivate

Have children turn to pages 96–97 in their books. Ask them to find the map key and tell what they have learned about maps and map keys. Next, provide each child with a sheet of drawing paper. Demonstrate how to fold the paper in half lengthwise and then in thirds to make six boxes. Ask children to think about how they would show plains, mountains, hills, islands, rivers, and lakes on a map. Have them draw their ideas in the boxes. Then invite children to share and compare their drawings.

Why It Matters

Have children read the text. Explain that knowing how to locate land and water on a map can help them understand what a place looks like.

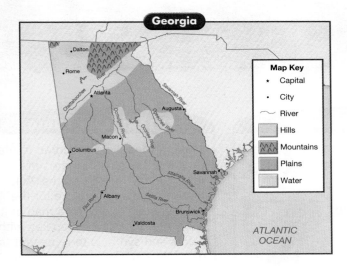

Georgia

Map Key
* ★ Capital
* • City
* ∿ River
* ▨ Hills
* ⋀⋀⋀ Mountains
* ▨ Plains
* ▨ Water

ATLANTIC OCEAN

READING SOCIAL STUDIES

Graphic Organizer Begin a K-W-L chart about using maps. Complete the chart as children read and discuss the lesson.

What We Know	What We Want to Know	What We Learned
Maps have map keys.	How to tell what is land and what is water on a map	
Map keys have symbols that stand for things.	How to find different kinds of land and water	
Map keys help us find places on maps.		

2 Teach

What You Need to Know

Remind children of the pictures they drew earlier that stand for different kinds of land and water. Invite children to look at the map on page 103 and to point out the different colors and symbols they see. Ask children to guess what each one means. Explain that this map uses colors and symbols to show the different kinds of land and water in the state of Georgia.

Direct children's attention to the map key and ask them to guess which symbol stands for a river, for example. Verify their guesses by reading aloud the label.

Q Why do you think the mapmaker used this symbol?

A It looks like a river and it is the color of water.

Then read aloud the labels for the remaining colors and symbols on the map key, helping children to note how some of the symbol shapes, such as mountains, look like the land and water features they represent. Call on volunteers to locate places on the map where each color or symbol appears.

Q How does this map key help you?

A It shows me what each color or symbol means on the map.

Call children's attention to the symbol for a city.

Q Why do you think the mapmaker used a dot symbol for a city?

A It is small so it does not take up too much space on the map.

Skills

MAP AND GLOBE

Find Land and Water on a Map

▶ Why It Matters

Seeing land and water on maps can help you imagine what places look like.

▶ What You Need to Know

Georgia has many kinds of land and water. Different colors show the different kinds of land and water.

▶ Practice the Skill

1. Describe the symbols for land and water on the map.

2. Name two rivers in Georgia.

3. Which city is found beside the Flint River?

102

INTEGRATE READING

Solve Puzzles Read aloud with children *The News Hounds in the Great Balloon Race: A Geography Adventure* by Amy Axelrod (Simon & Schuster Children's, 2000). The story is about three dogs who cover a hot-air balloon race over the state of Texas. After reading through the story, help children solve the geographical puzzles that are included.

EXTEND AND ENRICH

Make a Map Invite children to pretend that the United States of America now has 51 states. Ask them to make up a name for the newest state and draw a map of it. Have them include a map key with colors and symbols to represent the different kinds of land and water. Have children exchange their completed maps with partners and describe their new state by using the map key.

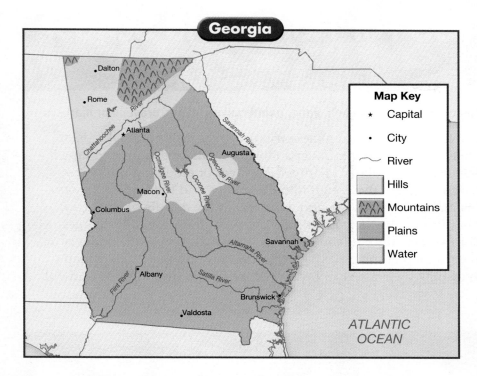

Georgia

Map Key
- ★ Capital
- • City
- ～ River
- Hills
- ⋀⋀ Mountains
- Plains
- Water

Dalton
Rome
Chattahoochee River
Atlanta
Ocmulgee River
Oconee River
Ogeechee River
Macon
Columbus
Augusta
Savannah River
Savannah
Altamaha River
Albany
Flint River
Satilla River
Brunswick
Valdosta

ATLANTIC OCEAN

▶ Apply What You Learned

Look at a map of your state. Find the different kinds of land and water.

Practice your map and globe skills with the **GeoSkills CD-ROM.**

103

MAP AND GLOBE SKILLS

As children distinguish between the different kinds of land and water, help them recognize that most of the land in Georgia consists of plains and rolling hills.

Q How does this map help you?

A It helps me know what the state of Georgia looks like.

Practice the Skill—Answers

❶ The colors yellow, purple, and green stand for land, and the color blue stands for water.

❷ Children should name any two of the following: Altamaha River, Chattahoochee River, Flint River, Ocmulgee River, Oconee River, Ogeechee River, Savannah River, Satilla River

❸ Albany

1 Close

Apply What You Learned

Children should be able to look at a map of their state and locate different kinds of land, such as plains, mountains, and hills, and water, such as rivers and lakes.

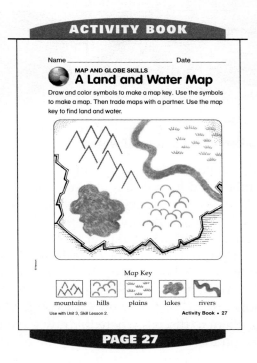

ACTIVITY BOOK

Name _____ Date _____

MAP AND GLOBE SKILLS
A Land and Water Map

Draw and color symbols to make a map key. Use the symbols to make a map. Then trade maps with a partner. Use the map key to find land and water.

Map Key

mountains   hills   plains   lakes   rivers

Use with Unit 3, Skill Lesson 2.   **Activity Book • 27**

PAGE 27

RETEACH THE SKILL

Use Maps Help children form small groups, and provide each group with a land and water map of the United States. Ask children to locate their state and the state of Georgia. Next, ask them to locate the map key and tell what the colors and symbols mean. Then invite each group member to identify one kind of land and one kind of water on the map.

TRANSPARENCY

Use SKILL TRANSPARENCY 3-2.

CD-ROM

Explore GEOSKILLS CD-ROM to learn more about map and globe skills.

Extension Activities For Home and School

A Tabletop Model

Materials: cardboard, masking tape, modeling dough, paint, paintbrushes, paper, crayons or markers

Invite children to create a tabletop model of an imaginary place that includes the kinds of land and water they have been learning about. Cover a tabletop with cardboard and tape it in place. Have children then coat the cardboard with a thick layer of modeling dough to begin their landscape. Have them shape the dough into mountains and hills, adding more dough as needed, as well as plains, lakes, rivers, and an island in the middle of a lake, for example. Once the dough has thoroughly dried, children can paint the landscape. Suggest they choose a different color for each kind of land and blue for water. When the model is complete, have children make a map of the place they created. Have them include a map key. Invite children to display their maps and demonstrate how to use them to find out what places look like.
(TACTILE/ VISUAL)

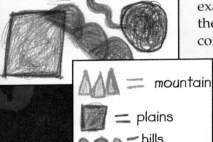

- ⋀⋀⋀ = mountain
- ▢ = plains
- ⌒⌒ = hills
- ◉ = lake
- ∿ = river

Finding Land and Water

Materials: maps

Invite children to explain how to find land and water on a map. List the suggested steps on the board and have children copy them onto a sheet of paper to take home. Then encourage children to gather any maps they have at home—road, city, county, state, country, world—and then look at the maps together with a family member, using the steps they came up with in class.
(VISUAL/ AUDITORY)

How to Find Land and Water on a Map

1. Find the map key.
2. Look at the colors and symbols in the map key to find out what each one means.
3. Choose a color or symbol in the map key and look for it on the map.

Chalk It Up

Materials: sidewalk chalk of varying colors, index cards with symbols for landforms and bodies of water

Have children form groups of five. Provide each group member with a symbol card for a different kind of land or water feature—mountain, hills, plain, island, river, lake—and a piece of colored sidewalk chalk to represent that kind of land or water. Then take children outside to a large open area with a concrete or blacktop surface. Designate space for each group, and invite groups to each make a map of an imaginary place using the symbols and chalk. Explain that each group member is responsible for drawing on the map and in the map key the land or water shown on his or her symbol card. Before group members begin, encourage them to discuss where to draw the mountain, hills, plain, river, and lake on their map. When groups have completed their maps, have them rotate from map to map and use the map key to locate land and water.
(TACTILE/ VISUAL)

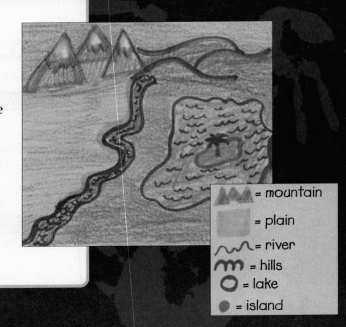

- ⋀⋀⋀ = mountain
- ▢ = plain
- ∿ = river
- ⋔ = hills
- ◯ = lake
- ● = island

Globes and Maps

OBJECTIVES

- Recognize the globe as a model of Earth.
- Identify the continents and oceans of the world.
- Locate places of significance on maps and globes.

 Focus Skill **Categorize** pp. 81, 105, 124

RESOURCES

Pupil Book/Unit Big Book, pp. 104–105

Word Cards V23–26

Activity Book, p. 28

⊕**Reading and Vocabulary Transparency 3–4**

Thinking Organizer T23

⊟Internet Resources

READING SOCIAL STUDIES

Study Questions To help prepare children for the lesson, pose the following questions.

How are a globe and a map alike?	
What places can you find on a globe and a map of the world?	

Tell children to think about these questions as you read the lesson.

● USE READING AND VOCABULARY TRANSPARENCY 3–4

3–4
TRANSPARENCY

Vocabulary

Earth p. 104　　　**globe** p. 104　　　**continent** p. 105

ocean p. 105

 ## When Minutes Count

Have pairs of children read the lesson together. Then ask them to list the similarities and differences between a globe and a map.

Quick Summary

This lesson focuses on globes and maps. It explores how to use both tools to find places on Earth.

 1 **Motivate**

Set the Purpose

Big Idea Before starting the lesson, read the Big Idea statement aloud. As they read and discuss the lesson, encourage children to note how people can use a globe and a map to find places on Earth.

Access Prior Knowledge

Using a classroom map or globe, invite volunteers to point out significant places such as the United States, your state, and your closest big city. Ask children when they think it would be better to use a globe (studying relationships between continents, countries, and bodies of water; working in small groups) and when a map would be more practical (using a road map when driving; working in a large group).

2 Teach

Visual Learning

Map/Globe Invite children to compare the pictures of the map and globe on pages 104–105.

Q How is this map like the globe? How is it different?

A They both show the continents and the oceans. The map is flat and the globe is round like Earth.

Have children point to the locations of the United States, Canada, and Mexico on the map on page 105.

CAPTION ANSWER: Pacific Ocean and Atlantic Ocean

Read and Respond

Geography Discuss the text. Ask children to tell what they know about North America or other continents. Display a globe and point to each continent as you slowly turn it. Then list the continents—North America, South America, Europe, Asia, Africa, Australia, and Antarctica—and help children find each one.

Q On what continent do we live? How do you know?

A North America. The United States is part of North America.

Display a map of the United States. Then call on a volunteer to point out the United States on the globe. Lead children to locate your state on the map and globe.

Tell children there are four great oceans—the Atlantic, the Pacific, the Indian, and the Arctic. Help them locate the oceans on the classroom globe and identify the oceans that separate North America from Europe and Asia. Then help them recognize that the oceans are really one body of water, by tracing a path from ocean to ocean around the globe without lifting your finger.

Lesson 3

Globes and Maps

Big Idea
People can use a globe and a map to find places on Earth.

Vocabulary
Earth
globe
continent
ocean

We live on the planet **Earth**. This globe shows how Earth looks from space. A **globe** is a model of Earth. The green and brown parts stand for land. The blue parts stand for water.

104

INTEGRATE MATHEMATICS

Compare Sizes Provide children with maps and globes of different sizes. Have children compare the size and shape of the same area, such as the United States, on the different maps and globes.

Guide children in understanding that the United States is larger on a larger globe, but it is the same size compared to other land areas.

EXTEND AND ENRICH

Write Globe and Map Riddles
Read aloud the following riddles for children to answer:

- I am not flat but round. I show all the continents and oceans on Earth. What am I? (globe)

- I am a large body of salty water. I separate North America and Europe. What am I? (Atlantic Ocean)

Invite children to write riddles about maps and globes to challenge classmates. As children answer a riddle, call on volunteers to point out the answer on a globe or map.

Like a globe, a map can also show all the places on Earth. The seven large areas of land are **continents**. We live on the continent of North America. Between most of the continents are oceans. An **ocean** is a very large body of salty water.

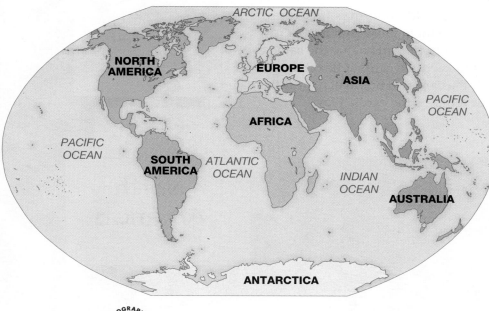

ARCTIC OCEAN

NORTH AMERICA

EUROPE

ASIA

PACIFIC OCEAN

PACIFIC OCEAN

AFRICA

SOUTH AMERICA

ATLANTIC OCEAN

INDIAN OCEAN

AUSTRALIA

ANTARCTICA

 GEOGRAPHY THEME **Which oceans are near North America?**

LESSON 3 Review

 Focus Skill ❶ **Categorize** Name two oceans and two continents.

❷ **Vocabulary** How is a map like a **globe**?

❸ Locate the United States on a globe.

105

ACTIVITY BOOK

Name _____ Date _____

Land and Water

Color the boxes in the map key to show land and water. Then color the map to match the key.
Key and map colors will vary.

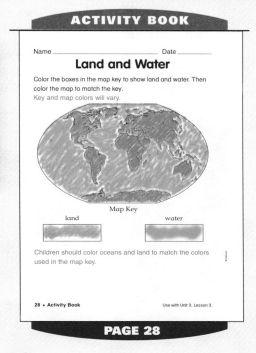

Map Key

land   water

Children should color oceans and land to match the colors used in the map key.

28 ▪ Activity Book   Use with Unit 3, Lesson 3.

3 Close

Summarize Key Content

- You can describe a globe as a model of Earth and compare it to a map.
- You can identify the continents and oceans on a globe and a map.
- You can locate the continent on which you live on a globe and a map.

READING SOCIAL STUDIES

Study Questions Revisit the questions posed in Motivate. Invite children to share answers to the questions. Add these answers to the chart.

How are a globe and a map alike?	They show places on Earth. They both show land and water.
What places can you find on a globe and a map of the world?	You can find continents and oceans.

● USE READING AND VOCABULARY TRANSPARENCY 3–4   **3–4** TRANSPARENCY

Assess

Lesson 3 Review—Answers

❶ Focus Skill **Categorize** Responses may include the Atlantic Ocean, Pacific Ocean, Indian Ocean, and Arctic Ocean; North America, South America, Europe, Asia, Africa, Australia, and Antarctica.

❷ Both a map and a globe show land and water found on Earth.

❸ **Performance Assessment Guidelines** Children should be able to point to the United States on a globe.

Extension Activities For Home and School

Match-Up Game

Materials: index cards, pencils, world map, globe

Invite children to name the seven continents and four oceans as you list them on the board. Provide children with 11 index cards each and have them write the names of the continents and oceans, each on a separate card. Next, have children form pairs to play a matching game. Have partners mix their cards and arrange them facedown in two rows. To play, each player, in turn, gets to turn over two cards. If both cards name the same continent or ocean, the player has made a match and gets to keep the cards if he or she can point to the continent or ocean on the map or globe. If the cards do not match, or if the player cannot locate the continent or ocean, the player replaces the cards. Play continues until all the cards have been matched.
(VISUAL/TACTILE)

North America

North America

X Marks the Spot

Materials: a large map of the world, globe, small self-stick note with an _X_

Display a large world map within easy reach of children. Have a volunteer close his or her eyes and lead that child to the map. Have the child press the note marked with an _X_ to the map. Then invite the child to ask the class up to ten yes or no questions before guessing which continent or ocean the _X_ is on. Suggest the following as examples:

- Is the _X_ on a continent (ocean)?

- Does the continent have two words in its name?

- Does the name of the continent begin with the letter _A_?

- Does the continent look like a big island?

- Is the continent along the Pacific Ocean?

- Is the continent next to Europe?
(VISUAL/AUDITORY)

A Look at the World

Materials: Thinking Organizer T23 (world map)

Have children use Thinking Organizer T23 to share with family members what they have learned about the continents and oceans of the world. Suggest that they label and color the continents and oceans. Then encourage children to use the map for the following family activities:

- Talk about continents the family might like to visit.

- Talk about where family ancestors are from.

- Locate the continents where important current events are taking place.

- Play games such as the continents and oceans Match-Up Game or _X_ Marks the Spot.
(VISUAL/AUDITORY/KINESTHETIC)

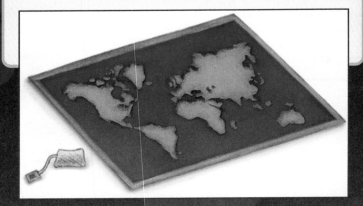

SKILLS

Find Directions on a Globe

North

West   East

South

Vocabulary

directions p. 106

1 Motivate

Invite children to play a game in which they take turns choosing a classroom object and describing its location using directional words for the others to guess. For example, a child might describe the flag by saying, "My mystery object is at the front of the room between the ceiling and the floor."

After playing the game, display a world map and point out North America, South America, the Pacific Ocean, and the Atlantic Ocean. Tell children that to show or tell where places are on a map or globe we do not use words like *left, right, up,* and *down,* but cardinal directions instead. Explain that they will learn about cardinal directions in this lesson.

Why It Matters

Tell children that knowing directional words helps us find places on a map and tell others how to find places on a map.

READING SOCIAL STUDIES

Make a List Help children recall the two continents you pointed out earlier on the map—North America and South America—and ask them to think about these names and what they mean. Then ask children to list what they think the cardinal directions are and write them on a sheet of paper. As they read, encourage children to check their ideas.

2 Teach

What You Need to Know

Recall with children that a globe is a model of Earth. Have children read the text, look at the drawings of the globe, and point to the North Pole. Point out that it is at the top of the globe at the northernmost point of Earth. Explain that the Arctic Circle is the area around the North Pole. Then have children point to the South Pole. Explain that the Antarctic Circle is the area around the South Pole.

Q What can you tell about the South Pole?

A It is the southernmost point on Earth.

Provide children with a globe and have them locate both poles. Then have them put their finger on the equator, or the area halfway between the poles. Emphasize that the poles help us determine directions on Earth—north, south, east, and west.

Tell children that north, south, east, and west are called cardinal directions. Then have children use cardinal directions to describe where each continent on the globe is in relation to the others and to the oceans around it.

Skills

MAP AND GLOBE

Find Directions on a Globe

Vocabulary

directions

▶ **Why It Matters**

Directions show or tell where something is. They help you find a place.

▶ **What You Need to Know**

Look at the drawings of a globe. Each drawing shows half of the globe. Both drawings show the North Pole and the South Pole. These poles help describe directions on Earth.

The main directions are north, south, east, and west. North is the direction toward the North Pole. When you face north, east is to your right. West is to your left.

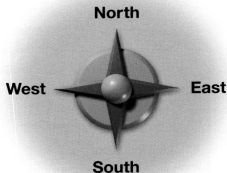

North

West · East

South

106

REACH ALL LEARNERS

Advanced Learners
Discuss with children how the sun always rises in the east and sets in the west. Challenge children to use this information to figure out which way is north and which way is south and to explain how they know.

INTEGRATE PHYSICAL EDUCATION

Simon Says Take children to the gym or playground. Use a compass to determine where north is, and have them face that direction. Remind children that east is to their right, west is to their left, and south is behind them. Then play a game of Simon Says, using cardinal directions in your commands. For example: *Simon says face east and hop on one foot. Simon says face west and run in place. Simon says face south and do ten jumping jacks.*

▶ Practice the Skill

① Which continent is east of Europe?

② Which continent is at the South Pole?

③ Which ocean is west of North America?

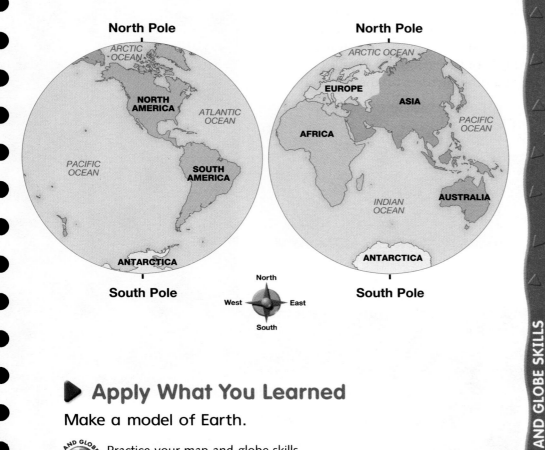

▶ Apply What You Learned

Make a model of Earth.

 Practice your map and globe skills with the **GeoSkills CD-ROM.**

107

Practice the Skill—Answers

① Asia is east of Europe.

② Antarctica is at the South Pole.

③ The Pacific Ocean is west of North America.

3 Close

Apply What You Learned

Provide children with balloons and papier-mâché to make models of Earth. Have them dip strips of paper into paste and wrap the strips around a balloon, making sure to overlap the strips and apply several layers. Once the strips are dry, have children paint the oceans and continents and mark the poles. Children's models should include the four great oceans, the seven continents, and the two poles.

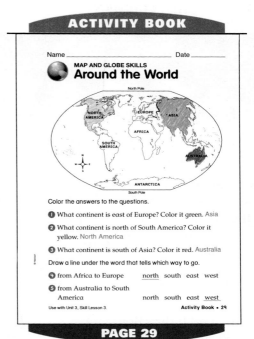

PAGE 29

TRANSPARENCY

Use SKILL TRANSPARENCY 3–3.

CD-ROM

Explore GEOSKILLS CD-ROM to learn more about map and globe skills.

EXTEND AND ENRICH

Create a Game Provide each small group of children with a world map. Have them label and color the continents and oceans. Then challenge each group to develop and play a game using the directions north, south, east, and west as clues. For example, players can give clues about a place for other players to guess or give directions to get from one place to another. Afterward, invite groups to share and compare their games.

RETEACH THE SKILL

Use a Globe Gather children around a globe. Point to a location, such as North America, and have children identify it. Then ask questions such as the following: *What ocean lies to the east? What continent lies to the south? What ocean lies to the west?* As children answer the questions, call on volunteers to point out each location on the globe. Then call on children to point to a location and ask directional questions.

Extension Activities For Home and School

Directions

Materials: blue construction paper, brown craft paper, scissors, red construction paper direction arrows labeled *N*, *S*, *E*, and *W*, pushpins, pictures of a ship, jet plane, lake, farm, town or city, mountains, forest, hills, and a family in a car

Cover a bulletin board with blue construction paper to represent the ocean. Use brown craft paper to construct a large area of land to represent an island or continent. Pin the direction arrow for north at the top edge of the map and call on children to pin the remaining direction arrows in place. Pin the family car in the middle of the island. Then give children directions such as the following to pin the remaining pictures on the map:

- Pin the ship to the east of the island.
- Pin the jet to the west of the island.
- Pin the mountains to the north of the car.
- Pin the lake to the west of the mountains.

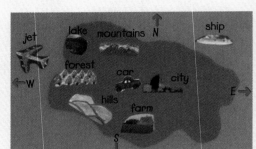

When the map is complete, encourage children to work in groups to create statements about the map and have classmates tell if the statements are true or false. For example: *The hills are to the north of the forest. The car is going north if it is headed toward the mountains.*

(VISUAL/ TACTILE/ AUDITORY)

Following Directions

Materials: masking tape, construction paper direction arrows marked *N*, *S*, *E*, *W*

Use masking tape to make a six-by-six grid on the floor, with each block about one square foot so that a child can easily stand in a block. Indicate *north, south, east,* and *west* by taping each direction arrow in place along an outside edge of the grid. Then place a number from 1 to 36 in each block.

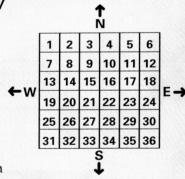

Have children follow a series of directions to move from one block to another. For example: *Stand in block 1. Face east and go 3 blocks. Face south and go 5 blocks. Face west and go 1 block. Face north and go 2 blocks. What number are you standing on now?* Children can take turns giving each other directions.

(KINESTHETIC/ AUDITORY)

Location Riddles

Materials: globe, world map, paper, pencil

On slips of paper, write several riddles using cardinal directions to describe where bodies of water, continents, and the poles are located. For example, *I am east of North America. I am west of Europe. Which body of water am I?* Have children work with partners or in small groups to read and solve the riddles using a map or globe. Lead children to see how they can use cardinal directions to describe places on Earth. Then challenge partners or groups to write riddles for others to solve.

(VISUAL/ AUDITORY)

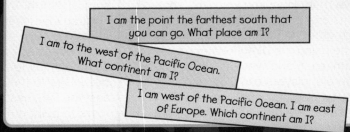

I am the point the farthest south that you can go. What place am I?

I am to the west of the Pacific Ocean. What continent am I?

I am west of the Pacific Ocean. I am east of Europe. Which continent am I?

People and Resources

OBJECTIVES

- Identify examples of and uses for natural resources in the community, state, and nation.
- Recognize how people depend on land and water.
- Understand the importance of natural resources.

 Categorize pp. 81, 124

RESOURCES

Pupil Book/Unit Big Book, pp. 108–111

Word Cards V25–V28

Activity Book, p. 30

🖘 **Reading and Vocabulary Transparency 3–5**

🖥 **Internet Resources**

READING SOCIAL STUDIES

Graphic Organizer Begin a chart about natural resources and how people use them. Complete the chart during Close.

Using Earth's Resources	
Resource	**How We Use It**
trees	paper, furniture
oil	gasoline
soil	growing food

● USE READING AND VOCABULARY
TRANSPARENCY 3–5

3–5
TRANSPARENCY

Vocabulary

resource p. 108 **farm** p. 108 **forest** p. 109

 When Minutes Count

Have children read the Big Idea and skim the lesson for Earth's five major resources.

Quick Summary

This lesson is about Earth's many resources: soil, forests, oil, gas, and water. It focuses on how people depend upon these resources for their needs.

 Motivate

Set the Purpose

Big Idea Before starting the lesson, read the Big Idea statement aloud. As children read and discuss the lesson, have them identify each resource, noting how people use it and why it is important to them.

Access Prior Knowledge

Ask children to think about or make a list of some items they use every day. Ask them if they know what each item is made from or where it comes from. Begin a discussion of natural resources such as trees, oil, and soil.

2 Teach

Read and Respond

Link Geography and Economics
As children read the text on page 108, emphasize that resources include land and water and the things that live and grow on land or in water. Point out that resources also include things that are found underground, like minerals.

Point out that the physical features of land, along with the water supply, determine what types of crops will grow there and how well they will grow.

Emphasize that plants, animals, and people depend on soil either directly or indirectly for food.

Q What foods do you eat that grow in soil?

A fruits and vegetables

Q What might happen if farmers did not take care of the soil or use it wisely?

A Crops would not grow well; farmers would not be able to feed and raise animals.

Remind children that farmers not only grow crops but also raise animals. Point out that some animals provide us with food as well as the resources to make clothing.

Lesson

4

People and Resources

Big Idea
Natural resources are important to people.

Vocabulary

resource

farm

forest

How are paper, bread, and gasoline alike? They are all made from Earth's resources. A **resource** is anything people can use. Earth has many resources.

Soil

Much of the land on Earth is covered with soil. Soil is important to plants, animals, and people. On a **farm**, workers use the soil to grow plants and raise animals that people use for food.

108

STUDY/RESEARCH SKILLS

Using Reference Sources
Brainstorm a list of countries around the world. Have small groups choose a country from the list and research how that country uses land. Have children use children's encyclopedias or books to find at least two ways people use the land. Groups can write and illustrate the facts they find and bind the pages to make a world resources book.

INTEGRATE SCIENCE

What's in Soil? Half-fill a jar with soil. Next, add water to the top. Replace the lid and shake. When the contents settle, have children observe the layers: dead matter, or humus (provides soil with nutrients); water; sand; clay or mud (gives structure); small stones; and bigger stones (help water drain). Children may want to try this at home with a family member.

REACH ALL LEARNERS

Tactile Learners Provide children with paper plates. Invite them to draw or cut out and paste on the plates pictures of what they had for lunch or breakfast. Help children name the resources from which food items come. For example: the flour used to make bread comes from wheat, which comes from the soil; cows provide milk; peanut plants grow peanuts for peanut butter.

Trees

A **forest** is a large area where many trees grow. Wood from trees is used to make furniture and buildings. Some trees give us food, such as apples and walnuts.

109

Pictures Invite children to describe what the farmer is doing in the picture on page 108. holding potatoes Then direct children's attention to the oak tree, noting that it is growing in soil. Emphasize that trees, like other plants, depend on the soil for water and nutrients.

Q **Why do you think trees are important?**

A The trees that grow in a forest provide us with wood and food.

Invite children to look at the remaining photos and describe how people are using trees for things they need.

Q **What examples do you see in our classroom of items that might have come from trees in a forest?**

A desks, bookshelves, tables, pencils, books, newspaper, craft sticks, rulers, wooden blocks

Focus attention on the child picking the apple in the picture.

Q **Other than apples, what foods do you eat that come from trees?**

A Possible answers are peaches, pears, plums, lemons, limes, grapefruits, cherries, apricots, oranges, walnuts, and pecans.

You may wish to mention that another way people use trees is to burn wood to keep their homes warm in cold weather.

INTEGRATE ART

Leaf and Bark Rubbings
Display photos of trees that are common to your region and discuss with children why they are an important resource. Then take children on a walk to identify and observe some of the trees. Provide white paper and crayons for children to make leaf and bark rubbings. Have children label their rubbings with the names of the trees and then use them to create a display entitled "Our Trees."

INTEGRATE READING

Add to a Poem Focus attention on the photo of the people framing a house. Then read this verse from "What Do We Plant?" by Henry Abbey.

> What do we plant when
>   we plant the tree?
> We plant the houses for
>   you and me.
> We plant the rafters,
>   the shingles, the floors,
> We plant the studding,
>   the lath, the doors,

> The beams and siding,
>   all parts that be;
> We plant the house
>   when we plant the tree.

Then write on the board *What do we plant when we plant the tree?* Challenge children to think of other ways people use trees and then make up new lines to answer the question. For example, *What do we plant when we plant the tree? We plant books to read for you and for me.* Have children share their lines.

Read and Respond

Link Geography with Culture and Society Discuss the text and pictures on page 110. Explain that oil and gas are fuels—something burned to provide heat, light, or energy to make things move. Ask children to describe how people are using natural gas and gasoline in the pictures. Point out that oil is made into fuel to run ships, trains, trucks, jet planes, and cars and is also used in making hundreds of products including plastics and cosmetics.

A CLOSER LOOK
Drilling for Oil

Emphasize that to reach the oil or gas trapped deep below Earth's surface and pump it out, a well must be drilled. Discuss the text and captions with children. Explain that gas and oil cannot be used over and over again or quickly replaced. Once they are used up, they are gone.

CAPTION ANSWER: by drilling holes deep into the ground

Visual Learning

Pictures Focus on the text and pictures on page 111. Point out that sunlight and water are the most important elements needed for the survival of living things. Discuss the different uses of water.

Q How do we depend on water?

A We drink water, water crops, cook and clean with water, and eat plants and animals that live in oceans, rivers, and lakes.

Discuss how we use our oceans, rivers, and lakes for recreation and as a way to travel and transport things from place to place as well.

Q How are ocean water and river water different?

A Ocean water is salty; river water is fresh.

Have children study this lesson and list the ways in which people make a living by using natural resources.

Oil and Gas

Oil and gas come from under the ground. People use oil and gas to heat their homes and cook their food. Some oil is made into gasoline for running cars and other machines.

110

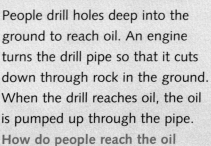
A CLOSER LOOK
Drilling for Oil

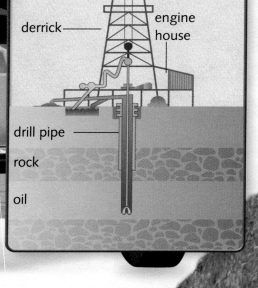
People drill holes deep into the ground to reach oil. An engine turns the drill pipe so that it cuts down through rock in the ground. When the drill reaches oil, the oil is pumped up through the pipe. How do people reach the oil under the ground?

derrick

engine house

drill pipe

rock

oil

MAKE IT RELEVANT

In Your Community Invite representatives from the different utility companies to speak with children about how resources such as natural gas, electricity, and water come into their homes.

EXTEND AND ENRICH

Make a Photo Journal Help children find and gather a variety of reference materials about your state, including information available on the Internet. Then invite children to make a photo journal about their state's resources and how those resources are used. Children can use postcard and magazine photographs, take photographs, or draw their own pictures.

Water

Water is a resource that all living things must have to live. People and animals drink it, and some plants and animals live in it.

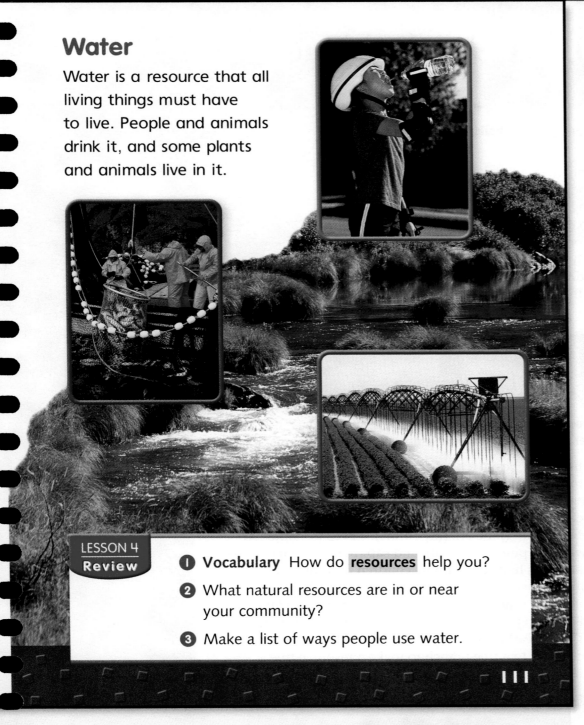

LESSON 4 Review

① **Vocabulary** How do **resources** help you?

② What natural resources are in or near your community?

③ Make a list of ways people use water.

111

ACTIVITY BOOK

Name _____ Date _____

Earth's Resources

Write the names of three resources you see in the picture. Draw something you use that comes from each resource.

soil

trees

water

30 • Activity Book   Use with Unit 3, Lesson 4.

PAGE 30

Summarize Key Content

- Resources are important because people use them to meet their needs.
- Water, oil, gas, trees, and soil are natural resources.
- You can explain how people use natural resources from the land and water.

READING SOCIAL STUDIES

Graphic Organizer Revisit the chart begun in Motivate. Invite children to share new ideas they learned. Add these ideas to the chart.

Using Earth's Resources	
Resource	**How We Use It**
trees	paper, furniture, wood, food, building
oil	gasoline, heat
soil	growing food
water	drink, cook, water plants
gas	heat, cook

● USE READING AND VOCABULARY TRANSPARENCY 3–5   **3–5** TRANSPARENCY

Assess

Lesson 4 Review—Answers

① Resources provide the things I need, such as water to drink, food to eat, a way to stay warm, and materials to build a place to live.

② Children should recognize that trees, bodies of water, soil, plants, and animals are natural resources in or near their community.

③ **Performance Assessment Guidelines** Children's lists should include any of the following ways people use water: drink, bathe, cook, clean, water crops and plants, eat plants and animals that live in water.

Extension Activities For Home and School

Earth's Resources Book

Materials: magazines, scissors, construction paper, paste, pencils, three-hole punch, yarn or fasteners

Organize children into small groups and invite them to make a book about Earth's resources. Have children begin by finding and cutting out pictures of natural resources from magazines and pasting them on separate sheets of construction paper. Remind children that resources include not only the land and water but also the things that live and grow on land or in water, as well as things that are found under Earth's surface. For each picture, ask children to list some of the ways people use that resource. Help children put together the pages to create *Our Earth's Resources Book*. Have each group make a cover for their book.
(TACTILE/VISUAL)

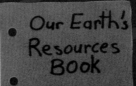

making furniture
building a house
making paper
source of food

A Resource Tree

Materials: bare tree branches, bucket, sand, rocks, crayons or markers, 6-inch construction paper circles, magazines, scissors, paste, hole punch, yarn

Arrange sturdy tree branches in a bucket. Using sand and rocks, prop up the branches so that they resemble a tree. Emphasize that trees provide thousands of products that people use every day, including foods, wood, and chemical products. Point out to children that even the bark (cork, dyes), gum (pine oil, turpentine), leaves (ornamental wreaths, pine-needle oil), and sap (maple sugar) of certain trees have uses. Invite children to draw or cut out and paste onto the construction paper circles pictures of products that come from trees and tree parts. Have children then punch a hole along the edge of the circle. Help them thread a piece of yarn or string through the hole, and tie it to a tree branch to make a resource tree.
(TACTILE/VISUAL)

Make a Chart

Materials: poster paper, package labels

Discuss the importance of soil as a resource (to grow food for people and animals, to grow plants for use in clothing and other products). Ask children to brainstorm crops such as wheat, oats, corn, rice, peanuts, barley, and cotton. Have children make a copy of the list to take home to share with family members. Suggest that together they read labels to find out what products they eat or use at home that contain these resources. Suggest that children and family members make a chart to show their findings.
(TACTILE/VISUAL)

Wheat	Rice	Cotton
bread, a cereal such as cream of wheat	puffed rice cereal, chicken and rice soup	T-shirt, bath towel and wash cloth, socks

Predict What Will Happen

OBJECTIVES

- Use a decision-making process to identify a situation that requires a decision, gather information, and predict consequences.

- Demonstrate the concept of scarcity.

RESOURCES

Pupil Book/Unit Big Book, pp. 112–113

Word Cards V27–V28

Activity Book, p. 31

⊘**Skill Transparency 3–4**

Vocabulary

predict p. 112   **weather** p. 112

Motivate

Read aloud the poem "Spring Rain" by Marchette Chute and ask children to imagine they are the child in the poem.

> The storm came up so very quick
>   It couldn't have been quicker.
> I should have brought my hat along,
>   I should have brought my slicker.
>
> My hair is wet, my feet are wet,
>   I couldn't be much wetter.
> I fell into a river once
>   But this is even better.

Q **What could you have done before leaving the house?**

A Possible responses: looked outside to see if it was cloudy, listened to the weather forecast, and taken an umbrella.

Invite children to explain how they can tell when a storm is coming and why knowing about an approaching storm can be important.

Why It Matters

Tell children that paying attention to clues and thinking about what they already know can sometimes help them tell what might happen next. Explain that knowing this can help them plan what to do.

REACH ALL LEARNERS

English as a Second Language To help children understand the poem, explain that a slicker is a kind of glossy raincoat. If possible, display a picture of a slicker. Have children share the name of a raincoat in their first language by saying "A raincoat is called _____."

2 Teach

What You Need to Know

Explain that *weather* includes the temperature of the air, the wind conditions, and the moisture—rain or snow, for example. Invite children to look outside the classroom window and describe the current weather. If you have an outdoor thermometer, help children read the temperature. Ask children if the weather has changed between the time they left for school this morning and now. If it has, encourage them to explain how. For example, it may be warmer, the early morning fog may be gone, the sun may be shining, or it may be windier.

Then focus attention on the picture of the clouds and invite children to describe their color and shape. Explain that clouds like these often appear across the sky before rain and that by observing such clouds, they can predict, or tell ahead of time, that rain is coming.

Q What would you do if you were about to ride your bike to a friend's house and saw clouds like these?

A Possible responses: take my umbrella and raincoat and walk; ask an adult to give me a ride; stay home and wait until the rain is over

Tell children the water that clouds bring as rain or snow is important to all life—people, plants, and animals.

Q What might happen if there were not enough rain?

A Crops could dry up; plants, animals, and people could suffer.

Emphasize that clouds can also bring hail and destructive storms such as tornadoes. Observing clouds and thinking about what they know can help children plan what to do to stay safe well before a predicted storm hits.

Skills READING

Predict What Will Happen

Vocabulary

predict

weather

▶ Why It Matters

When you know how things happen, you can **predict**, or tell ahead of time, what will happen next. Knowing what is going to happen can help people plan what to do.

▶ What You Need to Know

People can predict the weather by looking at clouds. **Weather** is what the air outside is like. Dark clouds often mean rain is coming.

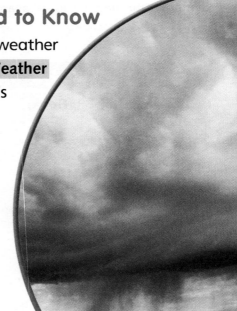

112

▶ Practice the Skill

1 If it did not rain for a long time, what would happen to growing food?

2 Think about the people who make, sell, and buy food. Tell what you think would happen to them.

▶ Apply What You Learned

What do you think would happen if people caught all the fish they could find?

113

Practice the Skill—Answers

1 Without enough water, crops cannot grow well and may even die. This means there would be less food for people.

2 Possible responses: because there is less food, it may cost more; people may only be allowed to make, sell, or buy a certain amount of food; people could lose their jobs or be forced to close their businesses.

3 Close

Apply What You Learned

Children's predictions should reflect an understanding that over time there would be fewer and fewer fish to catch and eventually fish might disappear completely.

ACTIVITY BOOK

Name _____ Date _____

READING SKILLS
What Might Happen?

Draw pictures to show what might happen.

What might happen if it rains for five days?

What might happen if there is a thunderstorm?

What might happen if it doesn't rain all summer?

Use with Unit 3, Skill Lesson 4.   Activity Book • 31

PAGE 31

TRANSPARENCY

Use SKILL TRANSPARENCY 3–4.

EXTEND AND ENRICH

Research Clouds Tell children that scientists have names for the different kinds of clouds—stratus clouds, cumulus clouds, and cirrus clouds. Provide children with reference materials to find out what these three main kinds of clouds look like and how they help scientists predict the weather. Then have them make models using cotton balls, paste, and construction paper.

RETEACH THE SKILL

Collect and Check Weather Predictions Ask children to think about the weather over the last week. Has it been similar each day, or has it been changing? Has it been colder or warmer than usual? Has it been stormy? Then invite children to predict the weather for the coming week. Each day, have each child write a prediction for the following day on a sheet of paper and then sign it. Collect their papers and save. At the end of each day, have children check yesterday's predictions and discuss how they made their decisions.

Extension Activities For Home and School

Making Plans

Materials: magazines, scissors, glue, poster paper, crayons or markers

Invite children to imagine that a blizzard has been predicted. Explain that during such storms people often lose their electricity because of downed power lines. Organize children into groups. Have each group find and cut out magazine pictures of the appliances they have in their homes that need electricity to run. Then have them paste the pictures onto a sheet of poster paper. Challenge each group to come up with suggestions for coping without electricity during the storm. For example, *Use candles for light; Use logs to make a fire in the fireplace; Cook outdoors on a charcoal grill; Have a cellular phone and portable radio handy.* Invite groups to share and discuss their posters.
(TACTILE/VISUAL)

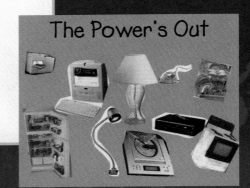
The Power's Out

Nursery Rhyme Fun

Materials: drawing paper, crayons or markers (optional)

Invite children to listen to the following reworked nursery rhymes. Have them predict what the characters might do by pantomiming a character's actions, by drawing a picture, or by role-playing and speaking as a character.

> Little Miss Muffet
> Sat on her tuffet
> Eating her curds and whey.
>
> When along came a mouse,
> It ran through her house.
> Predict what Miss Muffet did say.
>
> Pease porridge hot,
> Pease porridge cold,
> Pease porridge in the pot
> Nine days old.
>
> Some like it hot,
> Some like it cold,
> Predict how porridge tastes
> When it's nine days old.

(AUDITORY/ KINESTHETIC)

Your Best Guess

Materials: wooden building blocks, heavy cardboard, books, toy cars

Set up the activities described below. Invite pairs of children to choose one of the activities, predict the results, and then check their predictions. Suggest children try these activities with family members as well.

Invite partners to each build a wooden block tower. Have one partner stack the blocks on top of each other and the other partner use two blocks side by side at a time, alternating each row as shown below. Have partners predict which tower is likely to topple first.

Invite partners to each build a ramp using cardboard and books. Tell children that one ramp must be higher than the other. After the ramps are built, provide each partner with a small toy car of identical size and weight. Have partners predict which car will go farther when released at the top of the ramp.
(TACTILE/ VISUAL/ KINESTHETIC)

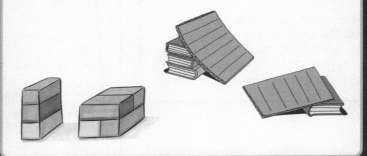

Saving Our Resources

OBJECTIVES

- Recognize that we need to protect resources for the future.
- Describe personal responsibility for protecting the environment.

 Categorize pp. 81, 116, 124

RESOURCES

Pupil Book/Unit Big Book, pp. 114–117

Word Cards V29–V30

Activity Book, p. 32

⊕ **Reading and Vocabulary Transparency 3–6**

Activity Pattern P6

⊡ **Internet Resources**

READING SOCIAL STUDIES

Study Questions To help prepare children for the lesson, pose the following questions.

What are resources?	
Why must we save our resources?	
How can you help save Earth's resources?	

Tell children to think about these questions as you read the lesson.

● **USE READING AND VOCABULARY TRANSPARENCY 3–6**
 3–6 TRANSPARENCY

Vocabulary

pollution p. 114   **litter** p. 115   **recycle** p. 117

 When Minutes Count

Have children skim the lesson to find the meanings of *reduce*, *reuse*, and *recycle*.

Quick Summary

This lesson focuses on protecting Earth and its natural resources. It explores the importance of reducing, reusing, and recycling materials.

 1 **Motivate**

Set the Purpose

Big Idea Before starting the lesson, read the Big Idea statement aloud. As children read and discuss the lesson, help them identify the different ways they can help protect their environment.

Access Prior Knowledge

Before reading the lesson with children, show them photographs of litter and pollution. Ask children to describe the damage to the environment that each photo presents.

Read and Respond

Culture and Society Read aloud the text on page 114 with children. Point out that there are now over 6 billion people on Earth and we are all sharing the same resources. Invite children to take a deep breath as you point out that the air they are breathing is another important resource.

Q Why do you think the air, land, and water are so important?

A People and animals cannot live without them.

Emphasize that everything on our planet—air, land, and water—is connected, and pollution is a serious threat to our resources. Explain, for example, that rain can wash dangerous chemicals in factory smoke onto the land and into our streams, rivers, lakes, and oceans. These chemicals in turn can affect the plants and animals that live or grow on the land or in our waterways or under the ground.

Q What could happen to the fish in a polluted river or stream?

A The fish could get sick or die.

Q What could happen if the soil on a farm becomes polluted?

A The farmer can have trouble growing crops for food.

Lesson 5

Saving Our Resources

Big Idea
People need to take care of Earth's natural resources.

Vocabulary
pollution
litter
recycle

Many people live on Earth. They all use the same resources.

Protect Our Resources

It is important to keep Earth and our resources clean. **Pollution** is anything that makes air, land, or water dirty.

114

Environmental Concerns
Brainstorm key terms children can use to research environmental concerns in their community. Then organize children into pairs, and help them use the key terms to research the topic on the Internet. Have pairs share with the class the information they found.

Acid Rain Describe acid rain as rain, snow, sleet, fog, and hail that has been polluted by harmful chemicals in the air from cars, factories, and power plants. To demonstrate the effects of acid rain, have children water two small plants of the same kind for two weeks, one with tap water and the other with a mixture of one cup of tap water and a tablespoon of vinegar. Have children observe and record the results.

Things To Do Invite children to read *Just a Dream* by Chris Van Allsburg (Houghton Mifflin, 1990), a story about a boy who is not at all concerned about pollution until he has a dream about the future on Earth. After reading the story, challenge children to suggest things they can do to take care of the environment.

JUST A DREAM

Laws help. You can help, too. Do not **litter**, or throw trash, on land or in water.

115

MAKE IT RELEVANT

At School and in the Community Invite children to form a litter patrol and act as litter scouts. Take them on a walk around the school grounds and the surrounding neighborhood to look for and pick up clean litter. NOTE: Have children bring rubber or gardening gloves from home and wear them when picking up litter. When you return to school, help children decide which items are trash and which items can be recycled.

Read and Respond

Civics and Government Help children recall that a law is a rule enacted by a city, state, or country and that everyone must obey it. Note that many laws have been passed to help clean up the environment and to reduce pollution.

Q **How do you think laws can help?**

A Everyone knows what he or she can and cannot do.

Discuss how children can help the environment by not littering. Define *litter* as unwanted items that people have tossed on the ground or in the water instead of properly discarding. Ask children to name the kinds of items they have seen discarded in this way, such as drink cans, paper and plastic, and bottles.

Q **What should we do with things we don't want so they don't become litter?**

A Put them in trash cans, dumpsters, and recycling bins.

Marjory Stoneman Douglas

Responsibility Help children recall an earlier discussion about responsibility in relation to Thomas Jefferson (Unit 2, Lesson 3). Explain that people who demonstrate responsibility are people who take charge and get things done. Share with children that Marjory Stoneman Douglas created a group that worked to preserve the environment. After reading about her on page 115, ask children if they think she demonstrated responsibility. Children may point out that she assumed responsibility for protecting the Everglades by organizing a group and working to get laws passed to protect this natural resource.

Visual Learning

Pictures Invite children to describe the land and water in the picture on the bottom of pages 114–115. Note that it is the Florida Everglades. Display a map of Florida and help children locate the area.

Read and Respond

Civics and Government Explain that to help protect our resources we must use them wisely. Invite children to read the text to find out how. Write *reduce, reuse,* and *recycle* on the board as you read the sentence that relates to each word. Point out the recycling symbol in the picture. Encourage children to suggest things they can reuse and ways to reduce the use of resources. For example, use plastic bags and jars again; turn off the water when you brush your teeth; when you leave a room, shut off the lights to save electricity; or walk or ride your bike to save gasoline. List children's ideas on the board.

Explain that paper can be reprocessed to make different paper products, and plastics can be melted down and used to make such things as fences, benches, and carpeting. Distribute recyclable plastic containers for children to examine. Have them locate the recycle symbol and number. Explain that the symbol means the container can be recycled.

Q What other things can you name that people recycle?

A glass, metal cans, old tires

DEMOCRATIC VALUES
Common Good

Call attention to Earnest's words. Emphasize that we all have a responsibility to protect Earth and its resources, not just for ourselves and our families today, but also for families in the future. Invite children to tell how they reduce, reuse, and/or recycle.

Use Resources Wisely

You can reduce, or use less of a resource.

You can reuse, or use some things over and over again.

116

READING SKILL

Categorize Organize the class into three groups. Assign one group the word *reduce*, one group the word *reuse*, and one group the word *recycle*. Have each group brainstorm and list ways or items to conserve.

EXTEND AND ENRICH

Role-Play Organize children into two groups, one representing citizens who do not recycle and the other representing citizens who do. Have children create a role-play in which the second group tries to convince the first group to recycle, while the first group gives reasons not to recycle. Groups can then reverse their roles.

Reduce, reuse, recycle.

You can recycle, or make something old into something new.

Recycle

LESSON 5 Review

❶ **Vocabulary** Why is it important not to **litter**?

❷ Why should people use less of a resource?

❸ Make a poster showing how you can use resources wisely at home.

117

3 Close

Summarize Key Content

- Everyone must help take care of Earth's resources.

- You can explain how to reduce, reuse, and recycle to protect Earth's resources.

READING SOCIAL STUDIES

Study Questions Revisit the questions posed during Motivate. Invite children to share answers to the questions. Add these answers to the chart.

What are resources?	Soil, trees, water, gas and oil are some resources.
Why must we save our resources?	We must save our resources so they don't get used up.
How can you help save Earth's resources?	You can use some things over. You can use less of some things. You can not litter. You can recycle.

● USE READING AND VOCABULARY TRANSPARENCY 3–6

3–6 TRANSPARENCY

Assess

Lesson 5 Review—Answers

❶ Litter can cause harm to the land, water, plants, and animals.

❷ People should use less of a resource so it will be there for the future.

❸ **Performance Assessment Guidelines** Children's posters should reflect ways to use less of a resource such as water, electricity, or paper products; to reuse items such as plastic bags and boxes; and to recycle items such as bottles, paper, metal cans, and plastic containers.

RETEACH THE LESSON

Sort to Recycle or Reuse Fill a trash bag with clean reusable and recyclable items such as an aluminum can, foil, newspaper, orange juice can, milk carton, shoe box, lunch bag, yogurt container, plastic berry basket, plastic lids, baby food jars, plastic soda bottle, and construction paper scraps. Have children first remove and sort the items into paper, glass, plastic, and aluminum and then tell how they would reuse or recycle the items. Encourage children to tell why it is important to reuse or recycle these items.

ACTIVITY BOOK

Name _____ Date _____
The Recycle Challenge
Look at all the trash. Think of something that you could make out of these things. Then draw a picture of it.

32 • Activity Book   Use with Unit 3, Lesson 5.

PAGE 32

Extension Activities For Home and School

Reduce, Reuse, Recycle

Materials: Activity Pattern P6 (Reduce, Reuse, Recycle Game), game markers, coin

Review Earnest Eagle's message to reduce, reuse, and recycle. Ask children to explain what each word means and give examples. Then invite children to form pairs to play the Reduce, Reuse, Recycle Game. Provide each pair with Activity Pattern P6, game markers, and a coin. To play the game, partners flip a coin to determine whether to move one space—heads—or two spaces—tails. To stay on the space, they must tell one way to reduce, reuse, or recycle the item or resource shown. The first partner to reach the end of the path wins the game. To extend the activity, provide each child with Activity Pattern P6 to take home. Encourage children to share what they have learned about saving our resources and then invite family members to play the game.
(TACTILE/VISUAL)

Turn out the lights when you leave a room.

Put cans in a recycling bin.

Take shorter showers.

Skits to Save Resources

Materials: assorted props, video camcorder (optional)

Invite children to work in small groups to create skits entitled "How We Can Save Our Resources." Encourage children to suggest ways to reduce, reuse, and recycle. For example: *Make a pencil holder from a can; recycle newspapers, glass, and cans; turn off the water while brushing your teeth; turn off the lights when you leave the room.* Have the group choose two suggestions and create a skit to demonstrate them. Encourage children to gather or make props to use in their skits. Give children time to develop and practice their skits before performing them for classmates. If a video camcorder is available, you might record all the skits. Then invite another class to watch and discuss the video.
(KINESTHETIC)

LESSON 6

Houses and Homes

OBJECTIVES

■ Identify and describe the physical characteristics of places such as landforms, bodies of water, natural resources, and weather.

■ Identify and describe the human characteristics of places such as types of houses.

■ Explain how the environment affects the types of homes people have.

 Categorize pp. 81, 118, 124

RESOURCES

Pupil Book/Unit Big Book, pp. 118–121

Word Cards V29–V30

Activity Book, p. 33

🌐 **Reading and Vocabulary Transparency 3–7**

💻 **Internet Resources**

READING SOCIAL STUDIES

Graphic Organizer Begin a chart about homes. Complete the chart during Close.

	My Home	Other Homes
What is the home made of?	brick	
What does the land look like	flat	
What water is nearby?	river	
What is the weather like?	It is cold in winter. It is hot in summer.	

● USE READING AND VOCABULARY TRANSPARENCY 3–7

3–7
TRANSPARENCY

Vocabulary

desert p. 119

 When Minutes Count

Have children examine the pictures on pages 118–121. Use the pictures to discuss the Big Idea in the lesson.

Quick Summary

This lesson focuses on the various kinds of homes that people live in around the world. It explores how environment accounts for differences among them.

Motivate

Set the Purpose

Big Idea Before starting the lesson, read the Big Idea statement aloud. As children read and discuss the lesson, encourage them to note how the homes and environments are alike and how they are different.

Access Prior Knowledge

Ask children to recall the fairy tale "The Three Little Pigs." Call on volunteers to describe the three pigs' houses (straw, sticks, brick). Which home was the strongest?

Visual Learning

Pictures As children examine the pictures on pages 118–119, explain that they show some of the different kinds of homes around the world—Canada, Germany, Brazil, Mexico, and Congo in Africa. Lead children to describe the different homes, noting details such as the kind of homes, the resources used to build them, and the land surrounding them. Display a world map and help children locate each country.

Q **Although these homes look different and are in different parts of the world, in what ways are they alike?**

A Each home protects the family that lives in it against bad weather and danger and provides them with a place where they can eat, sleep, and spend time together.

Read and Respond

Link Geography with Culture and Society Remind children that the different homes in the photos are examples of shelters, a basic need of every family.

Q **What are some other kinds of homes where people live?**

A mobile homes, log cabins, houseboats, tents, huts

Lesson

6 Houses and Homes

Big Idea
People around the world live in all kinds of homes.

Vocabulary

desert

People around the world have different kinds of homes. Some live in houses. Others live in buildings with many apartments.

Germany

Canada

Brazil

118

Focus Skill **READING SKILL**

Categorize With children, observe the homes in the photos. Have children categorize the homes in different ways—for example, according to what they are made of and whether they are for one or many families. Point out that although these homes can be categorized in different ways, they are all alike in that they provide shelter.

MAKE IT RELEVANT

In the Community Take children on a walk around the school neighborhood and nearby community to observe the different kinds of homes and landscapes that surround them. Take pictures if possible. Then invite a builder to answer questions from the class about the kinds of materials used to build homes in your area and about any special features needed because of land or weather conditions.

INTEGRATE MATHEMATICS

Measurement Explain to children that a builder must take a great many measurements when building a house. Provide samples of building materials such as bricks, cinder blocks, scraps of lumber, and shingles. Invite children to use a tape measure or ruler to measure the materials.

People build homes using the resources of the land where they live. These homes in Congo have roofs made from straw, or dried grass.

Congo

Mexico

People also have to think about the weather where they build their homes. This place in Mexico is built of clay bricks dried in the hot desert sun. A **desert** is land that gets little rain.

Read and Respond

Geography Help children locate Congo and Mexico on a map or globe. Point out that the homes pictured are in parts of these countries that receive very little rainfall. The people in each place built their homes with materials and resources that were available to them and suitable for their weather. Mention that both brick, or *adobe*, and mud houses stay cooler than do wood or stone houses in hot, dry weather, but they are not suitable for rainy weather or periods of freezing and thawing.

Q Why do you think people do not build mud or adobe houses where it rains a lot or where the weather is cold?

A The mud and adobe walls would probably come apart or crumble.

Q Adobe houses are common in the southwestern United States. What does this tell you about the weather there?

A It is probably hot and dry.

Lead children in a discussion about how the kinds of land in different parts of the world affect the types of homes people have.

· GEOGRAPHY ·

Sonoran Desert

Explain to children that, although little rain falls in a desert, it is not a wasteland. Deserts have a variety of plant and animal life. The saguaro, the state flower of Arizona, grows only in the Sonoran Desert. The saguaro can grow as tall as 60 feet (18 m), and live for more than 100 years. Point out that the saguaro itself is home to bats, birds, and insects. Encourage children to use books and the Internet to identify and describe other kinds of plants and animals that live in desert regions.

INTEGRATE READING

Making Comparisons Invite children to read and discuss *Houses and Homes*, a photo essay by Ann Morris (William Morrow & Co, 1995). Encourage them to compare and contrast the different homes in the book with the kinds of shelters in their community.

REACH ALL LEARNERS

Tactile Learners Invite children to make adobe bricks. In a paper milk carton cut in half, have them mix two cups of outdoor soil with one-half cup of powdered clay. Add water to make the mixture fluid. Then add straw until it stiffens. Press down to flatten it. After the bricks dry in the sun, have children remove the molds. They can use the bricks to build a model of a house.

Visual Learning

Pictures Help children locate Norway and the Amazon rain forest on a map. Then ask children to study the two houses in the pictures.

Q **The log cabin is in Norway. What can you tell about the weather in Norway? How can you tell?**

A I can tell from the snow on the roof that it is cold in Norway and probably snows a lot.

Q **How can you describe the roof on the log cabin?**

A It is not flat. It is sloped.

Explain that in places where there is heavy snowfall, people build houses with sloping roofs strong enough to hold the weight of the snow. The snow will slide off easily and the roofs won't collapse. Mention also that logs help to keep the cold out and the heat in.

Q **The house on stilts is in the Amazon rain forest. What can you tell about the weather in the rain forest?**

A It probably rains a lot, causing the river to rise and even flood.

Read and Respond

Geography Continue by reading the text on page 121 and having children describe the homes in Italy and the houseboats, or *junks*, and apartment buildings in Hong Kong. Emphasize that a city is a place where many people live and work. Encourage children to suggest reasons why the homes are so close together in Italy and why there are so many tall apartment buildings in China. Help children understand that tall buildings and homes built close together take up less space, making it possible for more people to live and work in a place.

Conclude by having children think about all the different houses and homes they read about in this lesson.

Q **Why do you think there are so many different kinds of homes?**

A The land, weather, and resources are different in different places; people like and need different kinds of homes.

This house is in Norway. It is made from the trees in the forest around it.

Norway

When it rains a lot, this river in the Amazon rain forest can flood. This house in Venezuela is built on stilts. They keep it dry above the river's water.

Venezuela

120

BACKGROUND

Junks People in the Far East have used these wooden sailing boats for centuries to transport goods along their waterways. A junk may have from two to five masts to hold its sails. People also live on junks and on another kind of boat called a *sampan*. It has a cabin with a mat roof and is rowed with oars. In China today there are floating villages of junks.

EXTEND AND ENRICH

Make a Chart Invite children to identify and find out about other kinds of homes, such as igloos, yurts, beach huts, tepees, mobile homes, hogans, and sod houses. Have them show the results of their research on a chart that includes a picture of each home, what it is made of, and where it is or was used as a form of shelter.

Some places are crowded.
These homes in Italy
are built close together.
There is little open space
between the homes.

Italy

China

This city in China has very
little land for new homes.
Some people live on boats.

LESSON 6
Review

❶ **Vocabulary** How is a **desert** different
from a forest?

❷ Why do people have to think about the
weather when they build their homes?

❸ Describe the types of houses in
your neighborhood.

121

Summarize Key Content

- You can describe what a place is like.
- You can identify and describe various kinds of houses.
- You can explain how the environment is a factor in the kinds of homes people build.

READING SOCIAL STUDIES

Graphic Organizer Revisit the chart begun in Motivate. Invite children to share new ideas they learned. Add these ideas to the chart.

	My Home	Other Homes
What is the home made of?	brick	stone, wood, mud and straw, adobe
What does the land look like?	flat	hilly, rocky
What water is nearby?	river	lakes, rivers, streams
What is the weather like?	It is cold in winter. It is hot in summer.	hot, dry, cold, wet, snowy

● USE READING AND VOCABULARY
TRANSPARENCY 3–7

3–7
TRANSPARENCY

Assess

Lesson 6 Review—Answers

❶ A desert is land that gets little rain. A forest is a place where many trees grow.

❷ Homes must be built to protect the families who live in them from weather conditions that are typical for the area.

❸ **Performance Assessment Guidelines** Children's descriptions should reflect the homes in their neighborhoods.

RETEACH THE LESSON

Make Up Riddles Invite children to make up riddles about the homes in this lesson. For example, *I live near a big city, but not in an apartment. My house floats on the water. Which home is mine?* Or *I live in a place where it is hot and dry. The roof is flat and the walls are bricks made from sandy soil. Which home is mine?* Have classmates take turns posing the riddles and locating the correct homes on pages 118–121.

ACTIVITY BOOK

Name _____ Date _____

Different Kinds of Homes

Look at the different kinds of homes. Then draw to show what the land and weather are like where the homes are.

Use with Unit 3, Lesson 6.   **Activity Book • 33**

PAGE 33

Extension Activities For Home and School

What Belongs Where?

Materials: magazines with photos of various environments and homes that would be found in each environment, scissors, crayons or markers, pushpins

Divide a bulletin board into several sections and attach a magazine photo of a different environment in each one. Encourage children to identify and describe the environments, noting the physical characteristics. Then have children form groups and each choose a different environment. Challenge groups to find and cut out magazine pictures of the kinds of homes people might build in the environments. Children can also draw, color, and cut out their own pictures. As group members add to their environments, encourage them to explain their choices. For example, a house on stilts is a good home for people who live by a rain forest river because it will stay dry. As a variation, place homes in environments where they do not belong, such as a stilt house in a city. Challenge children to tell why each home is out of place and then put it in the correct environment. Point out that some houses may be suitable for more than one environment.
(TACTILE/VISUAL)

Build a Model Home

Materials: assorted art and craft supplies such as cardboard boxes and lids, clay or modeling dough, craft sticks, straw, twigs, stones, construction paper, cotton balls, glue, poster paper, crayons or markers

Review with children the different kinds of homes they learned about in this lesson and the various resources and materials that people used to build them. Then invite children to make models of different homes. When models are complete, have children display the homes that belong in similar environments together. Then have groups of children create a backdrop scene to show the environment for their homes.
(TACTILE)

Houses and Homes

Ask children to look on the Internet, flip through magazines and books, or watch travel videos with family members to find examples of homes from other parts of the world.

Homes Around the World

Encourage children to share what they know about different kinds of homes and why resources and weather are important in determining the kinds of homes people build. Ask children to print out, clip, or draw pictures of the homes they found and bring them to class. Provide a bulletin board labeled "Houses and Homes from Around the World."
(VISUAL)

VISIT · A Butterfly Garden

Summary

In this lesson, children see how a group of students planned, planted, and tended a butterfly garden at their school.

OBJECTIVES

- Recognize the importance of caring for our natural resources.
- Sequence and categorize information.
- Obtain information about a topic using a variety of visual sources, such as pictures, television, and computer images.

RESOURCES

Pupil Book/Unit Big Book, pp. 122–123

Video

💻 **Internet Resources**

1 Motivate

Get Ready

Explain to children that they will discover how a group of students helped to make their school a more beautiful place by planting a butterfly garden. Invite children to share what they know about butterflies and butterfly gardens. Record their responses in a chart such as the following:

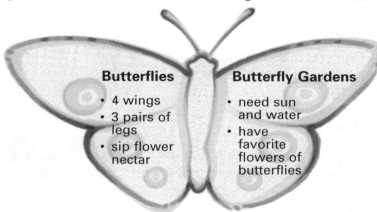

Butterflies
- 4 wings
- 3 pairs of legs
- sip flower nectar

Butterfly Gardens
- need sun and water
- have favorite flowers of butterflies

BACKGROUND

Butterflies and Plants Butterflies and plants have a special relationship. Butterflies play an important role in the life cycle of plants. As they travel from flower to flower, feeding on nectar, they carry pollen from flower to flower, thus helping the plants to reproduce. Plants are equally important. As well as a source of nectar for the adult butterfly, plants also provide shelter and food during the other stages in the life cycle of a butterfly. Female butterflies lay their eggs on the leaves of a plant. When the eggs hatch, the caterpillars feed on the leaves until their metamorphosis, during which they change to become butterflies.

2 Teach

What to See

Invite children to study the student's plan on page 122 and then follow along as you read aloud the caption. Ask children to describe the plan, noting details such as the office entrance, garden, and dimensions.

Q Why do you think it is important for each student to draw a plan?

A The students can share their plans and decide the best place to plant a butterfly garden.

Explain that the students had to consider other things while planning the garden. Have children share their ideas. Remind them that butterflies prefer certain kinds of flowers. Help children recognize that the students would have to know the kinds of butterflies common in their area and the kinds of plants that attract them.

Focus attention on the picture at the top of page 123, and have children read the caption to learn what else a butterfly garden needs. Explain that plants use the sun's light to make food.

Q Why do you think a butterfly garden should not get much wind?

A Too much wind would make it difficult for butterflies to fly from flower to flower.

Ask children what they think the students did after choosing a sunny spot and deciding what flowers to plant.

As children study the next picture and read the caption, have them describe how the students are caring for the flowers. Point out that they are pulling weeds.

Q What else do flowers need besides sun and soil to grow?

A water

Have children look at the last photograph on page 123 as you read aloud the caption. Emphasize that it takes hard work to plan, plant, and care for a garden. Ask children how they would celebrate a new garden.

VISIT

A Butterfly Garden

Get Ready

Planting a flower garden makes any place more beautiful. Some flowers are favorites of butterflies. These students decided to plant a butterfly garden outside their school.

What to See

Each student draws a plan for the new butterfly garden.

REACH ALL LEARNERS

English as a Second Language Children may be confused when they read or hear the term *butterfly garden*. Help them to understand that a butterfly is not a plant but rather an insect and that a butterfly garden is one that attracts butterflies because of the flowers and plants growing in it.

REACH ALL LEARNERS

Advanced Learners Invite children to do research to create a booklet called "Facts About Butterflies." Encourage them to discover answers to questions such as *How many kinds of butterflies are there? How do butterflies drink the nectar from flowers? How are butterflies and moths different? What happens to a butterfly when the weather gets cold?* Suggest they illustrate their booklet and share it with the class.

Butterfly gardens need to get lots of sun but not much wind.

The students work in the garden to care for the flowers.

Students celebrate the new garden with a party.

Then

Now

Take a Field Trip

GO ONLINE

A VIRTUAL TOUR Visit The Learning Site at **www.harcourtschool.com** to take virtual tours of other parks and scenic areas.

A VIDEO TOUR Check your media center or classroom library for a video featuring a segment from Reading Rainbow.

123

3 Close

Invite children to make a list of steps for planning, planting, and caring for a butterfly garden based on their discussions, prior knowledge, and the visit.

Take a Field Trip

A Virtual Tour Depending on the availability of computers, have children work individually, in pairs, or in small groups to view the virtual tour. Suggest they identify plants and animals as they tour different parks and scenic areas.

GO ONLINE **INTERNET RESOURCES**

THE LEARNING SITE Visit The Learning Site at **www.harcourtschool.com** to take virtual tours of parks and scenic areas.

A Video Field Trip Have children watch the Reading Rainbow video in small groups. Have the members of each group then draw pictures that show the order of events in the tree-planting process and write captions on separate strips. When all the groups have watched the video, have them exchange pictures and captions. Tell them to arrange the pictures in order and then match the correct caption to each drawing. You may want to show the video a second time.

VIDEO

Use the Reading Rainbow TAKE A TRIP videotape of a tree-planting project.

Unit 3 Review and Test Preparation

PAGES 124–128

 Focus Skill **Categorize**

Children should be able to add at least two words or pictures to each box that fit the category. Words and pictures under *land* might include *hill, plain,* and *island*. Words under *water* might include *river* and *ocean*. Words and pictures under *resources* might include *trees, water, air, oil,* and *gas*.

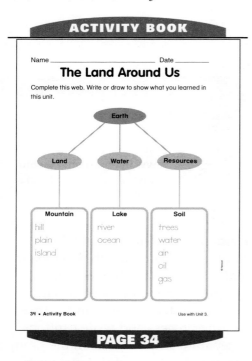

ACTIVITY BOOK

Name _____ Date _____
The Land Around Us
Complete this web. Write or draw to show what you learned in this unit.

Earth
Land — Water — Resources
Mountain: hill, plain, island
Lake: river, ocean
Soil: trees, water, air, oil, gas

34 • Activity Book   Use with Unit 3.

PAGE 34

Think & Write

Children should look for clues in the pictures, such as the structure, building materials, and setting of the house, to determine what the weather might be like in the area where the house is located. Their caption should be a complete sentence that makes a reasonable assumption of the weather based on clues in the pictures children chose.

TRANSPARENCY

This graphic organizer appears on READING AND VOCABULARY TRANSPARENCY 3–8.

Unit 3 Review and Test Preparation

 Focus Skill **Categorize**

Use what you have learned to complete the web.

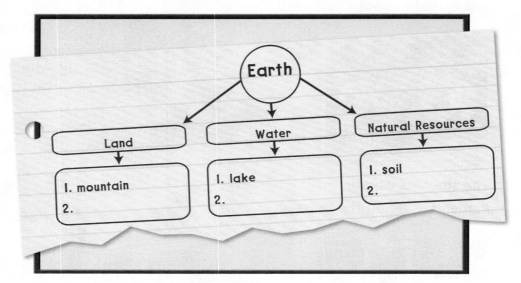

Earth
- Land
  - 1. mountain
  - 2.
- Water
  - 1. lake
  - 2.
- Natural Resources
  - 1. soil
  - 2.

THINK & WRITE

Look at Pictures Look at homes in books and magazines. Look for clues that show what the weather is like there.

Write a Caption Choose one of the homes. Write a sentence telling about the weather in that picture.

124

TEST PREPARATION

Review these tips with children.

- Read the directions before reading the questions.
- Read each question twice, focusing the second time on all the possible answers.
- Take the time to think about all the possible answers before deciding on an answer.
- Move past questions that are giving you trouble, and answer the ones you know. Then return to concentrate on the difficult items.

Use Vocabulary

Draw a picture to show the meaning of each word.

1 **neighborhood**
(p. 94)

3 **resource**
(p. 108)

2 **ocean**
(p. 105)

4 **weather**
(p. 112)

Recall Facts

5 How many continents are there?

6 How are a river and an ocean different?

7 Name two kinds of resources.

8 How do farmers use soil?

9 On which continent do you live?

A Africa

C North America

B Australia

D South America

10 Which resource do people use to build homes?

F water

H oil

G soil

J trees

125

Use Vocabulary

Children's drawings should illustrate a neighborhood, ocean, resource, and form of weather.

Recall Facts

5 There are seven continents.

6 An ocean is a large body of salty water; a river is a stream of water that moves across the land.

7 Children's answers may include soil, water, trees, and oil and gas.

8 Farmers use soil to grow food for people and animals.

9 C—North America

10 J—trees

Think Critically

11 Children's responses should show that they understand that to predict is to guess what will happen ahead of time. Answers should give examples of how people could prepare for specific events.

12 Many of Earth's resources can be used up or spoiled. If we do not take care of our resources, they will not be available for the people to use in the future.

Apply Chart and Graph Skills

13 Accept South America or Antarctica

14 the Indian Ocean

15 south

16 the Arctic Ocean

Think Critically

11 How can being able to predict what will happen help people plan what to do?

12 Why is it important to take care of Earth's resources?

Apply Map and Globe Skills

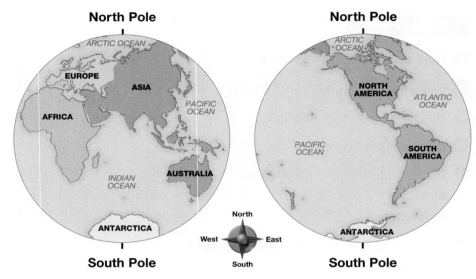

13 If you traveled south from North America, on what continent would you be?

14 Which ocean is west of Australia?

15 Is Antarctica north or south of Africa?

16 Which ocean is at the North Pole?

126

South Carolina

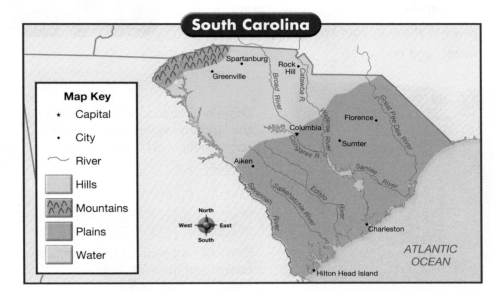

Map Key
- ★ Capital
- • City
- ～ River
- Hills
- Mountains
- Plains
- Water

Spartanburg
Greenville
Rock Hill
Columbia
Florence
Sumter
Aiken
Charleston
Hilton Head Island

Catawba R.
Broad River
Wateree River
Great Pee Dee River
Congaree R.
Santee River
Edisto River
Salkehatchie River
Savannah River

North
West East
South

ATLANTIC OCEAN

⑰ Name the ocean that is east of South Carolina.

⑱ What kind of land is around Rock Hill?

⑲ What kind of land is in the southern part of the state?

⑳ Name a city that is on the plains.

127

ASSESSMENT

Use the UNIT 3 TEST on pages 9–12 of the Assessment Program.

Apply Map and Globe Skills

⑰ the Atlantic Ocean

⑱ hills

⑲ plains

⑳ Aiken, Hilton Head Island, Charleston, Sumter, Florence, or Columbia

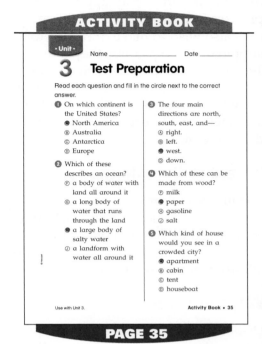

ACTIVITY BOOK

• Unit •
Name_____ Date_____

3 Test Preparation

Read each question and fill in the circle next to the correct answer.

❶ On which continent is the United States?
- Ⓐ North America
- Ⓑ Australia
- Ⓒ Antarctica
- Ⓓ Europe

❷ Which of these describes an ocean?
- Ⓕ a body of water with land all around it
- Ⓖ a long body of water that runs through the land
- Ⓗ a large body of salty water
- Ⓘ a landform with water all around it

❸ The four main directions are north, south, east, and—
- Ⓐ right.
- Ⓑ left.
- Ⓒ west.
- Ⓓ down.

❹ Which of these can be made from wood?
- Ⓕ milk
- Ⓖ paper
- Ⓗ gasoline
- Ⓘ salt

❺ Which kind of house would you see in a crowded city?
- Ⓐ apartment
- Ⓑ cabin
- Ⓒ tent
- Ⓓ houseboat

Use with Unit 3.　Activity Book • 35

PAGE 35

Unit Activities

Organize the class into small groups of three or four children to work on the collage together. Allow time for children to discuss what pictures they might use in their collage. Have children locate and cut out appropriate pictures from magazines. Children may also wish to make drawings to supplement the pictures they found. Tell children to arrange their pictures on a large sheet of posterboard. When the whole group is satisfied with the arrangement, children should glue down the pictures.

Where to Get Information

Encourage children to use a wide variety of reference sources, including encyclopedias, library books, travel brochures, social studies books, picture atlases, magazines, and the Internet.

Ways to Share

Display the collages on a wall, and have each group stand near its collage. Name a resource, such as soil, trees, water, or oil and gas. Call on volunteers to point to and describe the pictures on their collage that relate to the resource you named. Allow time for volunteers to describe any remaining pictures and to explain why the group chose the pictures. Repeat this activity with land and water.

Performance Assessment Guidelines Note whether children's collages include pictures that show all the resources mentioned in the unit. Listen to hear whether children's descriptions and explanations indicate that they understand why each resource is important and that our resources must be protected.

Visit Your Library

Encourage independent reading with these books or others of your choice after children have completed their study of land and resources. Additional resources are listed in the Multimedia Resources on pages 81J–81K of this Teacher's Edition.

Unit Activities

GO ONLINE
Visit The Learning Site at **www.harcourtschool.com** for additional activities.

Complete the Unit Project Work with your group to finish the unit project. Decide what you will show in your collage about land, water, and resources.

Land and Water

Draw or find pictures that show the land and water around your community. Add these to your collage.

Using Resources

Draw or find pictures that show how people use these resources.
- soil
- oil and gas
- trees
- water

Visit Your Library

Compost! Growing Gardens from Your Garbage by Linda Glaser. Find out how a family recycles food leftovers.

Me on the Map by Joan Sweeney. A young girl shows where she is in the world.

Haystack by Bonnie and Arthur Geisert. See how important a haystack is on a farm.

128

Easy *Compost! Growing Gardens from Your Garbage* by Linda Glaser. Millbrook Press, 1996. A young girl starts a family compost pile, helps care for it, and uses the compost during spring planting.

Average *Me on the Map* by Joan Sweeney. Dragonfly Books, 1998. A young girl creates a variety of maps and pinpoints her location on each one.

Challenging *Haystack* by Bonnie and Arthur Geisert. Houghton Mifflin, 1995. Old-fashioned haystacks played an important role in the life cycle of a prairie farm.

For Your Reference

281

Biographical Dictionary

The Biographical Dictionary lists many of the important people introduced in this book. The page number tells where the main discussion of each person starts. See the Index for other page references.

Addams, Jane (1860–1935) American who started Hull-House to help poor people in Chicago. p. 207

Aesop Greek who told fables that children still enjoy today. p. 150

Bell, Alexander Graham (1847–1922) American who invented the telephone. He also trained teachers to help people with hearing losses. p. 216

Bellamy, Francis (1855–1931) American minister. He wrote the Pledge of Allegiance in 1892. p. 41

Bethune, Mary McLeod (1875–1955) African American teacher. Her work gave other African Americans the chance to go to school. p. 15

Bush, George W. (1946–) 43rd President of the United States. His father was 41st President. p. 54

Carver, George Washington (1864–1943) African American scientist. His work helped farmers grow better crops. p. 208

Clemente, Roberto (1934–1972) Famous Puerto Rican baseball player who helped many people. p. 209

Columbus, Christopher (1451–1506) Italian explorer who sailed to the Americas. p. 194

Douglas, Marjory Stoneman (1890–1998) American writer. She worked to protect the Florida Everglades. p. 115

Edison, Thomas (1847–1931) American inventor. He invented the lightbulb and many other things. p. 211

Flagler, Henry (1830–1913) Businessperson who helped Florida grow. He built hotels and gave money to build schools and hospitals. p. 69

Franklin, Benjamin (1706–1790) American leader, writer, and inventor. He helped write the Declaration of Independence. p. 206

Gálvez, Bernardo de (1746–1786) Leader from Louisiana. He helped the Americans win their freedom from England. p. 68

Gonzales, John (1955–) A Native American leader from New Mexico. p. 70

Jefferson, Thomas (1743–1826) Third President of the United States. He was the main writer of the Declaration of Independence. p. 57

282

King, Martin Luther, Jr. (1929–1968) African American minister and leader. He worked to win civil rights for all Americans. p. 200

Kwolek, Stephanie (1923–) American inventor. She found a way to make a cloth that is stronger than steel. p. 70

Lincoln, Abraham (1809–1865) 16th President of the United States. He made it against the law to own slaves. p. 201

McLoughlin, John (1784–1857) Worked as a trader in the West. He helped settle Oregon. p. 189

O'Connor, Sandra Day (1930–) First female Justice of the United States Supreme Court. p. 209

Ochoa, Ellen (1955–) American astronaut. She was the first Hispanic female to go into space. p. 257

Oglethorpe, James (1696–1785) English settler who started the colony of Georgia. p. 189

Penn, William (1644–1718) English settler who started the colony of Pennsylvania. p. 188

Pitcher, Molly (1754?–1832) Nickname of Mary Hays McCauly. She brought pitchers of water to soldiers in the Revolutionary War. p. 207

Ross, Betsy (1752–1836) Seamstress from Philadelphia, Pennsylvania. She is thought to have sewed the first American flag. p. 63

Sacajawea (1786?–1812?) Shoshone woman who helped explorers in the West. p. 207

Sequoyah (1765?–1843) Cherokee leader. He created a way to write the Cherokee language. p. 207

Tubman, Harriet (1820–1913) An escaped slave. She helped lead many slaves to freedom. p. 69

Wagner, Honus (1874–1955) One of the greatest baseball players in history. He played shortstop. p. 269

Washington, George (1732–1799) First President of the United States. He is known as "The Father of Our Country." p. 56

Wells, Ida B. (1862–1931) African American newspaper writer. She helped get laws passed for the fair treatment of African Americans. p. 208

Wheatley, Phillis (1753?–1784) African American poet. p. 206

Wright, Orville (1871–1948) and **Wilbur** (1867–1912) First Americans to fly a motor-powered airplane. p. 208

283

Picture Glossary

address
The numbers and words that tell where a building is. (page 84)

border
A line on a map that shows where a state or country ends. (page 52)

ballot
A piece of paper that shows the choices for voting. (page 58)

business
The making or selling of goods or services. (page 252)

bar graph
A graph that uses bars to show how many or how much. (page 262)

calendar
A chart that shows the days, weeks, and months in a year. (page 158)

cause
What makes
something happen.
(page 190)

citizen
A person who lives
in and belongs to a
community. (page 68)

celebration
A time to be happy
about something
special. (page 154)

city
A very large town.
(page 50)

change
To become different.
(page 175)

communication
The sharing of ideas
and information.
(page 214)

285

community
A group of people who live or work together. (page 46)

culture
A group's way of life. (page 143)

continent
One of the seven main land areas on Earth. (page 105)

custom
A group's way of doing something. (page 160)

country
An area of land with its own people and laws. (page 52)

desert
A large, dry area of land. (page 119)

286

I have a pet cat.

Her name is Snowball.

She is white.

detail
An extra piece of
information about
something. (page 8)

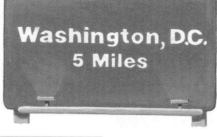

distance
How far one place is
from another. (page 152)

diagram
A drawing that shows
parts of something.
(page 182)

E

Earth
Our planet. (page 104)

direction
The way to go to find
something. (page 106)

effect
What happens
because of a cause.
(page 190)

287

explorer
A person who goes first to find out about a place. (page 194)

factory
A building in which people use machines to make goods. (page 244)

fable
A made-up story that teaches a lesson. (page 150)

fair
Done in a way that is right and honest. (page 11)

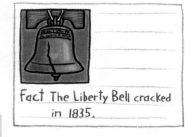

Fact The Liberty Bell cracked in 1835.

fact
A piece of information that is true. (page 66)

farm
A place where crops are grown and animals are raised for food. (page 108)

fiction
Stories that are
made up. (page 66)

freedom
The right of people
to make their own
choices. (page 199)

flag
A piece of cloth with
a special design that
stands for a country
or group. (page 62)

future
The time that is to
come. (page 186)

forest
A very large area of
trees. (page 109)

G

globe
A model of Earth.
(page 104)

goods
Things that can be bought and sold. (page 240)

group
A number of people working together. (page 12)

government
The group of citizens that runs a community, state, or country. (page 51)

 H

hero
A person who has done something brave or important. (page 206)

governor
The leader of a state's government. (page 51)

hill
Land that rises above the land around it. (page 100)

290

history
The story of what has happened in the past. (page 178)

lake
A body of water that has land all around it. (page 99)

holiday
A day to celebrate or remember something. (page 154)

language
The words or signs people use to communicate. (page 132)

island
A piece of land that has water all around it. (page 101)

law
A rule that people in a community must follow. (page 46)

291

leader
A person who helps
a group plan what
to do. (page 48)

location
The place where
something is.
(page 18)

M

learn
To find out something
new. (page 6)

main idea
What the information
that you are reading
is mostly about.
(page 8)

litter
To leave trash on the
ground. (page 115)

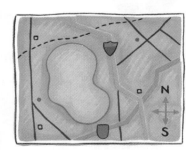

map
A drawing that
shows where places
are. (page 20)

292

map key
The part of a map that shows what the symbols mean. (page 96)

mayor
The leader of a city or town government. (page 50)

map scale
The part of a map that helps you find the distance between two places. (page 152)

money
The coins and paper bills used to buy things. (page 252)

market
A place where people buy and sell goods. (page 258)

mountain
The highest kind of land. (page 98)

N

needs
Things people must have to live. (page 138)

neighborhood
The part of a community in which a group of people lives. (page 94)

nonfiction
Stories that have real information. (page 66)

O

ocean
A very large body of salty water. (page 105)

P

past
The time before now. (page 184)

peace
A time of quietness and calm. (page 203)

294

picture graph

A graph that uses pictures to stand for numbers of things. (page 250)

pollution

Anything that makes the air, land, or water dirty. (page 114)

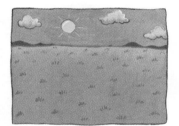

plain

Land that is mostly flat. (page 100)

predict

To say what will happen. (page 112)

point of view

A way of thinking about something. (page 146)

present

The time now. (page 186)

295

PICTURE GLOSSARY

President
Leader of the United States government. (page 54)

principal
The leader of a school. (page 14)

problem
Something that causes trouble. (page 136)

R

recreation
The things people do in their spare time, such as playing sports or having hobbies. (page 215)

recycle
To use things again. (page 117)

religion
A belief in a god or gods. (page 144)

resource
Anything that people can use. (page 108)

river
A stream of water that flows across the land. (page 101)

responsibility
Something that a citizen should do. (page 73)

robot
A machine run by a computer to do work. (page 257)

right
A freedom. (page 72)

role
The part a person plays in a group or community. (page 134)

297

route
A way to go from
one place to another.
(page 204)

scarce
Not in good supply,
or hard to find.
(page 266)

rule
An instruction
telling what must or
must not be done.
(page 10)

school
A place where
people go to learn.
(page 4)

save
To keep something,
such as money, to
use later. (page 260)

season
One of the four parts
of the year that have
different kinds of
weather. (page 175)

298

services
Work done for others for money. (page 242)

shelter
A safe place to live. (page 138)

settler
One of the first people to make a home in a new place. (page 196)

solution
The answer to a problem. (page 136)

share
To tell others what we know or think. (page 7)

state
A part of a country. (page 52)

299

symbol
A picture or object that stands for something else. (page 20)

technology
New inventions that we use in everyday life. (page 210)

table
A chart that shows information in rows and columns. (page 28)

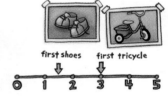

time line
A line that shows when events happened. (page 176)

teacher
A person who helps others learn. (page 14)

today
This day. (page 174)

300

tomorrow
The day after today.
(page 174)

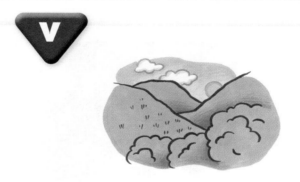

transportation
Ways of carrying
people and goods
from one place to
another. (page 212)

V

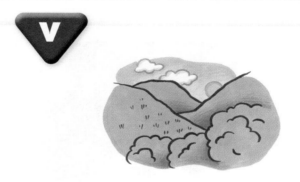

tool
Something a
person uses to do
work. (page 24)

valley
Low land between
mountains. (page 98)

trade
To give one thing to
get another. (page 268)

veteran
A person who has
served in the
military. (page 203)

301

volunteer
A person who works without being paid. (page 253)

weather
What the air outside is like. (page 112)

vote
A choice that gets counted. (page 58)

world
All the people and places on Earth. (page 30)

W

wants
Things that people would like to have but do not need. (page 264)

Y

yesterday
The day before today. (page 174)

302

Index

303

INDEX

INDEX

For permission to reprint copyrighted material, grateful acknowledgment is made to the following sources:

Atheneum Books for Young Readers, an imprint of Simon & Schuster Children's Publishing Division: Cover illustration by Barry Root from *Messenger, Messenger* by Robert Burleigh. Illustration copyright © 2000 by Barry Root.

Curtis Brown, Ltd.: "School Bus" from *School Supplies: A Book of Poems* by Lee Bennett Hopkins. Text copyright © 1996 by Lee Bennett Hopkins. Published by Simon & Schuster Books for Young Readers.

Marc Brown Studios: From *Arthur Meets the President* by Marc Brown. Copyright © 1991 by Marc Brown. Published by Little, Brown and Company (Inc.).

Charlesbridge Publishing, Inc.: Cover illustration by Ralph Masiello from *The Flag We Love* by Pam Muñoz Ryan. Illustration copyright © 1996 by Ralph Masiello.

Children's Press, a Scholastic Library Publishing imprint: From *George Washington: First President of the United States* by Carol Greene. Copyright © 1991 by Childrens Press®, Inc.

Chronicle Books, San Francisco: Cover illustration by Donna Ingemanson from *Something's Happening on Calabash Street* by Judith Ross Enderle and Stephanie Jacob Gordon. Illustration copyright © 2000 by Donna Ingemanson.

Cobblehill Books, an affiliate of Dutton Children's Books, a division of Penguin Putnam Inc.: Cover photographs from *Emeka's Gift: An African Counting Story* by Ifeoma Onyefulu. Photographs copyright © 1995 by Ifeoma Onyefulu.

Crown Publishers, an imprint of Random House Children's Books, a division of Random House, Inc.: Cover illustration by Annette Cable from *Me On the Map* by Joan Sweeney. Illustration copyright © 1996 by Annette Cable.

Farrar, Straus and Giroux, LLC: Cover illustration from *Madlenka* by Peter Sis. Copyright © 2000 by Peter Sis.

Harcourt, Inc.: Cover illustration from *Market Day* by Lois Ehlert. Copyright © 2000 by Lois Ehlert. Cover illustration from *Check It Out! The Book About Libraries* by Gail Gibbons. Copyright © 1985 by Gail Gibbons.

HarperCollins Publishers: Cover illustration by Diane Greenseid from *Get Up and Go!* by Stuart J. Murphy. Illustration copyright © 1996 by Diane Greenseid.

Holiday House, Inc.: Cover illustration from *First Day, Hooray!* by Nancy Poydar. Copyright © 1999 by Nancy Poydar.

Henry Holt and Company, LLC: From Here to There by Margery Cuyler, illustrated by Yu Cha Pak. Text copyright © 1999 by Margery Cuyler; illustrations copyright © 1999 by Yu Cha Pak.

Houghton Mifflin Company: Cover illustration by Arthur Geisert from *Haystack* by Bonnie Geisert. Illustration copyright © 1995 by Arthur Geisert. From *Rush Hour* by Christine Loomis, illustrated by Mari Takabayashi. Text copyright © 1996 by Christine Loomis; illustrations copyright © 1996 by Mari Takabayashi.

Little, Brown and Company (Inc.): "Four Generations" from *Fathers, Mothers, Sisters, Brothers: A Collection of Family Poems* by Mary Ann Hoberman. Text copyright © 1991 by Mary Ann Hoberman.

The Millbrook Press: Cover illustration by Anca Hariton from *Compost! Growing Gardens from Your Garbage* by Linda Glaser. Illustration copyright © 1996 by Anca Hariton.

Scholastic Inc.: Cover illustration by Nila Aye from *When I'm Big* by Tim Drury. Illustration copyright © 1999 by Nila Aye. Published by Orchard Books, an imprint of Scholastic Inc.

SeaStar Books, a division of North-South Books, Inc., New York: Cover illustration from *The Inside-Outside Book of Washington, D.C.* by Roxie Munro. Copyright © 1987, 2001 by Roxie Munro.

Simon & Schuster Books for Young Readers, an imprint of Simon & Schuster Children's Publishing Division: Cover illustration by Michael P. Paraskevas from *On the Day the Tall Ships Sailed* by Betty Paraskevas. Illustration copyright © 2000 by Michael P. Paraskevas.

State of Louisiana, Secretary of State: Lyrics and music from state song "Give Me Louisiana" by Doralice Fontane, and Louisiana State Seal.

Walker and Company: Cover illustration by Eric Velasquez from *The Piano Man* by Debbi Chocolate. Illustration copyright © 1998 by Eric Velasquez.

Albert Whitman & Company: Cover illustration by Paige Billin-Frye from *This Is the Turkey* by Abby Levine. Illustration copyright © 2000 by Paige Billin-Frye. Cover illustration by DyAnne DiSalvo-Ryan from *If I Were President* by Catherine Stier. Illustration copyright © 1999 by DyAnne DiSalvo-Ryan.

PHOTO CREDITS

Cover: Doug DuKane (children on swing); Ric Ergenbright Photography (schoolhouse); Tom & DeeAnn McCarthy/Corbis Stock Market, (children running), Photodisc.com (flag).

PAGE PLACEMENT KEY:

(t)-top (b)-bottom (c)-center (l)-left (r)-right
(bg)-background
(fg) foreground

TABLE OF CONTENTS:

iv (tl) Shelburne Museum; v (tl) Newlab; ix (tl) Smithsonian Institution

UNIT 1

Opener (fg) Shelburne Museum, 2 (cr) Ellen Senisi/The Image Works; 3 (cl) Bob Daemmrich Photography; 3 (cr) Superstock; 9 (t) J.C. Carton/Bruce Coleman, Inc.; 12 (br) Superstock; 14 (b) Bob Daemmrich Photography; 14 (tr) Christine Osborne Pictures; 15 (b) Gordon Parks/Hulton/Archive Photos; 15 (t) Jim Pickerell/Stock Connection/PictureQuest; 16 (t) L. O'Shaughnessy/H.Armstrong Roberts; 17 (t) Bob Daemmrich Photography; 18 (b) Peter Cade/Stone; 22 (c) Mark E. Gibson Photography; 22 (b) Jeff Greenberg/Stock, Boston; 23 (c) Richard T. Nowitz; 23 (bl) West Sedona School; 23 (br) James Marshall/The Image Works, 24, 29 (t),(tl) Blackwell History of Education Museum; 24, 29 (c), (bl) Blackwell History of Education Museum; 24, 25 (b) Jack McConnell/McConnell & McNamara; 24 (bl) Blackwell History of Education Museum; 26 (br) Michael Newman/PhotoEdit/PictureQuest; 28 (t) Blackwell History of Education Museum; 29 (bl) (cl) Blackwell History of Education Museum; 29 (bcl) Gloria Rejune Adams/Old School Square; 30 (cr) Bob Daemmrich Photography/Stock, Boston; 31 (br) Jay Ireland & Georgienne E.

Bradley/Bradley Ireland Productions; 31 (cr) Nicholas DeVore, III/Bruce Coleman, Inc. 31 (cl) Sheila McKinnon/Mira; 32 (bl) Burbank/The Image Works; 32 (t) Victor Englebert; 33 (c) D. Donadoni/Bruce Coleman, Inc.; 34 (b) Photopia; 35 (ti), (tr), (br), (cl) Photopia.

UNIT 2

Opener (fg) Newlab; (bg) Robert Frerck/Odyssey Productions, Chicago; 41 (tl) Newlab; 43 (tl) Reuters NewMedia/Corbis; (bl) B. Daemmrich/The Image Works; (cr) John Henry Williams/Bruce Coleman, Inc.; 46 (c) Alan Schein/Corbis Stock Market; (br) DiMaggio/Kalish/Corbis Stock Market; (cb) Rodney Jones/Harcourt; (cr) Joe Sohm/Pictor; 47 (c) Diane M. Meyer; 48 (b) Michael Newman/PhotoEdit; 49 (t) Ken Chernus/FPG International; (cl) PhotoDisc/Getty Images; 50 (t) Photovault; (b)Courtesy of the City of Santa Fe, NM; 51 (t), (b) Jeff Geissler/Getty Images; (c) Paul Slaughter/Omni Photo Communications; 52 Joe Sohm/Alamy Images; 54 (b) Michael Hubrich/Photo Researchers; 55 (t) Time For Kids Magazine; (br) Tim Sloan/Corbis; (cr) Robert Essel/Corbis Stock Market; 56 (bc) Peggy and Ronald Barnett/Corbis Stock Market; (cr) Visions of America; (bc) Peggy & Ronald Barnett/Corbis Stock Market; 60 (b) Phil Degginger/Color-Pic; 61 (c) Corbis; (tr) Ed Wheeler/Corbis Stock Market; (br) Joe Sohm/Visions of America; (br) B. Bachmann/The Image Works; (cl) D. Boone/Corbis; 63 (t) Bettmann/Corbis; (cl) Bob Daemmrich/The Image Works; 64 One Mile Up; 65 (l) The Granger Collection; (r) South Caroliniana Library/The University of South Carolina; 68 (t) Louisiana Secretary of State; (b) The Granger Collection, NY; 69 (t) Bettmann/Corbis; (bl) Corbis; (br) Florida State Archives; 70 (t) Macduff Everton/Corbis; (bl) Courtesy of DuPont; (br) E.R. Degginger/Bruce Coleman Collection; 71 (c) Anton Oparin/Corbis SABA; 72 (bl) PictureQuest; (br) Bob Daemmrich/Stock, Boston/PictureQuest; 73 (tl) Michael Newman/PhotoEdit; (cr) Photodisc; 74 (b) Larry Evans/Black Star; (cr) Bettmann/Corbis; 75 (c) Larry Evans/Black Star; (tl) Chicago Historical Society; (tr) Public Art Program/Chicago Cultural Center, (bl) Todd Buchanan/Black Star; (cr) Hulton-Deutsch Collection/Corbis.

UNIT 3

Opener (bg) Mark E. Gibson; 82 (t) Richard Pasley/Stock, Boston; (br) Nigel Press/Stone; 83 (tl) Buddy Mays/Travel Stock; (bl) W. Perry Conway/Corbis; (br) R. Walker/H. Armstrong Roberts; 94 (b) Bob Daemmrich Photography; 96 (b) Robert Winslow/The Viesti Collection; 98, 99 (bg) Richard H. Johnston/Taxi/Getty Images; 98 (fg) Michael McDermott/Getty Images; 99 (t), (fg) First Light Photo (b),(fg) Joseph R. Melanson/Aerials OnlyGallery/Aero Photo; 100 (t) David Muench/Corbis; (b) Superstock; 101 (l) Bill Strong; (r) Ricky Hudson/CB4GO.com; 102, 103 Phillip Gould/Corbis; (inset) Ed Jackson; 108 (bl) Bruce Hands/Stone; (bc) Ken Kenzie/Harcourt; 108, 109 (bkg) John Lawrence/Stone; 109 (tr) Fred Habegger/Grant Heilman Photography; (br) B. Daemmrich/The Image Works; (cr) Bob Daemmrich/Stock, Boston; 110 (bl) Mark E. Gibson Photography; 110, 111 (bg) Jan Butchofsky-Houser/Houserstock; 111 (tr) PhotoEdit; (br) Bob Daemmrich/The Image Works; (cl) Jim Nilson/Stone; 112 (b) A. & J. Verkaik/Corbis Stock Market; 113 (c) Larry Lefever/Grant

Heilman Photography; 114 (b) Dan Guravich Corbis; 114, 115 (bg) Randy Wells Photography; 115 (cr) Kevin Fleming/Corbis; 116 (tr) Geri Engberg Photography; 117 (cl) Mark E. Gibson Photography; 118 (c), (br) Superstock; (bg) Buddy Mays/Travel Stock Photography; 119 (tr) W. Jacobs/Art Directors & TRIP Photo Library; (tr) Jay Ireland & Georgienne E. Bradley/Bradley Ireland Productions; (bl) Inger Hogstrum/Danita Delimont, Agent; (cl) K. Rice/H. Armstrong Roberts; 120 (b) Superstock (tr) Siede Preis/PhotoDisc/PictureQuest; 121 (tc) Superstock; (tr) Sami Sarkis/Getty Images/PhotoDisc; (bc) PhotoDisc/Getty Images; (cl) Wolfgang Kaehler Photography; 122 (tr) Ian Adams/Garden Image; (bl) Sara Demmons; (cr) Laurie Dove/Garden Image; 123 (tl) Judith Lindsey; (tr) Phillip Roullard/Garden Image; (bl) Judith Lindsey; (cl) Judith Lindsey; (cr) Woodbridge Williams/Garden Image.

UNIT 4

130 (tl) Norbert Schafer/Corbis Stock Market; 131 (tl) Lee Snider/The Image Works; (tr) Bachmann/Unicorn Stock Photos; (bl) Bob Daemmrich/Stock, Boston; 132 (bl) Marilyn "Angel" Wynn/Nativestock.com; (br) Melanie Weiner Photography; 133 (t) Melanie Weiner Photography; 140 (tl) John Elk III; (tr) H. Thomas III/Unicorn Stock Photos; (bl) Bob Daemmrich/The Image Works; (br) Dave Bartruf/Corbis; 141 (tl) Eric Chrichton/Bruce Coleman, Inc. (tr) Topham/The Image Works; 142 (cr) Ted Streshinsky/Corbis; 143 (tr) Superstock; (bc)Momatiuk Eastcott/The Image Works; (cl) Susan Lapides/Woodfin Camp & Associates; 144 (tl) Hanan Isachar-Herzlia/Dieses Bild ist urhe-berrechtlich geschutzt; (bc) Macduff Everton/The Image Works, (bc) David R. Frazier; 148 (bl) The Newark Museum/Art Resource, NY; (cr) Corbis; 149 (t) C Squared Studios/PhotoDisc/PictureQuest; (bl) Feldman & Associates; (br) Lawrence Migdale; (cr) Mimmo Jodice/Corbis; 150 (cl) The University of Southern Mississippi; 151 (cr) Michigan State University/Feldman & Associates; (cr) UCLA Fowler Museum of Cultural History, photograph by Don Cole/Feldman & Associates; 154 (bc), (br) Superstock; 153 (tc) Ray Morsch/Corbis; (tr) H. Rogers/Art Directors & TRIP Photo Library; (bl) Suzanne Murphy/DDB Stock Photo; (br) Alyx Kellington/DDB Stock Photo; 156 (tr) Billy Hustace/Stone; (br) Paul Barton/Corbis Stock Market; (cl) Kathy McLaughlin/The Image Works; 157 (tl) Richard T. Norwitz/Folio; (tr) Ray Juno/Corbis Stock Market; 160 (cr) Bob Krist/PictureQuest; 161 © Tom & See Ann McCarthy/Corbis Stock Market; (tr) PhotoEdit.

UNIT 5

Opener (fg) Eric Lessing/Art Resource, NY; 169 (tl) Erich Lessing/Art Resource, NY; 170 (tl) S.A. Kraulis/Masterfile; (cr) Jon Gnass/Gnass Photo Images; 171 (bl) Paul Barton/Corbis Stock Market; (cr) Science Photo Library/Photo Researchers; 175 (tl) Superstock; (tr) Mark E. Gibson; (cl) Rommel/Masterfile; (cr) Superstock; 178,179 (b) Sarah H. Cotter/Bruce Coleman, Inc.; 181 (cl) Pat Lanza/Bruce Coleman, Inc.; 184 (l) Downtown Thomasville.com; (r) Gary Doster; 185 Downtown Thomasville.com; 186 (b) Downtown Thomasville.com; 187 (b) Mark Wall/Getty Images; 186,187 Jay Taffet/Affordable Aerials.com; 188 (tl) Historical Society of Pennsylbania; (b) Oregon Historical Society; 189 (tl) Hulton/Archive; (cr) Texas State Library &

Archives Commission; 190,191 (t) Reality X; 191 © Kevin Horan/Stock, Boston Inc./PictureQuest; 194 (tr) Bettmann/Corbis; 196 (b) Bert Lane/Plimoth Plantation; 197 (b), (tr) Ted Curtain/Plimoth Plantation, 198 (c) George F. Mobley/Courtesy U.S. Capitol Historical Society; (b) Joseph Sohn/Corbis; 199 (tr) Joe Sohm/Photo Researchers; 200 (b) Hulton-Deutsch Collection; 201 (tr) United States Postal Service/Harcourt; (br) Denise Cupen/Bruce Coleman, Inc; 202 (c) James P. Blair/Corbis; (b) Frank Siteman/Stock, Boston; (tl), (cl), (cr) United States Postal Service/Harcourt; (tr) John Neubauer/PhotoEdit; 203 (c) Joe Sohn/ChromoSohm Media; (tr) National Archives; 208 (bc) Bettman/Corbis; (br) Bettman/Corbis; 209 (c) Bettman/Corbis; (tr) Reuters NewMedia/Corbis; 210 (bl) Anthony Meshkinyar/Stone; (br) Michael Boys/Corbis; 211 (c) H.H. Thomas/Unicorn Stock Photos; (tc) Phylllis Kedl/Unicorn Stock Photos; (tr) Anthony Marsland/Stone; (br) Corbis; (cl) PictureQuest; 212 (c) Chad Slattery/Stone; (bl) AFP/Corbis; (tl) Phillip Wallick/Corbis Stock Market; 212, 213 (t) D. & J. Heaton/Stock, Boston; 213 (c) Leo de Wys Photo Agency/eStock Photograpy/PictureQuest; (b) Torleif Svensson/Corbis Stock Market; (tc) Superstock; (cr) Brian K. Miller/Bruce Coleman, Inc.; 214 (c) D. Young-Wolff/PhotoEdit; (tl) Topham/The Image Works; (tc) Archivo Iconografico, S.A./Corbis; (br) NASA; (cl) John Elk III/Stock, Boston; 215 (c) L. Hafencher/H. Armstrong Roberts; (tc) Rudi Von Briel; (tr) DiMaggio/Kalish/Corbis Stock Market; (bc) Don Mason/Corbis Stock Market; (cr) Roger Wood/Corbis; (bl) The Museum of Independent Telephony; (br) The Museum of Independent Telephony; (cr) Corbis; 217 (tl) The Museum of Independent Telephony; (tr) Superstock.

UNIT 6

Opener (fg) Smithsonian Institution; (bg) Nick Gunderson/Stone; 225 (tl) Smithsonian Institution; 226 (br) Mark E. Gibson Photography; (cl) Richard Hutchings/Photo Researchers; 227 (bl) David Young-Wolff/PhotoEdit; (cr) Katie Ciccarello/The Image Works; 240 (b) Aneal S. Vohra/Unicorn Stock Photos; 241 (tl) John Millar/Stone; (tr) PhotoEdit; (br) Christopher Bissell/Stone; (cl) Richard Eskite/Harcourt; (bg) PhotoDisc/Getty Images; 242 (tl) Bob Daemmrich/The Image Works; (bl) Dan Bosler/Stone; (cr) Aaron Haupt/Photo Researchers; 243 (tr) Steven Peters/Stone; (c) Art Directors & TRIP Photo Library; (cr) Bob Clay/Visuals Unlimited; 253 (c) Hans Reinhard/Bruce Coleman Collection; 254 (bl) Burke/Triolo/Brand X Pictures/PictureQuest; (bc) H. Armstrong Roberts/Corbis Stock Market; 255 (bl) Hulton/Archive Photos; 256 (tr) Bettmann/Corbis; (bl) Pittsburg Post-Gazette; (br) Hulton/Archive Photos; (cl) Hulton/Archive Photos; 257 (tl) Ray Juno/Corbis Stock Market; (tr) NASA; (cr) Agence France Presse/Corbis; (cl) Doug Martin/Photo Researchers; 258, 259 (bg) Van Bucher/Photo Researchers; 262, 263 (b), (bl) Morton Beebe, S.F./Corbis; 264 (br) Superstock; (bg) Don Mason/Corbis Stock Market; 267 (cr) Anthony Meshkinyar/Stone; 268 (b) Craig Hammell/Corbis Stock Market; 270 (t) George Hall/Corbis; (b) Donnezan/Explorer/Photo Researchers; 272 (b) Stephen Kline/Bruce Coleman, Inc. 272 (tr) David R. Frazier; 274 (tr) Carlo Hindian/Masterfile; (bl) Jef Zaruba/Corbis; (br) Sven Martson/The Image Works; 275 (tl) Bob Dammerich/Stock, Boston;

(tr) Rolf Bruderer/Corbis Stock Market; (bl) John Lei/Stock, Boston; (cl) Michael Philip Manheim/The Image Finders.

All other photographs by Harcourt photogrphers listed below:
Harcourt: Weronica Ankarorn, Bartlett Digital Photography, Victoria Bowen, Ken Kinzie, Gibson Pasley Sohm/Vi Daeee

Activity Patterns

Activity Patterns

The reproducible patterns in this section are for use with the extension activities described in your lesson plans. You may also want to use the patterns to create other activities appropriate for children in your class.

Contents

School Workers

teacher

bus driver

principal

food server

custodian

librarian

secretary

nurse

student

© Harcourt

School Scenes

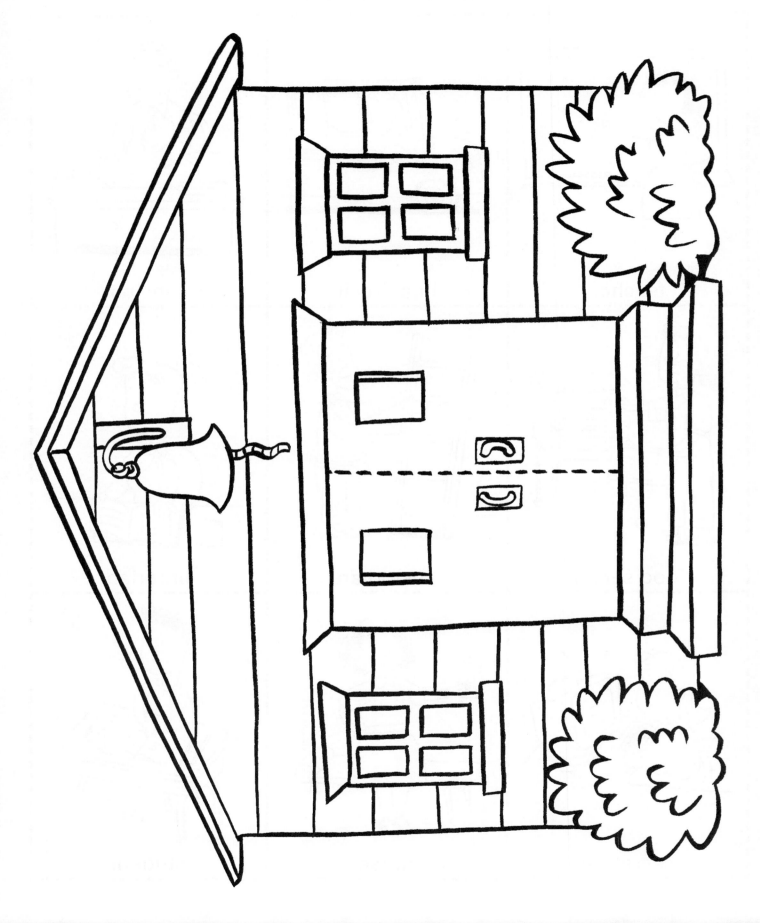

United States Map

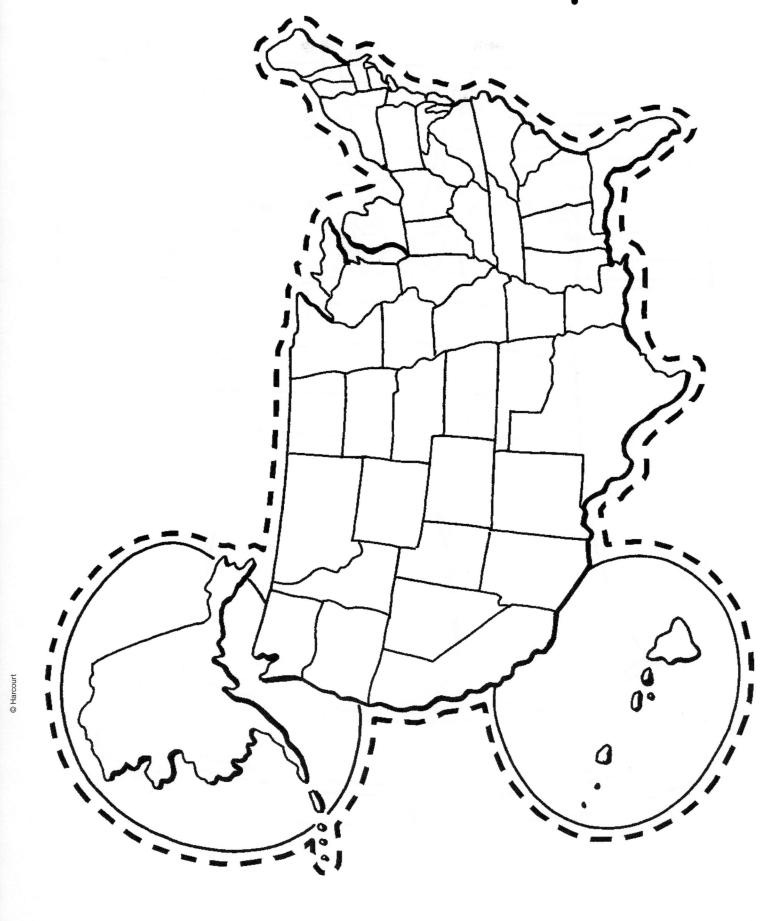

Our Freedoms

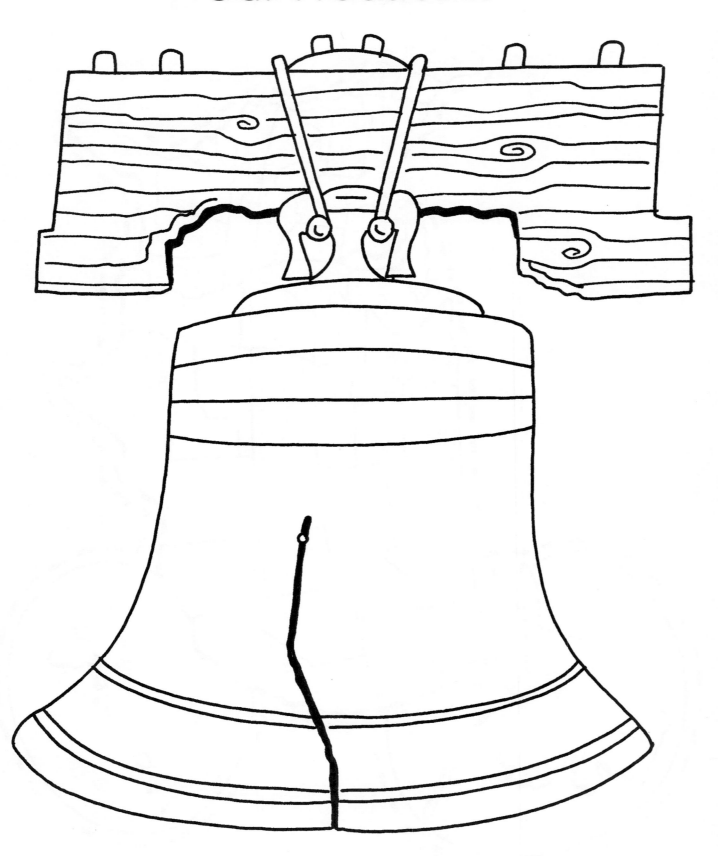

Picture Dictionary

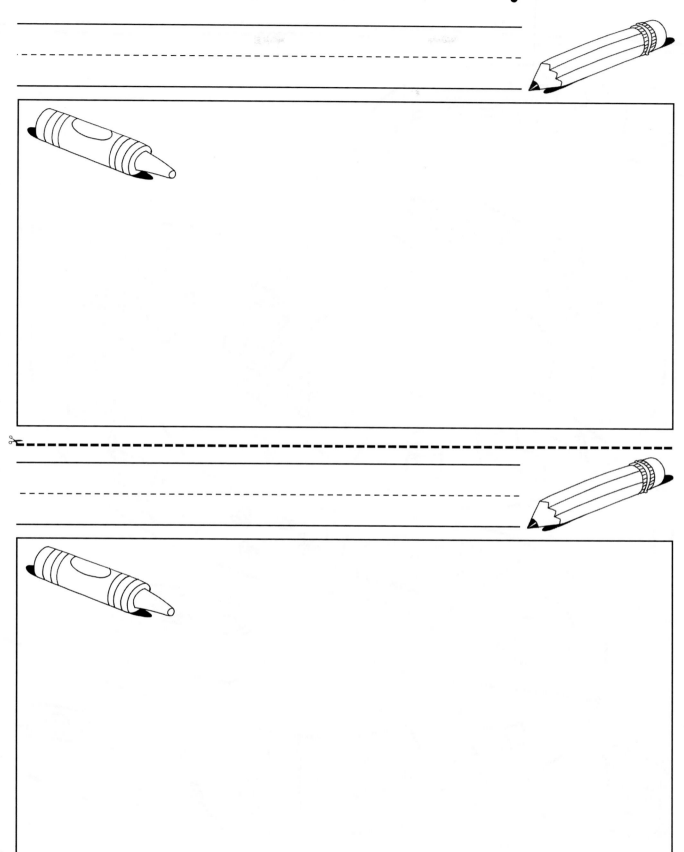

Reduce, Reuse, Recycle Game

© Harcourt

Community Map

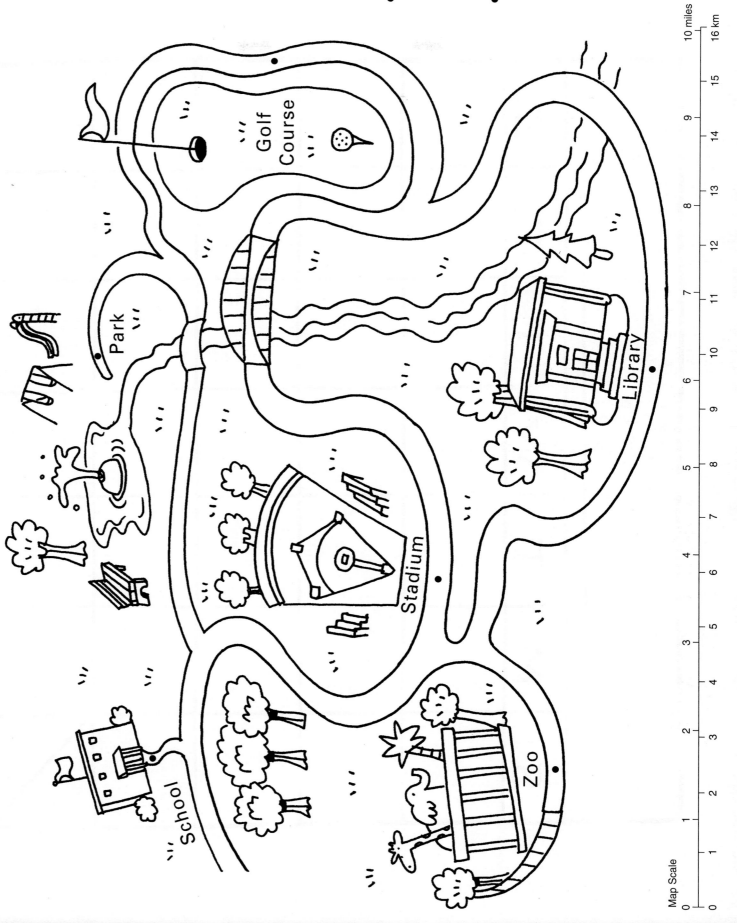

© Harcourt

Calendar

	S	M	T	W	T	F	S

© Harcourt

Time Line

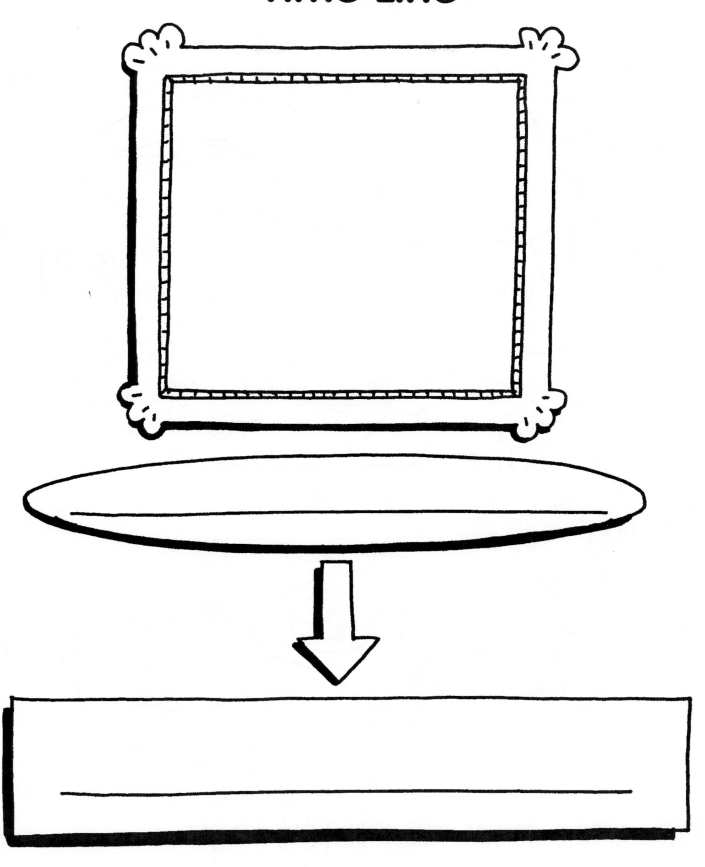

Everyday Life Game

© Harcourt

Well-Done Job Award

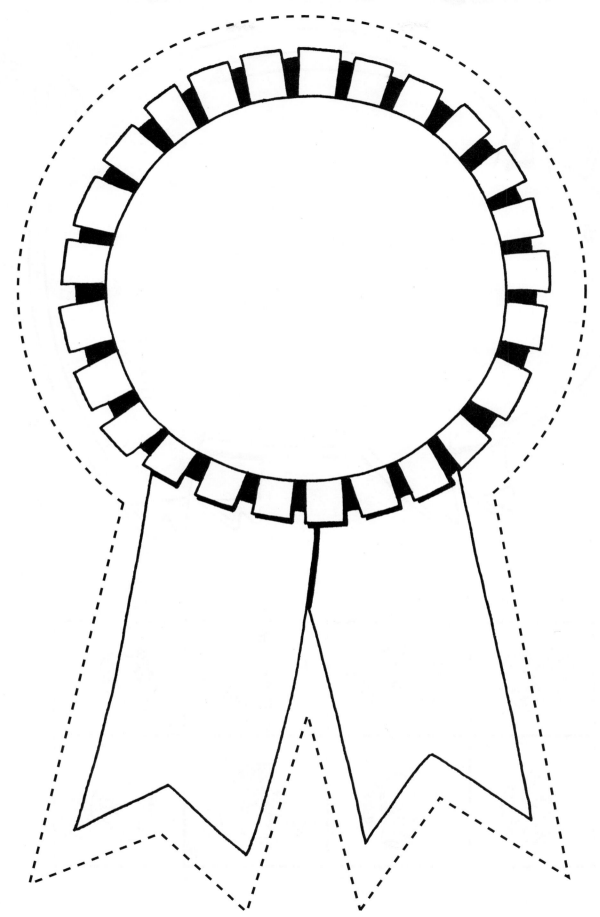

© Harcourt

Piggy Bank Savings

Thinking Organizers

Thinking Organizers

Ideas and concepts may be organized in many different ways. The contents of the following pages are intended to act as guides for that organization. These copying masters may be used to help children organize the concepts in the lessons they have read. They may also help children complete the wide variety of activities that are assigned throughout the school year.

Contents

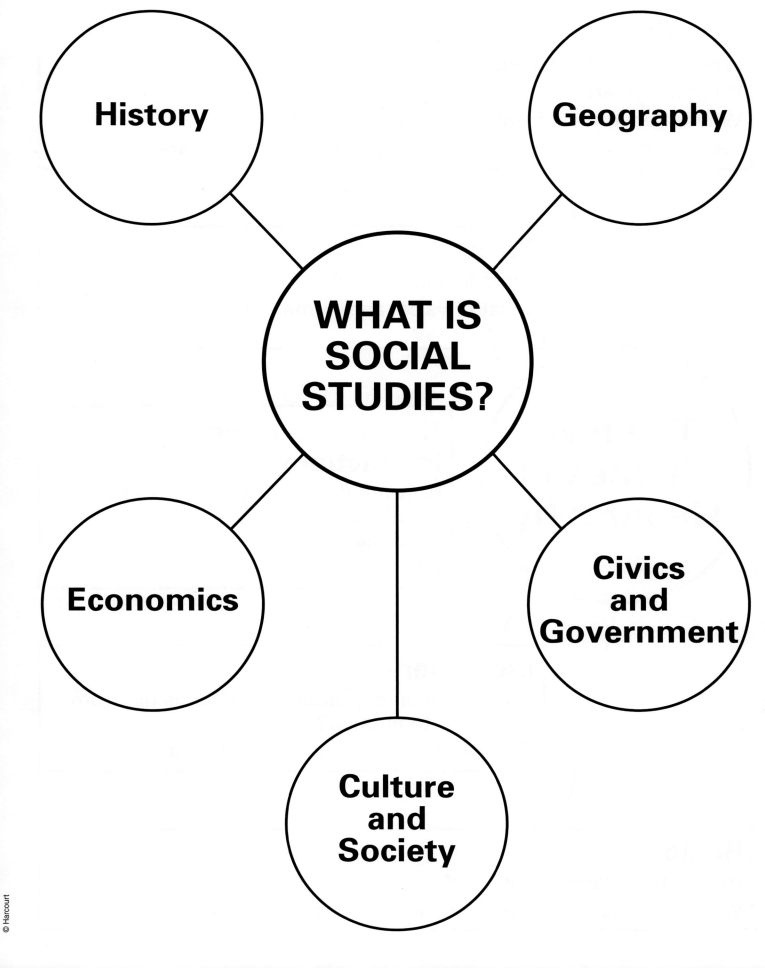

History

Geography

WHAT IS SOCIAL STUDIES?

Economics

Civics and Government

Culture and Society

© Harcourt

Location

Where is a place located?

What is it near?

What direction is it from another place?

Why are certain features or places located where they are?

Place

What is it like there?

What physical and human features does it have?

The Five Themes of Geography

Human-Environment Interactions

How are people's lives shaped by the place?

How has the place been shaped by people?

Movement

How did people, products, and ideas get from one place to another?

Why do they make these movements?

Regions

How is this place like other places?

What features set this place apart from other places?

Current Events

Summary of an important event:

WHO:

WHAT:

WHEN:

WHERE:

HOW:

Prediction

**What do I think
will happen next?**

**Personal
Reaction**

**My reaction
to the event:**

© Harcourt

Social Studies Journal

The most important thing I learned was . . .

Something that I did not understand was . . .

What surprised me the most was . . .

I would like to know more about . . .

© Harcourt

Reading Guide

K	What I **K**now

W	What I **W**ant to Know

L	What I **L**earned

© Harcourt

Main Idea and Supporting Details

Supporting Detail	Supporting Detail

Main Idea

Supporting Detail	Supporting Detail

© Harcourt

Fact and Opinion

	Fact
✓	**Fact**
✓	**Fact**
✓	**Fact**
✓	**Fact**

	Opinion
✗	**Opinion**
✗	**Opinion**
✗	**Opinion**
✗	**Opinion**

© Harcourt

Cause and Effect

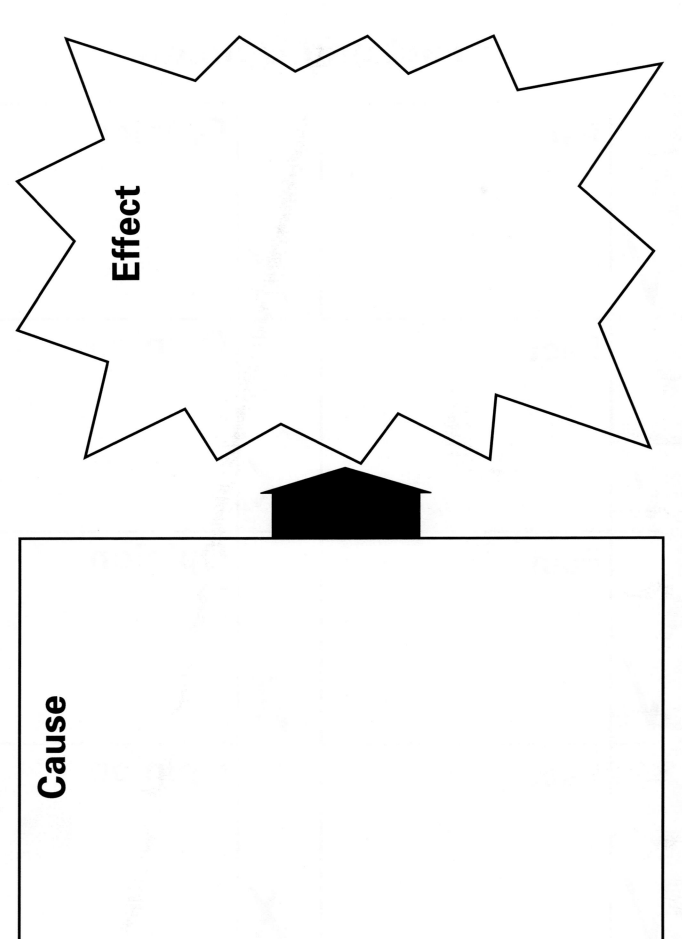

Effect

Cause

Compare and Contrast

Information About "A"	Information About "B"

© Harcourt

Categorize

Sequence

Event

Order

Event

Event

Event

Event

© Harcourt

Summarize

Important Facts

SUMMARY

Important Facts

Make a Generalization

Fact

Fact

GENERALIZATION

Fact

Fact

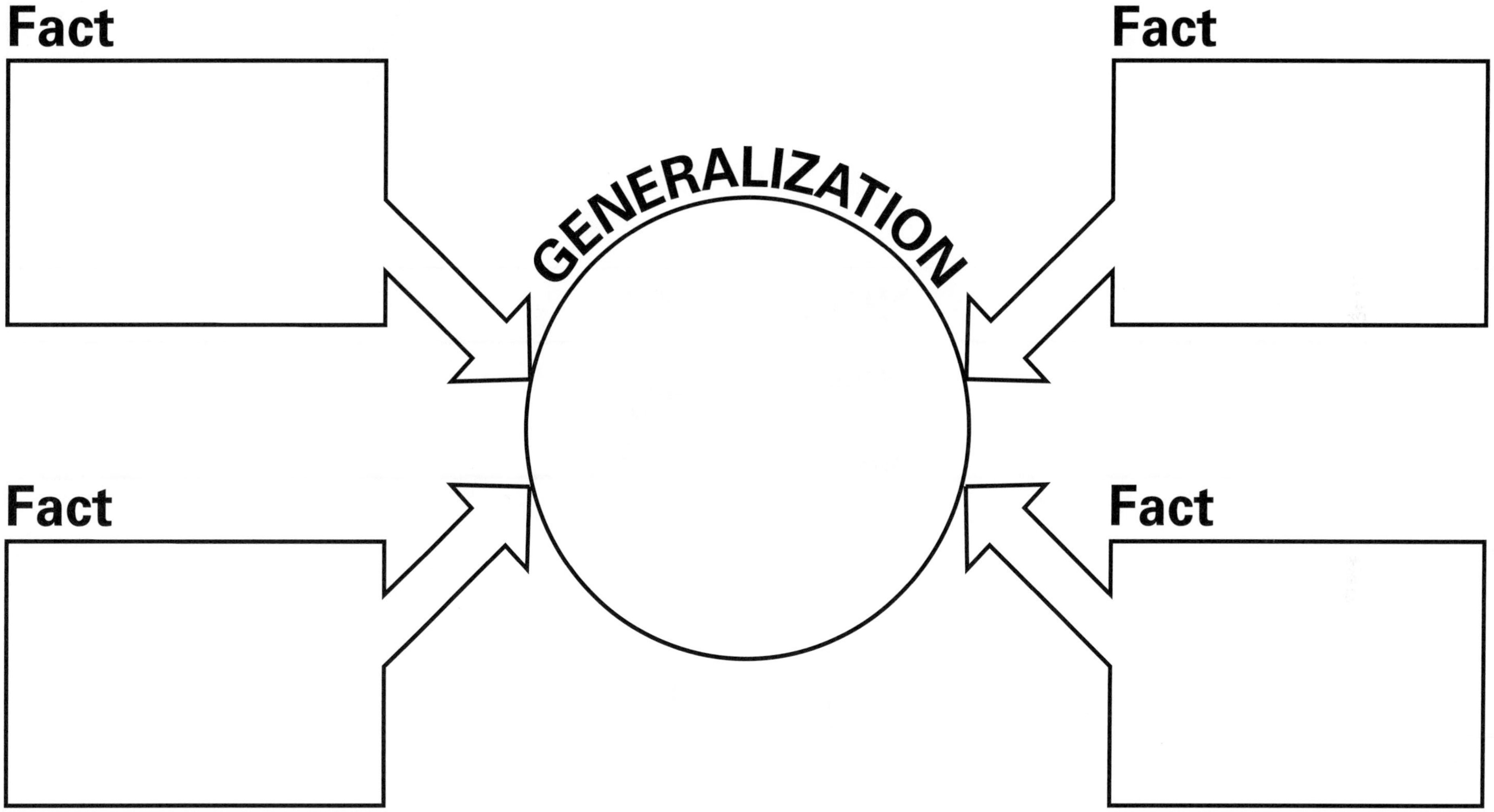

Draw a Conclusion

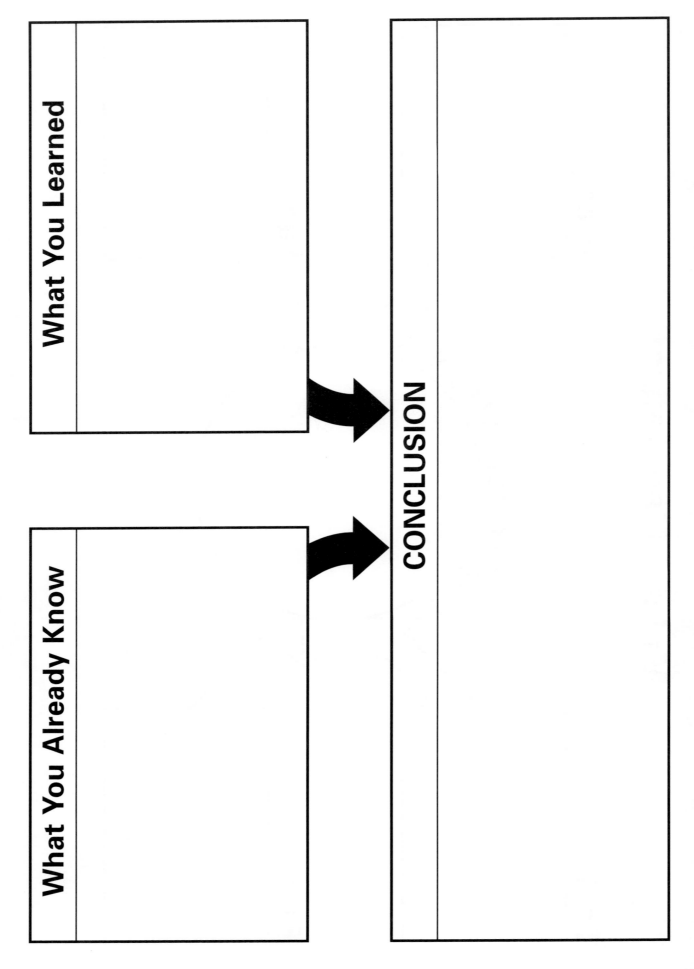

What You Learned

What You Already Know

CONCLUSION

Point of View

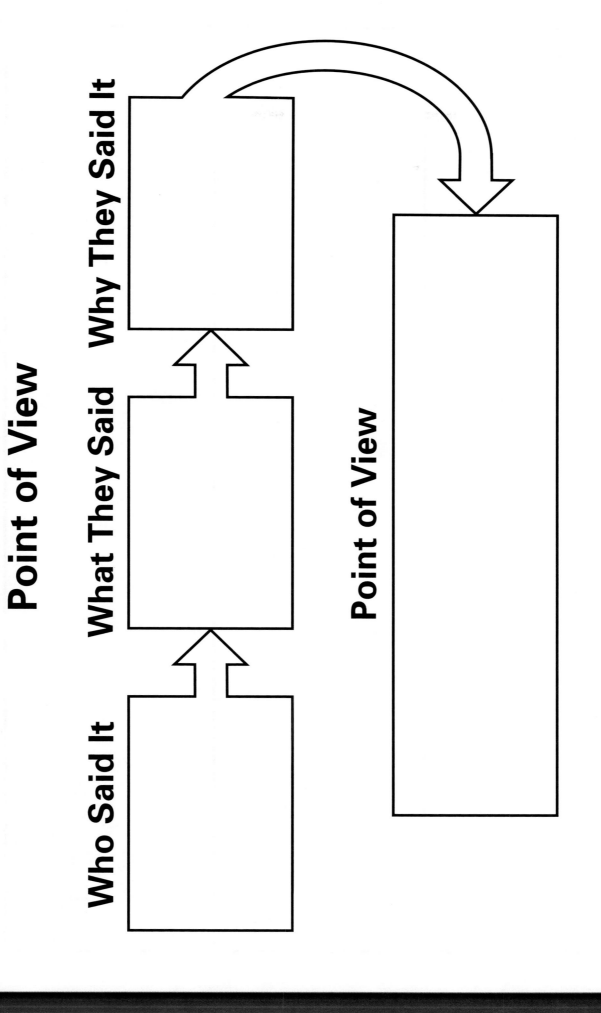

Who Said It · **What They Said** · **Why They Said It**

Point of View

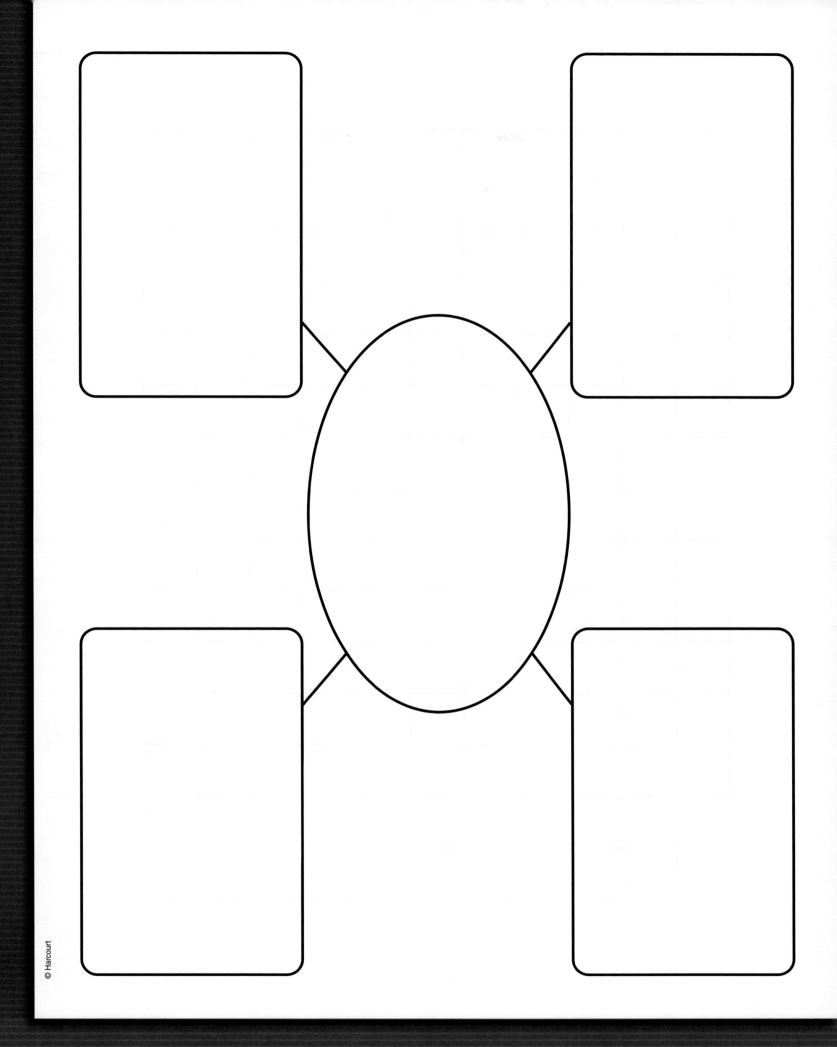

© Harcourt

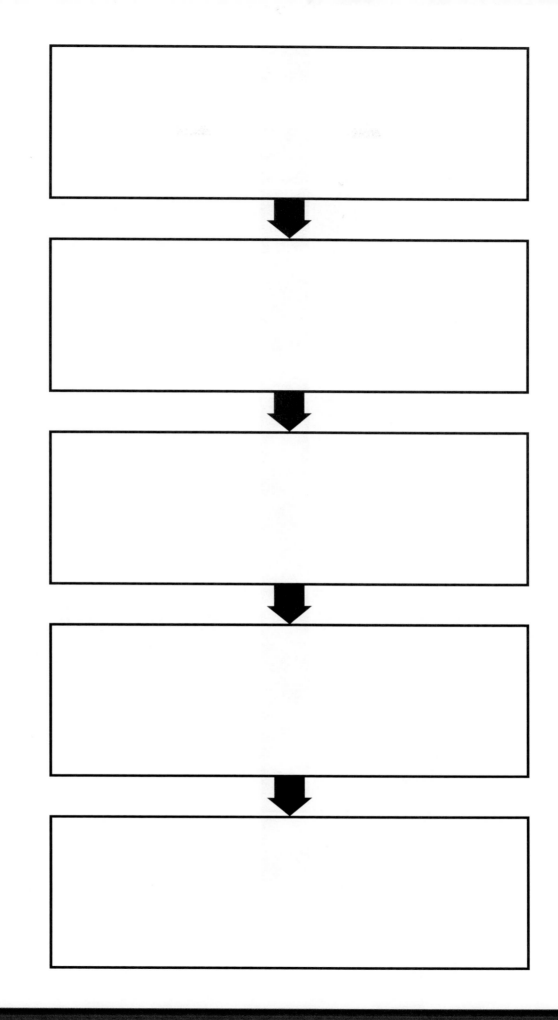

The United States

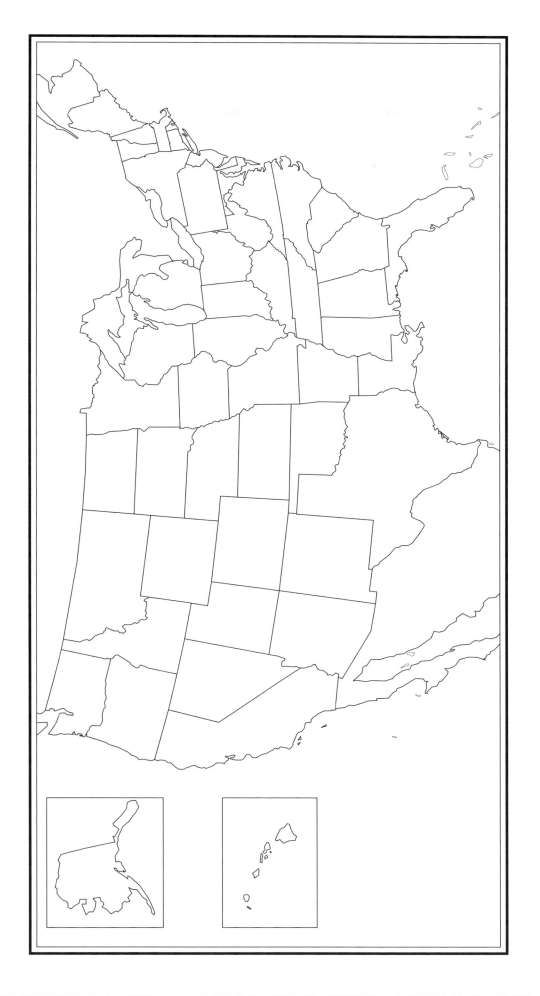

North America

© Harcourt

The World

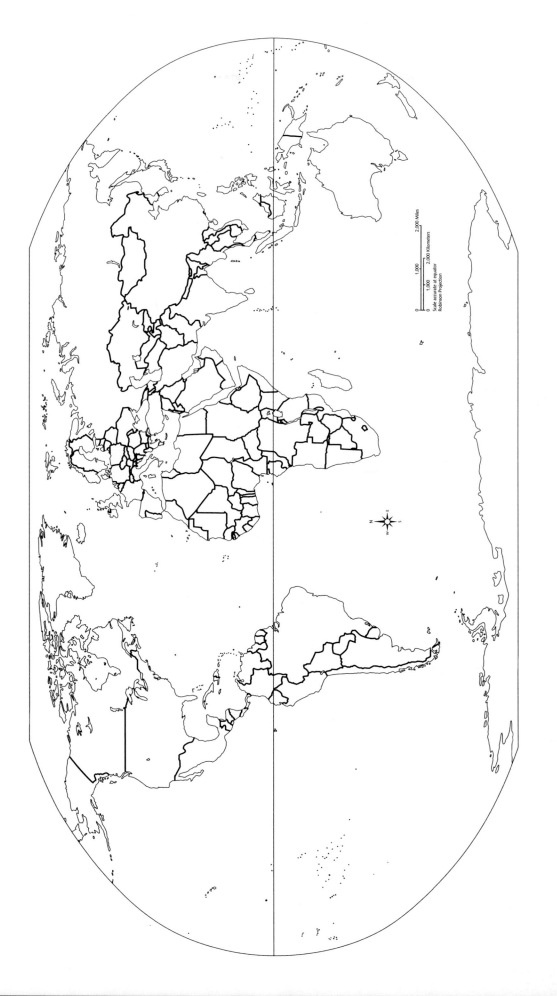

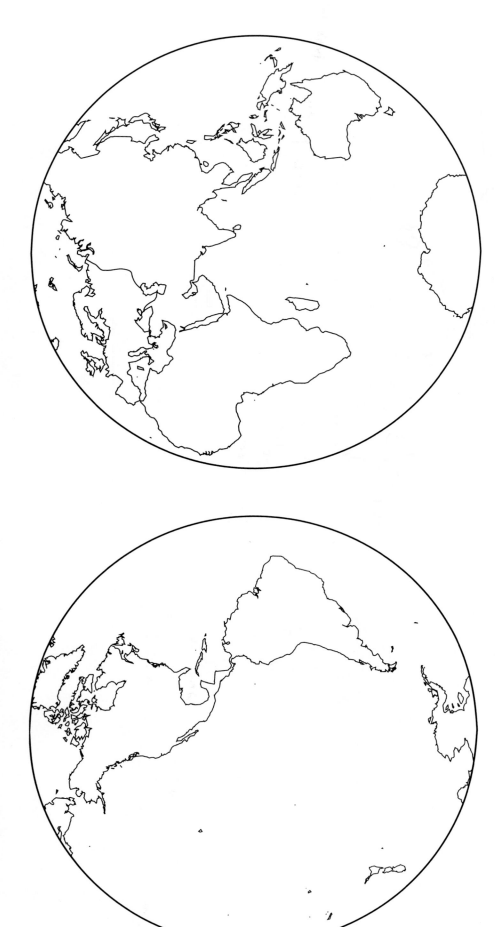

Northern Hemisphere

Southern Hemisphere

Holiday Activities

Holiday Activities

At appropriate times of the year, the holiday backgrounds and activities provided in this section can be used to introduce or reinforce concepts related to important holidays. The holiday activities explore a variety of individual and community celebrations. They can prompt discussion of the similarities and differences in the traditions and cultures found in the United States.

Contents

Labor Day

Labor Day

Labor Day is a day to celebrate the many workers in our country, who work hard to help others. Labor Day is celebrated on the first Monday in September, and for many school children, it signals the beginning of the school year. When the holiday was first proposed, parades were suggested to honor the workers. Afterwards, a festival was added so the workers and their families could have fun. The first Labor Day parade was held in New York City in 1882. In 1894, President Grover Cleveland signed a bill into law making Labor Day a national holiday. Many people do not work on Labor Day and spend the day relaxing or going to picnics. Often there are fireworks displays at night. Other places, like Puerto Rico and Canada, also celebrate Labor Day.

There are many kinds of workers. Some workers provide services to others, like doctors or bus drivers. Others make products we eat, like bakery workers who bake bread. Still others make things we need in order to do our jobs, such as computers. Some workers entertain us, like baseball players or musicians. It certainly takes many kinds of workers to make our world a better place! Think about the kinds of businesses in your neighborhood or town. What kinds of workers are needed to keep these businesses running well?

Workers Word Search

Make grids with half-inch squares (ten across, ten down). Have children name ten kinds of workers and list them on a chart. Distribute the grids to children. Tell them to write one letter per box in either horizontal or vertical form for each worker listed. Have children hide the workers' titles first and then have them fill in the remaining boxes with random letters. Invite children to switch papers and complete each other's puzzles.

Who Made Me?

Take children on a tour of your classroom and have them help you make a list of all the products they see that help them to do their jobs as students. Take a few minutes to discuss what each item is used for, and ask children to tell what it is made of. Then ask them to speculate on how the item is made and how long it might take to make it. When they have an understanding of the length of time needed to produce the item, ask how they think it gets to their school. Give children art paper and

crayons and invite them to draw a time line to show how one such item finds its way to their classroom. There are commercially prepared videotapes that explain how milk gets from the cow to the grocery store, for example, and you may wish to borrow something appropriate from your school library for a visual tour of how products are made and distributed.

What Makes Our School Tick?

Create a hallway bulletin board highlighting the many workers who help children in your school. Have children help you list the kinds of workers in your building, such as other teachers, principal, security or crossing guard, nurse, counselor, librarian, cafeteria workers, and secretaries. In advance, ask workers if your students could interview them about their jobs, and set up times that are convenient. Ask children to think of two or three interview questions, and discuss some pointers for having a good interview. Let children practice reading their questions to you before the actual interviews. You could take photographs of children speaking into a tape recorder and post the photos on the bulletin board, or you could videotape the entire process. You may want to follow up by having children write thank-you notes to the people who participated in your activity.

Columbus Day

Christopher Columbus

Christopher Columbus was an Italian explorer. In 1492, Queen Isabella and King Ferdinand of Spain provided money for Columbus to make a voyage. They wanted him to find a shorter route to the Indies and to the gold, spices, and other riches that could be found there. Columbus readied his three ships, the *Niña*, the *Pinta*, and the *Santa Maria*. Instead of finding a route to the Indies, however, Columbus first landed on an island in the Bahamas. Columbus named the island San Salvador, claiming it for Spain. Columbus thought he had landed in the Indies and called the people there *Indians*. Instead of the Indies, Columbus found a whole new continent, which was later named North America.

Four hundred years after Columbus found the new land, people in the United States decided to name a holiday in his honor. Columbus Day is celebrated on the second Monday in October. Americans celebrate with parades and speeches. Many schools, government offices, and businesses are closed.

Making Flags

Explain to children that a ship's flag helps people tell it apart from other ships. Have children pretend they are the captain of a ship and are in charge of making its flag. Encourage them to show something that is important to them or something that they like, such as their family, a pet, or a favorite sport. Precut and distribute 4" x 3" rectangles of white art paper and crayons or markers to children. When their flags are complete, have children glue them to craft sticks for display in a foam block. For an alternate Columbus Day display, complete the next activity and use the flags in the ships.

Edible Ships

Review the three ships that sailed on Columbus's voyage: the *Niña*, the *Pinta*, and the *Santa Maria*. Tell children they are going to make edible ships for Columbus Day. You will need small paper plates, half a peach for each child, a tub of whipped topping, blue food coloring, craft sticks, and a spoon. (CAUTION: Check records for allergies first, and read the ingredients in the topping.)

Give each child a paper plate, and spoon a small amount of whipped topping on each plate. Squeeze a drop of food coloring on the topping and have children carefully mix it in with the craft stick to make the topping blue to represent the ocean. Then place the peach in the center of the topping and have children anchor the flag from the previous activity on their ship. (If you did not complete the first activity, you can make a small flag from a marshmallow on a toothpick.)

Singing in Rounds

Teach children the following verse to be sung to the tune of "Row, Row, Row Your Boat." Tell children that they will be singing the song to Christopher Columbus to thank him for landing in North America. Practice singing the verse in unison several times. Then let each child select a colored paper slip from a basket. One third of the slips should be red, one third blue, and one third yellow. Have children stand in three groups according to the color they chose. When children have learned the song, teach them how to sing in rounds. Give signals to each group so they know when to begin singing.

> *Sailed, sailed, sailed his ships,*
> *Sailed across the sea,*
> *Found new lands, found new lands,*
> *Just for you and me.*

Veterans Day

Veterans Day

On November 11, 1918, World War I came to an end. This day became known as "Armistice Day." The word *armistice* means that both sides agreed to stop fighting. A treaty, or promise, was signed by both sides to keep the agreement. The United States Congress made November 11 a federal holiday in 1938. After World War II, the date became known as Veterans Day, and in 1954 Congress declared that it would be a day to honor veterans who served or fought in all wars. It became a celebration to honor all of America's veterans for their patriotism, love of country, and willingness to serve and sacrifice for the common good.

- Veterans, or former members of the armed forces, such as the Army, Navy, Marine Corps, or Air Force, often celebrate Veterans Day with parades and speeches.

- Many veterans' groups plan activities in their towns or cities to teach young people about patriotism and remember those who served their country.

Patriotic Music

Gather a collection of patriotic music to play to children. Check with the band teacher and librarian for tapes or CDs you can borrow. Ask children to tell what they know about parades and the bands that play in them. Tell children that you are going to play some parade music such as "The Stars and Stripes Forever" for them. Encourage them to stand and move to the music. Then lead children in a march around the room in time to the music.

Veterans Day Streamers

Show children pictures of parades. Have them examine the pictures to find out what kinds of decorations are used. Point out flags, bunting, and banners and the colors used. Discuss why red, white, and blue are used as patriotic colors. Have children name things that are red, white, and blue.

Let children use various books to find more red, white, and blue items and their uses as decorations.

Provide a paper plate and red, white, and blue crepe paper or streamers. Use construction paper if the other materials are not available. Punch three holes evenly spaced along the bottom half of the outer rim of each paper plate. Have children cut the crepe paper into two-foot lengths, one of each color. Show them how to twist the crepe paper end into a point and push the point through one of the holes in the paper plate. Then use masking tape to anchor the streamers to the plate. Children can hold the plate high in the air as they march around in a classroom parade. The streamers will billow out behind them as they move.

Patriotic Speeches

Decorate a podium (or desk) with red, white, and blue bunting. Discuss the meaning of *patriotic* with children, and tell them that people often make speeches on patriotic holidays, such as Veterans Day. Ask children to ask their families if any family members are veterans, and if so, if they would be willing to visit the classroom to tell what the holiday means to them. If you have no volunteers, contact a local veterans' organization to see about arranging a classroom visit. You may wish to serve your guests refreshments that are red, white, and blue, such as blueberries and sliced strawberries over angel food cake with milk, as a thank-you for their visit.

Thanksgiving

Though it was not called Thanksgiving at the time, a feast of thanks was celebrated by the Pilgrims in 1621. They had come from England to what is now known as America in search of a place where they could worship in the way they wanted. So they set sail for a new land on a ship called the *Mayflower* and settled in America. Many people died on the long trip from England. The trip was difficult, and they did not have good food, medicine, or clean drinking water. In their new land, the people worked hard to build warm homes and to find food. They did not know how to grow food in this new land.

One day, a band of Indians came to Plymouth to greet the Pilgrims. They showed them how to plant corn and other crops they could harvest for food. When the crops had grown, the Pilgrims had an outdoor feast to celebrate their good fortune. They gave thanks for a wonderful harvest and for having survived their first year in America.

Now Americans celebrate Thanksgiving to give thanks for each other and for their blessings. Turkey, sweet potatoes, corn, cranberries, and pumpkin pie are often served.

Pilgrim's Porridge

Explain that the Pilgrims worked together to make food for their feast. Invite children to name each vegetable as you chop it. (carrots, celery, green beans, potatoes, peas, corn) Add them to vegetable broth in a crock-pot and cook until the vegetables are tender. You may wish to have children invite their parents to join them for Pilgrim's Porridge. (CAUTION: Check records for allergies first.)

Beadwork

Make Thanksgiving headbands and necklaces with various kinds of pasta. Display a few pictures of Indian beadwork from an encyclopedia or magazine, and discuss the patterns that appear. Explain that some Indian tribes are known for their beadwork, and point out on a United States map where these tribes are located.

Demonstrate how to glue pieces of pasta to a piece of oak tag, and invite children to design their own patterns using different shapes. When the glue is dry, have children paint the pasta with food coloring or tempera paint to accentuate their patterns. When the headband or necklace is dry, staple it into a circle that fits the child's forehead or neck.

Thanksgiving Collage

Discuss with children why the Pilgrims gave thanks for their first harvest. Help them understand that just as the Pilgrims were thankful for many things, we can be thankful for many things in our lives, too.

Have children browse through old magazines and cut out pictures of things for which they are thankful. Provide large outlines of Indians and Pilgrims, and help children paste their pictures inside the outlines. Teach children the following song to the tune of "Twinkle, Twinkle, Little Star" to sing as they display their collages.

> *Let's be thankful for today,*
> *For our friends with whom we play,*
> *For our moms and for our dads,*
> *For the things we're glad we have,*
> *Let's be thankful for today,*
> *Oh, we love Thanksgiving Day.*

Hanukkah

Hanukkah

Hanukkah is the Jewish Festival of Lights, celebrated in December. It commemorates the victory of the Jews over the Syrians. Long ago, the Syrians had ruled over Israel and had not allowed Jews to study or practice their religion. When the Jewish people in Judea reclaimed their temple in Jerusalem, they found only one small vessel of oil to light the holy lamps. Normally it would be enough to burn for only one day. Miraculously, the lamps burned for eight days. That was enough time to obtain new oil. The holiday of Hanukkah lasts for eight days in memory of this miracle. Candles are lit in windows using a special candleholder, called a *menorah,* to honor the miracle. A menorah has eight branches, and one candle is lit on each night of Hanukkah. Some Jewish families exchange gifts each night of the celebration. They sing songs and have family dinners with traditional Jewish foods such as *latkes,* which are pancakes made of shredded potato. Games are also played, such as spinning the dreidel, which is a kind of top.

The Eight Days of Hanukkah

Have children plan eight gifts they would give to a parent or friend—one for each day of Hanukkah. But tell children they are to think of gifts that do not cost any money. Discuss gifts from the heart, and explain that sometimes these are the best gifts we can get. Help children make their lists and share their favorite ideas with the class.

Hanukkah Customs

Arrange with the media specialist to bring your class to the library to find out about more Hanukkah customs in books or on videotapes, filmstrips, or computer software. Also, arrange for children to visit the computer lab to use the Internet to find Web sites on Hanukkah.

Make a Tzedakah Box

Explain to children that a *tradition* is a practice that people carry out year after year for a special reason. Ask children if they know of any traditions their family has and to describe them. Tell children that one Hanukkah custom is the receiving of *gelt,* which is a word for *money* in Yiddish. Gelt can appear as a savings bond, as a check, or as small chocolate coins wrapped in gold foil. Gelt-giving is an ancient custom that dates back to the Syrian ruler's giving Jews the right to mint their own money after their victory.

Explain that another Hanukkah tradition is to put some of the gelt you receive into a special box known as a Tzedakah. The box is shared with someone less fortunate or the gelt is donated to another good cause. Tell children that they are going to make a Tzedakah Box.

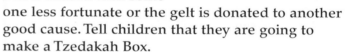

Have a small box with a removable lid for each child. Let them paint their boxes with a dark color, then decorate them with metallic paint or glitter. Give children drinking straws and glue. Have them cut the straws into different lengths and glue them to the box in a design of their choosing. Use multicolored straws or have children paint white straws.

Role Play the Festival of Lights

Remind children that during the eight nights of Hanukkah, candles are burned in a candleholder called a menorah. Invite eight children to be "candles" on a menorah and a ninth to be the candle lighter. Before darkening the room, give each of the volunteers a flashlight. Role play the Festival of Lights by having the candle lighter light his or her candle (flashlight) and then light each "candle" on the menorah.

Christmas

Christmas

Many people around the world celebrate Christmas on December 25. For Christians, Christmas is a day to honor the birth of Jesus. It was even celebrated in ancient Rome more than a thousand years ago! Over the years, it has become a family tradition that includes decorating a Christmas tree, sending Christmas cards, visiting Santa Claus, and giving gifts.

The first Christmas tree in America is said to have been decorated in Virginia in 1842. Since then, people have decorated trees with colored lights, tinsel, and Christmas ornaments. Some people make homemade decorations. Some people even decorate outdoor trees with popcorn and cranberry strings to feed the hungry birds in winter!

People have different ways of celebrating Christmas. In America, children leave cookies and milk for Santa Claus on the night before Christmas. Santa is known as St. Nick in Holland, and children leave bundles of hay for his horse. Santa Claus is known as Papa Noël in Brazil and Père Noël in France.

Luciadagen Breakfast

In Sweden, people celebrate Saint Lucia Day, also known as Luciadagen. The oldest girl in the family dresses up in a white gown and wears a crown of evergreens decorated with candles. She serves her parents coffee and sweet rolls for breakfast. The younger children also dress up, and boys wear tall cone-shaped hats with stars on them. Help children make a batch of sweet rolls to serve to their parents with juice as they visit the classroom.

The Stockings Are Hung

A popular custom in the United States is to hang stockings on a fireplace, door, or windowsill. It is believed that Santa will fill the stockings with treats such as small toys, nuts, coins, or candy. Have children cut out two pieces of felt in the shape of stockings. Punch holes around the edge of the stockings and let children sew in and out of the holes to attach the pieces.

Merry Christmas, Birds!

There is a legend that birds and animals are given the ability to speak at the stroke of midnight on Christmas Eve. Perhaps because of this, animals and birds are given special recognition in many parts of the world at Christmas time. People may put out seeds and suet for wild birds or give their pets extra food as a special treat.

Explain to children that birds find it harder to get food in the wintertime because it is so cold. Invite them to help prepare a special treat for the birds in their neighborhood by making birdseed balls. Use balls or any small shape. Give children craft sticks, and have them spread peanut butter over the ball and then roll it in birdseed. Use newspaper on tables to catch spills. Then wrap a ribbon around each treat when the seed has set a bit, tie it in a bow, and tell children to hang the treat on a tree branch visible from their window. Then invite the birds to a Christmas feast!

Luminarias

Explain to children that in Mexico the people begin celebrating Christmas on December 16. Las Posadas is celebrated for nine days! People sometimes make *luminarias,* which are small paper lanterns with cutouts that reveal the light of a candle inside.

Provide children with paper lunch bags and scissors. Demonstrate how to fold and cut out shapes in the front and back of the bags. Tell them not to cut any shapes in the bottom half of the bag. Fold the bags down neatly at the top and have children take them home as a family gift. At home, parents can place a small flashlight or glowstick inside the luminary to light it. Remind children to tell the story of the luminarias to their parents, brothers, or sisters.

Kwanzaa

Kwanzaa

Kwanzaa is an African American celebration. The holiday was begun by Maulana Karenga in 1966 to bring African Americans together. He hoped they would look back with pride at their African roots. He adopted seven ideas that were important to building strong families and communities. These seven ideas celebrate the African harvest. The word *Kwanzaa* means "first fruits" in Swahili, an African language.

Kwanzaa begins on December 26 and lasts for seven days. During Kwanzaa, families reflect on what is important in life. They think about what will make next year better and make promises for the new year. It is a time of joy and sharing. Some families exchange gifts. Traditional African foods are served, and families may sing, dance, and tell stories.

Red, green, and black are the special colors of Kwanzaa. A *kinara,* or candle holder, is displayed, which holds one black, three red, and three green candles. One candle is lit each night of the celebration. At that time, the families discuss one of the seven ideas, or principles, of Kwanzaa.

Rock Passing Game

Tell children that they are going to play a game that comes from Ghana, a country in Africa. Display a map and point out Ghana's location. Explain that one of the seven principles of Kwanzaa is *ujima,* which means "cooperation," which they will need to play this game. Have them sit in a circle, and play a tape of African music. The first child taps a rock on the floor in time to the music and then passes the rock to the next child, also in time to the music. The rock continues around the circle. If a student breaks the rhythm, he is out.

The Seven Principles of Kwanzaa

Explain to children that the holiday of Kwanzaa lasts for seven days, one for each of the seven ideas, or principles, of Kwanzaa. Make a chart of these seven principles and their meanings, and explain each to children.

- Umoja (oo•MOH•jah)—unity
- Kujichagulia (KOO•gee•CHA•goo•LEE•ah)—self-determination
- Ujima (oo•GEE•mah)—collective work and responsibility
- Ujamaa (oo•jah•MAH)—cooperative economics
- Nia (NEE•ah)—purpose
- Kuumba (koo•OOM•bah)—creativity
- Imani (ee•MON•ee)—faith

Provide each child with 7 pieces of art paper, about $8 \frac{1}{2}$" x $5 \frac{1}{2}$" in size. Explain that each page will represent one of the seven principles. Have children write one principle at the top of each page.

Using various books as references, such as *Imani's Gift, Bringing the Rain to Kapiti Plain, Jambo Means Hello,* and *My First Book of Kwanzaa,* invite children to create illustrations that demonstrate knowledge of each of the seven principles. Let children make covers for their books when complete.  You may wish to provide an African map to paste to book covers and have children color it using red, black, and green.

Kwanzaa *Mkeka*

Tell children that another symbol of Kwanzaa is the *mkeka* (em•KAY•kah). Explain that it is a traditional mat that represents a firm foundation. Cut 1" x $8 \frac{1}{2}$" strips of red and green construction paper. Provide children with a piece of black construction paper with vertical bars that you have cut to one inch from the top and bottom of the paper. (This should resemble a cage with bars.) Have children alternately weave the red and green strips into the black mat.

New Year's Day

New Year's Day

One of the oldest holidays we know might be the celebration of the coming new year. Although most Americans celebrate New Year's Day on January 1, some people of different religions and cultures celebrate it on different days. For example, the beginning of the Chinese new year falls between January 20 and February 19. In Japan, people celebrate the new year from January 1 to 3. Jewish people celebrate Rosh Hashanah anywhere from mid-September to early October. India's new year, Diwali, is celebrated in October. The Cambodian new year is in mid-April. But in most cultures, the beginning of the new year is a symbol of change and growth. Many people make promises, or resolutions, to better themselves in the coming year.

People celebrate New Year's Day in many different ways. Fireworks are set off at midnight to welcome in the new year with a bang! Many cities have parades on New Year's Day. People in some cultures clean their house from top to bottom to welcome in the new year. Others throw old things away in a giant bonfire to start fresh on New Year's Day. Still others start the new year by wearing brand new clothes. Many families enjoy sharing a wonderful meal together.

Who's the First?

Explain to children that over 2,000 years ago the ancient Greeks started the tradition of honoring the first baby born in each new year. In some towns, stores give the first baby presents. Sometimes, the lucky baby may even be on television! Make a chart of children's names and write their birthdays beside the names. Have children help determine who was born closest to New Year's Day. You may wish to sing "Happy Birthday" or celebrate with cookies and juice.

Catching the Dragon's Tail

In China, the dragon is an important part of the new year celebration. Children enjoy playing this game indoors or out. It should be played with at least ten children, but the more there are, the longer the dragon's tail will be. Choose one child to be the dragon's head. You may wish to make a dragon mask from a large paper bag with large eye and nose openings cut in it.  Have the other children line up behind the dragon's head with their hands on the shoulders of the person in front of them.

At your signal (ring a bell, clap your hands), the dragon's head tries to catch the tail, which is the last person in line. This is harder than it sounds because the children must keep holding on to the shoulders of the child in front of them and the dragon's head will be twisting and turning to get its tail. If the dragon's head catches its tail, it remains the head. A child who breaks the line must become the tail.

Chi Chiao Bang

Explain that a tangram, or *chi chiao bang*, is a seven-piece puzzle that originated in China. It is often a part of new year celebrations. Point out that the pieces can be fitted together in many different ways to make designs or pictures.

Provide a tangram pattern for each child. Ask children to color each piece a different color. Then, have them cut out the 7 pieces and explore different ways to make pictures. Demonstrate how to make a giraffe. Then invite children to put the pieces together to make a dragon in honor of the Chinese new year.

Celebrating Heroes

American Heroes

A hero is someone who is remembered for acts of bravery, outstanding achievements, or kindness toward others. A hero can be a man, woman, or child. What makes a hero is the content of your character, as Dr. Martin Luther King, Jr., said long ago.

Heroes are soldiers who fight to preserve freedom, doctors or scientists who cure people of illness, or someone who does something that changes your life for the better. Heroes raise money or volunteer their time to help disaster victims. Heroes can be people who have enough courage to stand up for something they believe in, even though others disagree. But all of us can agree that the world is a better place because of them. Clara Barton, Benjamin Franklin, and George Washington Carver are three American heroes.

- During the Civil War, **Clara Barton** carried supplies to soldiers and cared for the wounded soldiers on the battlefields. She also founded the American Red Cross and was its first president (1881–1904).

- **Benjamin Franklin** was one of the founders of our country. He was also an inventor, a scientist, a writer, and a printer. He was one of the signers of the Declaration of Independence.

- **George Washington Carver** was a scientist. His research showed farmers that planting peanuts would enrich soil that had become worthless for other crops. He is best known for his research into the industrial uses of the peanut, soybean, and sweet potato.

Day of Roses

Encourage children to think of an everyday hero they know at school. It could be a child who befriended them, or a security guard who waited with them till they were picked up from school. Tell children you will have a "Day of Roses" to honor their heroes. Help them make a rose to give as a thank-you at school. Wrap red crepe paper around a pencil to form the rose, then remove the rose and attach it to a green pipe cleaner. Then have children deliver their roses to their school heroes.

Poor Richard's Almanac

Read aloud and discuss sayings from Benjamin Franklin's *Poor Richard's Almanac*. Invite children to copy and illustrate their favorite sayings. Let children make up new sayings that match Franklin's wit and wisdom.

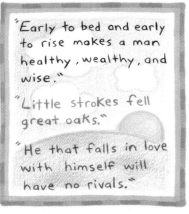

"Early to bed and early to rise makes a man healthy, wealthy, and wise."

"Little strokes fell great oaks."

"He that falls in love with himself will have no rivals."

Hero Puppet Show

Read stories or view videotapes about Clara Barton, Benjamin Franklin, and George Washington Carver. Invite children to use puppets to tell the story of one of these heroes. To make the puppets, use construction paper, yarn, glue, ribbons, fabric, and other assorted materials. You can attach each to a craft stick if the puppet is small or to a dowel stick if it is larger. Then, using a puppet theater, have children perform an impromptu puppet show. You can make a puppet theater by stretching a sheet across a doorway and having children stand behind it, raising the puppets above the level of the sheet.

Peanut Butter

George Washington Carver did not invent the peanut, but the work of this great African American inventor and scientist helped develop many products that are made from peanuts and peanut oils. Some of the products include hand lotion, instant coffee, and peanut butter. Have children add to the list. Then make homemade peanut butter.

You Will Need:
$1\frac{1}{2}$ cups roasted peanuts
1 tablespoon peanut oil
food processor

Put the peanuts and the peanut oil into the food processor. Process the mixture until it's very smooth. (NOTE: Check allergies before serving any food items.)

Dr. Martin Luther King, Jr., Day

Dr. Martin Luther King, Jr.

Dr. Martin Luther King, Jr., was born on January 15, 1929, in Atlanta, Georgia. His father and grandfather were ministers. Martin was very bright and skipped two grades in school. He went to college and was awarded many degrees. He became a minister, married, and had four children. As an adult, he was arrested many times for his participation in civil rights movements. He believed that people should be judged, not by the color of their skin, but rather, by the kind of people they are. He led many protests against the unfair treatment of African American people, but he did not believe in violence. Instead, he wanted people to live together peacefully.

When Rosa Parks refused to give up her seat on a city bus for a white man, she was taken to jail. Dr. King organized a protest against the bus companies to show them that the unfair law needed to be changed. Many people boycotted the buses and did not ride them. This caused the bus companies to lose money, and people began to work to change the law. Though Dr. Martin Luther King, Jr., was a gentle man, many people did not agree with his beliefs and practices. He was shot and killed in 1968. But we remember him as a man of great wisdom. His words and actions reflected his belief that violence was not the way to create change. We celebrate his birthday on the third Monday of January each year.

I Have a Dream

Place a picture of Dr. Martin Luther King, Jr., on a bulletin board with a blue background. Title the board "I Have a Dream." Have children write or dictate their dreams for the future on white construction-paper clouds and illustrate them with crayons or markers. Post children's creations on the bulletin board and read them aloud.

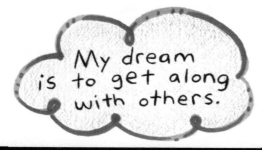

We Are All Special

Talk with children about Dr. Martin Luther King, Jr., and the qualities that made him a leader. Establish that he was kind, fair, brave, and helpful. Ask children to share the special qualities they have.

Have children work in pairs to trace onto craft paper around each other's bodies. Ask children to color the cutout to resemble them. Then have children write in their good qualities on their figure.

Multicultural Wreath

Have children stand in a group around you. Put your hand into the middle of the group and have all children place their hands near yours. Have them discuss the many different colors that make up our skin tones. Tell children that just as their hands are many different colors, people of the world also have different skin colors. Ask if skin tone has anything to do with what kind of a person they are. Share this famous quote of Dr. Martin Luther King, Jr., from his "I Have a Dream" speech: *"I have a dream that my four little children will one day live in a nation where they will not be judged by the color of their skin, but by the content of their character."*

Have children trace their hands three times on a piece of white construction paper and color each hand with a different multicultural crayon, or select alternate colors. Have children cut out the hands and then overlap them to form a multicultural wreath. Discuss what they think the wreath symbolizes. Point out that the world is made up of many different groups of people who must learn to live in harmony.

Valentine's Day

Valentine's Day

No one is really sure how Valentine's Day began, but it might have started in ancient Rome. During a feast called Lupercalia, young women wrote love messages that were put into a big pot. Men who were not married picked a message and then found out who had written it. Sometimes a man married the woman who wrote his note. Also in ancient Rome lived a kind-hearted doctor named Valentine. One day, the Emperor of Rome brought his young daughter to Valentine to cure her blindness. Valentine tried his best, but the little girl did not regain her sight. Roman soldiers arrested Valentine because they felt he was at fault. They put him in jail. Valentine wrote a note to the little girl. He put a bright yellow flower inside. The note was signed, "From your Valentine." When the little girl opened it, she saw a bright yellow flower for the first time in her life! It was a miracle. Her blindness was cured! Perhaps Valentine's Day was named for this kindly doctor who died on February 14.

Today, people often buy or make valentine cards for each other. Some people give candy hearts to others to show that they love and care for them.

Love Stamps

Discuss the post office with children. Ask if children know how a letter gets from one place to another. Explain the purpose of stamps and point out that as costs rise, the price of stamps also rises. If possible, display a few current stamps to children.

Invite children to design their own love stamp to commemorate Valentine's Day. Provide children with stamp outlines and crayons or colored pencils to complete their designs.

We Are All Special!

Ask children what makes them feel special. Invite children to tell about special times at school and at home. Tell children that they are going to make special valentines for each other.

Have oak-tag patterns precut in the shape of a valentine, about 8" tall by 6–7" wide. Let children trace and cut out the hearts on a variety of white, pink, and red construction paper. There should be one heart per child. Help children write their names, one on each heart, and put the hearts into a container such as a big hat or a basket. Mix them up and invite each child to pick a heart. Have them try again if they pick their own.

Provide pencils, crayons, and markers, and invite children to think of something nice about the child whose name appears on their heart and draw a picture of it. Then have children dictate a sentence about it as you write it on the heart. When each heart is finished, have children deliver their personalized heart to the recipient. When all children have received their hearts, help them interpret and read the heartfelt messages.

Thank-You Hearts

Discuss with children the workers in school that help them each day. Write a list on the board. Your list might include the principal, the school nurse, cafeteria workers, and the bus driver.

Make a big heart for each person on your list and have all children sign their names. Then decorate the heart with assorted stickers, buttons, yarn, or glitter. Invite the people to a celebration on Valentine's Day and present them with their thank-you hearts.

Presidents' Day

Presidents' Day

Presidents' Day is celebrated on the third Monday in February to honor two of our greatest Presidents, George Washington and Abraham Lincoln.

When **George Washington** was born on February 22, 1732, America belonged to England, but America later fought in a war to get free. Washington was an American general in that war. When it was over, our country had a brand new name—the United States of America—and George Washington was elected the first President. He is known as the father of our country.

Abraham Lincoln was born into a poor family on February 12, 1809. He lived in a small house made of logs cut from trees. The family had no electricity, but Abraham read by the fire. He walked long distances to get more books to read. When he grew up, he studied hard and became a lawyer. He was elected President in 1860. We remember him today as the man who freed the slaves.

There are special places in Washington, D.C., to honor these Presidents: the Washington Monument and the Lincoln Memorial. Many people visit these places to reflect on what these men did to make our country strong and free.

Lincoln Logs

Display pictures of a log cabin and discuss how it was built. Reproduce an outline of a simple log cabin with one window and a door. Show children how to use white glue on pretzel logs to build their own log cabin in the outline.

CAUTION: Tell children that because of the glue, the pretzel log cabin is not edible.

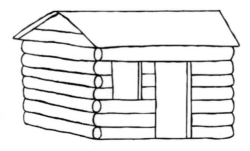

Presidential Facts

Using your school library, provide children with appropriate nonfiction books about the Presidents. Tell children that while Presidents' Day was begun to honor the birthdays of George Washington and Abraham Lincoln, there are other Presidents who have done important things for our country. Have children select a different President to read about. Set their purpose in reading, which is to find one interesting fact about that President and share it with the class.

Define the word *fact* for children. When children have found their facts, have them share them before the class in a Presidents' Day remembrance. You may wish to help children find a symbol that represents each President and display it to the class when they share.

Building Monuments

Show children pictures of the Washington Monument, the Lincoln Memorial, the Jefferson Memorial, and the Franklin Delano Roosevelt Memorial, or borrow a videotape from the school library about Washington, D.C. Discuss with children why these memorials were built and how they are alike and different. Ask children how they might have designed a monument, and for whom.

Provide children with sugar cubes, frosting, craft sticks and oaktag. Demonstrate how to spread frosting on a sugar cube and stack it to build a structure. Encourage children to use their imagination to create a monument to honor a President that they have learned about. As a variation, they could create their monument for a person who is important to them, such as a parent, a teacher, or a friend. When monuments are complete, children can decorate the "ground" with grass and acorns or cut paper glued to the base with frosting.

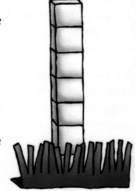

St. Patrick's Day

St. Patrick's Day

St. Patrick's Day is a traditional holiday in the United States. On March 17, many people wear green clothes, put green shamrocks in their windows, gather for parades, and have parties.

On this day some people honor St. Patrick, who was a missionary in Ireland over 1,500 years ago. He brought Christianity to the people and taught them how to read and write.

- St. Patrick often carried a shamrock when he preached. The shamrock is the symbol of Ireland. It grows in green bunches and can be seen in fields throughout the country.

- The potato is a very important food to the people in Ireland. Many Irish people came to the United States during a period when their potato crops were ruined by a plant disease.

- St. Patrick's Day is a holiday on which many people think about all the different places people came from to settle in America.

Irish Potato Prints

Point out Ireland on a map. Explain that potatoes are an important food for the people of Ireland. Tell children that they are going to make some prints using a potato. Cut some potatoes in half and give one half to each child. Using a craft stick, show children how to "carve" a simple shape by drawing it with a marker and then carving away the excess to leave a raised shape. Dip the shape into tempera and invite children to make a repeated print on white paper using their potato.

Limericks

Tell children that a limerick is an Irish poem that has five lines. Write the following limerick on the board and read it to children. Then have them read it with you. Ask if they can find the rhyming words. Circle *smart, start,* and *heart* in one color and *long* and *song* in a different color so children can see the AABBA rhyming pattern. (Insert your school's name in line 2.)

> *A leprechaun silly but smart,*
> *Came to _____ School to get a good start.*
> *But he played all day long,*
> *And heard a great song,*
> *But he never could learn it by heart.*

Sing a Rainbow

Display a prism to children, and let them experiment with it to make rainbows in the sunlight. Have them describe rainbows they have seen, and ask if they know when a rainbow can be seen. Identify the colors in an actual rainbow, and then teach the following song to children:

> *Red and yellow and pink and green,*
> *Purple and orange and blue,*
> *I can sing a rainbow,*
> *Sing a rainbow,*
> *Sing a rainbow too.*

Have children sing the song, and then compare the colors with the actual colors of a rainbow. Then give children brown paper grocery bags, sponge pieces, and tempera paint. Demonstrate how to dip the sponge into the paint and then make wide sweeping semi-circle strokes to create a rainbow on the paper bag. When the rainbows are dry, ask children to use crayons or markers to add Irish symbols, such as a leprechaun, a pot of gold, or a shamrock, to complete their paintings. You may wish to display their creations in the hallway.

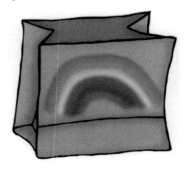

Memorial Day

Memorial Day

Memorial Day is celebrated on the last Monday in May. It is a day that traditionally marks the beginning of the summer holidays. It is a time to remember the United States men and women who lost their lives serving their country. Originally known as Decoration Day, it was established in 1868 to remember the dead from the Civil War. Over the years it came to serve as a day to remember all United States men and women killed or missing in action in all wars. We give thanks on Memorial Day that we live in a free nation, and we honor those who gave their lives for our freedom. Since World War I, Memorial Day has also been called Poppy Day. Volunteers sell small, red artificial flowers as a fund-raiser for disabled veterans. Today, almost everywhere around the world, people have a special day to honor not only those who gave their lives in battle, but also family members and friends whom they wish to remember. Some veterans' organizations put flags on the graves of people who were veterans of a war. Schools, banks, the post office, and other government agencies are closed on Memorial Day. Many businesses are also closed. There are parades, speeches, and military ceremonies, such as a 21-gun salute, to honor those who lost their lives for our country.

Are You a Hero?

Tell the class that children can also be heroes. Discuss times that children have shown courage, helped someone who was having difficulty, found a lost kitten, or done something nice for someone for no special reason. Explain that because of these actions, they are heroes, too. Have children make small medals using an oak-tag circle decorated with patriotic stickers attached to a ribbon. Encourage them to find others who perform kind acts for others and reward them with a memorial medal.

Color Me a Hero

Discuss what it means to be a hero. Read an appropriate biography to children about a hero such as Harriet Tubman, Abraham Lincoln, or Dr. Martin Luther King, Jr. Discuss the genre of biography by making it clear to children that the stories are true and are about real people. Then display a comic strip to children and read through it with them. Point out how the illustrator showed action by using a second or third frame. Give children a piece of art paper that has been blocked out in three horizontal frames.

Have children choose a hero they have learned about. Ask them to think about what made that person a hero. Point out the three frames on their papers. Explain that they are to tell a story about their hero using pictures they draw. Let them use crayons, markers, or colored pencils to make their hero story. Then have them share their comics with the class.

America the Beautiful

Teach children the words to this beautiful song. Explain any unfamiliar vocabulary. Play a recording of the song if you have one available. Otherwise, perhaps the music teacher could join you to help in teaching the melody to children. Encourage children to visualize what the song is about, and help them to understand that Memorial Day celebrates all those who gave their lives so we could have freedom.

O beautiful for spacious skies,
For amber waves of grain,
For purple mountain majesties
Above the fruited plain.
America, America,
God shed his grace on thee,
And crown thy good
With brotherhood
From sea to shining sea.

Flag Day

Flag Day

A flag is a piece of fabric with a specific design on it. The United States flag is a symbol of our freedom. The original design for our country's flag was adopted on June 14, 1777. This is the day we remember on Flag Day.

The original design of our flag was thirteen alternating red and white stripes, with thirteen stars that stood for the thirteen original colonies. The plan was to add a new stripe and star each time a state came into the Union. Congress realized, however, they would have a very long flag, so they decided to have only thirteen stripes and just add a star for each new state. Today our flag has fifty stars. The American flag is the best-known symbol of patriotism in our country.

■ Flag Day is celebrated with flags waving at parades, picnics, assemblies, and in front of homes and offices.

Betsy Ross's Cap

You Will Need:
> 24" circles of white felt
> hole punch
> yarn

Tell children that Betsy Ross was a special American. Some people say she made the first American flag. On Flag Day, we think about Betsy Ross and the flag she made. Tell children that Betsy Ross was born in 1752 and that she lived during the Colonial period. During this period of our history, many women wore white caps on their heads. Have children make a white cap similar to the one Betsy Ross wore.

Help children punch holes two inches apart about an inch from the outside border of the felt. Then have children string yarn in and out of the holes. When the stitching is complete, help children pull both ends of the yarn to gather the material. Tie the ends together.

Weave a Flag

Look at the flag of the United States. Count the stars and stripes. There are 13 stripes and 50 stars. Explain the significance of these numbers. Then, have children work together to make a flag. If there is a chain link fence around your school playground, ask permission to weave a flag for Flag Day. Weave long strips of red, white, and blue crepe paper in and out of the fence. Crumple 50 pieces of white crepe paper and stuff them into the blue part of the flag to represent the 50 stars.

(CAUTION: Remove paper flag at the end of the day if rain is expected.)

There Are Many Flags

There are many patriotic songs about the flag. Invite children to share flag songs they know. Then teach children the song "There Are Many Flags in Many Lands." If possible, borrow a recording of the song from the music teacher or media center specialist to use as accompaniment as you sing.

> **There Are Many Flags in Many Lands**
> *There are many flags in many lands,*
> *There are flags of ev'ry hue;*
> *But there is no flag, however grand,*
> *Like our own Red, White, and Blue.*
> *Then hurrah for the flag,*
> *Our country's flag,*
> *Its stripes and white stars, too;*
> *There is no flag in any land*
> *Like our own Red, White, and Blue.*

Independence Day

Independence Day

Independence Day is celebrated on July 4 each year in honor of the signing of the Declaration of Independence. The declaration announced to England that we were independent from their rule. It spelled out what was important  to our people, such as freedom of speech and the freedom to worship as we wanted. Thomas Jefferson was asked to write a first draft. Because it was such an important but difficult job, he worked for days in secret. He brought it before the Congress to read. They made changes and then agreed. These people were very brave to stand up for what they believed. We owe them a great deal of thanks for making our country the land of the free and the home of the brave.

The holiday was first observed in Philadelphia in 1776. The Declaration of Independence was read aloud to the people gathered in the square, city bells rang, and bands played in celebration. There were fireworks and candles were lit and placed in windows all over the city. Today people celebrate with picnics or cookouts, fireworks displays, and parades.

It's a Grand Old Flag!

Show pictures of how the American flag has changed since it was first created. Point out the difference in the number of stars. Explain that each star now stands for a state in the U.S. Have children describe the pattern of stripes. Point out that a red stripe always appears first. Give children an $8 \frac{1}{2}$" x 11" piece of white construction paper, a handful of cotton balls, and craft sticks. Have children paint the blue section of the flag on paper and then paint the craft sticks with red and white tempera paint. When the paint is dry, have children glue craft sticks for stripes and cotton balls for stars. Hang the flags around your room.

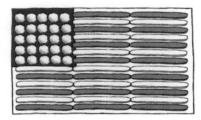

Gelatin Stars

Ask children to name the colors of the flag. Tell them that the colors were originally not chosen for any particular meaning, but that over the years, people have brought meaning to them. Some say that the red stands for the hardiness and bravery of those who fought for freedom, the white stands for purity and innocence, and the blue stands for vigilance and justice. Tell children that now they will get to create a red, white, and blue snack for Independence Day.

Prepare two packages each of cherry and blueberry gelatin in 13" x 9" pans, enough so that each child will get a serving. When the gelatin is set, run a knife around the edges of the pan and invert it onto a cookie sheet or tray. Give children star-shaped cookie cutters and let them cut a gelatin star in their favorite flavor and then top it with vanilla yogurt. Top the red gelatin treat with a few blueberries, and the blue treat with a cherry. (CAUTION: Be sure no one is allergic to these snacks.)

Bike Parade

Have children describe what they see at a parade. Ask if they have ever been in a parade, and if not, what they would like to do in one. Tell them that they can have their very own parade right in their own neighborhoods. Help children think of ways to decorate their bikes to show patriotism. Provide an outline of a bike and have children decorate it as a reference. Discuss ways to decorate a bike or a scooter. Suggest that they could use crepe paper or pipe cleaners to wrap their handlebars, make streamers for their handlebars, and decorate their basket, if they have one. Have children ask their friends to ride in their Independence Day parade, and invite their families and neighbors to be the audience. Remind children to get permission first and to ask for help in determining a route for their bike parade.

Vocabulary Cards

Vocabulary Cards

This reproducible section will help you create word cards for the vocabulary found at the beginning of each lesson in your Teacher's Edition. Throughout the lesson plans, you will find suggestions for using the vocabulary cards with the children. The cards may also be used to preview the unit, build vocabulary notebooks, assist ESL children, and review vocabulary at the end of the unit. Use blank cards to add vocabulary to meet the special needs of your class.

Contents

learn

main idea

I have a pet cat.
Her name is
Snowball.
She is white.

school

share

learn

To find out something new.

school

A place where people go to learn.

main idea

What the information that you are reading is mostly about.

share

To tell others what we know or think.

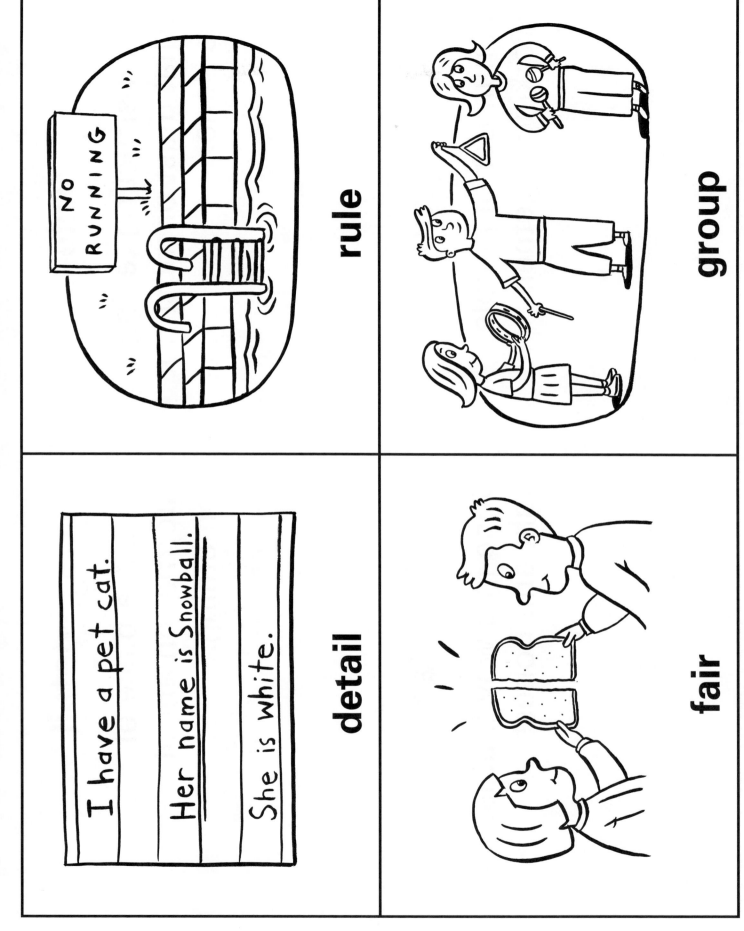

rule

group

detail

I have a pet cat.

Her name is Snowball.

She is white.

fair

© Harcourt

rule

An instruction telling what must or must not be done.

detail

An extra piece of information about something.

group

A number of people working together.

fair

Done in a way that is right and honest.

principal

map

teacher

You are here.

location

© Harcourt

principal

The leader of a school.

teacher

A person who helps others learn.

map

A drawing that shows where places are.

location

The place where something is.

tool

world

symbol

mountain

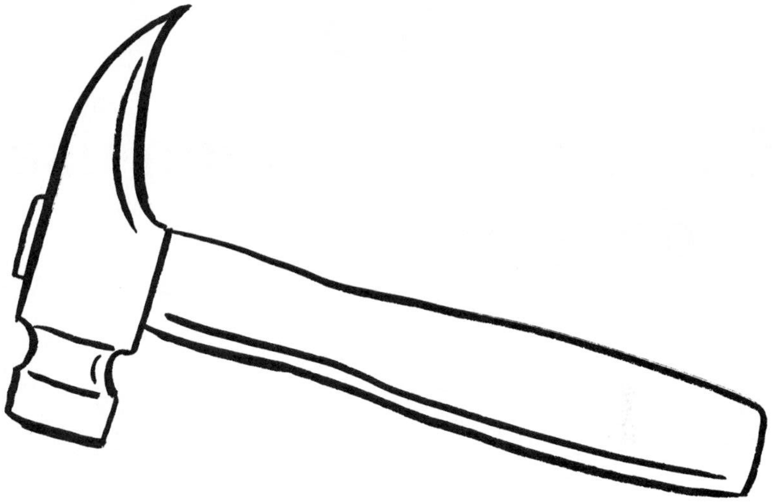

table

School Lunch Times

CLASS	TIME
Mr. Turner	11:00 a.m.
Mrs. Rojas	11:15 a.m.
Mrs. Brown	11:30 a.m.

© Harcourt

tool

Something a person uses to do work.

symbol

A picture or object that stands for something else.

world

All the people and places on Earth.

table

A chart that shows information in rows and columns.

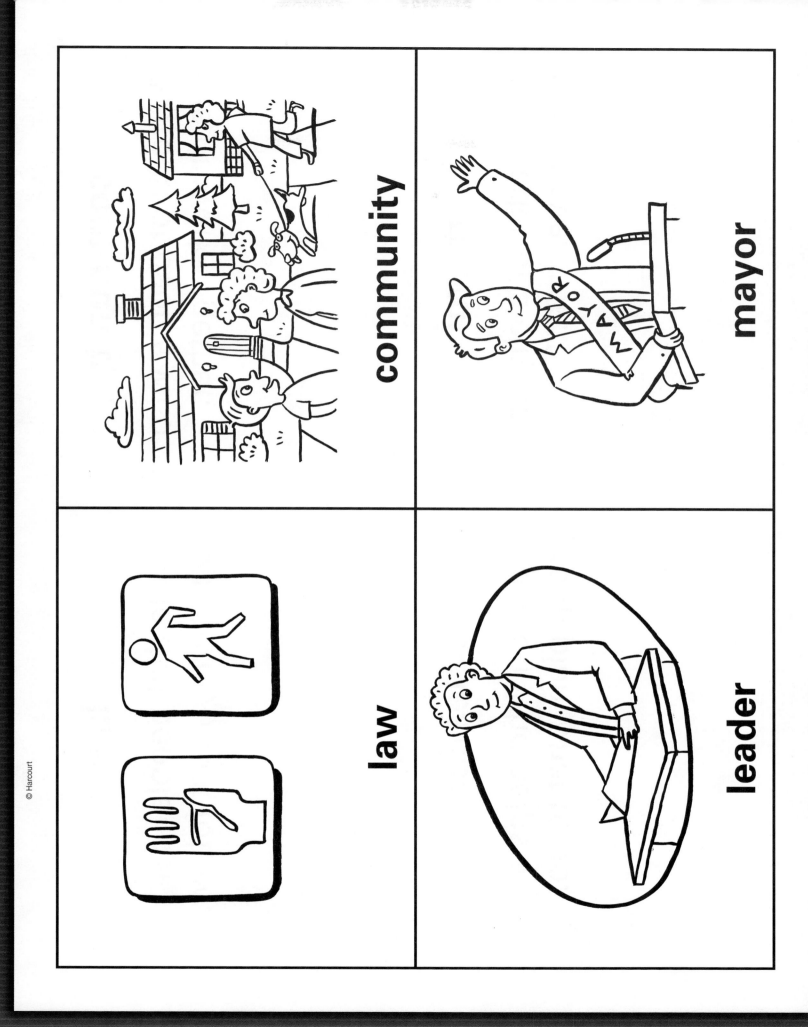

community

mayor

law

leader

© Harcourt

community

A group of people who live or work together.

law

A rule that people in a community must follow.

mayor

The leader of a city or town government.

leader

A person who helps a group plan what to do.

governor

country

city

government

© Harcourt

governor

The leader of a state's government.

city

A very large town.

© Harcourt

country

An area of land with its own people and laws.

government

The group of citizens that runs a community, state, or country.

border

vote

state

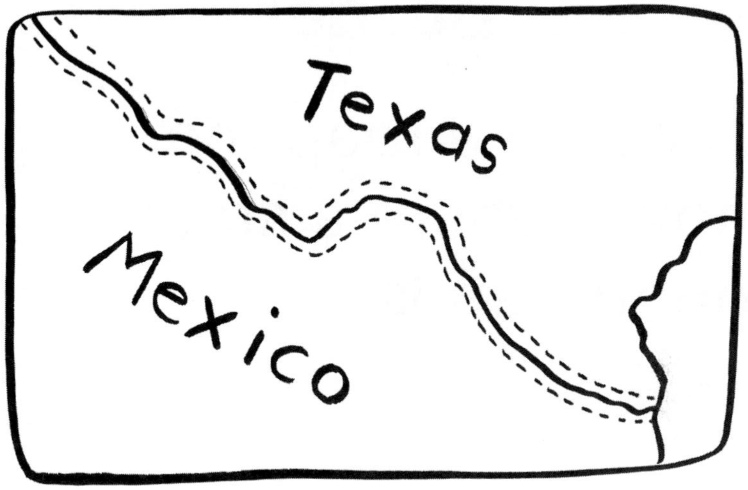

President

© Harcourt

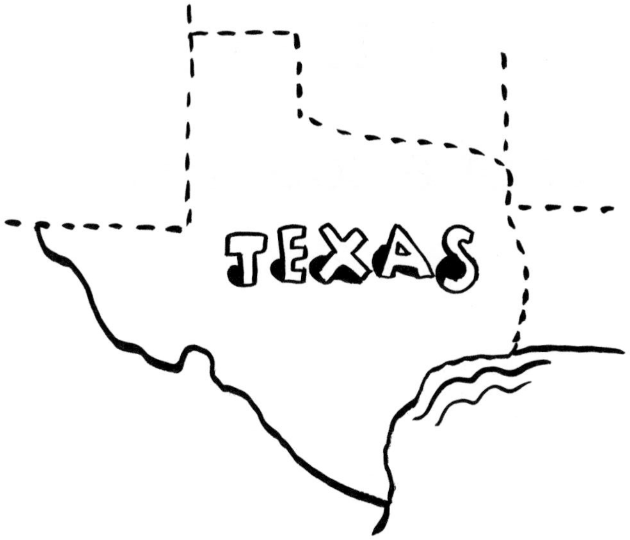

border

A line on a map that shows where a state or country ends.

state

A part of a country.

vote

A choice that gets counted.

President

Leader of the United States government.

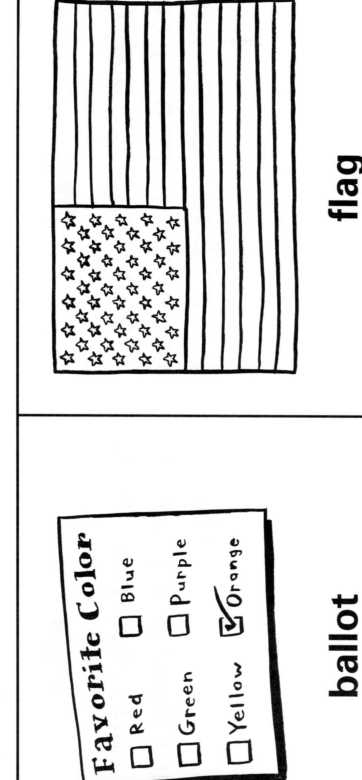

flag

nonfiction

ballot

fiction

© Harcourt

flag

A piece of cloth with a special design that stands for a country or group.

nonfiction

Stories that have real information.

ballot

A piece of paper that shows the choices for voting.

fiction

Stories that are made up.

citizen

responsibility

fact

right

© Harcourt

citizen

A person who lives in and belongs to a community.

fact

A piece of information that is true.

responsibility

Something that a citizen should do.

right

A freedom.

neighborhood

mountain

address

Mr. Lee
6 Park Street
Canton, OH 44730

map key

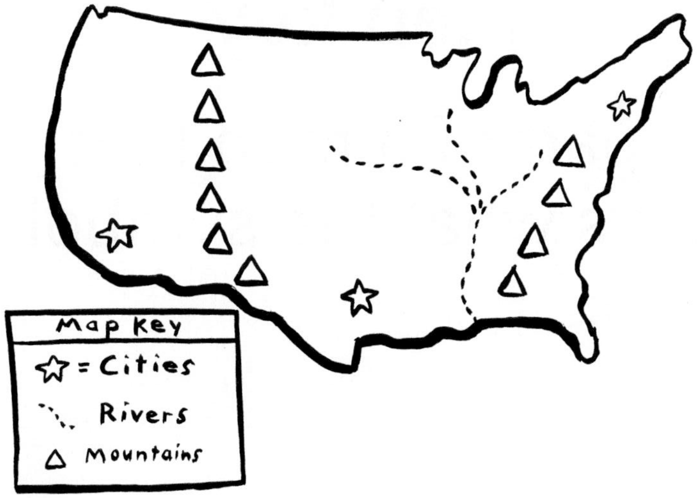

Map Key
☆ = Cities
∿ Rivers
△ Mountains

© Harcourt

neighborhood

The part of a community in which a group of people lives.

address

The numbers and words that tell where a building is.

mountain

The highest kind of land.

map key

The part of a map that shows what the symbols mean.

© Harcourt

lake

hill

valley

plain

lake

A body of water that has land all around it.

valley

Low land between mountains.

hill

Land that rises above the land around it.

plain

Land that is mostly flat.

river

globe

island

Earth

© Harcourt

river

A stream of water that flows across the land.

island

A piece of land that has water all around it.

globe

A model of Earth.

Earth

Our planet.

© Harcourt

ocean

resource

continent

direction

© Harcourt

ocean

A very large body of salty water.

continent

One of the seven main land areas on Earth.

resource

Anything that people can use.

direction

The way to go to find something.

© Harcourt

forest

weather

© Harcourt

farm

predict

forest

A very large area of trees.

farm

A place where crops are grown and animals are raised for food.

weather

What the air outside is like.

predict

To say what will happen.

litter

desert

pollution

recycle

© Harcourt

litter

To leave trash on the ground.

desert

A large, dry area of land.

pollution

Anything that makes the air, land, or water dirty.

recycle

To use things again.

role

solution

language

problem

© Harcourt

role

The part a person plays in a group or community.

solution

The answer to a problem.

language

The words or signs people use to communicate.

problem

Something that causes trouble.

© Harcourt

shelter

religion

needs

culture

© Harcourt

shelter

A safe place to live.

needs

Things people must have to live.

religion

A belief in a god or gods.

culture

A group's way of life.

fable

map scale

point of view

distance

© Harcourt

fable

A made-up story that teaches a lesson.

point of view

A way of thinking about something.

map scale

The part of a map that helps you find the distance between two places.

distance

How far one place is from another.

© Harcourt

holiday

custom

celebration

calendar

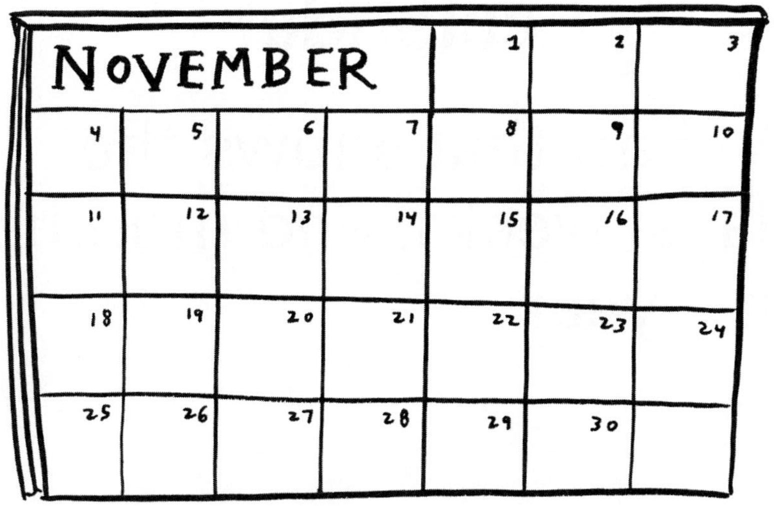

NOVEMBER

© Harcourt

holiday

A day to celebrate or remember something.

celebration

A time to be happy about something special.

custom

A group's way of doing something.

calendar

A chart that shows the days, weeks, and months in a year.

© Harcourt

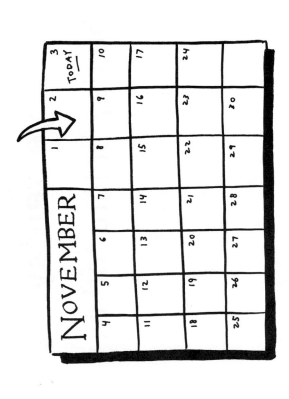

today

change

NOVEMBER

yesterday

NOVEMBER

tomorrow

© Harcourt

today

This day.

yesterday

The day before today.

change

To become different.

tomorrow

The day after today.

time line

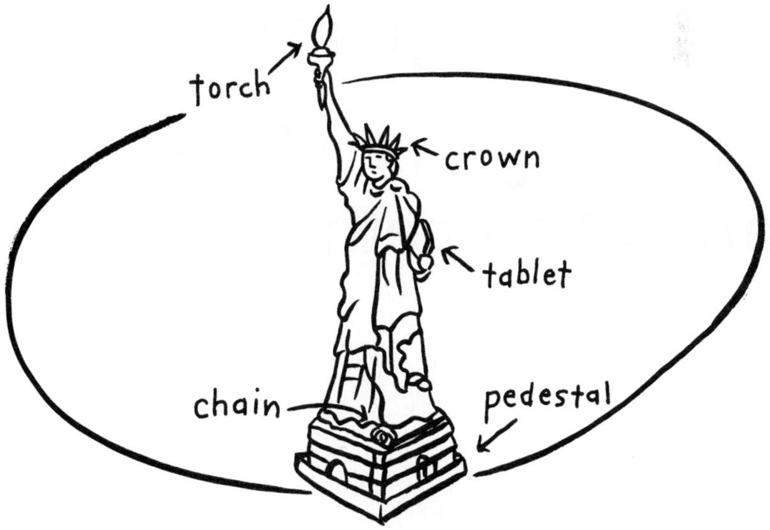

diagram

torch
crown
tablet
pedestal
chain

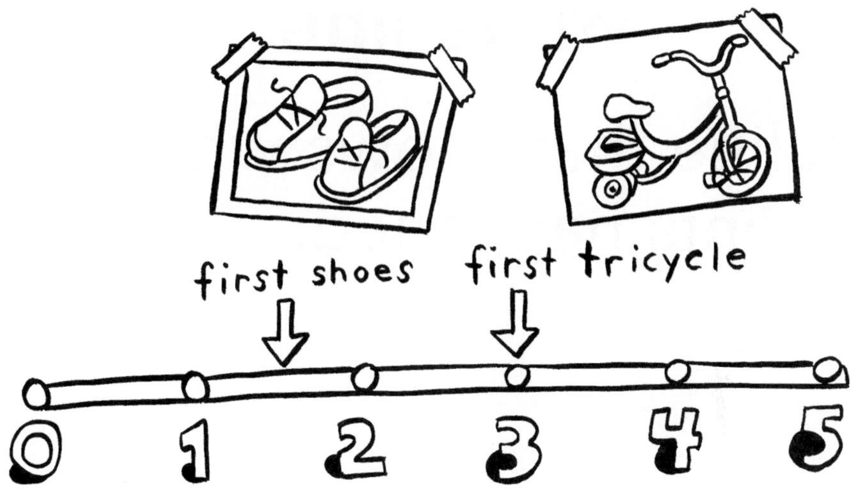

season

history

time line

A line that shows when events happened.

diagram

A drawing that shows parts of something.

season

One of the four parts of the year that have different kinds of weather.

history

The story of what has happened in the past.

© Harcourt

present

cause

past

future

© Harcourt

present The time now.	**past** The time before now.
cause What makes something happen.	**future** The time that is to come.

© Harcourt

explorer

freedom

effect

settler

© Harcourt

explorer	**effect**
A person who goes first to find out about a place.	What happens because of a cause.
freedom	**settler**
The right of people to make their own choices.	One of the first people to make a home in a new place.

© Harcourt

peace

hero

veteran

route

© Harcourt

peace

A time of quietness and calm.

veteran

A person who has served in the military.

hero

A person who has done something brave or important.

route

A way to go from one place to another.

© Harcourt

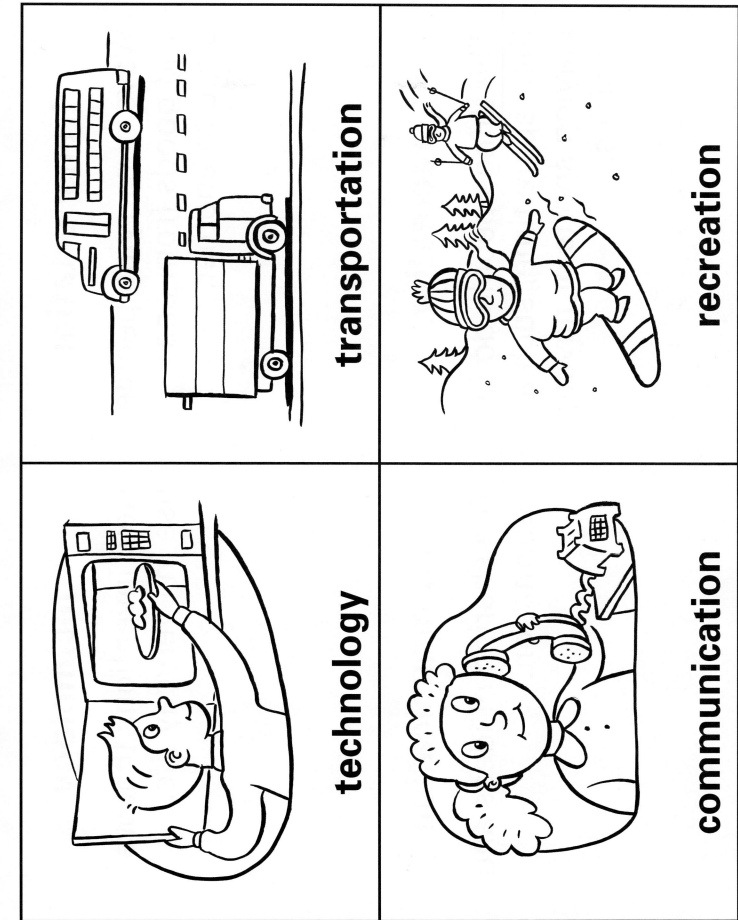

transportation

recreation

technology

communication

© Harcourt

transportation

Ways of carrying people and goods from one place to another.

recreation

The things people do in their spare time, such as playing sports or having hobbies.

technology

New inventions that we use in everyday life.

communication

The sharing of ideas and information.

services

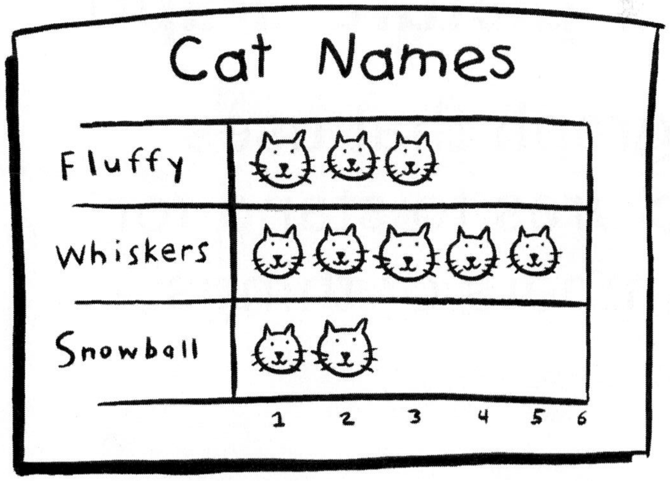

picture graph

Cat Names

Fluffy
Whiskers
Snowball

1 2 3 4 5 6

goods

factory

© Harcourt

services

Work done for others for money.

goods

Things that can be bought and sold.

picture graph

A graph that uses pictures to stand for numbers of things.

factory

A building in which people use machines to make goods.

money

market

business

volunteer

© Harcourt

money

The coins and paper bills used to buy things.

business

The making or selling of goods or services.

market

A place where people buy and sell goods.

volunteer

A person who works without being paid.

© Harcourt

bar graph

scarce

save

wants

© Harcourt

bar graph

A graph that uses bars to show how many or how much.

save

To keep something, such as money, to use later.

scarce

Not in good supply, or hard to find.

wants

Things that people would like to have but do not need.

© Harcourt

robot

trade

robot

A machine run by a computer to do work.

trade

To give one thing to get another.

School to Home Newsletter

School to Home Newsletters

These school to home letters offer a way of linking children's study of social studies to the children's family members. There is one newsletter, available in English and Spanish, for each unit. The newsletters include family activities as well as books to read.

Contents

School to Home

Harcourt Horizons • About My World Unit 1

Newsletter

Content to Learn

Your child is about to begin studying his or her relationship to the classroom, school, and community. In the first unit, Going to School, some of the topics that will be covered include:

- School is a place to learn and share.

- Good rules are fair and help people work together.

- There are many workers at school.

- You can describe a location.

- Schools long ago were like schools today in some ways. They were also different.

- Schools around the world are alike in many ways.

✏️ Activities to Try

- Have your child list school helpers, such as cafeteria workers, office workers, librarians, or crossing guards. Then have your child choose one person who is special in some way. Together, think of a way to thank that person, such as with a thank-you note, a baked treat, or a handmade gift.

- Invite your child to make a visitor's map or brochure of his or her school. Talk about important places to include, such as the office, the

cafeteria, the library, and his or her classroom. Then help your child fold a sheet of paper into fourths and draw and color a picture in each of the panels. You and your child can draw a map on the back.

- Find a relative, friend, or neighbor who went to your child's school, or another school in your community, at least ten years ago. Have your child interview that person and ask questions about how going to school has changed and how it has stayed the same. Use the information to make a chart that shows similarities and differences.

💡 Ideas to Discuss

- What are some school rules that everyone must follow? What happens if people don't follow the rules?

- Why do people use maps?

- How do you think schools have changed since long ago?

Books to Read

The Bus for Us by Suzanne Bloom. Boyds Mills Press, 2001.

Rex and Lilly Schooltime by Laurene Brown. Little, Brown, 2001.

The Brand New Kid by Katie Couric. Doubleday, 2000.

The Giant Carrot by Jan Peck. Dial Books, 1998.

Ebb and Flo and the New Friend by Jane Simmons. McElderry Books, 1999.

© Harcourt

GO ONLINE Visit **The Learning Site** at www.harcourtschool.com/socialstudies for additional activities, primary sources, and other resources to use in this unit.

Carta para la casa

Boletín

Tema de estudio

Su hijo va a comenzar a estudiar sus relaciones con la clase, la escuela y la comunidad. Éstos son algunos de los temas de la primera unidad titulada: Vamos a la escuela:

- la escuela es un lugar para aprender y compartir
- las reglas buenas son justas y ayudan a las personas a trabajar juntas
- hay muchos trabajadores en la escuela
- se puede describir una ubicación
- algunos aspectos de las escuelas de tiempos pasados eran como las escuelas de hoy. También había diferencias
- las escuelas de todo el mundo se parecen en algunos aspectos

✏️ Actividades

- Pída a su hijo que liste algunos trabajadores de la escuela, como los trabajadores de la cafetería, de la dirección, bibliotecarios o guardias del cruce de peatones. Luego pida que elija a una persona que tenga algo especial. Juntos, piensen en una manera de darle gracias a esa persona, como una tarjeta de agradecimiento, un dulce o una manualidad.
- Invite a su hijo a hacer un mapa o un panfleto para visitantes de su escuela. Hablen

sobre sitios importantes que se pueden incluir, como la dirección, la cafetería, la biblioteca y su salón de clases. Luego ayude a su hijo a doblar una hoja de papel en cuatro y dibujar y colorear un dibujo en cada panel. Ustedes y su hijo pueden dibujar un mapa en la parte de atrás.

- Busque un familiar, amigo o vecino que haya asistido a la escuela de su hijo o a otra escuela de su comunidad, hace por lo menos diez años. Pida a su hijo que entreviste a esa persona y pregunte cómo han cambiado las cosas desde que fue a la escuela y qué ha seguido igual. Usen la información para hacer una tabla de semejanzas y diferencias.

💡 Ideas para comentar

- ¿Cuáles son algunas reglas escolares que todos deben seguir? ¿Qué sucede si las personas no siguen las reglas?
- ¿Por qué las personas usan mapas?
- ¿Cómo creen que han cambiado las escuelas?

© Harcourt

Libros

The Bus for Us por Suzanne Bloom. Boyds Mills Press, 2001.

Rex and Lilly Schooltime por Laurene Brown. Little, Brown, 2001.

The Brand New Kid por Katie Couric. Doubleday, 2000.

The Giant Carrot por Jan Peck. Dial Books, 1998.

Ebb and Flo and the New Friend por Jane Simmons. McElderry Books, 1999.

Visiten The Learning Site en www.harcourtschool.com/socialstudies para obtener actividades adicionales, fuentes originales y otros recursos para usar en esta unidad.

School to Home

Newsletter

Content to Learn

Your child is going to begin learning about communities and citizens. In this unit, Good Citizens, some of the topics that will be covered include:

- Communities have rules called laws.
- Leaders help people.
- The President is the leader of our country.
- Symbols remind us to show respect for our country.
- Good citizens help others.
- Citizens have rights and responsibilities.

Activities to Try

■ With your child, look for pictures of symbols of America, such as the flag, the bald eagle, or the White House. Trace or cut out the pictures and use them to make a collage about America. Then let your child decide on a place in your home to display the collage.

■ Help your child become more aware of the President of the United States. Go through newspapers and magazines together, and circle pictures and articles about the President. Use the Internet (usually available at your local library or school library) to research biographical information about the President.

Make a picture story to share with other family members.

■ Ask your child to help you make a list of the responsibilities citizens have. For example, good citizens vote, take an interest in local government, and obey laws. Write the items on a sheet of paper, and share the list with family members. Each family member can choose one item and tell how he or she has fulfilled that responsibility.

Ideas to Discuss

■ What are laws?

■ How do rules and laws help you get along with others? How do they keep you safe?

■ How do you think being a leader of our country is different from being a community leader, such as a mayor or a governor?

Books to Read

Soaring with the Wind by Gail Gibbons. William Morrow, 1998.

Cat Up a Tree by Ann Hassett. Houghton Mifflin, 1998.

I Read Symbols by Tana Hoban. William Morrow and Company, 1999.

The Honest-to-Goodness Truth by Patricia McKissack. Atheneum Books, 2000.

Citybook by Shelley Rotner and Ken Kreisler. Orchard, 1994.

© Harcourt

 Visit **The Learning Site** at www.harcourtschool.com/socialstudies for additional activities, primary sources, and other resources to use in this unit.

Carta para la casa

Boletín

Libros

Soaring with the Wind por Gail Gibbons. William Morrow, 1998.

Cat Up a Tree por Ann Hassett. Houghton Mifflin, 1998.

I Read Symbols por Tana Hoban. William Morrow, 1999.

The Honest-to-Goodness Truth por Patricia McKissack. Atheneum Books, 2000.

Citybook por Shelley Rotner y Ken Kreisler. Orchard, 1994.

Tema de estudio

Su hijo va a comenzar a aprender sobre comunidades y ciudadanos. En esta unidad, Buenos ciudadanos, algunos de los temas que se cubrirán son:

- las comunidades tienen reglas llamadas leyes
- los líderes ayudan a las personas
- el presidente es el líder de nuestro país
- los símbolos nos recuerdan que debemos mostrar respeto por nuestro país
- los buenos ciudadanos ayudan a los demás
- los ciudadanos tienen derechos y responsabilidades

Actividades

■ Con su hijo, busque ilustraciones de los símbolos de Estados Unidos, como la bandera, el águila calva o la Casa Blanca. Tracen o recorten las ilustraciones y úsenlas para hacer un collage de Estados Unidos. Luego deje que su hijo decida en qué lugar de la casa se puede exhibir el collage.

■ Ayude a su hijo a saber más del presidente de Estados Unidos. Juntos, vean periódicos y revistas y encierren en un círculo fotos y artículos sobre el presidente. Usen Internet (por lo general se puede hacer en la biblioteca local o la biblioteca de una escuela) para investigar información biográfica sobre el presidente. Hagan un cuento con dibujos para compartir con otros familiares.

■ Pida a su hijo que lo ayude a hacer una lista de responsabilidades que tienen los ciudadanos. Por ejemplo: los buenos ciudadanos votan, se interesan por el gobierno local y obedecen las leyes. Escriban la lista en una hoja de papel y compártanla con sus familiares. Cada familiar puede elegir una de las responsabilidades y contar cómo la ha cumplido.

Ideas para comentar

■ ¿Qué son las leyes?

■ ¿Cómo nos ayudan las reglas y las leyes a llevarnos bien con los demás? ¿Cómo nos mantienen fuera de peligro?

■ ¿En qué se diferencia ser el líder de nuestro país de ser un líder de una comunidad, como un alcalde o un gobernador?

© Harcourt

Visiten The Learning Site en www.harcourtschool.com/socialstudies para obtener actividades adicionales, fuentes originales y otros recursos para usar en esta unidad.

School to Home

Newsletter

Books to Read

River by Debby Atwell. Houghton Mifflin, 1999.

Moo in the Morning by Barbara Maitland. Farrar, Straus & Giroux, 2000.

Snow by Uri Shulevitz. Farrar, Straus & Giroux, 1998.

Turtle and Snake Go Camping by Kate Spohn. Viking, 2000.

Hello Ocean by Pam Muñoz Ryan. Talewinds, 2001.

© Harcourt

Content to Learn

Your child is about to begin studying land, water, and natural resources. In this unit, The Land Around Us, some of the topics that will be covered include:

- People in a neighborhood share things.
- There are many kinds of land and water.
- People can use a globe and a map to find places on Earth.
- Natural resources are important to people.
- People need to take care of Earth's natural resources.
- People around the world live in all kinds of homes.

✏️ Activities to Try

- Take a walk with your child around the neighborhood. Talk about what makes each home different from the ones around it. Spend some time discussing the things that make your own home special. Then help your child draw and color a picture of your home, including things that make it unique.

- With your child, keep a list for a few days of all the ways your family uses water in your home. Look at the list together, and discuss how important water is in everyday life. Encourage your child to think of ways that he or she can conserve water at home.

- Go on a nature hunt with your child and gather natural resources such as leaves, pinecones, acorns, berries, and stones. When you return home, talk about ways in which the items are alike and different. Your child may want to make a collage or a sculpture with the items, using glue and scrap materials.

💡 Ideas to Discuss

- What are some things all neighborhoods have?

- What is a globe? How is it different from a map?

- What are natural resources?

GO ONLINE Visit **The Learning Site** at www.harcourtschool.com/socialstudies for additional activities, primary sources, and other resources to use in this unit.

Carta para la casa

Boletín

Tema de estudio

Su hijo va a comenzar a estudiar la tierra, el agua y los recursos naturales. Éstos son algunos de los temas de la tercera unidad titulada: La tierra a mi alrededor:

- las personas de un barrio comparten cosas
- hay muchos tipos de tierra y agua
- las personas pueden usar un mapa o un globo terráqueo para ubicar lugares en la Tierra
- los recursos naturales son importantes para las personas
- las personas necesitan cuidar los recursos naturales de la Tierra
- las personas de todo el mundo viven en muchos tipos de hogares

Actividades

- Con su hijo, camine por el barrio. Hablen de en qué se diferencia una casa de las otras a su alrededor. Pasen un tiempo comentando las cosas que hacen que su propio hogar sea especial. Luego ayude a su hijo a dibujar y colorear una ilustración de su hogar, incluidas las cosas que son únicas.

- Con su hijo, haga una lista durante varios días de todas las maneras en que su familia usa el agua en su casa. Miren juntos la lista y comenten la importancia del agua en la vida diaria. Anime a su hijo a pensar en maneras de conservar el agua en su casa.

- Vaya a una cacería natural con su hijo y reúnan recursos naturales, como hojas, conos de pinos, bellotas, moras y piedras. Cuando regresen a su casa, hablen de las semejanzas y deferencias entre los objetos. Quizá su hijo quiera hacer un collage o una escultura con los objetos usando pegamento y restos de materiales.

💡 Ideas para comentar

- ¿Cuáles son algunas cosas que tienen todos los barrios?

- ¿Qué es un globo terráqueo? ¿En qué se diferencia de un mapa?

- ¿Qué son recursos naturales?

Libros

River por Debby Atwell. Houghton Mifflin, 1999.

Moo in the Morning por Barbara Maitland. Farrar, Straus and Giroux, 2000.

Snow por Uri Shulevitz. Farrar, Straus and Giroux, 1998.

Turtle and Snake Go Camping por Kate Spohn. Viking, 2000.

Hello Ocean por Pam Muñoz Ryan. Talewinds, 2001.

© Harcourt

APRENDE en línea

Visiten The Learning Site en www.harcourtschool.com/socialstudies para obtener actividades adicionales, fuentes originales y otros recursos para usar en esta unidad.

School to Home

Newsletter

Books to Read

All the Way to Morning by Marc Harshman. Cavendish, 1999.

Daddy Calls Me Man by Angela Johnson. Orchard, 1997.

The Fox and the Stork by Gerald McDermott. Harcourt, 1999.

Different Just Like Me by Lori Mitchell. Charlesbridge, 1999.

Yoko by Rosemary Wells. Hyperion, 1998.

© Harcourt

Content to Learn

Your child is going to be learning about people's needs, cultures, and celebrations. In this unit, All About People, some of the topics that will be covered include:

■ People have different roles in different groups.

■ People have needs that they meet in different ways.

■ People around the world have different cultures.

■ People celebrate special times.

■ Americans share many customs.

Activities to Try

■ Invite your child to pretend you are going on a family camping trip. Look at magazines and catalogs and ask your child to decide what he or she would bring if only six items were allowed. Help your child think in terms of needs by asking questions such as *What do we have to have? What will we do when it gets dark? How will we stay warm?*

■ With your child, make a memory bag of the special smells, tastes, textures, and sights of a family event or holiday. For example, for a birthday you might collect photographs, a candle, scraps of wrapping paper, ribbon, and a list of people who attended.

Put the items in a bag and have your child decorate it.

■ Have your child "interview" important people in his or her life about favorite holidays. Help him or her think of good questions to ask, such as *What is your favorite holiday? Why? What do you do to celebrate on that day?* Help your child take notes during the interview.

Ideas to Discuss

■ What groups are you part of? Why do people sometimes work in groups?

■ What are some things you need? What are some things you want? How are they different?

■ Do all families celebrate the same special days? Tell why or why not.

GO ONLINE Visit **The Learning Site** at www.harcourtschool.com/socialstudies for additional activities, primary sources, and other resources to use in this unit.

Carta para la casa

Boletín

Libros

All the Way to Morning por Marc Harshman. Cavendish, 1999.

Daddy Calls Me Man por Angela Johnson. Orchard, 1997.

The Fox and the Stork por Gerald McDermott. Harcourt, 1999.

Different Just Like Me por Lori Mitchell. Charlesbridge, 1999.

Yoko por Rosemary Wells. Hyperion, 1998.

Tema de estudio

Su hijo va a comenzar a aprender sobre las necesidades de las personas, las culturas y las celebraciones. Éstos son algunos de los temas de la cuarta unidad titulada: Nosotros y todo lo que nos rodea:

- las personas cumplen diferentes funciones en grupos diferentes.
- las personas tienen necesidades que satisfacen de diferentes maneras.
- las personas de todo el mundo tienen culturas diferentes.
- las personas celebran ocasiones especiales.
- los americanos comparten muchas costumbres.

Actividades

■ Invite a su hijo a pretender que van a una excursión con la familia. Miren revistas y catálogos y pidan a su hijo que decida qué llevaría si solo se permitiera llevar seis objetos. Ayúdenlo a pensar en términos de necesidades preguntando: *¿Qué tenemos que tener? ¿Qué haremos cuando oscurezca? ¿Cómo nos mantendremos calientes?*

■ Con su hijo, prepare una bolsa de recuerdos (con olores, sabores, texturas e imágenes especiales) de una ocasión especial o de un día festivo. Por ejemplo: para un cumpleaños, podrían reunir fotos, una vela, pedazos de papel de regalo, un lazo y una lista de los invitados que asistieron. Pongan los objetos en una bolsa y pida a su hijo que la adorne.

■ Pida a su hijo que "entreviste" a personas importantes en su vida sobre los días festivos. Ayúdelo a pensar en buenas preguntas, como: *¿Cuál es su día festivo favorito? ¿Por qué? ¿Qué celebra en ese día?* Ayude a su hijo a tomar notas durante la entrevista.

Ideas para comentar

■ ¿A qué grupos pertenecen? ¿Por qué a veces las personas trabajan en grupos?

■ ¿Cuáles son algunas de las cosas que necesitan? ¿Cuáles son algunas cosas que quieren tener? ¿En qué se diferencian?

■ ¿Todas las familias celebran los mismos días especiales? Digan por qué.

© Harcourt

APRENDE en línea

Visiten The Learning Site en www.harcourtschool.com/socialstudies para obtener actividades adicionales, fuentes originales y otros recursos para usar en esta unidad.

School to Home

Newsletter

Content to Learn

Your child is about to begin studying time and change and the history of our country. In this unit, Looking Back, some of the topics that will be covered include:

- Things change all the time.
- Families share their history through stories.
- Like people, places also grow and change over time.
- Many groups lived in North and South America before Columbus arrived.
- Our country's history is made up of many people and the things they did.
- We celebrate on holidays to remember our history.
- People who do important things are heroes we remember.
- Technology has made many changes in our lives.

Activities to Try

- Help your child think of an event that involved change, such as a move from one home to another, a trip you have taken, or even an overnight with a friend. Have your child act out what happened first, next, and last. You can help him or her remember by asking questions such as *What did you do first? What happened after that?*

- Invite your child to imagine that the two of you are sailing with Christopher Columbus. Talk about what you see, hear, feel, and smell on your sailing vessel. Then help your child write a letter or a diary entry about your adventures. He or she might like to share the writing with classmates at school.

- On a globe or world map, help your child locate the continents of Europe, North America, Africa, and Asia. Use a finger to trace the route Europeans took when they sailed from Europe around Africa to Asia. Then trace the route west from Europe to Asia. Which continent is in the way?

Ideas to Discuss

- Which places in your community were built a long time ago?

- Who were the first people to live in America?

- Why do we celebrate holidays?

Books to Read

The 4th of July Story by Alice Dalgliesh. Aladdin, 1995.

Down the Winding Road by Angela Johnson. DK, 2000.

I Am Me by Karla Kuskin. Simon & Schuster, 2000.

Pedaling Along: Bikes Then and Now by Steven Otfinoski. Benchmark Books, 1997.

George Washington Carver by Martha Rustad. Capstone, 2002.

© Harcourt

 Visit **The Learning Site** at www.harcourtschool.com/socialstudies for additional activities, primary sources, and other resources to use in this unit.

Carta para la casa

Boletín

Libros

The 4th of July Story por Alice Dalgliesh. Aladdin, 1995.

Down the Winding Road por Angela Johnson. DK, 2002.

I Am Me por Karla Kuskin. Simon & Schuster, 2000.

Pedaling Along: Bikes Then and Now por Steven Otfinoski. Benchmark Books, 1997.

George Washington Carver por Martha Rustad. Capstone, 2002.

Tema de estudio

Su hijo va a comenzar a estudiar tiempo y cambio, y la historia de nuestro país. Éstos son algunos de los temas de la unidad titulada: Miramos el pasado:

- las cosas cambian todo el tiempo
- las familias comparten su historia por medio de cuentos
- al igual que las personas, los lugares también crecen y cambian con el tiempo
- muchos grupos vivían en América del Norte y del Sur antes de la llegada de Colón
- la historia de nuestro país está compuesta de muchas personas y las cosas que hicieron
- celebramos los días festivos para recordar nuestra historia
- las personas que hacen cosas importantes son héroes que recordamos
- la tecnología ha cambiado muchas cosas en nuestras vidas

✎ Actividades

- Ayude a su hijo a pensar en un evento en el que hubo cambios, como mudarse de una casa a otra, un viaje que hayan realizado o incluso cuando se haya quedado a dormir en casa de un amigo. Pida a su hijo que represente lo que sucedió primero, después y último. Lo pueden ayudar a recordar haciendo preguntas como: *¿Qué hiciste primero? ¿Qué sucedió después de eso?*

- Invite a su hijo a imaginarse que ustedes están navegando con Cristóbal Colón. Hable de lo que ven, oyen, sienten y huelen en su barco. Luego ayude a su hijo a escribir una carta o una entrada de un diario sobre sus aventuras. Quizá su hijo quiera compartir lo que escribió con los compañeros de clase.

- En un mapamundi o globo terráqueo, ayude a su hijo a ubicar los continentes de Europa, América del Norte, África y Asia. Use un dedo para trazar la ruta que los europeos tomaron alrededor de África hasta Asia. Luego tracen la ruta occidental desde Europa hasta Asia. ¿Qué continente se encuentra en el camino?

☼ Ideas para comentar

- ¿Qué lugares de su comunidad se construyeron hace mucho tiempo?

- ¿Quiénes fueron los primeros habitantes de América?

- ¿Por qué celebramos los días festivos?

© Harcourt

Visiten The Learning Site en www.harcourtschool.com/socialstudies para obtener actividades adicionales, fuentes originales y otros recursos para usar en esta unidad.

School to Home

Newsletter

Content to Learn

In this social studies unit, Jobs People Do, your child will learn about work people do to earn money, and about goods and services. Some of the topics that will be covered include:

- People depend on one another for goods and services.
- People work together to make goods in a factory.
- People work to earn money to buy what they need.
- The kinds of work that people do and the ways they do them change over time.
- People can be buyers or sellers or both.
- People must make choices about what they want.
- People around the world depend on one another.

Activities to Try

- Give your child old catalogs, magazines, and advertisements. Have him or her cut out ten pictures of goods and foods he or she would like to have. From those ten, your child may choose only five. Ask him or her to tell at least one reason for each choice.

- Ask your child to be "a consumer for a day." Together, make a shopping list for a particular store in your neighborhood. Show your child

how you prepare for the trip, including bringing enough money to pay for your purchases. At the store, let your child find the items on the list. He or she can pay the cashier and be responsible for any change.

- If possible, arrange for your child to go to work for a few hours with you or another family member. After your child sees the area where you work, walk around to see what other people do there. Have your child tell other family members about the experience. Your child can also "shadow" you on a Saturday as you do chores around your home.

Ideas to Discuss

- What are goods? What are services?

- Why do people have to choose what they buy? Why can't most people buy everything they want?

- How are volunteers different from paid workers? How is being a volunteer different from doing jobs in your home?

Books to Read

Pigs Will Be Pigs: Fun with Math and Money by Amy Axelrod. Aladdin, 1997.

The Night Worker by Kate Banks. Frances Foster, 2000.

Deena's Lucky Penny by Barbara DeRubertis. Kane Press, 1999.

Just Enough Carrots by Stuart Murphy. HarperCollins, 1997.

Career Day by Anne Rockwell. HarperCollins, 2000.

© Harcourt

 Visit **The Learning Site** at www.harcourtschool.com/socialstudies for additional activities, primary sources, and other resources to use in this unit.

Carta para la casa

Boletín

Tema de estudio

En esta unidad de estudios sociales, Trabajos que hacen las personas, su hijo va a aprender sobre el trabajo que hacen las personas para ganar dinero, y sobre los bienes y servicios. Éstos son algunos de los temas:

- las personas dependen unas de otras para obtener bienes y servicios
- las personas trabajan juntas para hacer bienes en una fábrica
- las personas trabajan para ganar dinero para comprar lo que necesitan
- los tipos de trabajos que hacen las personas y las maneras en que los realizan cambian con el tiempo
- las personas pueden ser compradores o vendedores o ambos
- las personas deben tomar decisiones sobre lo que quieren
- las personas de todo el mundo dependen unas de otras

✏️ Actividades

- De a su hijo catálogos o revistas viejas y avisos publicitarios. Pídale que recorte diez ilustraciones de bienes y alimentos que le gustaría tener. De esos diez, su hijo debe elegir solo cinco. Pídale que diga por lo menos una razón por la cual eligió cada opción.

- Pida a su hijo que sea "un consumidor por un día". Juntos, hagan una lista de compras para una tienda específica de su barrio. Muestre a su hijo cómo prepararse para ir de compras, incluido cuánto dinero llevar para pagar. En la tienda, deje que su hijo busque los artículos de la lista. Él o ella puede pagarle al cajero y ser responsable del cambio.

- Si es posible, haga arreglos para que su hijo los acompañe al trabajo por unas horas o vaya con otro familiar. Después de que él o ella vea el área de trabajo, camine por la oficina para ver lo que hacen las otras personas. Pida a su hijo que les cuente a otros familiares sobre la experiencia. Su hijo también puede "seguirlos" durante un sábado a medida que hace sus quehaceres en la casa.

💡 Ideas para comentar

- ¿Qué son bienes? ¿Qué son servicios?

- ¿Por qué las personas tienen que elegir lo que compran? ¿Por qué la mayoría de las personas compra todo lo que quiere?

- ¿En qué se diferencian los voluntarios de los trabajadores asalariados? ¿En qué se diferencia ser un voluntario de hacer trabajos en el hogar?

© Harcourt

Libros

Pigs Will Be Pigs: Fun with Math and Money por Amy Axelrod. Aladdin, 1997.

The Night Worker por Kate Banks. Frances Foster, 2000.

Deena's Lucky Penny por Barbara DeRubertis. Kane Press, 1999.

Just Enough Carrots por Stuart Murphy. HarperCollins, 1997.

Career Day por Anne Rockwell. HarperCollins, 2000.

APRENDE en línea

Visiten The Learning Site en www.harcourtschool.com/socialstudies para obtener actividades adicionales, fuentes originales y otros recursos para usar en esta unidad.

Index

writing, 33A, 57A, 181, 276
Questions Kids Ask, 22, 54, 92, 99, 129, 218, 236, 247, 271
Quilting, 173, 224
Quotations, 1, 41, 81, 225

Railroads, *See* Trains
Rain, 112A, 112, 113, 114, 120
Rain forest, 120
Rainbows, H13
Reading activities
   adding to a poem, 109
   end of slavery, 201
   legends, 192
   literature, 12A
   making comparisons, 120, 213
   predicting, 136A
   reading about Benjamin Franklin, 206
   reading about community history, 186
   reading about homes, 139
   reading about transportation methods, 30
   reading aloud, 176, 192
   solving puzzles, 102
   tall tales, 66
Reading guide, T5
Reading/language arts activities
   advice for a classmate, 1I
   busy day stories, 225I
   Earth verses, 81I
   German language, 182
   good neighbor puppet show, 41I
   reviewing stories, 129I
   settler stories, 169I
Reading/literature activities
   cultural traditions, 142
   life in the past, 211
   origami, 148
   sharing a poem, 140, 245
   sharing stories, 178
   things to do to protect resources, 114
   weather folklore, 112
   work around the world, 234
Reading skills
   categorize, 81, 99, 101, 105, 116, 118, 124
   compare and contrast, 1, 17, 27, 31, 36
   fiction or nonfiction, 66A–67A
   finding main idea, 8A–9A, T6
   generalize, 129, 141, 155, 157, 160, 164
   graphic organizer, 81, 129
   K-W-L chart, 41

point of view, 44, 146A–147A, T15
predicting, 112A–113A
prior knowledge, 41, 48, 51, 54, 73, 76
sequence, 169, 174, 175, 189, 199, 200, 220
summarize, 225, 233, 248, 249, 256, 257, 276
tables, 1, T16
Reading Social Studies
   anticipation guide, 30A, 33, 138A, 141, 160A, 161, 192A, 195, 252A, 253
   compare and contrast, 132, 213, T9
   context clues, 68
   creating mental images, 178, 235
   graphic organizers, 6A, 7, 18A, 19, 22A, 27, 46A, 47, 68A, 71, 98A, 101, 108A, 111, 118A, 121, 129, 132A, 133, 142A, 145, 200A, 203, 206A, 209, 210A, 215, 238, 254A, 257, 264A, 265
   K-W-L chart, 14A, 17, 48A, 51, 60A, 65, 102A, 196A, 199
   making a chart, 98A, 101, 203, 209, 210A, 215
   making a list, 106A
   making predictions, 4A, 5, 34A, 42, 72A, 73, 82, 84A, 89, 93, 136A, 170, 172A, 173, 184A, 189, 228A, 239, 244A, 249, 255
   paraphrasing, 31, 62, 270
   personal response, 44A, 45, 94A, 95, 134A, 135, 154A, 157, 174A, 175, 258A, 261
   picture clues, 172
   previewing the unit, 2, 130
   reading ahead, 143
   sequence, 136, T11
   study questions, 10A, 11, 54A, 57, 104A, 105, 114A, 117, 178A, 181, 240A, 243, 268A, 273
   summarizing, 139, 233, T12
   synonyms, 41R
   using text structure and format, 229, 258
"Recess Rules" (Shields), 11A
Recreation, 215
Recycling, 81I, 116–117A, P6
Red Cross, 69, 71A
Reference sources, 1R, 52, 56, 242
Region, 98
Religions, 72, 144, 154, 188
Reports
   on comic strips, 260
   on culture, 129N
   See also Research and report
Research, 151, 214, 217, 263, 267

Research and report, 32, 50, 160, 180, 242
Research skills. *See* Study/research skills
Resources, 83, 108, 110, 111
   capital, 244–249
   human, 244–249
   human-made, 109, 110
   natural, 108–111
   saving, 114A–117A
   types of, 108A–111A
   using, 197, 244, 248
   See also Internet resources
Responsibility(ies), 72A–73A
   as character trait, 56, 57, 69, 115
   of citizens, 41I, 43, 73, 116, 117A
Reteach activities, 7, 9, 11, 17, 19, 21, 27, 29, 33, 51, 53, 57, 59, 65, 67, 71, 73, 95, 97, 101, 103, 105, 107, 111, 113, 117, 121, 135, 137, 145, 147, 151, 157, 159, 161, 175, 177, 181, 183, 189, 191, 195, 199, 203, 205, 209, 215, 217, 243, 249, 251, 253, 257, 261, 263, 265, 267, 273
Review questions, 154
Rhymes, 113A, 139, 229, 259
   See also Poetry
Riddles, 1N, 43A, 83, 104, 107A, 121, 157A, 209
Rights
   Bill of, 72
   of citizens, 72A–73A, 200
   civil, 200
   right to privacy, 72
Rio Grande, 102
River, 81R, 101, 102, 110
River Town **(Geisert),** 186
Robot, 256, 257
Role(s), 51A, 57A, 129N, 130, 131, 134A–135A
Role-play, 21, 43A, 46, 72, 116, 135A, 151, 219, 252, 267, 275, H5
Roof, 120, 141
Roop, Connie, 40
Roop, Peter, 40
Roosevelt, Theodore, 222
Ross, Betsy, 63
Routes, 53A, 204A–205A, 223
Rubrics, 1Q, 41Q, 81Q, 129Q, 169Q, 225Q
Rules, 2, 3, 38
   at home, 10
   on playground, 11A
   at school, 3, 10A–11A, 13, 38, 46–47A
   writing about, 11
"Rush Hour" (Loomis), 228A–239A
Rushmore, Mount, 60, 61

Russia, 268
Ryan, Pam Muñoz, 80